A
Sister's
Promise

A
Sister's
Promise

RENITA D'SILVA

bookouture

Published by Bookouture

An imprint of StoryFire Ltd.
23 Sussex Road, Ickenham, UB10 8PN
United Kingdom

www.bookouture.com

ISBN: 978-1-910751-14-5
eBook ISBN: 978-1-910751-13-8

Acknowledgements

I would like to thank everyone at Bookouture for their continued belief in me. Especial thanks to Oliver Rhodes for his advice and support, and also for the title. Thank you to Kim Nash who is absolutely lovely and the best person ever to have championing my books.

Huge thanks to Lorella Belli of Lorella Belli Literary Agency for all her brilliant efforts in making my books go places.

A big thank you to Jenny Hutton who is the BEST editor once could wish for and who knows just what needs to be done to make my stories the best they can be.

Thank you to Lydia Newhouse for her wonderful and insightful comments and to Nichola Lewis for her amazing eye for detail.

Thank you to all my lovely fellow Bookouture authors and to all the fabulous book bloggers and twitter/fb friends for their enthusiastic and overwhelming support.

Thank you to Suresh Babu, Amber Pinto and Rupal Menezes for their knowledge, time and patience in answering all my medical queries.

Thank you to my lovely friend Judy Nappa for all her support.

Thank you to my lovely sister-in-law Levin D'Souza and to our mutual friend Gomathy Paramasivan; my amazing neighbours, the McKays and the superb Tristan Barnett for their time and tolerance in answering all of my many questions.

A huge thank you to my mum, Perdita Hilda D'Silva, who is always there to talk things through, calming me down and making me laugh. Thank you also to my aunt, Lucy Pinto and my dad, Cyril D'Silva for their prayers.

I am immensely grateful to my long-suffering family for willingly sharing me with characters that live only in my head and for accepting that half the time I am but a shell, physically present but that's about all. My daughter voiced what they were all thinking when she said, after having kept her counsel for as long as she possibly could: 'Mum, which character are you talking to now!' Love always.

Thank you, as ever, to you, reader. In the words of Samuel Johnson: 'A writer only begins a book. A reader finishes it.' Thank you for choosing to finish A Sister's Promise.

Dedication

In memory of my grandfather, Simon Rodrigues, Aba, (1918 - 2002) – the vanquisher of pythons; the nemesis of cockroaches, spiders and sundry bugs; the herald of our achievements; soft voiced and big hearted, protector and provider.

And in memory of my grandmother, Mary Rodrigues, Ba, (1929 - 2015) – the repository of anecdotes and old wives' tales, gossip and ghost stories and recipes; the dispenser of advice and wisdom; the owner of magic hands that healed and fed, cooked and created. Loved.

Prologue
Benedictions from a Benevolent God

Two girls frolic on a summer's evening, and while shadows slant grey in emerald fields, they revel in the golden taste of happiness, basking in the warm radiance of childhood, innocence and freedom.

Touch-me-nots, their blooms, the soft, sugar-embroidered pink of a happy ending, shrink from the kiss of grumbling yellow bees. Butterflies coyly flutter their emerald-tipped silver wings as if dispensing benedictions from a benevolent god. High up in the coconut trees, the crows squabble and gossip.

The taller girl, pigtails swaying in the fragranced breeze, closes her eyes and counts. The smaller girl hides among the copse of trees at the edge of the field as the lone cow, tail twitching, keeps watch and envelops her in its mildly curious, liquid mahogany gaze.

'Here I come,' shouts the seeker and she darts among the fields, her churidar ballooning around her.

The other girl peeks from behind the base of the mango tree as she breathes in the tart green smell of ripening mangoes, her hands attuning to the knobbly brown feel of bark.

'Got you,' the taller girl yells, coming up behind her, but the smaller girl screams as she slips on the moss at the base of the tree, her knee exploding in a spurt of red as she cuts it on a sharp-edged stone.

The taller girl holds the smaller one in her arms and gently wipes away the blood oozing through the torn churidar bottoms.

The cow strains at the rope that tethers it to the post and comes up to them, nudging their faces with its soft wet nose: the slimy feel of fish guts, the earthy tang of manure.

The girls laugh, syrup and sweetness, their angst forgotten, dispersed into the evening air that brings cooking smells wafting up to them. The cow bellows, a long, mournful moo.

'Here,' says the taller girl, rubbing at the blood that still sprouts in scarlet droplets from the wounded girl's knee. 'Let's make a promise to love and look out for each other forever.'

The wounded girl hesitates for one protracted beat during which the other girl's smile slips.

Then, she too dips her pinkie finger in the blood and ignoring the summons to dinner that carry over the gurgling of the stream, and drift across the fields, they link their fingers together and recite, 'We will always look out for each other and love each other best.'

Chapter 1
Kushi

Bhoomihalli, India
The Ghost of Daring to Dream Too Big

In my fevered dreams, in this peculiar half-awake state, I see myself writing the letter.

The seemingly innocuous wad of papers penned in meticulous joined-up letters, in my best handwriting, and my mother's voice echoing in my ears: 'Remember, for some people, your handwriting is their first, and perhaps only, introduction to you.' My brain fired up, vivid images of amber flames dancing in front of my eyes, my ink-marked fingers working zealously.

Now, my agitated mind whispers a warning from the confines of this strange bed in which I find myself strapped; medicinal sheets swaddle me in a claustrophobic embrace, as I watch my younger, naive self making copies, penning addresses, sealing envelopes.

I am unable to do any more than gag on the bitter taste of glue, damp paper and remonstrance, my hollow stomach dipping, knowing that it is done and in the past. My words posted and in the relevant hands, set into action events which will culminate in the here and now: this delirious state; this bizarre prison.

The letter then:

To

The Chief Minister of Karnataka

CC: The Minister for Higher Education; The Minister for Law, Justice and Human Rights.

Dear Sirs,

My name is Kushi Shankar. I am seventeen years old and a resident of Bhoomihalli village. I am writing this letter to you because, in my opinion, even though you have been elected to represent the people of this state and have pledged to do your best by them, you sometimes forget how they, i.e. we, the common people, live.

Mr Chief Minister, I know that you grew up in the city, started your political career there and now reside there in a huge mansion in the poshest part of the city. I am not faulting you for this. I just wonder if you know what it is really like for the people in the villages, that's all. The people you are supposed to protect and look after, whose concerns, you assure us, are your priority.

Well, we don't feel that way here in Bhoomihalli and I am sure this is the case in other villages as well. We feel let down, disillusioned. You promise us all these things so we vote for you: clean roads, drinking water, medical facilities, a good education and then you renege on these promises as soon as you are elected. Is this fair?

Why do we have to suffer power cuts every single evening and through the night while your city mansions have electricity day in and day out? Why do we still not have the medical facility that has been promised us by every politician before every election since my father was a boy, and have to travel to Dhoompur to get medical help and medicines? Why do we have to queue for hours at the one communal tap every summer when our wells dry up, for water the colour of sludge that comes for one hour each day, at different and entirely random times? Where are the borewells you have promised us? Where is the clean, running water?

All of these concerns I have raised here are important, of course, but they are not the real reason I am writing to you. I have a specific purpose in writing this letter, which I will tell you about in a minute. But mostly, this letter is a plea, showing you how it is for us and asking you to please do something.

Now, I am going to present to you a scenario.

Picture this:

The Engineering College on the outskirts of Dhoompur. The one with the imposing gate and the leafy, tree-lined drive leading up to the formidable two-storey building, with its cement roof and its tall gables; with its chattering, confident students who wear their sense of entitlement like an extra set of clothes. The one whose

*glossy prospectus promises 100% placement at the end
of the four-year course, a white-collar job guaranteed.*

*Every child in Bhoomihalli and the neighbouring
villages seeks admission into the hallowed portals of this
college, dreaming of being one of the revered students
with their poise and their absolute belief in a sunny
future. The parents of Bhoomihalli's aspiring children
are farm labourers who work so very hard to make sure
their kids get the education they themselves were denied, which is why they perform back-breaking labour
in other men's fields for little return.*

*These farmers would like their children to be of-
ficers, to wear shirts and trousers, not lungis and holey
vests. They would like their children to carry briefcases
spilling over with documents—which they, mere labourers, cannot read—and not bricks and rubble, or
yokes and bales of hay. They would like their children
to have an upright bearing, not a back permanently
bent with lugging the cares of the world. They would
like their children's skin to be pampered and soothed by
the air-conditioned interior of offices, not burnt to a
crisp by the unforgiving sun.*

*They would like their children to speak the Eng-
lish of the educated, not the Kannada and Tulu of the
masses. They would like their children to have soft,
well-fed bellies sagging contentedly over their belts, not
concave stomachs that ache with hunger and struggle to
hold up lungis like their own.*

They would like their children to eat meat at least three times a week, not once every few months when the cow that was their livelihood finally gives up on life and has to be butchered, the paltry, stringy meat clinging to the bones tasting of worry. For how will they replace Nandini, who was so very loyal and gave milk every single day even though she lived only on a diet of scorched, yellow grass?

And the villagers can conceive of only one way that their children can have all of this, and that is through education, that magic word that promises entry into the echelons of the rich and the well settled.

At the local school which the children of these labourers attend, the teachers change like the weather, they appear and disappear like apparitions, like gods who every once in a while give a darshan to favoured supplicants. When the teachers disappear—they are not paid enough, they say, and go to the cities in search of better recompense and the big break they know is their due—there is no choice but to club two or three classes together, no matter the pupils' ages. These range from eleven to fifteen, with some of the older children stepping in to teach the younger ones. Is it any matter then that there is such a disparate success rate between schools in the city and those in the villages?

The teachers who do stay more than a month or two all recite the same mantra, unintentionally echoing the message that is drilled into the village children by their parents so many times that they know it by heart: Study hard, bag a seat at the Engineering College, get out of here.

And so, the children of the labourers study and their parents work extra-long hours to procure the requisite textbooks. As the exams loom, the villagers forgo meals for a week or two to send their children for tuition in Dhoompur, to centres that claim 'Sure-fire Success in Pre-University and CET Exams'.

And these village kids, who lack textbooks and teachers and classroom space, pass the exams with fly-ing colours, their high ranks in the CET assured to win them entry into the Engineering College. They are invited to the city to choose their seat, their shiny, as-sured future gleaming tantalisingly before them.

On paper, of course, that is what is supposed to happen.

But does it?

Now my ma says that it was a different system while she was growing up. In those days you chose the schools you wanted by post. You sent off the form and either you were offered a place or you weren't. So, the travesty I am about to narrate was much easier to execute then and not as transparent, you see.

Anyway, the surprising thing is that my ma, yes, you heard right, was offered a place to study medicine at Hosahanapur College! This is because she won the first rank in the entire state and the education board couldn't in all honestly refuse her a place at the college of her choice. She, after all, had first claim on any or all of the seats. If they had refused, it would have caused too big a furore to sweep under their scandal-studded carpet.

Now, back to my scenario. To make this easier, I am going to narrate it from the point of view of Somu, the boy who scored the top marks in the entire village last year.

Somu and his da arrive in the city to choose a place at the Engineering College. Somu shakes the grime off his clothes as best he can, and pats his hair down using the dust-smeared, cracked glass of the groaning, overstuffed city bus window as a mirror, as he and his da journey to the interview hall. His father stands beside him, too close due to the press of commuters. Both of them are uncomfortable in the shiny new clothes purchased for this day from money obtained by emptying the rainy day fund. Somu's father is desperately missing his lungi and tries to discreetly adjust his crotch which feels confined and trapped inside the unfamiliar trousers.

Once in the vicinity of the interview hall, they join the queue of hopeful students snaking all the way to the end of the road and beyond.

Somu eyes the other applicants, every one of them effortlessly self-assured and better dressed than him. Despite his new clothes, Somu thinks he looks out of place and all wrong here in the city. His heart flares with the hope he hasn't dared give voice to until now, convincing him that when he exits this building, the proud owner of an engineering seat, he'll be well on his way to becoming one of them, these confident city boys. He hopes that in time, some of their poise, their sense of purpose will rub off on him, bestowing him with the ability to choose the right clothes, look like he belongs.

And then, it is Somu's turn to go inside, and he forgets everything else as he concentrates on what he has to do, this important step that will secure for him a future as bright and promising as every one of the people he has seen and envied outside.

There are big electronic boards displaying the number of seats available and the building is air-conditioned no less!

Ah, this is the life, Somu's da thinks, feeling the cool air soothe the itch in his crotch, his mind racing ahead to a future where his son has a house, complete with air-conditioning, in the centre of the city where they will all reside in luxury.

Do Da and I stand out? Somu worries. Do I smell? He sweats more when he is nervous.

The board says eleven seats available in Electronic Engineering, which is the discipline Somu aims to pursue at the Dhoompur Engineering College. He does a quick assessment. There are ten students ahead of him. Even if all ten of them choose the same discipline in the same college, he will get the seat.

The person in front of the queue chooses and the board changes the display. Somu blinks, waits a beat and blinks again. He's seeing things surely? Only one person has chosen and the number of seats available has gone down to seven.

He looks at the other disciplines offered by Dhoompur Engineering College and quickly makes up his mind. Even if he doesn't get Electronics, he can choose Electrical (eight seats avail-

able) or even Mechanical (ten seats). All good disciplines with guaranteed jobs. He's not worried. He has plenty of leeway. And then, there are four people ahead and no seats in Electronics, one in Electrical and only three left in Mechanical.

How did this happen?

'Please, Lord Ganapathy,' he entreats, seeking comfort from a god, who until now he had prayed to by rote and only at his mother's insistence. He looks at his da, pulling at the collar of his shirt as if it is strangling him. His da is clearly itchy in these unfamiliar clothes and is waiting eagerly to change into his regular uniform of vest and lungi. He grins at Somu and squeezes his hand. He doesn't have a clue, being unable to read. But then, Somu can read and he doesn't understand either.

What on earth is going on here?

By the time he gets to choose there are no seats left in Electronics Engineering, or Electrical or even Mechanical. There is one seat available in Civil Engineering and he goes to choose it, but before he does, that too disappears, and with the board making that whirring noise like a frenzied bee, the '1' changes right before his blurry eyes and sinking heart to zero.

What is he going to do? How did this happen?

His father goes to clap him on the back, and then seeing Somu's face, does not say a word. Silently he leads his dejected son outside.

There are seats available in other colleges of course, but they are too far away and how is Somu going to get there, and afford the cost of staying in a hostel? At least at Dhoompur College, he would have been a day student, travelling to and from the

college every day and helping his father out in the fields in the
evenings.

Somu's da tries to look upbeat for the sake of his son but it is
hard to keep a smile fixed on his face. His grin wavers, yearning
to be upended, his lips tilting down at the corners of his mouth.
Somu was their family's only chance out of poverty; he was bank-
ing on him.

Father and son barely register the crush in the bus back to
the bus station, side by side, but not speaking. The prickly new
clothes stick to their backs from the heat, and they try not to
think of the hopes and the excitement they had carried inside
them as the bus was traversing this same route only going the
other way. The buildings which had seemed so full of promise
and possibility, the confident people, all seem to mock them, for
daring to presume they could be one of them, that they could
belong here. They are, and always will be, outsiders.

And thus, they make their way back to the village, their disil-
lusionment trailing behind them like an out-of-favour pet, their
lost hopes haunting them like a ghost. The Ghost of Daring to
Dream Too Big.

Somu is still on the waiting list for Dhoompur Engineering
College but he doesn't hold out much hope. What is the point?

From now on, he will regard hope as his enemy, he will retreat
from anticipation, he will stay clear of joyful fantasies, and he
will be deeply suspicious of happy endings. He will be a farmer
like his father, and he will cry as he trudges up and down urging
the bullocks on through the dry, drought-cracked land that will
never be his, and his anger will burn in his chest like the relentless heat from the sun's orb beating down on his head. For he has

done his research, he has solved the Mystery of the Lost Seats. He knows why no child of the village, no matter how bright, has ever crossed through the imposing gates of the Engineering College and made it to the other side.

The Lost Seats are not lost, you see, but absorbed into the system, bought by people like you, sirs, ministers and lawyers, politicians and doctors, people rich enough to grease palms and purchase their children's way into futures denied the children of the villages.

So, here is the truth. The only people assured good futures are those who have enough money to buy their way in. Their children will go to the Engineering College and they will not study. They will drink alcohol and play truant and when the principal dares suspend them, they will go on strike. They will shut the college down. They will demand less hours of study and more breaks. Their influential parents will lean on the local police and politicians who in turn will lean on the principal, and he will give in like he always does. And in a few years, even though these students have failed every exam ever set, they will pass the final exam of the final year with distinction, newly minted engineers who will go on to build multi-storied buildings on foundations as weak and unstable as theirs, that will collapse after a few years killing the throngs of families living within. But will they be held accountable? Will they lose their jobs?

What do you think?

They will go on to other jobs where they will once again buy their way into the echelons of power and create figureheads like you, Chief Minister, and they will run our state and our country through you.

Didn't you start your career as a civil engineer, Mr. Minister for Justice, Law and Human Rights? Weren't you one of the engineers involved in the construction of that bridge near Mangalore which collapsed, killing one hundred and fifty people, seventy of them children travelling in a school bus?

You might say: 'Kushi, you are but seventeen years old, how do you know all this? Why are you making up these things? On whose authority are you spouting these tall tales?'

Ah, that brings me to the painful subject here—to the real reason I am writing this letter. That brings me to my father. He told me all of this.

My da taught in the village school all these years, but then he was promoted to the Engineering College in Dhoompur and his disenchantment began.

My da was perfectly happy teaching here in the village. He did not want to go to the Engineering College, be another of those teachers who abandon the village children for better pastures. He dithered and dallied. But then he thought that if he did teach at the Engineering College, he might be able to get some of the village students in. He was puzzled as to why they were not getting the seats they deserved. You see, none of us knew the true extent of the scam then. So, finally, he decided to take up the offer.

It was the worst decision of his life.

He soon discovered where all the 'lost' seats were going. He was going to do something about it but before he could, the horror I am about to narrate happened:

My da was the one who suspended that student, that influential politician's son (I am sure you know who I am speaking about). Da was summoned to the principal's office and was told in no uncertain terms not to suspend anyone again, no matter how provoking the circumstances. My father refused. His students misbehaved and he suspended them, not caring how powerful their parents were. And so, the students went on strike. And not content with just that, they went on a spree of destruction. They set fire to the library.

Now, my father loved books more than anything else, a love he has passed on to me, and he couldn't bear the wilful destruction of these tomes his pupils in the village school would have given anything to be able to have access to.

I picture my da in that library—the swirling saffron flames, the blanket of smoke—his eyes stinging and his breath being squeezed out of his chest by the acrid fumes, as he ushers the students out, saving all of them. And then . . . the crisp, scorched yellow smell of pain, the ravenous flames voraciously licking at his legs, depositing their blistering caresses as they travel up his body amidst the devastation of burning pages—distorted spines, cream pages shrivelling; all the knowledge contained in those black squiggles on white leaves disintegrating into wispy grey ash—and finding the next breath, a lungful of clean white air is suddenly a matter of life or death . . .

Did da regret going into that building? Did he exhale his last breath, choked out by smoke, thinking of us? Did he hurt? I try to will these pictures away, these horrible visions of my father's last moments that hijack my dreams and dog my waking moments.

I try.

My father's killers haven't been punished. They have not even spent a day in jail. I am sure they didn't mean to murder anyone; they were vandalising public property, that is all. Property that is public for the likes of them but not for the village children. They caused thousands of rupees worth of damage. Money that could have fed our entire village for weeks.

As I write this, these arsonists are sailing through the corridors of Dhoompur Engineering College, not attending lessons, not taking notes, confident in the knowledge (the only knowledge they have amassed so far in the course of their education) that they will pass their exams with distinction. They have not paid for what they did, for robbing me of my father and our village of a great teacher and provider.

That is all I have to say.

Kushi

PS: I know you may not do anything about this letter, you might dismiss it as the ranting of a schoolgirl, if you read it at all. Well, I am tired of feeling useless, tired of feeling like my hands are tied. I am sending a copy of this letter to the editors at the Deccan Herald, The Hindu and the Times of India.

Chapter 2
Kushi

Iridescent World

A year since my da passed. Six months since I wrote that letter.

I stand at the window of the sari shop in Dhoompur, our nearest town, and wait for a signal from Asha within.

Shapely, bindi-sporting mannequins, draped in turquoise, red and gold, grin at me from the cloudy glass window—a dingy shade of weary grey—smudged by a thousand handprints.

A year on and I miss Da so much every single day. His loss is a constant and unappeased ache in my chest. Ma has been my saving grace, my strength. And there have been my causes, of course. They have given me purpose. Campaigning to get the people living in slums moved into accommodation with walls and a roof never mind that it is mud walls and a thatch roof, (anything is an improvement on flimsy tarpaulin), is one of them.

That letter I wrote. It was published in all the newspapers. And it changed things.

The ministers finally made a pretence of seeming interested. They visited Bhoomihalli and met with me. That picture of me shaking hands with the Chief Minister, the letter held up in his other hand, made the news, along with a picture of him stooped in the entrance of Guru's hut, designed to endear the Chief Minister to the masses and undo, to some extent, the damage my letter had done to his credibility.

The Chief Minister promised that the system of seats allocated for entry to the Engineering Colleges would henceforth be based on merit only. And they have stuck to that principle, more or less, during the recent seat allocations, not least because journalists have been waiting outside the seating allocation hall, and interviewing students going in and out, who have dutifully reported any discrepancies.

Many of the village students have gained entry into the Engineering College, and what pleases me the most is that Somu was offered a seat at Dhoompur Engineering College to study Electronics Engineering. The picture taken of the Chief Minister with Somu and his family: his mother, two sisters, and his grinning father, unrecognisable in a shirt and trousers, clicked at the unfortunate moment when Somu's father was trying to adjust his crotch, made the news too, the proudest moment so far in the history of Somu's family.

'There will be many proud moments to celebrate from now on,' Somu's father said, beaming at Somu, when they came to thank me with a gift of their biggest marrow, coaxed from the cracked red soil on the tiny patch of land adjoining their hut.

There have been other changes. The arsonists who caused my da's death have been expelled and barred from studying engineering, even though their parents, who must be very high up in the influential chain—the ones funding all the politicians—tried hard to avoid this happening, and lobbied to have them moved to a different college in the city. I still feel they've escaped lightly. I think they should have served a sentence, or been cautioned at the very least. Ma says their punishment is having to live with the unavoidable fact that their actions took Da's life.

Bhoomihalli now sports two borewells (although they are not nearly enough, especially now that we are suffering a drought—I have been campaigning for more), a medical store and a doctor, who visits once a week, driving up self-importantly each Monday in his car. Every villager has now added an additional prayer to their daily list: 'Please God, if I or any member of my family has to fall ill, let us do so on a Monday.'

So, most of the concerns I raised in that fateful letter conjured out of bone-crunching grief have been addressed. The power cuts are still just as frequent, but we cannot have everything I suppose.

There was one other unexpected and yet very welcome outcome in the aftermath of the letter. What with all the interest in the village, Ma's fledgling catering business took off, and people came from far and wide to sample 'Sharda's melt-in-the-mouth delicacies' as Ma's wonderful culinary concoctions came to be known.

Also, the college finally accepted some responsibility and offered remuneration for inadvertently causing Da's untimely death. Ma didn't want to take it, but I pressed her to, pointing out that, with all the orders flooding in, she needed to think of proper premises instead of running her trade from our small cottage.

'We could buy that abandoned plot near the hill, Ma, convert one of the sheds there into a factory, hire the village women to help,' I urged.

Now, Ma's business (called Sharda's Kitchen), is flourishing. She employs most of the village in her factory: all the women and the men who are too old or infirm to work in the fields. She now supplies many of the big distributors in Bangalore and even to a few in Mumbai!

If Da is looking down on us, and I want to believe he is, he would be pleased. We are providing for the villagers like he used to, distributing most of the profit from Ma's business amongst people who need it more than us.

Da would have been so proud of me, I know. That letter changed me.

Since then, I have become the spokesperson for our village. I campaign about the lack of proper healthcare and education facilities in the villages and ask for more to be done for the desperately poor; I organise food drives and vaccination clinics, clothing banks and refuge centres for girls and women who are victims of rape and domestic abuse.

I am their representative because I have the ear of the newspapers—I can write a mean letter you see, one that will have the ministers sitting up and taking action, as they don't want to slip in public estimation.

I have been getting missives from people voicing their concerns, asking for help, and there has been the odd threatening letter amongst all the pleas. The first time I got one, written in bold, red letters, screaming the words, 'If you don't stop right now, we will hurt you,' I dropped the paper as if it had bitten me.

Ma had looked up then, her gentle, loving gaze scrutinising me.

'What's the matter?' she asked.

'I-I. . .' I held the offending sheet out to her.

Her face went pale, but that was the only visible sign of inner turmoil. Otherwise, she was as composed as ever. She ripped the letter into minuscule shreds and put her arms around me. 'There will always be people who'll be against you, no matter what you do, Kushi. And there will be more letters like this one. You must ignore them and do what *you* think is right. The people who pen such notes,' a contemptuous glance at the flecks of paper that lifted in the tamarind-scented breeze fanning through the open front door, 'are cowards, resorting to empty threats because they do not have the courage to do what you are doing.' Ma paused. She cupped my face between her palms and looked into my eyes. 'One thing, Kushi. I know you feel deeply about what you do. But remember to take the girls' feelings into account. Put yourself in their shoes. Don't project what you think is best

for them onto them. They need to make their own minds
up. I know it frustrates you when some of them don't want
to change. It's a long process, sweetie.'

'Oh Ma, yes, I know.'

Since then, there have been a few more vitriolic letters,
scarlet ink voicing similar threats, but they haven't had the
same effect as that first one. I get the odd look thrown at me
sometimes, men frowning and spitting, hecklers at my rallies: husbands angry about their newly vocal wives, mother-
in-laws of women who are no longer acquiescent puppets,
even mothers whose daughters are refusing to marry the men
they have chosen for them.

I do get scared but have learned not to show my fear. I
have taken Ma's advice, celebrated my successes and learnt
to ignore the threats and the jeerers, treating them as a con-
sequence of my job, brushing them away as nothing peskier
than the whine of a persistent mosquito.

I am here now to help Asha, imprisoned amidst new saris
and old fears, beading sweat, and looming decisions. Asha, a
slight waif of a girl, squished between her mother on one side
and her mother-in-law-to-be on the other, an opening and
closing parenthesis crowding a comma. A waterfall of saris
in various shades, cascade in front of her nose as her mother
and mother-in-law-to-be hold up one after the other for her
approval.

Asha's parents have four girls of whom Asha is the oldest.
The man she is betrothed to, against her will, (not that she

had a say in the matter, nobody asked for her opinion), is a divorcee, thirty to her seventeen with a young child that needs looking after. But he lives in a house, not a hut like Asha's parents and he is refusing dowry, which to Asha's parents, with four girls to marry off, is a godsend.

Asha wants to study at the Engineering College, get a job, and not get married this early. She's tried telling her parents, but they will not entertain what they call 'her whimsical fancies', and so she's asked me to intervene on her behalf.

Something flits back and forth in my line of vision. I look up, and realise it is Asha, waving to me, her eyes huge and afraid. I smile reassuringly at her, use the back of my arm to wipe my face of the sweat that has collected, take a deep breath and enter the shop.

The sari shop is like entering an opulent, iridescent world, so different from the one outside with its pungent reek of fish and drains and spices, blood from the butcher's shop and rotting garbage. It smells of shiny smooth fabric, the promise of new clothes and something else, something exotic. Rows and rows of saris in all the hues of the rainbow shimmer and glisten in racks behind the counter and tumble from the table in front of Asha.

'Welcome, ma'am, what can I do for you?' the proprietor asks me in a voice as slippery as melted butter.

'Sorry, I am with her,' I say, pointing towards Asha and he retreats, his face falling in a dismay he does nothing to hide.

'Hi Asha,' I say cheerily as I approach the trio.

Asha's mother and mother-in-law turn in unison and scrutinise me suspiciously. Asha flashes a cautious smile, fear dapping her face, and shadows shivering in her eyes. The women's gaze is questioning and I get straight to the point.

'Have you asked your daughter if this is what she wants?' I say, fixing my gaze on Asha's mother.

Huffing, the mother-in-law to be—or not, if I have anything to do with it—stands up abruptly, dislodging a pile of saris, which the shop assistant rescues just in time.

'Who are you to interfere in personal business? We are offering Asha a great proposal. My son has a good job. She will be well looked after and we do not even want dowry!' Her bulbous eyes jiggle furiously in their sockets with every vehement word she utters.

I keep my eyes on Asha's mother whose gaze wavers between her daughter and me.

'You know of course that Asha is the brightest girl in her class. She will get a place in the Engineering College here easily.'

'Engineering!' the soon-not-to-be mother-in-law gasps.

'Once she finishes her degree, Asha will get a good job and she'll be independent,' I say, looking only at Asha's mother, 'Isn't that what you want for your daughter? Or do you want her to be tied to a man almost twice her age, looking after another woman's child, when she is barely an adult herself?'

As I say this, I thank God that I have been brought up in an educated household, that my mother would not dream of forcing me to marry anyone against my will, old-fashioned through she might be in some ways.

The soon-not-to-be mother-in-law unleashes her ire on Asha's mother.

'Why are you entertaining this nonsense? Everything has been decided. We are offering your daughter the world. If you break off this match, she will get a bad reputation. It will not help if she does what this mad girl here is suggesting. Who will marry Asha if she goes to a college where she is the only girl in the class? And how will you get your other girls married if your eldest amasses an unsavoury reputation bringing disgrace upon your whole family?'

Asha's mother's gaze falters. I know I have to do something and fast.

'Asha will *not* be the only girl in class. I don't know why everyone seems to think engineering is a boys' profession when the computer engineering course in Dhoompur College, which is what Asha wants to do, boasts more girls than boys.'

Asha's mother is watching me intently now, interest piqued. I make the most of it.

'And Asha will get a good job at the end of it, she will support herself and she will find someone to marry, an engineer like her, who'll see past this nonsense about reputation. She'll have a life you've never dreamed of, the fulfilling sort of life that I bet,' and here I cross a line I know, and go a bit too far, 'you haven't had. Do you want her to have a future that mirrors yours? A future where she will slog day and night for little return and no thanks? She can be so much more! Times are changing now. Okay, let's say you won't be able to marry off your other daughters. What's so wrong with that? We can live without men, you know. Give your girls an education instead. Let them stand on their own two feet.'

When I see the hope blooming in Asha's mother's eyes, nudging away the doubt, I know Asha and I have won. I insulted Asha's mother, yes, but I spoke the truth. Like most women in the village, she has endured a life she did not pick, a life that was chosen for her, a life she has sometimes resented, and she would rather not have her children subjected to the same life, especially if there is another way out.

With my insistence that Asha will get a job, and be independent, she realises that what Asha told her and her husband was not a fanciful whim but the truth. There *is* another way and she will take it, and persuade her husband.

Asha's mother looks apologetically at the not-to-be mother-in-law. She wrings her hands as she says, 'I am sorry.'

The woman storms off, yelling, 'You will be,' slamming the door so forcefully behind her, that the whole shop shakes and the proprietor rushes out from behind the counter, his face pale as watered-down milk, and spends the next few minutes checking the hinges and the latch to make sure everything works.

I wink at Asha.

Asha's mother squeezes her daughter's hand. 'You have to study hard and bag that engineering seat now,' Asha's mother says, 'while I work on convincing your da. I have a battle on my hands you know.' But she is smiling fondly at her daughter.

Asha's face glows like the sky at sunrise bestowing the golden assurance of another beautiful day.

'I will, Ma,' she says, and, to me, 'Thank you.'

I leave the shop and squash the proprietor, who is standing behind the door inspecting the hinges, against the wall.

I ignore his heated 'Lo!' My heart is replete with the thrill of a job well done.

Outside, I blink as my eyes adjust to the relentless yellow glare, thinking of what I will tell Ma. As I do so, I realise that the normal sounds of the street have been masked by a roar and the mad revving of a vehicle, rare even here in Dhoompur. Almost immediately, I become aware of shouts, screaming, horrified yelling.

'Arre,' I hear. 'What is that vehicle doing?'

I scarcely have time to register the car that is coming too fast up the road, raising a squall of tawny grit, and scattering peddlers and pedestrians like fish through a hole in the net, when I catch my name stumbling from agitated lips, and then breaking into multiple fragments.

'Kuuuushiiii . . .' I hear. 'Get away from there.' Asha's voice, barely recognisable—shrill with panic.

I step backwards, tripping over the doorstep of the sari shop. The car swerves and comes right at me. I stare, unable to believe what I am seeing.

And then there is cacophony: high-pitched wails, screeches and cries, wide-ranging octaves encompassing human panic, a splintering and a shattering.

The gasping fuzzy taste of shock, the acrid smell of rust, the sensation of being pricked and punctured in myriad places at once, a burst of red; something flutters and then settles; scarlet words on a fuzzy beige background blaze before my blurring eyes.

Chapter 3
Raj

London, UK
Realm of Shadows and Smoke Screens

Raj lights a cigarette, leaning against the bin and taking a deep drag, and with the release of each intoxicating lungful of smoke, feels the stresses of the day leave him: told off by Mr Grey for not bringing in his maths book, detention for talking during Geography, detention for arriving late to Mrs McCray's class, and a fight with his mum this morning.

His mum—'I am late for work,' she had called, her face a grim mask of intense displeasure mingled with frustration, 'Are you coming or not?'

He had made her wait for a good ten minutes, watching from his bedroom window as she stormed up and down the drive, looking at her watch and tutting impatiently.

'Work is all you care about,' he had yelled, opening his window and sticking his head out. A gust of air ruffled his hair, requiring it to be gelled into shape again.

She had sighed, and looked up at him. He noticed the violet rings that shadowed her eyes. How very drained she looked. He was surprised by a sharp pang of guilt which was dispelled the very next moment by her words, each one precise, soft, deadly. 'The same old argument. You never tire of it do you?'

'No mum, I don't,' he'd spat out, gripping onto the windowsill so hard that his knuckles hurt. 'Because it's the fucking truth.'

She had blinked but not commented on his language. 'My work is what gives you all of this,' a sweep of her hand indicating their detached house, the manicured sweep of lawn beside the drive. She'd glanced at her watch, 'I'm going. I have a meeting at nine.' That look again. Disapproval and disappointment as she appraised him. 'You can walk to school.'

If I disappoint you so much, why did you have me? he had opened his mouth to ask, but she was inside the car, door shut, probably thinking of work, son already forgotten. Anyhow, he had asked it many times before and had got no reply, only a sigh—another one of her interminable sighs.

Raj closes his eyes, and lets the cigarette work its magic. When he opens them again, Ellie is in his line of sight, under the awning by the bus stop, standing slightly apart from the giggly group of girls she hangs out with. Her sunshine coloured hair spills out of its loose ponytail, and her eyelashes fan downy gold-dusted cheeks. Her strawberry lips pucker as she checks her phone and she frowns.

Raj stubs out his cigarette and lights another one just as Ellie's bus arrives and she climbs in. He takes another drag, and searches for her, then watches as she swipes her card, as she floats down the bus, as she grabs a seat by the window, as she looks up and across right at him and smiles, those perfect lips executing a perfect bow just for him.

She lifts a palm and places it against the window of the bus and buckles up her fingers just slightly; the charm bracelet she is never without, catches the light and glints gold. He blinks, not daring to breathe, the fresh cigarette burning down to a nub. Her gaze, glossy azure—lake water twinkling in the late afternoon sunshine—locks with his.

'Hi,' she mouths.

He looks round swiftly, just to make sure there is nobody beside him or behind him that she could be talking to instead of him. When he turns back, she is smiling at him, those enticing dimples dancing in her velvet cheeks. His lips move upwards of their own accord.

Ellie points a finger at herself, cups her palms together, bending her fingers inward to form a heart, then points to him, a gesture that he is pretty sure means, 'I heart you'.

He blinks. Did she just say what he thinks she said?

The bus starts with a groan and moves away and he is galvanised into action, running down the pavement, wanting to hold on to Ellie, his eyes never leaving hers until the bus turns the corner and picks up speed, leaving him behind.

Bereft, he bends down, and inhales huge gulps of silvery blue air that tastes of smoke and excitement. His heart strains against the constraints of his rib cage, as it pounds out in pulsing booms: *She likes me. She does. She likes me back.*

'Hey, Raj,' his friends say, catching up with him, slapping his back, handing him a can of lager. 'What was all that about? Running away from us, were you?'

He sits with his friends and swigs from the can. All is right with his world at least for a little while. Ellie smiled at him and waved from the bus window. She had held his gaze while he pursued her bus as far as he could. She had said 'Hi' and mimed that she liked him, he is convinced she did, pretty sure that he hadn't just imagined it, even if it felt like she had been following the script of one of the myriad fantasies he conjures up on a daily basis, with her starring in the lead role.

Raj listens to his friends' banter as the evening glides into night. He lights a cigarette, its red-tipped yellow glow punctuating the gloom, and watches as shadows steal down the walls of the flats opposite, stealthily at first and then boldly taking the whole estate hostage until there are only shadows swirling, grey contrasting with a darker grey, rendering solid objects mere silhouettes.

I wouldn't mind living in a realm of shadows and smoke-screens, he muses, his thoughts mellow, *a world with no rules, where nothing is solid or constant, where nothing is set in stone.*

He breathes in the scent and flavour of night: oil and smoke, perfumed breeze spiced with intrigue, fried yellow chips flecked with salt and tangy with vinegar, soft morsels of steaming white fish wrapped in crispy brown battered coats, comfy slippers and bubble baths, hot chocolate and warm duvets promising the sweetest of dreams.

Inside the flats on the other side of the road, children are being tucked into bed, with a story and a cuddle, goodnight kisses and assurances of love, their parents' soothing voices swelling in their ears, the last thing they hear before sleep gently claims them.

His eyes prickle, suddenly hot. He shakes his head to dispel his momentary despondency and joins in the impromptu sing-song that has started up, woozily mouthing words to songs he had no idea he knew. When his friends suggest beer-can football on the road, he joins in.

They are laughing and singing and drunkenly punting the cans about when one of the residents, a balding man with bushy eyebrows that meet over his nose in a hirsute bridge, opens his window, a spotlight of slanting yellow light briefly dispersing the shadows, and yells at them to, 'Shut up, people are trying to sleep here. Don't you have homes to go to?'

After he has closed his window, they go up to his door and pound it a few times, ring his doorbell and rattle the postage slot for good measure, before resuming their game.

Then, just as his team is winning the beer can football, Raj kicks a can right at the car idling up the street, which pulls to a stop in front of them. It bounces off the window and the flashing blue lights dance a tango on the washed out faces of his friends, their lost eyes suddenly sober as two policemen climb out of the car and walk towards him.

Raj bites down on the cigarette he is smoking and tastes paper and tobacco, copper and rust as he accidentally bites down on his lower lip as well and it starts to bleed.

Chapter 4
Sharda

Bhoomihalli, India
An Onion to Hot Oil

Dearest Ma,

I am cooking samosas for Kushi when howling starts in the fields beyond.

I knead the dough until it is nice and supple in my hands, as soft and yielding as my daughter's young, butterscotch skin when I shower it with kisses. I roll out the pastry and cut it into rectangles. Then I set to work on the filling, heating the oil, adding mustard seeds and curry leaves, waiting until they pop and sizzle and rend the air with the piquant aroma of frying spices. I add the chopped onions, the shredded ginger and crushed garlic and stir and finally, that knot of uneasiness stamping upon my heart, making it throb like an open wound seems to ease a tiny bit.

'You are so intuitive, Sharda,' you used to say, Ma, cupping my face in your knobbly hands, smiling down at me.

All day I have felt the imminence of the past I have kept at bay for so long, its looming shadow pressing down upon my chest, and clutching it in a throttlehold.

Even at the factory, I couldn't relax, despite the comforting noise and flurry beside and around me, my trusty team boiling and frying, chopping and stirring, washing up and drying, sorting and scooping, packing and labelling, laughing and chattering all the while; smells rising and wafting, spicy and tangy, sweet and sour. An amalgamation. A merging.

Now, the weight pressing on my heart has alleviated slightly but is refusing to disappear entirely. I imagine, as I stir, and the mixture achieves a translucent golden sheen and the wonderful perfume of roasting onions envelops me, that the claws of all the crabs I have sautéed, marinated and fried, are extracting their revenge, and crushing my heart in a pincer grip.

What is this warning that is so potent, threatening to choke the sins of my past out of me?

Don't dwell on it, I chide myself and instead think about my factory, the bustling hive of lively activity, a place that originated from just my love of cooking and has grown into this enterprise, thanks to my daughter and, in an oblique way, the huge sacrifice my beloved husband inadvertently had to make.

What would you say if you saw it, Ma?

I often speak to you in my head, Ma, and when I have pen and paper to hand, like now, I write letters to you. Letters that are never posted; a pile that has grown thick over the years, steeped in stark yellow regrets, pickled in brackish self-blame, tinged lilac with guilt.

Remember how you taught me to cook, how we stood side-by-side, you holding my hand and guiding it at the ladle? We cooked with the barest of ingredients, using mud utensils on a charcoal fire, and yet, those dishes are among the tastiest I have ever eaten. All my life I have tried to recreate your dishes, Ma, but they never taste quite the same, as they are not cooked by your hand, and seasoned with all the love you felt for me.

But it looks like I have succeeded, if not in living up to your wonderful standards, exactly, then at least in producing tasty food. My factory has had orders from all over India, Ma, can you believe it? It seems my products fly off the shelves, the customers say my food is authentic, that it tastes exactly like the fare they remember eating while they were growing up. All of this because you taught me to cook, and I took to it like an onion to hot oil, Ma, your analogy that.

I still cannot quite believe it. I wanted to be a doctor, but life had other plans. And after all that pain, that hurt, that loss, here I am. I have had such a wonderful life, Ma, a life I had not expected or dared to hope for after what happened—I am blessed, Ma, I truly am.

Once the onions, ginger and garlic have browned, I add the crushed chillies, the boiled potatoes, the chopped carrots and peas and think of what Kushi will say when she dances in from helping her friend Asha in Dhoompur, bringing with her a gust of air smelling of overripe fruit and tasting of eagerness, and news of the day she's had bursting from her lips even before she comes through the door.

Kushi lives true to her name—which means happiness, as you know—and brings joy wherever she goes. Kushi, who has been my reason to keep going after we both lost the man we adored: my husband, her Da. She is so full of life, Ma, so passionate about everything, fighting for what she feels strongly about, unlike others who rail against injustice but then sit back and do nothing. She brightens up even the gloomiest day with just the suggestion of a smile. She lights up her surroundings, Ma. She lights up my life.

Kushi is not quite eighteen, and yet, she is the leader of this village. People listen to her. She is not afraid to fight the bigwigs, the politicians and the lawyers. I don't know where she gets her courage, her fervour from. She makes me proud and terrified in equal measure.

I used to worry when she stayed out late at her rallies, even though I knew there were people looking out for her—

you know how traditional I am. But Kushi has taught me so much, she has changed me, softened me, showed me that I have been too rigid, very set in my ways, which is part of the reason why it all went so wrong with us, Ma . . .

I add garam masala and chilli powder, coriander powder and cumin to the fragrant mixture. It is as I squeeze in a pinch of lemon that I feel the grasp on my heart tighten into a vice and at the same time, the howling starts, long and low in the fields, and approaches nearer and nearer. It sounds like all the neighbourhood dogs are converging on our little cottage.

What has happened?

I rush to the doorway and peer out, even as my legs drag me back, knowing somehow that what I will learn will change my world forever. Involuntarily, my mind harks back to that other time—so long ago now and yet so immediate in my mind—to the reek of smoke and charred devastation, to tears burning on stunned flesh. Such ruin, so much loss, caused by the reckless indiscretions of one unruly matchstick.

I think of the recent past and another fire, this one taking my husband, wisps of ash-laden smoke bathing the spice flavoured air, painting it the deep aubergine of shock and panic. I picture the yellowish amber lick of flames, the blue-black of smoke that trail my destiny.

My nostrils are suffused with the smell of burning. I turn around, away from the fields where it looks as if a black, keening cloud is gathering closer to my cosy, much-loved kitchen. I take it in, and sense that nothing will be the same again.

The samosa mixture is singed.

Another omen.

Like the constriction in my chest.

Even as I take the pot of charred mixture off the hearth, my stomach cramps in remembered deprivation. Although it's been years since I have experienced the spasms of hunger that come from having nothing to eat and no means of obtaining food, I hate wasting even a tiny morsel. The thought of throwing food away when there are people starving makes my stomach twist from evoked malnourishment.

I'll need to cook something else for Kushi.

Kushi . . .

My tongue is suddenly thick, refusing to do my bidding as I desperately try to inhale a lungful of air. The ladle, escaping my clutch, falls to the floor with a thud.

I can hear them clearly now. The entire village seems to be convening at my doorstep. The ladies are moaning and hitting their heads. The men are more sober than I've ever seen them. The dogs dancing around their feet, and the lowing cows ambling behind add to the clamour.

I scan the crowd for a glimpse of my daughter, willing her slender form to come weaving, unscathed, through the press of people and animals, but knowing, deep inside where the premonition of peril is choking the breath out of me, that I won't find her, knowing this is why the villagers are here.

My legs give way and I collapse against the doorjamb.

Then arms are smothering me, propping me up.

'Kushi . . .' I cry out . . . Or do I?

'Amma,' someone says.

I hold on to the doorjamb for dear life.

She was spiralling in the air like a perforated balloon, I hear. *The car went straight for her. It wanted to harm her. She was the intended target. The sari shop shattered, shards of glass erupting in a deadly fountain.*

No. Nononono. Please God, you have taken so much from me, not her too. Not my beloved only child.

'Where is she? Where is my daughter?' My voice is a scream—a never ending shriek.

I see a face contorting in consternation, a mouth opening in a cry.

'There was a letter beside her. Some sort of threat,' someone says.

'Why would they go for Kushi?' someone else wails. 'That girl is a saint. After all she has done for this village, for us . . . '

I picture my daughter's face when she got the first threat, the colour draining from it like water evaporating from mown fields leaving furrowed earth behind.

'It is nothing,' I had said to Kushi. 'Ignore them. They are cowards.'

My fault. All mine. Why didn't I take the threats seriously? Why didn't I watch over her?

'Take me to her,' I manage to mouth, grabbing hold of the person next to me. 'Take me to my daughter.'

I see huge, slightly squint, gram-flour-hued eyes widen with worry; glistening specks of perspiration dot an upper lip; pitted skin like a much tacked, well-worn map; the curvy groove of double chin like the ripe interior of a juicy yellow papaya; a mustard seed mole on a left nostril; a chilli-coloured bindi awry on a forehead; wiry hair, like coconut coir, glued to a head with perspiration and terror. I do not see the face I want to, the face whose features I have traced a million times. Kushi . . .

Then there is the spicy, sweat-infused smell of fear, the taste of a thousand panicked entreaties dying on my lips, as insubstantial as the air I fail to breathe in, as I give in to the stranglehold on my heart.

Chapter 5
Puja

London, UK
Cauldron of Secrets

Puja sits in the living room, laptop balanced on her lap, seeing to her backlog of work-related emails: one from her accountant which needs attention, *five* from the chairman of the residents' association in one of her buildings, increasing in urgency and tone, the last one all in capitals.

As always, as she looks at the figures her accountant has sent across, she allows herself a flash of pride, a brief glow of accomplishment. How far she has come! After everything that has happened, here she is. Successful businesswoman. Owner of several properties across London.

She looks at the clock blinking in the corner of her screen and falls back to earth, her good mood evaporating like bubbles from a flute of champagne. Almost midnight. Where is her son? She tries to shrug off the prickle of unease, the blaze of anger, the bitter purple taste of regret and failure in her mouth. Raj is punishing her for this morning's argument, she knows. He'll be with his unsavoury gang of friends, haunting that estate by the school.

The first time it happened, when she had come home to find that he wasn't in bed as usual, she'd driven everywhere looking for him. She'd found him at the estate, smoking and drinking and laughing in a way she hadn't seen him do for a very long time. She had confronted him but he had ignored her, playing up all the more for her benefit. In the end she'd had no choice but to drive home and wait for him. He'd stumbled home very late that night trailing a miasma of cigarette smoke that permeated the house with its pungent smell. They'd had a huge fight.

She exhales deeply as she pictures what will happen when he does deign to come home. They'll have another spat. She'll cut his allowance. He'll yell and fume and sulk for days.

Sighing, she goes back to her emails, rubbing the back of her neck with a weary hand as she tackles the escalating complaint from the residents' association.

Fragments of the dream that had plagued her the previous night, the dream that she could not remember on waking, leaving only a lingering unease in its wake, are suddenly vivid before her tired eyes . . .

A woman, her hair wild: a bushy silvery tangle framing a face crocheted by delicate threads spun from the weary loom of a long life. Her stride purposeful, her sari in tatters. The shawl she has wrapped around her shoulders is grey as a drowsy sea in the wake of a storm, glints of dull green thread visible, perhaps relics from an earlier era when the shawl was new and shiny, full of promise.

She has changed over the years, folded into herself. Her eyes, though, are still the same: intense shards of steel grey. Her voice when it comes is high pitched, nasal, as if she is speaking from the pits of her soul: 'The cauldron of secrets is bubbling. It is set to overflow. You need to come clean. Release the confidences, flush out all the lies. It is time . . .'

Puja blinks; the email she's trying to compose and failing, blurs before her eyes. It's been a while since she's had these dreams.

This is why I was tossing and turning last night.

The past that she foolishly assumed she had subjugated and flushed away, is suddenly there, right in front of her, this woman has taken her back to the day it all ended: the ripe reek of manure and agony; swaying marrows; leering, yellow smiles. The woman's calm eyes: a sea of tranquillity in the panic-scented murk, an anchor amongst the confusion, the iron and ammonia taste of trepidation.

Flashing blue beams swoop and dive across the gloom of her living room, briefly illuminating it, and jerking her back into the present. She has been working in darkness, she realises, having forgotten to switch on the lamp or pull the curtains closed. The only light in the room stems from her computer and the images flickering on the muted television screen, desolate in their silence.

The doorbell rings, startling Puja into action, making her shut the computer screen and pull her cardigan close around her.

Ah, finally. Raj must have forgotten his key as usual.

She plasters a smile on her face as a peace offering for driving off that morning without him and opens the door, only to find her son sandwiched between two policemen on her doorstep. Shock robs her of breath, of voice.

Of course, she thinks inconsequentially. *The flashing blue lights in the living room; they were coming up our drive.*

She breathes her son in, every inch of him. He seems fine, nothing broken. *Thank you, God.*

Raj is biting his lower lip as he does when he's anxious. His eyes are swollen, the expression in them vulnerable, reminding her of the shy little boy who used to look up at her, holding out his arms, a plea for affection.

A pang in her heart. *Why didn't I indulge him? I couldn't. God help me, I just couldn't. I still can't, not that he craves my love anymore.*

He had learnt, in time, to not ask, the naked need in his eyes being replaced by a surly, sullen, glare; although glimpses of the little lost boy shine through the dour barrier he has constructed every once in a while, stabbing her.

My fault. I have failed him. In so many ways.

'Raj, are you okay, son? What happened?' she manages, her voice a pitiful squeak.

Raj's face is green. He is swaying on his feet. He looks like he might be sick any minute. The policemen let him go with a warning that his behaviour will not be tolerated again, that he's lucky the can he chucked did not mark the car, that the next time, Puja will be picking him up from the station. Raj nods meekly and rushes upstairs without a word to any of them.

Puja shifts her weight from foot to foot, her larynx clogged with residual fear, with thoughts of what might have been. What is the etiquette in this situation? Does she invite the police in?

They do not stay, thank goodness, and she closes the door after them and leans against it, the wood cool against the back of her head which is throbbing, sore.

She hears her son retching in the bathroom, and wishes she were a different woman, one who would go to her son and hold him, ease his pain, soothe his turmoil. Puja stays there like that until the pulsing blue lights from the departing police car draw an arc on the walls of her dark living room and then, she closes the curtains, switches off the TV and goes upstairs.

Raj is in bed, his long adult body sheathing the defence-less boy within, turned away from her.

'This cannot continue, Raj,' she says.

No response.

'What were you thinking?' she asks. 'What next? I'll be hauling you from the station? I thought you were just play-ing up, harmless teenage fun; a phase you're going through. But it keeps getting worse. I am so busy, I don't need this on top of everything else . . . '

He turns towards her and his face is knotted with rage. 'Work, work, work! That is all you bloody care about. If I am an inconvenience getting in the way of your success, why on earth did you have me?'

The yeasty vapours of alcohol, stale cigarettes and vomit swarm in the closed air of his room, making her want to gag.

'Look about you, Raj. Do you realise how lucky you are, with your PlayStation and Xbox, your TV and your designer clothes? Where do you think they come from?'

'All you care about is material things, making more money,' Raj yells, eyes flashing, '*I* don't care about all this, I could live without . . . '

'Really? Then why do you complain when I cut your allowance? What do you know about hunger? Have you experienced the tortured seizures of an emaciated stomach, the anxious tremors of not knowing where the next meal is coming from? You spoilt brat. Your room alone could house two of the huts I grew up in. I keep making allowances for you, thinking you're a teenager, that you're going through so much, but do you know what I was doing when I was your age? Have you any idea?'

All the anxiety, the dread she experienced when she saw Raj flanked by policemen, bursts out of her in one furious tirade. She just wanted to let Raj know that he had crossed a line, and that she would not entertain the law escorting him home on a regular basis. But instead of getting her point across calmly, she's lost her rag . . .

Why is she like this with her son? Why can't she tell him what she's really thinking, hold him like she wants to, show him she cares?

Because I am afraid. So afraid to love him in case . . . in case he gets hurt. In case I lose him.

Instead she rails at him, driving him further and further away.

He is *hurt. And I am losing him anyway.*

And why bring up her past? Why now? *Because of that dream. So real. Bringing it all back . . .*

Raj sits up, long legs bunching, staring a challenge at her. 'No mum, I don't know what you were doing when you were my age. I don't know anything about your past, because you haven't cared enough, or you haven't had the time to tell me. Maybe, it's because you're always fucking working.'

That does it. Something inside her breaks. She strides up to her son, lifts her hand and slaps him, hard, across his cheek.

Chapter 6
Sharda

Seething Silence

Dearest Ma,

I sit by Kushi's bedside and I write to you like I have over the years. These letters are my lifeline, and keep me tethered to the here and now. I want to be strong for my daughter, be there for her when she wakes.

I don't want to collapse again like I did when I found out what had happened —I have jotted that down in my previous letter. I am keeping a record of exactly what took place so I can produce it when we take the people who did this to my beloved Kushi to court.

Beside other beds along this long, illness-infused, grief-infected room, loved ones keep vigil like I am doing. We do not meet each other's eyes, preferring to keep our blame and our self-flagellation, our what-ifs and if-onlys to ourselves.

I look at Kushi, hitched to the bed, the myriad tubes keeping her alive sticking out of her like pins in a voodoo doll, her face ashen as clouds bereft of rain, and I will her back into my life. My vital girl, full of life, now just a shadow.

My fault.

Why did I ignore those threats?

How could I have wilfully let my perfect girl, naïve in the ways of the world, out of my sight when I, of all people, know the true, monstrous nature people hide behind false smiles and cloying grins?

I want to find the people who did this and hack them to bits, squeeze the heinous breath out of them. But I dare not leave my daughter's bedside, be lax in safeguarding her yet again.

I'd had a premonition all day, that sense of unease burdening my chest. Why didn't I act on it instead of ignoring it, tamping it down, and hoping it would go away? Granted I didn't know what exactly was going to happen—nevertheless, I should have gone in search of Kushi, found her and brought her home with me, and kept her safe. Or I should not have let her go out at all that day.

Now, here she is, my treasured child, her pale face motionless as the moon suspended in a nest of clouds in those tormented hours just prior to dawn's emergence from behind the stuffy curtain of night.

Does she know how very proud I am of her? How much she has taught me? How she has changed me, made me grow, own up to my mistakes, come into my own?

I want a chance to tell her. Please God, please Ma. I want her back. She is my life, my reason for living.

What will I do without her?

❋ ❋ ❋

Ma, when the doctor's eyes shied away from my needy gaze, desperate for a flicker of hope, when I noted the slump of his shoulders, I knew that it was not good news.

'Both her kidneys were destroyed in the accident,' he said. 'She needs a transplant or she'll be on dialysis for life.'

I jumped up. 'What are you waiting for?' I said.

I have been tested. Now it's just a question of transplanting my kidney into Kushi's body and, hopefully, she'll be fine and back with me sooner rather than later.

My beloved girl.

He's here, the doctor. And once again the darting eyes like a thief avoiding capture. The defeated stoop. What could possibly be wrong? How much more can I take?

Please God. Please.

He shakes his head. 'I am so sorry.'

'What . . . what do you mean?' I ask.

'You have only one kidney.'

'B-but . . . how?'

He twists his lower lip as if the words he is uttering hurt him. 'Having only one kidney is more common than people think.'

'So I can't. . . '

We look at my prone daughter, at her washed out face, at her machine reinforced body.

'No.' A deep sigh. 'I'm sorry.'

Punishment, I think, *for failing to protect Kushi.* I quickly make calculations in my head. Even after selling the factory and our cottage and taking out a loan, I will not be able to afford to keep Kushi on dialysis for long. Each treatment is frighteningly expensive. I have never coveted money, Ma, have always given it away to the more needy, but at this moment, I wish with all my heart that I was rich, that money was no object.

'We cannot afford dialysis for long,' I whisper.

I wish I could give her my one kidney. I don't mind dying so she can live unhindered.

But I know no doctor would agree to such a thing.

What kind of a cruel God are you, Lord? Why should my innocent girl who has not a bad bone in her body, who has fought to make life better for her fellow villagers, who loves so fiercely, lives so truly, pay for my mistakes?

The doctor sighs again, runs a hand across his drained face, and spreads the sweat beading on his upper lip all over it. 'Then it's imperative that we do a transplant, the sooner the better. Kushi's blood type is rare and trawling through donors to find a match will take a lot of time.'

Please God, Kushi deserves a lifetime of time. Please. Take me instead.

The doctor's voice cuts into my prayers, my fraught pleas. 'Does she have any other relatives?'

I stand there dumbstruck.

Is this your doing, Ma? Or Da's? Is all this part of a big joke God is playing on us?

I know of course, what I have to do.

I looked her up long ago, Ma, found her number. I carry it everywhere with me, tucked into my sari blouse, along with my letters to you. I just haven't had the nerve to call. I have never been the bravest, Ma. You know that. But now, I have to.

I look at Kushi and find my absconding courage right there. I plant a kiss like an offering, a blessing, an entreaty, a wish, on my daughter's soft, young, but impassive cheek and then go in search of the international phone booth in this vast hospital that houses the ailing and their petrified relatives in this impersonal town miles away from Dhoompur and Bhoomihalli.

The little clinic in Dhoompur was not equipped to deal with Kushi's injuries. They said this hospital was our only hope. And now, she, this woman whose number I have carried around close to my heart, is our only hope.

I take a deep breath and dial her number. I hate the fact that *I* cannot give my daughter the gift of life, that I have to ask *her*.

Will she make me grovel?

A beat that lasts a lifetime. Then the phone rings, once, twice.

'Hello?' Her voice, a British slant to her Indian vowels, bridges nearly two decades of seething silence.

Chapter 7
Puja

Raw Wedge of Lime

Puja's son looks at her with stunned eyes that reflect her shocked face; startled tears sprout as he lifts a palm to his cheek that now bears the imprint of her palm.

Raj scrutinises Puja as if seeing her for the first time, his face, with the exception of the reddened cheek, the pale, dazed cream of a newly whitewashed room.

In the traumatised silence, smelling of old secrets and new misgivings, an echo from the past she has kept hidden for years, resonates through the layer upon layer of armour that encompasses her heart: *the scent of shock, the taste of tears, pink-tinged brine.*

I am no better than my da, she thinks.

Her phone rings, shrill, puncturing the wounded atmosphere, colouring it with burnished sound, and she whips it out of her pocket, hand shaking, the offending palm stinging.

'Hello?'

A bruised heartbeat of static and then, 'Puja?'

You spend almost twenty years building a wall, she thinks, swaying on her feet. *You layer it, brick by brick with the silence of each month that passes with no communication with the past and then, like moss that creeps over the wall and travels to the other side, like ants that find the chinks in the age worn bricks and make their arduous way across from one side of the wall to the other, one voice leaps across the gap and bridges it—that cadence, that tone, as familiar as your own—capable of rousing so much love and so much hurt.*

A voice I have been hoping and fearing to hear, she thinks, as she lowers herself very gently onto the scuffed carpet of her son's room, *every time I have picked up the phone, every single day these past two decades.*

'Sharda?' She squeaks—the only sound her vocal chords seem capable of producing.

'It is you?' There is relief in the question, and apprehension and agony—hurt mingling with angst. Above all, there is urgency.

And just like that, the years that have elapsed since she last saw this woman, collapse like land assaulted by flood, washed away by the truant waves of a roaring, monsoon-incited ocean.

'What is it?'

She pictures the tangled coil that still connects them after a span of nearly twenty years and the distance of five-thousand miles. She wishes she could unravel the coil, smooth out the past, so there were no longer these bumps and hurts, no longer all the pain and guilt and allegations and misunderstandings, over which they are stumbling—a past like a thickly congealed river of tar that they must wade through to get to the other side, to reach each other.

'It's . . . my daughter, Kushi . . . she's dying.' Tears saturate Sharda's voice, and flood down the telephone line.

Puja closes her eyes. *Sharda. I am speaking to Sharda.*

'Kushi needs a kidney, urgently. Mine . . .' A sigh that is hijacked by a sob, 'I have only one it seems. Please. She needs you. We need you. Come home.'

Home . . . myriad nuances radiate from that one small word. Everything lost. Everything . . .

'It is not my home. It hasn't been for ages.'

'I know that. I know. But . . . I can't think what else to do . . .'

'So I'm your last resort?' Not what she meant to say, but the words come out in a bilious rush, sharper then she intended, like sucking the juice from a raw wedge of lime. Puja bites down on her lower lip, tastes iron and salt.

'Do you want me to beg? Then I will. Please, Puja, please help.'

'I . . .' Images from the past cascade behind Puja's closed lids, images that over the years she has consciously tuned out, and tried to ignore. Hurtful words and angry recriminations: marinated in grief, caked in the dust of almost twenty years of dormancy, the ubiquitous orange powder that embroiders the air of the country she has denounced, of the life she has buried.

'Kushi's on dialysis right now, but I cannot afford to keep her on it for long,' Sharda's desperate voice, cuts into Puja's musings, and brings her back to the here and now.

Puja takes a deep breath, and steadies herself. 'If it's money you want . . .'

'We don't want your money . . .' A blaze of heat bubbles through Sharda's ravaged, dread-soaked voice, making her sound clipped, abrupt.

'I need you. Kushi needs you. Please, Puja.' Sharda's anger dissipates as quickly as it flared, and is replaced by raw anguish.

Anguish that resounds in Puja's chest, which feels as if it has been spliced open, and all the protective armour built up over the years collapses.

Be careful. Her heart, which has never completely healed after the past had finished with her, warns. 'I don't know if I can . . .'

'Please . . .' Sharda whispers, wretchedly.

'I . . . I'll come,' Puja says, without thinking it through fully. Or, perhaps, thinking more clearly than she has in years. 'But I can't promise . . .'

'Thank you.' Sharda's voice blooms with gratitude like flowering jasmine buds. 'Thank you. Please, come as soon as you can.'

What have I just done? Puja wonders. And even though Sharda has cut the call, she holds the phone to her ear with her still-smarting hand, the taste of new fears on her suddenly parched lips.

Chapter 8
Raj

Fresh Wounds and Stale Alcohol

Raj stares at his mother, watching an alarming array of emotions parade across her face. His mother who is so cool and collected, except when she is raging at him. His mother the accomplished businesswoman and rubbish parent. His mother who's just given him a tiny glimpse into her secretive past—she grew up in a hut? His mother who's just hit him for the first time in his life.

Puja sits, uninvited, on the floor of his room, the phone still pressed to her ear. Now that the ultra-rare emotional display is over, she looks completely zoned out. Is she ever going to leave?

Raj is exhausted and wants to sleep away the horrendous evening he's had. The sobering ride in the police car had seemed to take forever, and he'd prayed that the nightmare he'd wound up right in the middle of would be over soon, and that his mother wouldn't flip; he'd sworn to himself that he would never drink or smoke or get into trouble again.

'Raj?' Puja's voice is tentative.

The room smells rankly of fresh wounds and stale alcohol. It tastes of blood, hot, red. It feels inflamed, like his throbbing cheek.

He does not want to talk to her. He is so angry. So hurt. So tired. He just wants her out of his room.

'Go away,' he mumbles, lying back down, pulling the duvet over his head.

'Raj,' her voice insistent. 'We have to go to India.'

He throws off his duvet, sits up, and glares at her. 'Have you gone quite mad? First you slap me, and now this.'

His mother blanches, wilts like a flower without water. 'Son, I'm so sorry.'

'Don't call me son. You sure as hell don't treat me like one.' His voice trembles and he is annoyed with himself for this weakness.

She stands, and goes towards him. He cringes. She hesitates and squats back down on the carpet again.

Raj sighs. What an evening this was turning out to be, going from horrible to abysmal in the space of an hour.

'You've barged into my room uninvited, hit me, and now you won't leave. In case you haven't noticed, I've had a terrible evening, made worse by you. I want to sleep.'

'I'll leave in a minute, but you need to know this. I'm not joking. We're going to India.'

He looks at her, properly this time. She is clutching the phone to her as if it is her talisman. She looks as knackered as he feels. For the second time that day he is surprised by a pang of guilt for what he is putting her through, but it is quickly replaced by righteous resentment when his sore cheek pulses with remembered pain.

'Why India for Christ's sake? That wasn't Dad on the phone, was it? I could have sworn you were talking to a woman?'

Another pang. This one of hurt at the thought of his dad, who moved to India years ago and has invited Raj to visit countless times since. Raj has refused on principle. Why should he go all the way to India when it is his dad who left? His dad finally gave up asking a couple of years previously when…

Raj suddenly, desperately craves a cigarette.

He knows, deep down that his mum is right in some ways, that he shouldn't resent her working. It is because of her that they are able to live more comfortably than most of his classmates.

What he begrudges is his mother not showing him an ounce of affection, always keeping him at a remove, treating him as if he is someone she has to put up with rather than someone she cares for. At least his dad used to be demonstrative, used to hug him, and kiss him goodnight.

After his dad left, Raj used to go to his mum, yearning comfort, a cuddle, a pat, *something*. But she would smile at him, give him food, a toy and fob him off on his nanny, who was lovely, whose arms were expansive, but who never belonged to him, who went home to her own kids at the end of the day.

But warring with the pangs of hurt when he hears his mum talking about going to India, there is a tiny blossom of hope—the first shoots budding after winter's thaw.

Perhaps his dad is trying again.

'No, not your dad.' Her voice brittle as old bones. And then it softens. 'He cares for you, you do know that?'

Raj turns away so she does not see the tears blistering in his eyes.

Who is this woman? This is not the remote mother he knows. First the slap, which, although it hurt, made his mother seem more real, more flesh and blood than the remote sighing and tutting robot he has come to expect.

And now this softer side he has never been party to . . .

They should have had this conversation when his dad left, not now! Back then, when he was that much younger and lost without his dad and more in need of her sympathy, there was only silence.

He's had enough. 'So who was it who called? Why did you say we had to go to India? Why are you speaking in riddles? What has happened to you?'

His mother's eyes are liquid—swirling pools of hurt. He cannot bear to look at her, so he worries the duvet instead.

'The woman who phoned is Sharda—my sister.' Puja puts her head in her hands. Her body slumps, a small brown comma punctuating his cream carpet.

Her words perforate the stifling, vinegary fug pervading his room, leaking shock, and the mothball odour of mystery. Countless, baffled questions trip over one another in their haste to slip from his tongue.

'What!' is all he can manage. He cannot believe it. All these years his mother has made not one mention of a sister.

But then his mother does not mention much of anything at all, really, except for her work. And his failings. His mother is a world unto herself, a world to which he has always been denied entry. He shouldn't be surprised that she has kept her sister from him. Come to think of it, he *can* believe it. He wouldn't be too shocked if he were to discover she has a brother too, or heck, a whole other family. Who knows what else she is hiding, or what else he will find out.

'Kushi her . . . her daughter is very ill. Her kidneys are destroyed and she's on dialysis. My sister . . . she wants me there. I . . . I have agreed to go . . . '

The rage that erupts blazes a trail through his alcohol-lined innards. 'Wait a minute. Let me get this straight. You're willing to put your precious work on hold and cross an ocean to go to visit this girl, your niece, who's in a hospital five thousand miles away—a girl you barely know, the child of a sister you've never mentioned—when you did not even stay with me that one time I was in hospital, when I desperately needed you?' he spits out and his mother's face crumples before she turns away from him to hide it.

It was just after his father had departed for India. Raj had been dreadfully ill, a spiking fever which refused to relinquish its hold on him, and stayed in the hundreds no matter how much Calpol and Neurofen his nanny administered. He was hospitalised and was being subjected to various tests to try and find out the cause.

Raj had been terrified, scared and lonely after his nanny left that evening. He had wanted his mother, had begged her to stay with him in that strange room with its whirring machines and wailing children. But his mother had abandoned him to the blue-smocked nurses with their well-meaning smiles that did not quite reach their tired eyes. Even then, *especially* then, she had chosen her work over him, not willing to give it up for a few hours to stay at her sick son's side.

That night the boy in the next bed had convulsed, and all the nurses and doctors in the hospital had converged on him, it seemed to Raj. He can still recall the strident panic in the air, the rasping sounds of curtains being drawn to shield the other children, the staccato clip of feet urgently slapping against the tiles, the frantic beep, beep of the machines, and the boy's face, pale and lifeless, as he was wheeled away. . .

Raj had sat up most of the night, terrified, shivering, and afraid to call out for the nurses. A nurse had found him rocking, and whispering, 'Mum, Dad,' over and over, as his sobs shuddered through his fevered body, the tears making slippery, wet tracks on his face, and his eyelashes crusted in salty clumps.

He has hated hospitals with a passion ever since. He looks at his mother now, and sees the memory of that hospital, of him begging her to stay, reflected in her eyes.

He had launched himself at her, his hot body trembling with relief and disbelief, when she visited the next morning, unable to trust the evidence of his sickly eyes, having convinced himself that this was it, that he would be wheeled away like that other boy, that he would never see his mum or his dad again. He had breathed her in—she smelled as always of a dewy, sun sprinkled, spring morning—had revelled in the unfamiliar luxury of her arms for all of a minute before she'd untangled him, gently backing away, patting her hair in place, smoothing her skirt, perching delicately at the edge of his bed, keeping him, as ever, at arms' length.

'I've promised my sister,' she says now, her voice low, hesitant.

'You haven't spoken to her, or of her, that I know of. And now she calls and you pack up your life, your work, which you've always maintained is so very important and will fall to pieces if you're not around, to embark on this trip to India . . .'

Why is this unknown sister so important and I am not? Why don't I matter? Why have I never mattered?

She sighs, fiddles with a thread on the carpet, not meeting his eye. 'Raj, she wants me there. I said I'd go . . . her daughter . . . Raj, we need to go to India. I'll book the first flight out.'

'*We* don't need to go to India. Dad's invited me there so many times. And I've always refused. If I didn't go for him, what makes you think I'll go now? For some aunt and cousin I haven't even heard of up until now. I'm not going. *You* go if you want to so desperately.'

She sighs again. 'I'm sorry son, you don't have a choice. Not this time.' She is referring to his dad and his pleas for Raj to come visit. Her voice is brisk, all emotion wiped out of it. 'Good job you only have a week left of school before you break up. I'll call the school, get special dispensation.'

'I am not travelling five thousand miles to a country I've never wanted to visit, to see a girl I do not know, who is in a hospital at that. I loathe hospitals.'

And whose fault is that?

'You are coming. You have no choice.' His mother's voice has morphed back into that efficient, no-nonsense tone he knows.

'I can stay here on my own.' He is so tired; he just wants to sleep. Can't she just leave him alone?

'You're coming with me.'

'You can't make me go.' Why does he behave like a toddler having a tantrum in his dealings with his mother?

'I can. I'm booking a flight now and I'll get leave of absence from your school.' Her voice softens suddenly, 'I know this is all very confusing, especially after the evening you've had. I'm . . . I'm so sorry for hitting you.' She hesitates and looks at him as if to say more, but then she rubs at her eyes wearily. 'Try and get some sleep. Good night.'

She leaves the room, closing the door softly behind her.

I hate you, he thinks. *A girl you barely know is ill halfway across the world and you are prepared to drag me over there, blithely making the decision for both of us, callously usurping my life without a thought as to how I might feel, what I might want, not caring that I'm leaving my life and everything I know, all that is familiar, behind.*

A picture forms in his mind of Ellie mouthing, 'Hi' through the bus window, and gesturing 'I heart you'. Ellie—the one good thing in his life at the moment.

It is instantly chased away by another wave of loathing toward his mother.

I want to go to school tomorrow, see if Ellie meant what she said, not come with you to a country I don't know and never meant to visit. And all this upheaval to travel to the other side of the globe, to visit a hospital of all places . . . and yet, when I was ill, you didn't even stay. You didn't stay. How can I forgive you?

Sleep, so desperately craved just minutes ago, eludes him. India—the country he's always hated, because it took his father from him. A provocative country full of surprises, now extending the consolation prize of aunt and cousin, in return for snatching his father. India, now showing him a different side to his mother. His mother, who has refused to give him anything of herself—except material things, certainly nothing like the love he has so craved—is now preparing to travel five-thousand miles to the hospital bedside of an unknown niece, jumping to obey the summons of a mysterious sister and in doing so, uprooting his life and hers. His mother, who has always been a closed book, is now marginally opening and promising pages full of secrets. What more will he find? And does he really want to?

Raj pulls the duvet over his head the way he did as a child. Breathing in the familiar smell of his sweat, alcohol fumes and stale cigarette smoke, he is assailed by new fears, clandestine worries and a vulnerability that he only unmasks privately, in the fusty dark.

Chapter 9
Kushi

The Bitter Tang of Medicine and Malaise

I am trapped, I cannot move. My hands and upper body feel trussed like the mutton carcasses suspended in Abdul's meat shack in Dhoompur. I cannot feel my legs. There's something sitting on my chest, seizing it in a stranglehold.

Where am I?

I feel tiredness like an ache deep in my bones, a weariness so heavy it weighs down my eyelids. There is a harsh taste of nails in my mouth as if I have swallowed whole, one of the tumbledown rust buckets that pass for buses in Bhoomihalli.

When the rush of blood whooshing in my ears dies down, I make out other sounds. The clatter of trolleys, the beep of machines, the smell of anaesthetic, the humming of electricity, sobs and moans and agonised entreaties.

The bitter tang of medicine and malaise.

I am in hospital.

Why?

Something scratches at the edges of memory, elusive, fluttering. I drag my sore eyes open, resisting an intense urge to close them immediately. The first thing I see is the framework of ugly apparatus surrounding me, contraptions holding me in place like the yoke on a bullock's back. No wonder I feel imprisoned.

My eyelids heavy, I move my throbbing eyes past the machinery hemming me in. Beside my bed, a chair and folded into it, is my ma, clutching a sheaf of papers, her mouth open, her eyes closed. Streaky grey hair escapes her bun. She looks as if she has aged ten years since I saw her last.

I obey my sinking eyelids and give in to the exhaustion that holds my body captive. I close my eyes.

Is this a dream? A strange, disorientating nightmare?

I could open my mouth and ask Ma but what if no words come? Can I even speak or have I lost my voice too, in this strange state that I find myself? Why does my body feel alien? Why do I have no control over it? What are all these machines? What has happened to me? The last thing I remember is talking with Asha's mother in the sari shop . . .

The sari shop . . .

Roaring sounds bear down upon me. The car . . . is coming right at me . . .

Glass splinters in a shower of dagger-edged crystal. The blazing burgundy stench of fear, the pungent smell of ammonia, the iron taste of rust . . . red letters on faded yellow . . .

The rush of urine slick on my thighs. Bright crimson droplets stain silvery shards glinting vulgarly in the sunshine . . .

Screams, laments, and then silence . . .

No, please, no . . .

My heart is jumping fit to escape the confines of my ribcage. I want to scream this nightmare away. I want to run, to rid my prone, unresponsive body of its mechanical cage—outpace this outlandish fantasy that feels so incredibly real.

'Kushi,' Ma's strangled voice utters my name as if it is a prayer she is offering to the gods. 'It's okay, my darling . . .' She consoles me as she used to when I was ill as a child. Her calloused hand, a legacy of years of chopping and stirring, cooking and cleaning, rests on mine.

My mother's touch—so familiar and reassuring, now signals the beginning of a waking nightmare, as the implications of feeling her hand on mine sink in.

This is real.

My eyes are still shut tight, but I must have displayed some agitation for Ma to soothe me in the way she used to when I awoke in the thick of night tormented by vivid dreams.

'You have too intense an imagination,' she used to say, smiling fondly at me as she brushed the sweat-slicked hair away from my forehead.

I am not imagining this.

I want Ma to lie, to tell me I'm dreaming.

I want to talk to Ma, make sense of this, but I do not want to open my eyes again, acknowledge this world I find myself in, this horror I have woken up to. I cannot afford to be here, like this, helpless, dependent on others, unable to move.

I have so many things I need to do. I have my causes to crusade, I have a rally scheduled. I don't want to be a victim, like the women I arrange counselling for on a daily basis, although it is gradually sinking in that I am.

I want to cry, rail, shout.

I keep my eyes closed and wish, like a deluded child, that when I open them again, my world will be back to normal.

I yearn for the dreamy numbness I was experiencing before I regained consciousness, the gentle balm of nothingness.

'We will fix this,' Ma is saying softly, as if she can read my mind, sense my turmoil. She's always been able to tell what's going on in my head even before I have voiced it. And now, here in the midst of this nightmare, broken as I am, eyes shut tight in denial of what is happening to me, she is still able to tune in to what I am feeling and offer comfort.

How, Ma? How can you sort this out for me?

I have always fixed other people's problems for them secure in the knowledge that if ever I was in trouble, Ma would be there for me. She is *my* problem solver. But now . . .

My faith in Ma is immense, but how can she get me out of this?

A male voice, right beside me, startles me. If I wasn't hemmed in by medical equipment, I would have jumped. 'How has she been?'

Something is yanked and pulled, one of the tubes feeding into my body causes a pinprick of discomfort to register in my left hand.

'She was restless just now. Thrashing about.' Ma's voice, distressed.

'It happens. She's not in any pain, I promise.' The doctor's—I assume he is my doctor—voice tries for assurance. It brings to mind the deep indigo of a summer's night settling over golden fields. It is threaded through with tiredness.

What is the hollowness I feel then? I want to ask. *This all-encompassing exhaustion.*

'She's doing fine in the circumstances. Her stats have stabilised. The dialysis is doing its job for now.'

Dialysis? Is that what the machines are for? I have heard that word before. What does it mean? I rack my brains to remember, but my head feels sluggish, it will not cooperate.

'Doctor, I have done the calculations and even if I sell the factory and the cottage, I can only afford to keep her on dialysis for another month or so. What are the chances of finding a donor before then?' Ma's voice throbs with pain and worry.

Sell the factory? The cottage? Oh God, no . . .

'Have you spoken with your sister?' The doctor sounds grave.

What is he saying? Is he talking to Ma? What does he mean?

'Yes.' Ma stumbles a bit over that one word of assent.

What? Ma's sister? Ma doesn't have a sister!

'She's agreed to come here.' Ma's voice is the colour of rain-washed tamarind gleaming in the morning sunshine.

A sister? Ma has a sister? Am I dreaming this?

Ma and I have laughed about the fact that I am an only child of only children, an oddity in a village where everybody is related to everybody else and have enough relatives to form an army.

'Well then . . .' The doctor says. I can picture him nodding.

'But . . . she did not promise anything . . . we haven't been in touch for years you see. Things happened in the past and I . . .' She chokes on her words.

There is a longish pause. The doctor clears his throat.

Then, Ma says, 'I am hoping that when she sees Kushi she will agree to donate her kidney . . . but in case she decides not to . . .' Ma's voice sounds as if it is drowning in a lake of sorrow, swirling with undercurrents of worry and ache. 'I curse the fact that I have only one kidney. I wish I could give it to her anyway . . . '

A kidney? So my kidneys have packed up then . . .

Now it comes to me what dialysis means: to purify the blood, as a substitute for the normal function of the kidney. I see the car bearing down. I hear the terrifying roar that crowds out everything else. I taste blood . . .

With effort, I direct my mind away from the memory of the accident and concentrate on what is being said. I still cannot believe Ma has a sister she has never mentioned. Why? She said something happened in the past. What did?

'We are trawling through donor registries, trying to find a match for Kushi.' The doctor takes a deep breath and his voice sounds as worn as the soles of a farm labourer's feet. 'But her blood group is rare and it is taking time . . . we'll step up the effort, do all we can . . . '

'Thank you, doctor.' I know Ma is frantic from the way she breaks up her syllables. I can tell that she has ever more questions, but is sealing them behind the barrier of her lips for now.

Suddenly I am beset by a horror worse than any I have envisaged. Will I die if they don't find a donor for me and the money for dialysis runs out? I don't want to die. Please God. Not yet. I have so many things to do.

'When do you think she will wake up?'

'All in good time. Her body has been traumatised. It is still recuperating. It needs the medium of sleep to heal. Why do you ask?'

'I have to go to the bank . . .' Worry paints Ma's voice the wet brown of muddy meadows.

How much money does dialysis cost? Can we afford it? Which hospital is this? We cannot be in Dhoompur clinic, it does not have the requisite facilities. So where am I?

'The nurses will keep a close eye on her. And I'll come by every half hour to check on her. She'll be fine. Please don't worry. You do what you have to.' The doctor is reassuring.

How long have I been sleeping? How much time have I lost? What day is it today?

I push down the rising waves of panic. I hate the fact that I am so completely out of control of my life.

'Thank you, doctor.' Ma says, her voice awash with gratitude and fear and anxiety and nerves.

What is this doing to you, Ma? Why did you lie to me, Ma, and tell me you are an only child, like me? Why did you wipe your sister from your life? What else have you lied about?

I hear the heavy drag of footsteps leading away—the doctor leaving, I presume—and then feel Ma's hand on mine again.

'Kushi,' her voice comes softly. 'I don't know if you can hear me, sweetie, but I have missed talking to you and I will talk as if you can hear me, okay? I have to go away, just for a bit, just to the bank. We are in Palmipur hospital, the dialysis ward—you were moved here from the ICU yesterday—so it will take me some time to get to Dhoompur and back, but the nurses and doctors here are very nice and will keep an eye on you. They have been absolutely brilliant so far, Kushi, and you will be fine, sweetie, that's a promise.' A breath, and then, 'I feel so terrible. This is all my fault.'

How? How is this your fault?

My face is cupped in the palm of Ma's hand, her touch as comforting as warm shelter on a wet day. I feel her cinnamon-scented breath on my cheeks.

Ma, the car . . . It came right at me, as if, as if, whoever was inside meant to harm me.

Voicing the horror of what I experienced, even in the privacy of my own head, and the suspicion that has been lurking since my memory of what happened has returned, makes me shiver and cringe. It is unbelievable. I am making it up, surely? Why would anyone want to hurt me?

Red letters on faded yellow fluttering beside me as I fall, just before everything fades to black . . .

As if she's heard what I am unable to utter out loud, Ma says, once again surprising me with her uncanny penchant for interpreting my thoughts, 'I should have realised those threats were serious. I should have looked out for you.'

Despite my fatigue, I am consumed by a welcome flood of rage that sends the adrenaline pulsing through my rigid body.

'You are not to blame,' I want to tell Ma, but the lethargy that pervades my body, instantly snuffing out the adrenaline, robs me of speech.

It is so much easier to pretend to be asleep, to not have to see in my mother's eyes what this is doing to her, to not have to clock the burden of her fear and heartache—which she will try and hide from me but which I can sense even with my eyes closed—especially when I haven't come to terms with my own fears yet.

'When I get better, I am going after the people who did this to me, and I will bring them down,' I want to say, but I lack the conviction I had in spades not so long ago. Am I going to get better?

Those people who did this to me have not only destroyed my kidneys, they also seem to have robbed me of my self-worth, the belief that I can do anything I set my mind to. I have always felt older than seventeen, I have always felt invincible. But now I am scared, a frightened little girl.

I am someone I do not recognise. Someone I do not want to be.

I am hiding behind my closed lids. It is hard enough to acknowledge my dread to myself; I do not want to see this new, fearful person I have become reflected in my mother's eyes.

'The police are looking into who did this and the villagers are on their case. Everyone in Bhoomihalli and beyond are up in arms and will not rest until they have caught and punished whoever did this to their beloved, young leader,' Ma says, gently. 'Kushi, the most important thing is getting you better. And you will, sweetheart,' her voice, shaky but determined, imparts faith. 'And don't you go worrying your pretty head about the cost either. I am going to sell the factory. '

No, Ma, not the factory.

I can feel her taking a deep breath. 'And there is something else, sweetheart. I have wanted to tell you this for a long time. But I . . .' she gulps and then the words come out in a burning rush like the murky water that gushes from the borewell after several gurgling false starts. 'Kushi, I have a sister. She is coming here to see you. I'm sorry I did not tell you earlier, Kushi. I . . . I meant to. But . . . so much happened in the past, and she and I . . . we're not close anymore and . . . the longer I left it, the harder it became.' A pause, then, 'I am leaving some letters for you to read here by your bedside, just in case you wake up before I come back, sweetie. They'll tell you what happened, why I haven't spoken of my sister . . .'

Letters. The sheaf of papers she'd been clutching when I opened my eyes and saw her beloved self snoozing in the chair beside me.

'In these letters which I've written over the years, I've penned our story: yours and mine, every word a prayer and a wish. Like you, I too find solace in words, Kushi. These letters are like my diary. I carry them everywhere with me, tucked into my sari blouse, adding more letters to the pile as and when I feel the need to write. They were with me when this happened to you and I've written a couple more and have been re-reading the earlier ones while waiting for you to wake. I hope they'll tell you what I have tried and failed to do so many times all these years. I hope they will explain what I cannot.' Her voice makes me think of marshmallow clouds in a rainbow sky at sunset.

'I am going now, my love. I will be back before you know it.' I feel her breath warming my cheeks, her lips pressing against my forehead. I am enveloped in her smell: sweat and sandalwood and worry and fear.

Then I hear the soft rustle of paper settling, the breezy swish of her sari skirt, her gentle footfall walking away. She is gone, and I am bereft. The displaced air beside my bed settles with a sigh. My heart is heavy with the weight of words unsaid.

I wait, listening to the sounds around me. The grumbles and the groans of pain. The determinedly cheerful chatter of nurses and the discordant drone of visiting relatives.

Then, slowly, I drag my unwilling eyes open, and look around.

I can make out rows of beds on either side of me, their occupants sprouting tubes like mine; only part of a hand, or a curl of ebony hair, or a flash of skin are visible.

Before I can take in any more, a nurse bustles up, smiling kindly. 'Awake, missy? And how are we doing?' She adjusts some of the tubes feeding into my body.

'Your ma has not left your bedside all this while, not even to eat.' The nurse nods toward the chair beside me. 'That's been her bed you know, that chair and a similar one when you were in the ICU. Just her luck that the moment she pops out, you wake up.'

I feel a stab of guilt. *I couldn't face you, Ma. Not when I'm all over the place. Sorry, Ma. I need some time to gather myself.*

'She'll be back soon. Meanwhile, you'll be seeing rather a lot of me.' The nurse winks. 'Your ma asked us no less than twenty times to keep an eye on you before she left.' She grins, yanking at a tube. It stings.

To distract myself, I look past the row of beds, breathing in the pale lemon smell of medicine and misery, urine and phenyl, hurt and entreaties, anguish and hope. I imagine I can hear the whisper of a thousand frantic prayers, heroic faith trumping desperate odds. I fancy I can taste the greenish orange of wretched despair at war with cautious optimism.

Doctors—fatigued gods in their smudged white coats and sallow grey faces—field, with each impeded step, the pleading, prostrate relatives, with their folded hands and their swollen eyes, begging them to rescue their loved ones from the dominion of death.

'All looking good. Your doctor will be along shortly. I will look in on you again in a bit. If you need anything just press this button here.' And with another kind smile, the nurse moves up to the next bed.

The chair beside me is devoid of Ma, but, as promised, she has left letters there in her stead.

I have a purpose now, something to distract me from my misery. My mother's story and why she has never mentioned her sister all this while.

The other Kushi, the girl I was before the accident, would have been annoyed with Ma for keeping such a big thing to herself, not sharing it with me. Especially when she has always stressed the importance of truth, taught me to prize honesty, and to live my life by it. Especially when I have always believed there were no secrets between us, that she was as transparent with me as I have always been with her, which is why I pretended to be asleep just now, so I didn't have to lie to her, by having to show a composure I do not feel. I did not want to show her how terrified I am, and for her to have to deal with that as well as the fact of my accident, and the frantic rooting around for funds to pay for my dialysis, and the desperate search for a kidney donor and the very real possibility of my considerably shortened lifespan.

Now though, I am relieved that there is something to divert me from this living nightmare. I am pleased to have something else to focus on other than my uncooperative, wrecked body.

I pick up the first letter, written in Ma's elegant handwriting.

'Ma, I know you wanted to be a doctor but you would never have passed muster, not with this beautiful handwriting,' I had said once.

She had looked up at me, her eyes puzzled, scrutinising me over her glasses.

'Aren't doctors' notes notoriously illegible?'

And she had laughed that cascading laugh of hers.

She has told me she had to give up studying medicine when her parents died, as she was unable to concentrate on her studies and failed her exams. Is that a lie too?

I suppose I will find out; the answers to all my questions right here in these letters, in her words. I remember her holding my hand and helping me form letters as a child. She had sat with me patiently every day until my handwriting became neat enough to pass muster. The teachers at school would mark my work but she would make me redo it until it was up to her standards.

'Presentation is important,' she said, again and again, 'whether you are cooking, or dressing up to go to school, or writing. Your handwriting says so much about the person you are.'

My fine handwriting, (although not as lovely as hers), is thanks to her.

I look at the first letter, my eyes burning. These are letters my ma has written to *her* mother.

I balk, not wanting to go further than 'Dearest Ma', but my eyes drag down the page, swallowing her words like brinjal soaking up oil in the cooking pot. She has given me permission after all.

Feeling like a voyeur, I lean back, my head nestling amongst the drug-permeated, linctus-scented pillows and start to read in earnest.

Chapter 10
Sharda—Childhood

Recipe for a Happy Family

Extract from the school report for Sharda Ramesh, Upper Kindergarten, Age 4.

Sharda is a quiet, shy, eager-to-please child who is a delight to have in the class. She is very hardworking and extremely bright also, being proficient at reading and writing, and showing a natural aptitude for numbers.

❊ ❊ ❊

Dearest Ma,

When I think back to my childhood, this is what I remember:

The dark hut, which Da had to bend to enter, with its soot-etched kitchen and the one room where we lived and ate and slept, the mud walls which cracked in summer and leaked during the monsoons, the hay which dripped in the rains, and we had to keep pans throughout the house to catch the drips, the tangy odour of disintegrating manure, the rotting stink of the woodlouse-ridden beams barely holding the thatch up. We would eat our meals to the music of the rain tangoing on the roof and drumming onto the pans. The smell of wet hay tickled my dreams.

The toilet and the cramped cubicle where we washed were in a lean-to outside—that coconut frond topped and walled shed—where the dog slept and where the coconut husks and twigs were stored. If I close my eyes now, I can almost inhale the smell of hot water and soap and dog and kindling and contentment as you lobbed warm mugfuls of water onto my wriggly body and scrubbed it clean of the adventures of the day.

Every once in a fortnight or so, we would have fish, when Da had saved up enough to negotiate for the rejects from the boats—fish too small and too plagued with bones to sell. I remember being shaken awake at the crack of dawn and taken to the fish market, the soft air, saturated with the drowsy dream-infused aroma of night, whispering lullabies as I dozed on Da's shoulders.

I hear the tantrums of the waves, the crashes and the rumbles as they collide with the rocks, long before the coconut fronds part, a swaying curtain, to reveal the rush of greenish turquoise depositing select gifts onto the moist, cream beach. Boats bob black on froth-capped blue. Yellow nets flash as they get closer to shore. The scales of thrashing fish glint in the sun. Seagulls swoop and crabs scurry into sandy shelters.

Da sets me down and I try to grab a crab with both hands, but it scoots into a hole and disappears, too fast for my clumsy efforts. The boats anchor in a rush of noise and smell, salt and ammonia. Fisherwomen are ready with baskets, haggling for fish.

Afterwards, Da and I would swan home with a bagful of rejects, a bargain for less than five rupees. I can almost taste the fish curry and fried fish we would eat later that evening; I see myself carefully prying the last sliver of flesh clinging stubbornly to the multitude of bones, a rare treat.

I remember long days steeped in joy spent at the little stall, Ma, that you and Da used to man in the patch of earth beside the highway that bisected our village, and which the villagers had appropriated for market in the hope that the buses that shuddered past would stop once in a while, affording business. I would place the vegetables you had coaxed out of our sorry-looking patch of land into their waiting bags, and carefully count out the change, and you would grin at me, pat my head, and mouth, 'My wonderful girl.'

We would eat red rice and pickle most days. We would only eat the vegetables you grew if we did not manage to sell them and they started to go bad. The milk we got was so watered down that we couldn't even make curd from it. But, despite all this, I was completely, incredibly content.

And then came the day which would mark the end of my life as I had known it, the day everything would change forever . . .

You haven't been yourself for some time, Ma. You have been sleeping a lot and when you wake, your face is the greenish yellow shade of the underside of banana leaves. I often hear you retching in the lean-to.

'Are you not well, Ma?' I query many times.

And you smile a smile that is a tad weary at the edges and assure me that you are fine.

One day, you sit me on your lap, cup my face in your palms and say, 'Since you're growing up so quickly, Sharda, into such a wonderful little girl, it is time you learnt a bit of cooking.'

I jump off your lap, skipping with delight at being treated like a grown up.

'We'll cook the okra we couldn't sell yesterday, what do you say?'

We squat together on the kitchen floor and you show me how to handle a knife. You give me a blunt one so I don't cut my fingers and patiently, you teach me to chop onions, garlic and ginger.

'The holy trinity of our cuisine,' you say smiling and I smile along, although I do not quite understand.

You heat the oil and add the mustard seeds and the curry leaves. I love the heady scent of frying curry leaves and put my face too close and one of the popping seeds nicks me in the face. I cry out, Ma, and you gently rub my cheek with your magic fingers.

You ask me to add the onions and I notice, as you thrust them at me that you have gone green again. I hear you heaving as I add the onions and watch them go from pinkish white to translucent gold, the piquant, tart reek of raw onion replaced by the heady aroma of comfort.

By the time you come back, I have added the garlic and ginger as well and am in the process of stirring everything together.

'Well done, my darling, you're a natural cook,' you beam and I preen as delight floods my being.

You ruffle my hair and together we add the okra, and you show me how to keep stirring it until the sticky gooey strands disappear. You add just a smidgen of water, put the lid on and leave it to cook.

'Now, since you're being such a star, shall we make kheer,' you say, 'just for today, as a treat? I feel like something sweet.'

I am beside myself. We are only able to afford one cup of watery milk a day and there is never enough for kheer, which is my favourite sweet in all the world.

'I've been saving milk for the past few days,' you say, smiling, 'for you, for this. Because today is a special day.'

'Why? Is it a feast day?' I go through the list of feasts in my head, wondering which one it is that I have missed. We did not get the day off at school, so it cannot be a major celebration, definitely nothing to do with any of the gods.

'No sweetie,' you say softly. 'It is a special day because I have to tell you something very important.'

'Okay,' I say, itching to get on with the making of the kheer, breathing in the spicy smell of the okra, pleased that I am good at cooking like you, Ma.

I am given the very important job of opening the cardamom pods and crushing the seeds. The dog pokes his nose in the kitchen doorway, drawn by all the smells wafting into the courtyard. Outside, the coconut tree fronds romp in the sudden wind that has started up, heralding rain; dust swirls marigold in the sunshine and the dog sneezes, his expression one of great surprise and I laugh and you say, 'What's so funny then?'

Your sari is dusted with flour from kneading chapathi dough to go with the okra. Our little hut smells of roasted cloves and cinnamon, of caramelising sugar and sweetening milk as it thickens into kheer.

'What did you want to tell me, Ma?' I ask unable to wait any longer.

Caressing your stomach, you look at me and smile, and your smile is radiant, even though your face is tired. 'You are going to have a little sister or brother soon, Sharda. A baby is growing in my tummy like you did not so long ago.'

I am going to be a big sister!

'Your da and I,' you say, 'will need your help in looking after the baby. Big sisters have big responsibilities, you know. They need to set a good example.'

I nod solemnly, excited and pleased. I touch your stomach and then kiss it, whispering, 'Hello, baby. I am your Big Sister and I promise to look after you, always.'

You laugh, Ma and tell me how lucky this baby is to be blessed with such a wonderful big sister. 'And are the cardamom seeds ready?' you ask.

I rush to finish the task assigned to me and in my haste, bring the pestle down hard on my hand instead of the cardamom seeds I am supposed to be crushing and scream with the agony of it and the dog barks and thunder growls and there is mayhem.

You take me in your arms, Ma, so I am settled in
your lap right beside the growing baby and I wish,
how I wish, that I was the one curled up within
you, safe and free from the pain that has claimed
my hand and will not ease no matter how hard you
blow on it and ply it with cold water and rub it with
your magic hands.

❊ ❊ ❊

Recipe for a Happy Family:

A man
A woman
A little girl

*Grow the little girl in the woman's belly until she's ready. Bring
her into a world where she's the sun, the brightest star lighting up
the stormy sky, the full stop that completes the man and woman's
world, the angel who is their greatest wish granted, the laughter
in their life, the word that makes up their sentence, the meaning to their existence, the sugar in their kheer, the spice in their
curry.*

No garnish necessary. No seasoning needed.

How is the little girl to know that she is not the full stop,
the ending that makes their story complete? That there is

more to come. A brighter sun, a shinier star, a more delightful angel, a better word, a zestier condiment, a more potent
spice . . .

＊ ＊ ＊

After the day you tell me I am going to be a big sister, Ma,
the life I have become accustomed to disappears; drastic
changes render our cosy household unrecognisable. As the
baby grows in your stomach, it seems to take you away from
me. When I wake up to go to school, you do not wake with
me. I learn to heat up last night's rice with water to make
conjee, which I eat with pickle for breakfast. You say I am a
brilliant girl, a godsend, but you don't beam at me like you
used to; you smile with great effort and then close your eyes
and go to sleep again.

You do not accompany Da to the market like before so he
is always rushing, continually busy and does not have time
for me. A worried frown permanently creases his forehead.
You are always lying down. Your face pale, your eyes heavy,
one hand cradling your stomach.

I worry that the baby is hurting you, that it is taking you
over. I worry that this is the ma I will have for always, that
the laughing, active Ma I have known and adored will become a distant memory.

I try very hard to put a smile on your face, to turn you
back into the ma you were before. I bring you food I have
carefully prepared myself, and I try gently to get you to sit
up. But your face goes green when you see the food and

you say, sighing, 'This looks wonderful but I can't today, sweetie.'

'Were you like this when I was growing in your stomach, Ma?' I ask.

Perhaps all babies do this and when the baby comes out, the ma I remember and greatly yearn for will be back.

You smile and pat your stomach fondly, and I wish it was my face you were touching. 'No, you were such an easy child, both inside my womb and when you came into this world. This one is giving me so much trouble.'

I beam at the thought that I was good even in the womb and then I am puzzled, Ma, that you are not upset with the baby for troubling you. But *I* am. I try not to be, but I am so mad with it at times. At school, I cannot concentrate, although I enjoy learning. I am thinking of how this baby is stealing you and the carefree da I knew away from me. I cannot remember the last time I heard Da laugh or even saw him smile. I cannot remember the last time you were up and about.

I do not know if I can like this baby who is already changing so much around our house, making me feel invisible sometimes, even though I try so very hard to be noticed, to be good, to help. I feel like I am fading away into the background, with this baby hogging the limelight and your affections, which until now had been focused brightly and solely on me.

I don't want to feel the hurt that makes my stomach cramp at night when I am lying next to you, Ma and you do not hold me close like you used to, because you have to lie on your back now, to be comfortable. I do not like the feeling I get when you stroke your stomach, when your face lights up as you speak about the baby, the feeling I cannot yet identify as envy.

I do not know if I even want this baby. Then I push the thought away. No, I cannot think like this. I am going to be a good big sister. I am going to love this sibling, look after it and make you and Da proud.

And then it is that time of year when exams loom. The last time I had an exam—my very first—you sat with me, Ma, massaging my hair, cooking my favourite dishes and feeding me as I practised my words and numbers. You and Da, although uneducated yourselves, believe very much in the power of education.

But now, even though my exams are forthcoming, I have to cook for Da and myself, I have to look after you, Ma. Despite this, I work extra hard as I do not want to let you and Da down.

On the day I get my report card, and find that I am at the top of the class, I skip the whole way home from school. This is the day you will forget about the baby for once, focus on me instead, I think. As I near our hut, the dog comes rushing at me, hurling his body at my feet, raising a tornado of dust.

'What's the matter?' I ask, scratching behind his ear. I never usually get this reception.

The hut is quiet, eerily so. I tumble inside anyway, holding out my report card, shouting breathlessly, 'Ma. Ma?'

Our hut is empty and I feel foreboding shooting daggers up my spine, rooting my legs to the ground. I look in the lean-to, behind the hut, in the fields, even inside the well. All empty.

Then I am running, bare feet flying, to the market, gulping in the smell of decomposing vegetables and raw fish, soil and spices, choking on the briny taste of fear. Our market stall is empty, Ma. I knew it would be, somehow, but I was holding out desperate hope. I stand there, in that stall bereft of you and Da but still haunted by Da's scent of stale sweat and hard work, and tasting salt and snot and panic with every gasping inhalation, I finally give in to the sobs that have been building in my chest, huge wheezing moans that rend my throat, and steal my breath.Soft arms envelop me, and for a brief minute, I think it's you, Ma. But the overpowering odour of dried fish, the crinkly feel of the sari, is all wrong, and I cry even harder, afraid to open my eyes, to acknowledge the fact that the world has turned upside down and I have lost you and Da. I fight the irrational conviction that this strange smelling woman whose embrace does not feel remotely like yours will be my mother from now on.

'What's the matter, sweetie? Sharda, what is it?' The woman whispers in my ear.

At her use of my name, I open my eyes. It is Sumatiakka, who squats in the mud next to our vegetable stall and sells fish.

'I don't know where Da and Ma are,' I hiccup.

Her worried face relaxes into a smile.

'Is that all?' she asks, wiping my eyes with her sari pallu, and I don't mind that the fish smell is now all over my face, that there might even be a fish scale or two stuck to my cheeks, my relief is so huge and all encompassing.

'Your ma went into labour suddenly, sweetie, earlier than expected. There were complications. The baby was stuck the wrong way and your ma had to be rushed to the clinic in Dhoompur. It all happened so fast, you see, so you must have slipped their mind . . . '

They only care for this baby. I am invisible to them.

Sumatiakka arranges for Modduanna to take me to the clinic in his rickshaw. At the clinic, I breathe in the alien, bitter odour of pills and I want to be sick. Then, I see you and Da and I run all the way up to you, my hurt and anger forgotten, as relief, sweet and golden effervesces in my chest.

'I thought you were lost,' I sob, trying to bury myself in your chest, Ma, yearning for the soothing luxury of your arms around me.

But you hold me at bay, even though your eyes shine with remorse as you knead my hair like you have not done in ages. 'I am so sorry, Sharda. It all happened so quickly, the baby was stuck, it almost died. Your da had to bring me here. By God's grace, the baby is fine. A real miracle.' Your voice softening, your gaze dissolving as you talk about the baby.

I want the comfort of your lap, Ma. I want to press my ear to your heart and hear your voice reverberate as it makes its way out of your throat.

But there is a bundle in your arms that is obstructing me from doing so and as I stand there, it emits a series of tremulous wails, much like the emaciated kittens that sometimes wander into the market in search of food.

I am intrigued by the bundle, but I have something important to tell you, first, Ma, something that will make you shine.

'I got my report card, and I came first,' I say, flapping the now crumpled sheet of paper in front of you.

But you are distracted, Ma, not paying attention to me. Not even looking at me anymore. Fuming and desperately hurt, my eyes stinging and fresh tears bubbling, I stare at the cause of all my upset. And my tears dry on my cheeks, and my distress is forgotten as I take in the perfect little being swaddled in cloth, with its miniature scrunched-up face that emits those plaintive mewls.

'Do you want to hold your sister?' you ask, Ma, and that is when I know the baby is a girl.

'She is very special,' you're saying. 'She almost died, you know. The nurse had to swing her upside down and slap her a couple of times, gently, of course, before she started breathing. She is a real marvel this one.'

Your words barely register as I hold the squirming, wiggling bundle in my arms. Her hands are tiny, with diminutive fingers bunched into delicate fists that she waves in the air as if railing against the world. And then, she turns her minuscule face in my direction and tries to open her eyes. She struggles to focus her new-born gaze on me and when she does, opens her little mouth in a huge yawn, a perfect 'O', displaying startling pink gums and a rosebud of a tongue. And just like that I fall in love with this vulnerable being.

My sister. Puja—meaning prayer.

'All our prayers answered,' you say, Ma, at the naming ceremony, and I nod in solemn agreement.

Chapter 11
Raj

Uneasy Truce

Raj slouches in his seat, jabs earphones into his ears, and turns the volume to its loudest setting. He does not want to go to India with his mother. He wants to be with Ellie.

He has loved Ellie since the very first day of Secondary School, when she sat in front of him and he was dazzled by her hair, a halo of gold glinting in the weak September sunlight that angled in slanting streaks into the classroom. Ellie, of course, had never given any indication of even knowing who he was, except for that incredible wave and mimed words from the bus that evening—was it only the day before yesterday?—that ended with him almost getting arrested. He hasn't been back to school since.

Did that wave and her subsequent declaration really happen or did he imagine it? If it did, then does it mean Ellie knows he likes her and that she likes him back? Will she acknowledge him when he comes back? When is he coming back?

Lord, he needs a smoke. What hell to be stuck next to his mother on a nine-hour flight, travelling to a country he never had any intention of visiting, especially after Raj's father chose it over him.

His mother is gesturing to him.

'What?' he growls, tugging an earphone out of one ear.

'I . . .'

If he didn't know her better, he would have thought she was blushing.

She gestures towards his cheek. 'I'm sorry about that.'

He nods, and goes to plug his earphone into his ear again.

'I . . .' his mum says, clearing her throat. 'I was quite a self-centred child. Can you believe it?'

Oh, so she wants to chat, tell him about her past. Perhaps it is because of his accusation that he doesn't know anything about her that triggered the slap. Or perhaps this is her way of apologizing for dragging him five thousand miles away from his life, to visit with an aunt and cousin he didn't know existed until the day before yesterday. He could do with an old-fashioned sorry and a bit of silence to be honest, so he can lose himself in his music and fantasise about Ellie. Will Ellie think he's given up on her when he doesn't turn up at school? Will she have hooked up with someone else by the time he's back?

Puja is looking expectantly at him, waiting for an answer. What does she think this conversation will achieve? Make him okay with being hauled on this pointless journey to the other end of the world? And does he really want to know? Does he really want to unlock the mystery that is his mother? Who knows what he'll find.

'Are you going to donate your kidney to your niece?' he'd asked her that morning, as he bit into toast slathered with lashings of butter and strawberry jam. Crumbs rained onto the carpet with each bite. He wilfully did not use a plate as she always nagged him to.

He had asked the question even though he'd been wary of disrupting their status quo, not really wanting to start a fight. They had both arrived at an uneasy truce after their argument (which generally meant ignoring everything that had been said—the hurtful words and accusations—and avoiding each other as much as possible until their next spat). But his curiosity and angst had got the better of him. He wanted to know why they were dropping everything at a moment's notice and leaving the country. He'd hoped, even then, that he might make Puja change her mind, rid her of this madness that seemed to have consumed her since her sister called. He wanted to make her see the foolhardiness of this venture—not that anything *he* ever suggested had the smallest effect on her.

His mother had stopped her maniacal rushing about, and, her hands full of clothes that she was trying to stuff into a suitcase that was already heaving, she looked up at him. 'I . . . I didn't promise anything . . .'

'Tell me again, why are we going then?'

She had sighed and ignored his question, as was her habit whenever they discussed anything of importance to him, and had resumed her frantic packing. Then she booked a taxi, sent emails, and made last-minute phone calls so her business would run smoothly in her absence.

He'd stood glaring at her until finally, she looked up. 'Have you had your shower yet? The taxi will be here in a few minutes.'

And that was when he had finally accepted that it was happening. They were going to India.

Fat lot of help this convoluted apology of his mother's will do, he thinks now. He's still going to be miles away from Ellie.

But . . . his mother's going to talk whether he wants her to or not. She has that determined look about her, the look she gets when she's read his school report and is preparing to launch into a lecture about how he's wasting his god-given talents by not working hard enough. Those times he escapes into his room, shuts the door, and shuts her out. Now he is trapped in this confined space beside her with nowhere to go. He should have chosen the aisle seat, he thinks.

Although truth be told, he is just a tiny bit curious to know more about the girl his remote mother once was, this girl who grew up in a hut. Sounds like a fairy tale, he thinks, especially compared with how she lives now, in a veritable mansion. He also wants to know more about his mother's sister whose phone call caused this upheaval, but whom his mother has never mentioned, or been in contact with in years, as far as he knows. If he's to be absolutely honest with himself, he's jealous. Jealous of this Sharda and her daughter, and the hold they have on his mother.

When Raj was too small to know better, he would launch himself at his mum, wanting reassurance, a hug, especially during those long, bleak days after his father left. She would push him away then, albeit gently, time and again. Gradually, he learned not to ask for affection, to hide his yearning, his need for his mother, behind a taciturn scowl, an armour of sullen resentment, a shield of rage, against the disservice done to him.

He learned not to be afraid of the dark, and to ignore the shadows skulking down the walls of his bedroom and taking his toys hostage, during those long, winter evenings when his mother forgot to inform his nanny that she was working later than usual, and his nanny left at her usual time and his mum had still not come home.

He learned to recognise the sound of her key in the lock, her soft tread on the stairs. He learned to tamp down hope when she opened his bedroom door to check on him. He would sense her standing above him, smell her perfume and her tiredness, and with his heart clenched and eyes shut tight, he would pray that this was the day she would bend down and kiss him goodnight.

He learned not to expect her at cake sales and school assemblies. He was the only child whose parents were not present; the only child whose nanny came to pick him up at three fifteen on the days when all the other kids went home early with their parents after book celebration morning, and he was the only one left in class, helping his teacher put the reading folders in order in the strangely echoing classroom bereft of the music of his classmates' voices.

In his mother's list of priorities he's always come last. Now he knows who comes first.

But why? Why a stranger, a woman his mother hasn't spoken of or been in touch with in years?

He wants to find out. And so he turns towards his mother.

'I can believe that you were a self-centred child, yes,' he says and she laughs, slightly hysterical.

He understands that she's nervous about this trip. She's already dropped their passports twice, causing him to stuff them into his own pocket. She's misplaced their boarding passes, making them wait for ten minutes at the door to their plane as she riffled through her purse, with the passengers behind them sighing and grumbling in frustration. If she's this nervous, then why on earth is she going to meet her sister, the woman who has achieved with one phone call what he hasn't managed in his life?

'I was the most beautiful girl in the village . . .' His mother says, her voice girlish, and tinged with nostalgia.

'Always so modest,' he mumbles and she laughs again, less hysterically this time and he can't help feeling a tad pleased that he's helped relax her nerves. This is a new side he is seeing to his proficient, distant mum—glimpses of a fumbling, unsure woman who seems to be hidden behind that accomplished façade.

It makes Raj even more curious about this stranger—his aunt—who is waiting for them on the other side of the world. A woman who has the power to reduce his efficient mother to a clumsy wreck; who, with one telephone call, has cracked his mother's shell of indifference, made her push aside the work that she lives for, and to embark, at a moment's notice, on an impulsive journey. His mother, the opposite of impulsive, who likes to plan everything—even their meals—weeks in advance.

'It was the happiest time of my life . . .' his mother says wistfully.

And so, as the plane taxies for take-off, Raj pulls his headphones out of his ears and crosses his feet, trying to find a comfortable position for them in this cramped space, and resigns himself to listening to his mum rather than his music.

Chapter 12
Puja—Childhood

Seeds from a Popped Pod

Extract from the school report for Puja Ramesh, First Standard, Age 7

Puja is an intelligent girl but she does not apply herself as much as she should. She is easily distracted. She gets into trouble mostly because she is not paying attention and/or talking too much to concentrate on her work, but she is quick to apologise. She is extremely popular and is loved by everyone.

❋ ❋ ❋

'You are very special,' Puja's sister tells her.

'Why?' Puja asks, a thrill running through her because she knows what's coming.

'Well . . . when you were born, you were not breathing. Everyone was sobbing and then . . .'

'And then?' No matter how many times Puja hears the story of her birth, she is agog, mesmerised by this bit.

'And then you joined in, a plaintive mewl, threading through the loud cries. It was the most beautiful sound in that sorrowful room. And everyone's tears turned to laughter as they thanked God for the miracle baby—the answer to their prayers—a special, perfect delight.' Sharda's voice is warm as a hug, as sweet as kheer.

Puja laughs, her joy bubbling over.

Sharda holds Puja high in the basket of her arms and asks her to describe what she sees.

'I can see way past the ocean to the very edge of the sky, that bit where the sky swallows the sun and vomits the moon, and which sometimes, but only on very precious days, gives us rainbows,' Puja says.

Sharda sets Puja down gently and runs inside the house to fetch the cane stool, which is falling to pieces, its threads unravelling like dry brown snakes.

'What are you doing, Sharda?' Puja asks, puzzled, hopping from one foot to the other. She is barefoot and it is mid-day, the sun a fiery ball of fury in the cloudless sky, and the earth is baked yellow, scorching hot.

'Wait a minute. Ah now,' Sharda says, climbing onto the stool and squinting into the distance. 'Do you think I am now as tall as you were when I was lifting you up high just then?'

Puja nods, distracted by a gold-winged dragonfly alighting on the hibiscus flower next to her. She goes to catch the dragonfly, but it flies away in a honey-flecked flutter.

'I cannot even see past Sumatiakka's hut,' Sharda says, jumping off the stool.

'Really?' Puja asks, dragonfly forgotten.

'Did you truly see the sea?'

'I did, I did,' Puja jumps, excited, flashing Sharda a huge, gap-toothed grin. She has just lost her two bottom teeth and the new ones haven't begun growing. Sharda gives Puja all her milk to drink as well as Puja's own portion so that her teeth will grow more quickly.

Sharda lifts Puja up and twirls her around.

Puja fancies herself a ballerina, her skirt and plaits flying behind her. When she is feeling dizzy with happiness, Sharda stops and hugs her close.

'You are the only one who can see all the way to the edge of the sky,' Sharda whispers in her ear. 'Nobody else can do that you know—see the sky's secret place, which sometimes gives us rainbows if we have been really, really good.'

Puja throws her arms around her sister's neck, breathing in her smell of Lifebuoy soap and coconut oil and sweat.

'Really?' she whispers, eyes shut tight, her head still tilting on the axis of her neck from being a whirling ballerina.

'You know why that is, Puja?' Sharda's spiced breath is warm in the crook of Puja's neck, tickling the hairs nestling there, making them wriggle and wrenching giggles out of her.

'Why?' she asks when she has finished laughing.

'Because you are unique—the baby who defeated death at birth. You are the most special girl in the world, loved by everyone, even the sky. It even says so in your school report.'

Puja laughs, and asks her sister to spin her again. Sharda does as she asks and the world around them splinters in a jumble of colours.

Puja opens her mouth and tastes the jackfruit flavoured air. Her stomach rumbles but her heart is replete with the complete conviction that what Sharda is saying is true.

Puja notices it in the way her parents' eyes soften when they see her. She clocks it in the way the villagers pinch her cheeks and remark that she is the cutest, most beautiful angel to ever grace their humble village.

'Even more beautiful than the butterflies?' she asks them.

'Even more so,' they say as they cackle, displaying paan-scored gums.

When she goes home with her clothes in tatters from climbing trees and squeezing through the thorny mimosa bushes by the pond, Ma shakes her head and pretends to frown. But Puja sees that she is really hiding a smile which escapes the corners of her mouth when Puja flings her arms around her and asks her not to be angry, please. Then, Ma gives up all pretence of scowling and hugs Puja close, kissing her eyes and her dusty nose.

When she spills all the guavas in their stall at the market, bruising them, Da's face darkens like the sky before a downpour. Puja's lower lip trembles as she tries to hold in her upset, her heart fit to burst with the effort and Da's face magically transforms and he opens his arms and engulfs Puja in them. He smells musty, of old sweat and hard work.

'It's okay Puja, we'll ask Ma to make something nice with them. It's okay, look, I have the mangoes and cashews to sell anyway,' he says.

Da's hug loosens her heart, and the hurt disperses like the seeds from a popped pod, and she is able to speak, the urge to cry gone.

'I can't eat those guavas,' she says, wrinkling her nose, 'they are injured and hurting and if I eat them my tummy might hurt too.'

Da throws back his head and laughs and Puja is fascinated, no matter how many times she sees it, by the way his tummy moves up and down as the laughter bubbles out of his throat.

Puja can make everyone in the village laugh, even when they are angry or upset. Sharda says it is a gift.

'I wish I had it,' she says.

'But you don't,' giggles Puja.

'No,' Sharda laughs. 'Only exceptional people have that ability.'

'Like me,' Puja says.

'Like you,' Sharda grins.

'You're a golden girl, my wonderful sister,' Sharda says.

'A minx,' Bijjuamma snorts, shaking her head.

'A sorceress,' Nagamma sighs, chewing her paan.

'A treasure,' Ma says.

'A delight,' Da laughs.

And Puja knows without a doubt that she is special and that she is loved.

❄ ❄ ❄

Extract from the school report for Puja Ramesh, Eighth Standard, Age 14

Puja needs to concentrate more in class and put in more effort. Her poor marks in the end of year exams reflect this. She has barely scraped by this year and if she does not work harder in the ninth standard, she will have to stay behind and repeat the year.

❊ ❊ ❊

Puja is hiding behind the jackfruit tree, the prickly green fruit stabbing her bare knees. Breathing in the smell of sandalwood and rose incense wafting from the temple by the river, she tries to stifle the torrent of giggles that threaten to erupt as she watches the bemused expressions of devotees, who come out of the temple to find that their chappals are missing.

Bored by the endless summer holidays stretching ahead, and with nothing to do in their tiny village except sit at the market stall and peddle their sorry looking vegetables as dutiful Sharda is doing, Puja couldn't resist stealing a few pairs from the haphazard pile of footwear outside the temple and hiding them behind Nagu's little shop underneath the rotting coconut fronds.

Her ears desensitised to the jarring clanging of temple bells and the blaring of the bhajans, she watches as the perplexed worshippers, their mouths stuffed with buttery prasadam laddoos and their foreheads smeared with vermilion, hunt for their missing chappals. They hitch up their lungis in bewilderment and scour the peepal trees for monkeys.

The hairs sticking wetly to the back of Puja's sweaty neck prickle. She drags her eyes away from the devotees who are now performing funny little dances due to their bare feet blistering from contact with the scorched mud, to see the leader of the gang of youths who congregate outside Nagu's shop grinning at her.

When her gaze meets his, he winks and indicates with a slight nod of his head towards the heap of decomposing coconut fronds. She looks down at her soiled skirt and busies herself trying to brush the worst of the mud away. He knows; he must have seen her stow the chappals. Will he give her away?

'Don't worry, my mouth is sealed.'

She jumps, startled. He has crossed the road and, leaning against the jackfruit tree, he smiles down at her. She has seen him and his friends often enough sipping badam milk and biting into spicy vegetable puffs outside Nagu's shop after having roared up and down Nandihalli and Dhoompur on their motorbikes raising 'all the ghosts of the peaceful dead along with a tornado of dust,' according to grumbling old Muthakka. 'I am deaf and even I can hear them!' Muthakka moans.

Puja looks right at him, not giving an inkling of her lurching heart and her fear. If Ma and Da hear of this, will it be the last straw? How will she charm her way out of this one?

'What are you talking about?' she asks, affecting nonchalance.

He laughs, and his eyes crinkle pleasingly in his stubbly, perspiration-soaked face.

'Well, your laugh is much better sounding than that racket your motorbike makes,' Puja says, and he laughs harder.

She gives a silent prayer of thanks to the god in the temple that she has always been able to make people laugh.

The devotees have given up looking for their chappals and have hailed the bus which comes to a trundling stop beside the temple. She watches them squat wearily on the rusty seats and gather their feet up onto their laps to massage their scalded soles.

'You are one mischievous girl,' the boy says.

Shall I? Oh why not? What else is there to do here?

'I have always wanted to know how it feels like to zoom around on a motorbike. It must be real fun to compensate for all that ugly noise it makes,' she says, and he laughs again, slapping his knees. 'So will you give me a ride?'

If he says yes, it will relieve the monotony at least a while, get me out of the village for a bit. If he says no, no harm done. If he tells Ma and Da on me, so be it.

The river laps softly at the shore. The boatmen call out to each other. The fisherwomen squatting on the bank gossip as they try to shift their sorry-looking catch of fish that are starting to reek in the unrelenting sun.

'Come on then, what are you waiting for?'

Puja lets out the breath she has been holding and crosses the road with him.

He gives the coconut fronds a kick, dislodging a chappal or two, but she pointedly does not look, which makes him laugh even harder.

His friends stare as Puja climbs onto his bike.

'How many times have we asked you for a ride?' they yell. 'But no, it is too precious for our ordinary backsides. And now you give this slip of a girl a ride?'

He grins at them, and kick-starts the engine.

A thrill of excitement tickles Puja's spine.

'You haven't given your friends a turn on your bike?' she asks.

The humid air is thick with adrenaline and the smell of gasoline and dust.

'It's the best bike around you know, the latest model. Nobody else in the surrounding villages or even in the whole of Dhoompur owns this make.' He gives the front of the bike an affectionate rub. 'Only special people allowed on.'

Puja opens her mouth and tastes the warm gold essence of bliss. 'How many people have you given a ride to?

She sees the side of his face visible to her turn red.

'Only you,' he mumbles.

'Sorry, I didn't hear that,' she teases.

He grins. 'Ready? Hold on to me or you'll fall off.'

Puja clutches his waist as the bike takes off. She throws her head back, her plaits jiggling, and savours the zesty air rushing past. She feels invincible.

'I'm flying,' Puja says, shouting to be heard above the roar of the wind and the growl of the motorbike, 'Thank you. You are the coolest person in the world.'

He laughs. 'So are you,' he says.

Chapter 13
Kushi

One Perfect Package

I put down Ma's letter in which she describes meeting her sister for the first time and blink, as I come back into myself. Everything aches—my body still complaining from the battering it has received. My head feels heavy and there is a rough dryness at the back of my throat.

With great effort, I push my physical discomfort aside and ponder instead over what I have always believed. Other families in the village boast more siblings, cousins and second cousins than they can keep track of, but I was told that we didn't have any relatives, that Da was an only child and so was Ma, and that their parents had long gone by the time I came along.

Ma used to say she'd wanted lots of siblings for me. But then God gave her just me.

'You are everything we ever hoped for and more,' she told me. 'All the answers to our prayers distilled into one perfect package. Da and I blessed many times over. Hence your name: "Kushi" meaning happiness.'

Two women sit on the bed next to mine, side by side, talking. One has a bush of hair the silver grey of a scouring brush; the other is bald. But they have identical sandalwood eyes set deep into gaunt faces. Sisters.

This sister Ma describes in her letter, this baby girl she fell in love with, this woman I can't quite believe is for real, is even now making her way here. Does she look like a younger version of my ma?

Tears glint on the bald woman's sparse eyelashes. The other gently wipes them away with her sari pallu.

My ma is the most loving person I know. And yet she has lived my lifetime pretending her sister doesn't exist. Why doesn't Ma speak of her? What happened to the bond between my mother and her sister? Why didn't they get back in touch before now?

The bushy haired sister sets a lime green sari on the bed beside mine. It contrasts brightly with the institutional yellow tinted cream of the hospital sheets. She pulls out a tiffin box from the cloth bag by her side and opens it up on the sari that serves as tablecloth. She breaks off a piece of chapathi, wraps it around some potato and feeds it to her distressed sister. The gesture is so tender that it makes me ache.

I suddenly, desperately, want my ma here with me. In the letters I have just read, Ma describes how she used to cook with *her* ma. Ma carried on that tradition with me, with the two of us cooking together every evening, when I got home from school.

'You know how to fix the world, Kushi. This is how you *own* the world,' she would say, setting out a chopping board and knives, red onions, a head of garlic and a knob of ginger.

'First we chop,' she said, and as if giving in humbly to a master, the onion would collapse into a hundred perfectly sized pearly pieces under her able fingers—her sprightly fingers jigging effortlessly as they wielded the knife.

'This is how we own the world?'

She would laugh at the disdain in my voice.

'Sweetie,' she said. 'Cooking is art, it is creation. It is, for me, the closest I get to knowing how God feels. If you are able to manipulate stubborn ingredients into imparting their flavour, and if you are able to make the obstinate onion dance to your tunes, if you are able to master it without shedding tears at its mutilation, then you can do anything. In my opinion, beautiful food, seasoned with love and affection, is the greatest gift you can offer someone. And when you do that, people want to give something back. Dictators buckle, kingdoms fold. You own the world, peacefully.'

I had shared in my ma's laughter then, called her a visionary, not quite believing what she said. Truth is, I have come round to her way of thinking. (Although, I'm still not convinced and doubt I ever will be about the 'owning the world' bit.) I love standing side-by-side with Ma, chopping and stirring, frying and poaching, flavouring it all liberally with gossip and laughter.

I wish I could do that now. I wish I could stand, walk to the end of this room and slip out the door of this hospital, into the sweet-smelling world outside, bathed in the amber glow of afternoon sun.

I am overcome by a blinding flash of frustrated rage. I want to pull off all these tubes binding me to this bed. Tears blind my eyes, and blur the letters I am holding. I hate that this has happened to me. I hate that my life is dependent on this unknown aunt's whims, on whether she'll agree to be my donor. I hate everything and everyone, even the sisters in the adjacent bed.

I want to cook, study, organise a rally. Anything would be better than being stuck here—with machines doing my body's work for me—counting down the hours until I meet this aunt whose existence I was unaware of. This aunt in whom I must place my trust, and hope that, whatever has happened in the past, my condition will rouse enough pity in her to agree to save me . . .

I turn my mind away from the only-ifs to cooking with Ma instead.

The first time I prepared a dish all on my own—green masala chicken garnished with coriander and served with a helping of steamed red rice—Ma had gasped in delight and with a smile that looked as if it would burst from her face, invited every woman in the village to sample it.

I understood then, the joy my ma gets from cooking. You mix together all these disparate ingredients that you would swear would never go together, that individually taste like nothing much at all, apply a bit of heat, add some well-chosen spices and hey presto, their communion is beautiful, delicious, heavenly—a perfectly matched marriage. The best part about cooking is the delight in sharing with others, seeing their taste buds jive, and their faces come alive, as they sample your latest concoction. I told Ma this and it was gratifying to see the joy light up her face like the moon on a cloudless summer's night.

You fell in love with your sister when she was born. Then what happened, Ma? What went wrong?

I pick up the next letter.

Chapter 14
Sharda—Childhood

Hot Barley Spiced with Nutmeg

Extract from the school report for Sharda Ramesh, Ninth Standard, Age 15

Sharda is a delight to have in class. Hardworking and extremely bright, she is an example to everyone, regularly topping all of her subjects.

❄ ❄ ❄

Dearest Ma,

I recall this period of time, which I am about to relate, as happy, and yet now, with the benefit of hindsight, I can see that even then a shadow loomed, casting a pall. A warning.

These letters to you, Ma, they are helping so much. Now that I am a mother myself, I want to put everything that happened down in writing, in the hope of seeing where it all went wrong. I want to pinpoint my part in all of this, so that I can then stay clear of the mistakes I made whether wilfully or in ignorance. So that I can bring up my innocent little girl well, without tarnishing her with the sins of the past, or marking her with new offences committed because I did not learn from bygone mistakes.

So then, to my account . . .

'Sharda,' Sister Rose says. 'You are the only person in this class who has grasped the concept of compound interest. Please could I ask you to explain it to this group over here?'

I glow, Ma, at this unexpected compliment from my strict teacher, and I squat underneath the peepal tree with the group I've been assigned. I brush the earth around us clear of pebbles and set about sharpening a twig to use as a pen on this makeshift board.

Our school, as you know, Ma, is too small to house all of its pupils, even though most village children do not attend school, and help out at home or in the fields instead. Hence, on days when there is no rain, we have lessons in the shade of the fruit trees in Anthu's orchard, which he kindly allows the school to use.

The air smells tart, of raw mango and ripe tamarind. It is dense with moisture and makes the wisps of hair escaping my plait stick wetly to my neck. The group I have been assigned consists only of boys, and it includes Gopi, the most handsome boy in the village, the one that all the girls collect in groups to admire, giggling and blushing if he so much as looks their way.

I see Rupa and Suggi frown as Gopi smiles at me and says, 'Go on then, Sharda, do your best. Try and explain this, let's see if it penetrates our thick heads.'

I feel colour flood my cheeks, and hating myself for acting just like the other girls simpering in Gopi's presence, I look down at the ground which serves as my board.

'So, imagine that you want to buy this house,' I begin, drawing a rectangle topped by a triangle in the dirt. The irony that the parents of most children in the school, with the possible exception of Gopi's father, can hardly afford to buy a cow let alone a house, does not escape me.

I patiently explain the mathematics of compound interest until the puzzled expressions of the boys clear and they begin to reward me with smiles of relieved comprehension.

A crow caws somewhere among the trees. A damp breeze rustles. It tastes sweet, of honeyed cashews, and makes my stomach twinge with hunger. Two women call to each other in the fields.

'You are the best teacher, Sharda,' Gopi says. He leans so close I can smell his hot breath, feel it prickling my ear, raising goose bumps. 'Even better than Sister Rose.'

My whole body feels warm, as if I am in the throes of a fever and I imagine my face must look as red as an overripe watermelon. I sense Rupa and Suggi's violent gaze branding me a traitor, labelling me a shameless slut. When Sister Rose bangs the stainless steel plate that serves as a bell, Rupa and Suggi loop their arms and flounce off, not waiting for me to walk with them as I usually do.

The next morning, as we squat in the mud waiting for Sister Rose to call out the register, Gopi swans in, late as usual. He makes a beeline for me, saying, rudely, 'Move,' to Rupa, pushing her out of the way when she doesn't move fast enough. He digs in his pocket, ignoring Sister Rose looking at him over the top of her glasses, and takes out a Campco chocolate éclair, a sweet I have always craved but never eaten, as we can't afford luxuries when necessities are in short order.

'Here,' he whispers. 'This is to say thank you for yesterday. My da was very impressed when I explained compound interest to him.' And then, when Sister Rose rushes back into the school building to get something, 'My da tests me on what I have learnt at school every evening,' he grimaces, 'and most days I do not pass muster. But yesterday, he couldn't fault me.' He grins at me, and it is as if I have been bestowed with a gift far more precious than the chocolate.

I take the sweet he is holding out, hot and wet from nestling in his pocket and palm. As I do so, I notice Rupa wiggling her hips and moving imperceptibly closer to Gopi.

'Thank you.' I murmur. And seized by an urge to continue our conversation, 'Is he very strict, your da?'

I have never talked during lessons, not being the sort of girl who does anything I am not meant to, and I feel a thrill tremble up my spine as I do so now, even though the entire class is raucously taking advantage of Sister Rose's temporary absence.

'Horribly,' Gopi grumbles. 'He wants me to be top of the class, which is impossible of course, given you are in it.'

I cannot help the rush of blood rouging my face. 'I . . .'

'Just joking, Sharda,' he grins. His eyes, the ochre of the sun at twilight, gleam at me.

'Why does he send you to this small school when you can go to the best school in Dhoompur?' I have always wondered about this.

'Oh,' he frowns. 'According to him this will teach me how to deal with the common man, which he says will stand me in good stead when I am older.' He leans closer to me, and I breathe in the musky tang of his sweat, 'I think he sends me here because it's free. He does not like spending money, my da, despite the fact that he has more than most.'

I nod, not knowing what to say, running my thumb over the chocolate, wondering if it will taste as deliciously sweet as I have fantasized.

'Can you teach me profit and loss as well in the break?' he asks.

'Of course,' I smile even as I wonder why he is singling me out.

❅ ❅ ❅

Tutoring Gopi in maths soon becomes a regular event.

One day, I gather up the courage to ask, 'Why don't you get Shimy to teach you? She is bright as well.'

He grins at me, his eyes glowing. Is that fondness I see in his gaze? 'I like you teaching me. You are an enigma, Sharda. So bright and yet so strangely innocent. So clever and yet so vulnerable.'

His words warm me like a tumbler of hot barley spiced with nutmeg and tart with lemon.

I think I know why he gravitates to me. It is because I do not fawn over him like the other girls. I am not coy with him, blushing and smirking and playing games.

I treat him as an equal, something he's not used to, with everyone always looking up to him, boys and girls alike. I do not give in to his charm, or bend over backwards to please him. I teach him, but do not indulge him. I take care never to be alone with him. I try not to get too close, and only help him with his maths at lunch time, in full view of all my classmates. I am very protective of my reputation, which is, as you have told me often enough, Ma, my 'most important asset'.

And yet, in the nights, after I have finished studying, after I have blown out the candle and settled down to sleep beside you and Puja, it is a boy with shining eyes whom I see flickering before my closed eyes. It is his face that eases me into sleep, his face inhabiting my dreams.

❊ ❊ ❊

Puja must sense something, for she asks me, one day, out of the blue, 'Have you ever been in love?'

Have I said his name in my sleep? I wonder. *Why am I beginning to care for him, of all people?* I worry.

Gopi embodies the very opposite of all the qualities I admire and hold dear. He is brash, cocky, someone who disregards rules just as much as I value them. And yet, every so often a chink of vulnerability perforates his smug exterior.

'Do you like me, Sharda?' he had asked just the previous day.

I laughed, making sure to keep my eyes on the ground, where I was teaching him the basics of algebra.

'I do, I suppose,' I said after a pause during which I pretended to consider his question.

I looked up just in time to see his face fall briefly, a puzzled little boy appearing through the veneer of bravado, before he righted it and laughed, saying, 'You tease.'

I do not want to be one of his conquests. I have seen the way he treats the girls who shadow him, who hang on his every word. I would much rather have the respect he affords me. But that look lodged right in my heart, and it blossomed—a ruby bloom unfurling.

'Answer me, Sharda, have you been in love? In fact, are you in love right now?' Puja asks, and her voice is as insistent as the Muslim call for prayer that blasts every sleeping body for miles around out of their slumber at daybreak.

Although Puja is lost in her own world much of the time, she is very perceptive and picks up on the slightest fluctuations in emotion. Puja, who doesn't give a jot about her reputation and does exactly as she pleases. Puja, who you say, Ma, only half-joking, is the cause of your prematurely grey hair. Puja, who, from the moment she entered this world, a squalling infant, not breathing at first, captured Da's heart, so he won't hear a bad word about her, won't see that she is, in fact, running wild.

You receive a visit from the village matrons every other day, Ma, with a blow-by-blow account of Puja's transgressions.

'She is growing up,' they say, spitting slivers of chewed paan with each grave word, their eyes like puris. 'She can't go around doing what she likes any more. She is so beautiful, and you will get her married very easily, perhaps even for no dowry at all, but she needs to guard her reputation.'

When Puja swans home, clothes torn, hair dishevelled, you begin to admonish her, but she grabs your hands and dances you around the courtyard and when your head is spinning and you are breathless, she kisses your cheek and says, 'Ma, I'm hungry, what lovely feast have you conjured up today?'

And you follow in her wake, smiling and sighing at the same time.

When Da gets home from work, you tell him about the matrons' visit, urging him to intercede. 'If you talk to Puja, she'll listen.'

But Da only laughs, his eyes softening as he looks at his favourite child, 'Oh she's still a kid. She'll grow out of it. Won't you, lovey?'

The choicest endearments for Puja. Endearments Da has never used on me.

Puja throws her arms around Da, kisses his ear. 'I was only playing, Da. The girls didn't want to play lagori, so I asked the boys.'

'She's only little. Why can't those witches mind their own business?' Da grumbles then.

You sigh, Ma. 'She's growing up,' you say, unintentionally echoing the matrons.

'If it was me doing that, you would be cross, Da,' I say.

'Oh but, Sharda, you wouldn't dare,' Puja says, laughter bursting out of her—a starry shower.

Now, I look up from the book I am pretending to read, adjusting my glasses—the ones with the rectangular, too-large frames, which Puja says do not do my face any favours, but which are the only ones you and Da can afford, Ma.

'Why do you ask?' I query, closing my book after carefully marking the page with a sliver of blue cotton torn from your old sari.

Puja clicks her tongue, and swipes at a mosquito alighting on her arm. It squishes in a splat of blood. 'Oh, why can't you just answer my question for God's sake! Are you in love?'

In the winking light of the lamp, her eyes are radiant, her skin glows gold and she looks even lovelier than usual.

'Love. It is not for the likes of us,' I say, finally, and push thoughts of Gopi firmly away. I mean it too. Gopi might intrude into my thoughts, but I know I will one day marry the man you and Da choose for me, Ma, as is my duty. 'Love is an indulgence only city girls can afford.'

'Who says so?' Puja scoffs.

From the kitchen wafts the sound of sizzling onions, and the smoky, slightly burnt smell of frying spices. You are cooking dinner, Ma. Da is washing himself in the lean-to. He is murdering a Kannada film song in his tuneless voice, snatches of which drift up to us. The dog flops in his habitual place, head on the kitchen stoop, long ears flapping, looking at you with mournful eyes, hoping you'll lob a crumb his way.

'Love causes havoc, Puja, tears a family apart. Remember when Sampa ran away with the butcher's son?'

Puja scrunches her face.

'You must have been too young to remember. Oh the scandal it caused! Sampa's mother committed suicide. She could not take the ignominy, the stain of disrepute.'

'Pah,' Puja mutters, looking disgusted. 'She obviously did not value her life enough.'

'Look at every woman in the village. Their husbands have been chosen for them. None of them have married for love. It is just not done,' I say, watching the play of shadows on the wall.

'That is why they always have their nose in other people's business, especially mine. They are forever trying to escape the depressing reality of their lives, their bullies of husbands . . .' Puja's voice is steeped with a bitterness I have not heard until now.

I look at her, curious. Where is this coming from?

'Look at Ma and Da,' I try. 'They only met properly on their wedding day. They're happy aren't they?'

Dusk has fallen outside and a soft breeze is rustling the aboli bushes. Now the smell of rising dough and boiling potatoes assaults my nose, making my stomach growl.

'Oh Sharda, there's no point talking to you. All you care about is doing your duty,' Puja huffs, saying the word *duty* as if it is something to be abhorred. 'And studying.'

Despite her obvious disgust, I decide that this is as good an opportunity as ever to expound the benefits of an education, as you are always urging me to do, Ma.

'Please talk to Puja,' you have begged, 'If you do, Sharda, she'll listen, perhaps.'

'A good education is important, Puja. Why do you think Da and Ma send us to school even though it would be easier if they took us out and put us to work like half the children of the village? They can't afford a huge dowry and if we have a good education, we'll get good husbands.' I parrot the words you have recited a thousand times, Ma, hoping Puja will take heed this time.

'I will find my own husband thank you very much,' she snaps, her rust coloured eyes flashing.

I take Puja's hand in mine. Her palm is warm and slightly moist. 'Puja, you are so bright but you don't apply yourself. If you only . . . '

'Huh, stop lecturing me . . . First Sister Seema and now you.'

'Oh, she's given you *that* lecture, has she?'

Puja rolls her eyes, meeting my gaze and we laugh together, tiff forgotten, recalling how all of us girls were herded outdoors, one class at a time, far from the boys, to the middle of the fields with only the languid cows and the singing stream, whispering coconut trees, and a gaggle of crows for company.

'You are growing up,' Sister Seema had squawked self-importantly piercing each of us with her prickly gaze. 'You will have thoughts about boys, and be tempted to sin with them. I have seen the looks some of you girls give the boys, as if inviting them to have their way with you. It is wrong. Forget about touching boys, even entertaining lustful thoughts about them is a sin. Banish wicked thoughts. You have to save yourselves for your husbands. It is your duty to keep yourselves pure.' Her vinegary voice had risen with each pompous word. 'Beware. Boys are not to be trusted. They will befriend you, bring your guard down and then try to steal your honour. Remember that your reputation is the most important jewel you own, more precious than all the gold your parents are setting aside for your dowry. Don't treat it lightly. Think of God when you are tempted to sin. He is watching your every move, keeping tabs on your immoral thoughts.'

Now, Puja says, chuckling, 'I asked Sister Seema who she was saving *her* reputation and honour for. You should have seen her face. She looked like she was choking on a frog she had accidentally swallowed!'

I start to snigger uncontrollably, as I imagine Sister Seema's gobsmacked face. Puja and I roll around the floor. Our laughter, like pealing bells, makes the dog bark, and ladle in hand, you come out of the kitchen, Ma, smelling of spices, with sweat from the cooking fumes beading your face, to ask us what in the world is so funny.

And just at that moment we overturn the lamp—oil spilling, the reek of kerosene, the stench of burning and the startled jitters of shock as our clothes catch fire—and if it had not been for Puja extinguishing the flames with her fingers and burning herself in the process, (I see her flinch and her fingers blaze red), our hut would have gone up in flames taking us with it.

A premonition, Ma, of what was to come. A dark, smoke-flavoured cloud to douse our mirth.

Chapter 15
Raj

A Splash of Vibrant Colour

'Mum, I cannot believe you let those poor temple-goers get their feet scorched!' Raj says, looking quizzically at his mother, trying to find in this woman, whose face he has searched for clues that she loves him, this woman he has loathed for what he believes is her neglect of him, that little girl who was loved by an entire village; the minx who hid devotees' shoes.

She laughs—a splash of vibrant colour on an arid landscape.

He doesn't think he has ever heard her laugh in this carefree way. It is as if, by reminiscing about her childhood, something coiled tight inside her has sprung loose. It makes her look younger, he thinks. And yet, even in this softer version of his mother, he cannot see the girl she once was. She *must* be in there somewhere.

'I can't equate that girl you are telling me about with you, Mum,' he muses.

'I know,' she sighs. 'I can't either.'

'How could you have changed so much?' Raj asks, not really expecting an answer, thinking his mother will ignore him or change the topic as she always does when faced with difficult questions, or things she doesn't want to talk about.

'Life. It squeezes you, wrings you out, until you don't know if you are facing forward or backward, until you don't recognise yourself.' Her voice is melancholy, a haunting melody. Her laughter gone.

Raj cannot recall the last time his mother had merited one of his queries with such an honest answer. He is surprised by the pang of sympathy he feels for her.

What happened to you? He thinks. *What happened to the girl you once were?*

The air hostess pushes her trolley down the aisle, offering drinks.

Raj takes a gulp of Coca Cola. His headphones have slipped off his ears and disappeared somewhere in the space around his seat but he couldn't care less. He is properly curious now, absorbed in his mother's story. He wants to know more about the girl she is telling him about; he wants to see if he can find something of her in the woman beside him, and to discover if that feisty child has left a small imprint of herself behind.

'You were close to your sister,' he says and she flinches, her face flooding with pain. 'She was such an important part of your life. Why didn't you speak of her before now, tell me about her?'

You haven't told me much of anything, up until now. I am surprised you are opening up so much to me today.

'I . . . I couldn't.' Distress dyes his mother's voice the blue black of old regrets and heartache.

'You haven't spoken to her, or been in touch with her, for years, have you? Before that phone call, I mean?'

'I haven't been in touch, no.' She says softly.

'Something major must have occurred to drive you two apart. What happened?'

His mother rubs at her eyes. 'I . . . I don't know if I . . . '

'Oh mum, come on!' He cannot help the anger. He jabs his Coca Cola onto the tray, not caring when some of it spills, a fizzy brown blob against the dull grey of the tray.

His mother flinches again.

He digs around in the pocket of the seat in front of him looking for his headphones. He bends down, groping about by his legs, almost upending the tray and spilling more of his Coca Cola.

Typical of her. Just when he was getting interested too. He's had enough. At least his music doesn't stop and start at anyone's whim but his own. Where on earth are his head-phones?

'You can't start telling me and then decide not to. God, you are dragging me halfway across . . . '

'It's hard for me, Raj, to revisit it all.' She bites down on her lower lip, hard.

He's sure it will split and start to bleed in a minute. Good.

'Then why are we going to India if not to revisit it all? Surely you owe me an explanation as to why you are taking me there, against my will, if I may . . . '

She takes a deep, shuddering breath. 'Yes. You are right. I owe you.'

He is so surprised by her capitulation, her admitting that he's right, that he bumps his head on the tray and spills the rest of the Coca Cola. He swabs ineffectually at the spreading mess with the measly napkin provided with the drink while his mother takes another deep breath and settles into her seat.

'I had skipped school . . . ' she begins and Raj gives up trying to clean up the gloopy spill with the disintegrating serviette and sits back to listen to his mother's story, her voice painting a picture of an audacious, devil-may-care girl, who she claims was her once upon a time . . .

Chapter 16

Puja—Childhood

Green-tipped Lullabies

Extract from the school report for Puja Ramesh, Ninth Standard, Age 15

Puja has done marginally better this year but her poor marks show that she still has a long way to go. Puja is a bright girl who needs to concentrate more in class. She is easily distracted and daydreams through her lessons, her mind clearly somewhere else. That said, Puja is a natural leader and is loved and looked up to by everyone.

❊ ❊ ❊

Puja has skipped school and is spending an illicit, luxuriously lazy afternoon by the lake, with the soft musical lick and splash of gentle waves communing with the reeds rocking her to sleep. The bluish emerald expanse is dotted with heart shaped leaves and water lilies, white with yellow middles, are perched like offerings on top.

Eyes closed, she leans back against the banyan tree, its perfumed branches whispering tender green-tipped lullabies as the soft breeze fans her face. A frog croaks hoarsely nearby, and she pictures it squatting on a lily pad, fat and slimy green, its bulbous eyes on the lookout for flies. A dog barks somewhere close and chickens squawk in uproar, sounding very much like the indignant fisherwomen squabbling with haggling customers at the market. Cooking smells drift up to her: roasted cinnamon and caramelising sugar. She thinks that Janakiamma, whose hut adjoins the lake, must be making kheer to celebrate her son's appointment as a taxi driver in Bangalore.

Puja imagines a mouthful of kheer, biting into syrup soaked raisins and ghee-coated cashews, the nutty sweetness exploding in her mouth. Her stomach rumbles.

When was the last time Ma made kheer? She can't remember. She hates being poor, she decides, uprooting a handful of the weeds beside her. A coconut tree branch tumbles to the ground with a crash in Janakiamma's orchard, she assumes. She drags her eyes open and turns to check. Yes, she is right.

The water in the lake undulates as the frog jumps in. She idly picks up a stone from beside her and throws it in, wishing she could make it skim. Dappled shadows play hide and seek with the sun.

She closes her eyes once more, giving in to the exquisite pull of sleep.

Thud, clunk, thump! A burst of noise explodes the languorous afternoon, a thunderous sound that careers closer and closer to Puja. She keeps her eyes squeezed shut, trying to still her pounding heart.

The hurtling sound stops directly in front of her. Someone pants, in noisy gasps, right next to her.

'Hey, this is *my* secret place. What are you doing here?' A man's voice. Gruff and croaky as the frog, and curiously familiar. 'Skipped school, have you? Why am I not surprised?' Laughter threads through the croakiness.

Puja opens her eyes and takes in grazed toes, endless legs, and a long, well-built torso culminating in a face she knows.

'You!'

'Stealing chappals from unsuspecting devotees; cutting school. Are you a Catholic? These sins could send you straight on the blazing path to hell, unless you confess of course . . .' His muscles ripple as he puts his hands on his hips and shakes his head, setting his floppy hair dancing.

'Are you a spy for the village matrons?' she snaps, enormously angry with him for disturbing her peaceful, indolent afternoon.

He throws back his head and laughs. 'I had forgotten how funny you are.'

She is still thinking up a suitable retort when he bends, rolls up his trousers and wades into the lake.

'What do you think you're doing?' she calls as she watches his legs disappear. 'It's deep in there. Can you swim?'

He turns and squints at her. 'No,' he grins. The water laps at his waist.

He takes a couple more steps, treading water backwards while looking at her, and then he slips, arms flailing. His grin freezes, mutating into bafflement and then, for a brief second, fright, before his body disappears underwater.

'No!' she yells, rubbing at her eyes, unable to believe what she is seeing. Puja can't swim either. What to do?

The air is yellow with fear. It tastes of horror, inky black.

Oh dear God, what will she do? She closes her eyes and starts to pray. *Please God, please.*

'Boo!'

Puja jumps. He is standing before her, dripping water from head to toe, and smelling slimy, of pond weed and algae.

'You lied!' she screeches. 'You . . .'

She lifts her hand to hit him, but he brings a wet hand from behind his back and holds out a posy of sopping water lilies.

'For you, ma'am,' he executes a mock bow, spraying droplets everywhere.

She laughs then, and accepts the water lilies, while her galloping heart slows to a canter. She lightly smacks his moist palm. 'Thank you. Did you come here by bike?'

He nods in the direction of the road and she sees the bike gleaming beside a peepal tree.

'I will only agree to a ride once you are completely dry,' she says, and he throws back his head and laughs.

❄ ❄ ❄

The next day when she comes out of school, he is waiting for her.

'Fancy a ride?'

'Why, thank you,' Puja says.

As they zoom away, her arms around him, she rejoices in the heady sensation of freedom from the constraints of the village, and the narrow minded people.

'Why me?' she asks him.

'You make me laugh,' he says simply.

'You know, this hanging out with you is not good for my reputation.'

'Do you care?'

'Not really. My reputation feels like a noose around my neck.'

She can feel his laugh start at the base of his stomach and rumble out of his throat.

He takes her to a Chinese restaurant in Palmipur, and plies her with delicacies: gobi manchurian, chilli chicken, chocolate milkshake.

Afterwards, he says, as if still answering her earlier question. 'You are amusing. You are unpredictable. You are different from all the other girls and more beautiful than any of them.'

She takes a big slurp of milkshake. 'Ha! I'm just another one of your conquests. But I don't mind as long as you buy me one of these every day.'

He smiles, but then he looks at her, suddenly serious. 'You bring much needed laughter into my life, Puja. My ma died when I was three. My da is a tyrant. He expects me to do everything *he* wants, never asking what *I* want . . .' his voice bitter. 'I just want to relax, enjoy myself.'

'And ruin me?'

'Maybe.'

'As long as I have fun in the process.'

He reaches across the table and takes her hand in his.

If this was the village, thinks Puja, everyone would be craning their necks, rumours already spreading to Dhoompur and beyond, her reputation tainted beyond repair. Here, a couple of people look askance at them but there is no danger of this tryst being reported back to her parents because nobody knows her, or her parents.

Puja imagines Sister Seema's reaction to their joined hands, and recalls her hectoring voice, 'And forget touching boys, even entertaining lustful thoughts about them is a sin.' She giggles.

'You're the most beautiful girl in the village. I'm not bad looking myself. We make a great couple.' His eyes glimmer like embers from a dying fire.

'Is that all? What if someone more beautiful comes along?'

'We get on, Puja. We are similar inside, tired of the village and its pointless restrictions, too good for it.'

'That we are.'

'Let's seal our friendship with some milkshake,' he says. 'If there is any left that is . . .' he tilts the glass, 'I can't believe it! You've finished yours *and* mine.'

She laughs. 'Serves you right.'

And so it begins.

❆ ❆ ❆

He takes to picking her up from school every day.

It helps that Sharda is not at school with her, always keeping tabs on her, and warning her of the dangers to her reputation. Sharda now attends the pre-university college in Dhoompur.

He waits for her by Nagu's shack but of necessity they are discreet, not letting on that they know each other. Puja walks on one side of the road while he pushes his bike along the other side, ignoring her, and once they are both free from prying eyes, she crosses the road, jumps on his bike and they zoom away.

Some days, she does not bother going to school at all, and spends the day with him instead, roaming the countryside on his bike.

They go as far away from the village as they possibly can. They sit on craggy rocks by the sea, listening to its boom and roar, tasting the salt from the spray, looking at the waves performing to the tunes of the tides.

'You're my best friend,' he declares, chewing on a stalk of grass. 'When I'm with you, I feel whole,' he says, gazing at her with his soulful eyes.

And, despite everything she's heard about him and his wild ways, she believes him.

One day, when she cuts classes and comes to Nagu's shack to surprise him, she catches him flirting with the girls from the sewing school.

She does not talk to him for two weeks.

He pursues her endlessly, relentlessly, until she consents to go for a ride with him on his bike.

'Why?' she shouts above the roar of the engine, her arms around him, her cheek resting on his jacket, revelling in the familiar leathery feel of it, breathing in his scent of lemon and motor oil. 'Why do you flirt with all the girls? Why do you want everyone to love you? You even flirt with that ogre Sunita ma'am. You treat it as a challenge to make people love you and then get bored of them and discard them like banana skins.' The wind scatters her words every which way, diminishing their gravity, but she has never been more serious as she asks, 'Will you discard me too?'

He stops the bike. They are on a mud road, sugarcane fields on either side, the river glinting silvery sage in the distance, the sweet honeyed fragrance of nectar flavouring the air.

The wind that strokes her face tastes of pushed boundaries. It smells of squirming embarrassment and regret. It is yellow with grit, heavy with humidity, making her eyes smart and blur.

She jumps off the bike. He doesn't, turning around and facing her instead, his expression inscrutable.

'So,' she tries for lightness. 'Why have we stopped here?'

'Because I wanted to answer your question.'

'Oh.'

'Come here.'

She goes up to him. He holds her hand. She prays no bus or rickshaw will pass by, no farmer on his bullock cart, no women carrying hay bales, to interrupt what he is about to say.

'I . . . I want people to like me, and like you said, I make it my business to win them over. I feel better when they capitulate.' His eyes, the colour of marigolds glowing in the sun, are solemn.

'Especially women,' she says.

He grins. 'There is that.' Then, as soft as the pink kiss of dawn brushing sleep from the inky horizon's bleary eyes, he says, 'But you . . . you're different. '

'How?'

He looks at her and it is as if he is looking inside her, to everything that she is, her good and her bad, the Puja who exasperates the matrons, the Puja who is put on a pedestal by her Da, the Puja who is her Ma's cross to bear, the Puja who is the complete antithesis of her sister. It is as if with his piercing tawny gaze, he can map the private depths of her soul and likes what he sees there.

'You are like me, inside,' he says softly. 'You yearn for more,' he sweeps his hand to indicate the mud road, the fields, 'than this.'

She nods, her hand in his as if it belongs there, as if it has found its rightful home.

'I do not give anyone else rides on my bike. Only you. You know that.'

She smiles. The air is celebratory, ringing joyful yellow, it smacks of fruit and happiness.

'I like you, Puja,' he says, 'very much.'

She believes him. 'I like you too.' And she does.

He makes her happy. When she is with him, the dream she's always had—of escaping the confines of the village, of being free of its limitations, and the senseless rules it imposes upon her, crushing her spirit—seems within reach.

Her village has always been too small for her and when she is with him, she can see beyond its precincts to different, wider horizons. When she's with him, she can flee the village and its oppressing restraints, its repressive rules, and for a brief while, she can pretend she is someone else, someone with a different, more glamorous life.

The villagers, who adored her when she was little, and smiled fondly at her antics, now purse their lips and give advice she hasn't asked for and doesn't want. She cannot walk two steps without someone stopping to lecture her on the importance of a good reputation. If she hears the word 'reputation' one more time, she sometimes thinks, she will jump in a well and drown. She does not know why everyone else cares more about *her* reputation than she does. She pictures it as a ferocious beast tracking her every move, pouncing if she takes one step out of line.

Her father indulges her, but even with her da she cannot go too far, show her true self. Sometimes, she feels like she is dying inside, her life-force being choked out of her by the narrow-mindedness, the *smallness* of the villagers.

This boy understands. He feels the same.

With him, she can be herself.

'I would like to run away,' he says.

'Can I come too?' Puja asks.

'Of course, I wouldn't want to go without you.'

And sitting beside him, she smiles, revelling in his throaty laughter and tasting contentment as she breathes in the piquant tang of a summer's evening. She is, at that moment, completely at peace with the world.

For once, she does not dread the inevitable return to the smothering confines of the village quite so much and the burden of not living up to her father's idealized version of her seems lighter and the aggravations of her family: her mother's perpetual worries about Puja's reputation, and Sharda's 'good' girl to Puja's 'bad', no longer seem insurmountable.

Chapter 17
Kushi

The Peach Embrace of Setting Sun

Ma wrote these letters to her mother after I was born, so she wouldn't make the same mistakes with me. What did she do?

Around me, in this unfamiliar present, nurses fuss, mosquitoes whine, trolleys wheeze, patients moan. The doctor comes by to check on me, his whole being radiating exhaustion, aubergine hued circles dogging his weary eyes. His visage: square face beneath thin, greying hair, a kind gaze that seems to take in everything at a glance, matches what I had envisaged when I heard him talking with Ma.

'Young lady, it's a real pleasure to be able to meet you properly,' he says, as he smiles and extends his hand, 'I've heard a lot about you, what you've done for your village and beyond. We're doing our very best to restore you to the best of health so you can carry on the good work.'

When he leaves, I close my eyes and imagine I am outside, skipping among fields glimmering greenish gold in the peach embrace of setting sun. The air sings as I dance past the men walking home from work, their vests soaked with sweat, their shoulders hunched, their thoughts turned to hot food and a warm bed, past the huts where fragrant smoke paints the sky a darker shade of grey and families are gathering for their evening meal. The coconut trees sway in the soft breeze aromatic with the fragrance of ripe mangoes, frying fish and cooling rice, hot chapathis and spicy potatoes.

I open my eyes and I am back in the malady-laden present, clutching my mother's letters, and breathing in the smells of phenyl and pain, of agony and entreaty.

I drag my mind away from the frustration I feel back to the letters.

Puja . . . despite myself, I like the picture I am getting of her. Devil-may-care, happy, outgoing. Ma, on the other hand seems to have been quite a stickler for the rules, afraid to do anything she wasn't meant to.

And yet, she let me do what I wanted. She was afraid for me and yet she encouraged my causes, revelled in my inquisitive, feisty nature. Was it because she was hell-bent on not repeating the mistakes of the past, as she says in this letter? Did she hold Puja back? Is that what pushed them apart?

I think of Ma having feelings for Gopi, but steadfastly denying them, a sweet girl, afraid to put one foot out of line. So very different from the person she has always encouraged me to be.

From there to here. What happened to change that innocent girl who loved her sister so? When did that love sour into hate, the laughter choke into broody silence? And why?

I pick up the next letter.

Chapter 18

Sharda—Cusp

The Yellow of Maturing Pineapples

Second PUC (Pre-University Course) Exam Results for Sharda Ramesh, Age 18

First rank holder in the state of Karnataka

Kannada 90/100

English 92/100

Maths 100/100

Physics 100/100

Chemistry 100/100

Biology 99/100

> *Extract from The Hindu:*
>
> *With the unprecedented score of 581/600, Sharda Ramesh of Dhoompur Pre-University College scores the first rank in the Second PU exam for the entire state*

of Karnataka. Sharda's exceptional score and her out-standing achievement is unparalleled in the history of Dhoompur Pre-University College, which services the children of all the neighbouring villages.

Sharda Ramesh hails from Nandihalli, a sleepy village snuggling on the banks of the river Varna. Most children in Nandihalli do not study beyond the seventh standard; the boys going on to work as labourers and the girls to work either as servants, or to prepare for marriage while helping their mothers look after their siblings. The children who do attend school have textbooks that are second-hand, with pages missing. The students do not have the facilities to undergo special coaching for the exam, as they do in the cities. And yet, this year, this village has produced a young girl who has gone on to get one of the highest recorded scores in the pre-university exam.

This reporter interviewed Sharda Ramesh, the shy girl who has put Nandihalli on the map. 'I like studying,' she said. 'I would like to be a doctor to set right some of the wrongs wrought unfairly on the innocents of this world.'

This jaded reporter who has interviewed countless people in his time, confesses himself humbled by the simple words of this amazing girl, who with fraying second-hand books and no extra tuition, has achieved this astounding score. Kudos to her and here's hoping that she holds on to that spark of ambition, ignites it and unleashes it on the world. This state and this country desperately need young people like you, Miss Sharda Ramesh.

❄ ❄ ❄

Dearest Ma,

The day my PUC results come through is one of the happiest days of my life. That is the only day I can remember since the birth of Puja, Ma, that I manage to overshadow my sister, to outshine her in Da's eyes.

Da laughs loudest for Puja. He is a different man when Puja is around. The worry lines on his forehead relax and he seems younger and you and I are both grateful to Puja for that.

I know Da loves me, Ma, I do. And I am not immune to Puja's charms myself. But I wish with all my heart that sometimes, his face would light up for me like it does when he sets eyes on Puja.

She fills our home with warmth, makes it radiate contentment, no matter how worried we might be of making ends meet. I love Puja and I am envious of her, my heart in constant tumult where she is concerned. I know I could never get away with the stuff she does, but then I wouldn't want to either. Puja is unique, a law unto herself, my beloved, infuriating sibling. I am delighted to be related to her and yet sometimes I wish she was someone else's sister, someone else's responsibility. You want me to look after her, Ma, and be a good role model for her. But she doesn't like being looked after.

'You are always studying, Sharda. You must learn to live a little,' she says, often.

What she says is true and yet I do not know how to be any other way. This is who I am.

I love learning. When I solve a maths problem or understand a scientific mystery, I feel like I have achieved something, I feel able to be outside myself, the chunky, clumsy girl that I am.

But Puja . . . Puja is sunshine and laughter. She is the moon shining silver on an overcast night and the rain after a long drought. She is sweetness and joy and the best of dreams. She gets into scrapes but is forgiven when she flashes her charming smile. The villagers are awed by her beauty and her vivaciousness; frustrated by her misdemeanours. She is a vision conjured out of the dust, our village's lucky charm, or so Da claims. She is like a rare bird landed in our midst, whose very presence lifts us, so we can bask in her reflected allure, share a tiny sprinkling of the fairy dust she is made of.

But that day, the day of my results, I—squat, chubby, unremarkable—am the rare bird, the repository of fairy dust! That day, I do not wish to be anyone else, not even Puja. For the first time, I am completely happy in my own ordinary skin.

I knew I had done my best but I had no idea I had performed this well. The principal of the college personally handed me my results.

'Wow!' he had said, eyes glistening behind his cloudy glasses. 'What an achievement! The newspapers are coming here, Sharda, to interview you and me.' He removed his glasses and rubbed his eyes. He was overwhelmed. As am I!

I clutch the piece of paper and run all the way home, gulping in the dense air, heady with the aroma of jasmine and over-ripe cashews.

I am not the fastest girl in the village, Ma, nor the most agile, as you know. I am short and heavy and I do love my food. But that day I have wings.

You glow, Ma, when I have explained my report card to you and Da as both of you never had the opportunity to go to school and thus cannot read or write.

'You have made me and your da so proud, Sharda,' you say, your eyes glimmering with joyous tears.

'I can stop working soon,' Da declares, beaming at me the way he does at Puja, and making my whole being shine. 'Because, you, Sharda are going to earn ten times in one day what I make in a month.'

And Puja wraps her arms tightly around my neck when she arrives home, a luminous butterfly, full of delight, trailing that special something in her wake. She skips around our small courtyard, a lithe danseuse, her sugar-spun curls twirling, screaming, 'Well done, Sharda, well done.'

That evening, there is a big celebration in the village grounds in my honour. The entire village congregates in the open field, bringing mats with them. Duja, who never misses a trick, circulates the crowd selling bhel puri from a cane tray slung across his neck, dispensing it, 50 paise apiece, in little paper cones fashioned from Udayavani, the daily newspaper—that day's news is oily and slick with spice, piquant with flecks of chopped red onions. Birakka, who is always in competition with Duja, does the same, but with roasted peanuts and goes one up, by circling the throng with a flask of cardamom and ginger tea.

You, Da and I have pride of place on the makeshift stage erected in a hurry that afternoon, when news of reporters arriving sent the principal into a frenzy. A generator has been borrowed at great cost from the electronic shop in Dhoompur and the fruit-scented gloom of early evening is dispelled by its flickering lights, which attract a plague of flies.

I'm wearing my best salwar, cerise with yellow flowers, the only one I own which isn't threadbare from use. My hair is in plaits. My eyes are shining. I cannot believe this: standing in the harsh yellow, moth-infested spotlight (courtesy of the grumbling generator) and squinting at the audience of villagers, a whispering hushed mass silhouetted in darkness, all of them submitting to being feasted upon by a buzzing pestilence of mosquitoes just for *me*. The rumble of applause builds up to a roar triggering a warm rush of happiness that permeates my entire being.

Gopi catches my eye, and gives me a thumbs up, and already saturated with well-being, I balloon with pleasure.

Flashes on my face as my photo is taken. Newspaper reporters shouting questions, one after the other, a staccato barrage. I don't know what I say, but later you tell me, Ma, that I was brilliant. You and Da are proud and tongue-tied by the attention. Like me, you are wearing your best, or to be more accurate, your least shabby clothes.

The principal makes a speech claiming that he always knew I was destined for great things. One of the reporters interviews Puja and she says, pointing at me, 'Yes, that is my sister,' and I am touched and overwhelmed because this is the first time I have heard her say it in that particular tone, her voice dripping with pride. Until now, it has always been the other way round, with *me* pointing to *her*, with unabashed pride: *My* sister, Puja.

✼ ✼ ✼

Dearest Ma,

You are waiting when I return from meeting friends in Dhoompur the evening after the celebration of my PU results, impatiently treading the nineteen steps between the mango tree at one end of our courtyard and the guava copse at the other. (I know it is nineteen because I counted one sweltering afternoon while you were comatose from the heat.)

When you spy me gingerly navigating the stepping stones down the hill, you hold up your sari and run across the field toward me breathless with news. I sprint to meet you halfway and you open your arms and fold me into them and I breathe in your smell of sweat and spices and comfort.

You dance me round and round, right there in the middle of the field for all to see, our feet slipping and sinking into the mud.

Duja's cow stops her placid cud chewing to stare at us, liquid eyes curious, soft brown nose twitching. Our dog barks delightedly, nipping at our dusty heels.

'What is it, Ma?' I laugh, when I can gather my breath.

'The landlord visited us at the market stall today asking for your hand in marriage.' The words come out in a rush as if you have been bursting with the effort of holding them in.

'To him?' I am not impressed.

You laugh, tweak my plaits. 'No, silly, to his son.'

It takes a moment for the news to percolate, to seep into my already overflowing heart.

Gopi. The boy I have secretly fancied for what seems like forever, always thinking, no, *knowing*, that he could never be mine, that we orbited two different planets. I cannot believe it. How can *all* my dreams come true in the space of just two days?

'Lost for words?' You are grinning from ear to ear, Ma, the care lines on your face disappearing so you look like the young woman who coloured my very first memories.

'Why me?' I ask when I trust myself to speak. I had always covertly hoped that Gopi reciprocated the feelings I had not dared acknowledge even to myself. Has he spoken to his father, told him how much I mean to him?

You cup my flushed, flabbergasted face in your hands. 'You deserve him, sweetie,' you whisper, your voice warm and brimming with all the love you feel for me.

'There are a hundred girls waiting in the wings to marry him, the richest and most handsome boy in the village. Why me?' I ask again. I want to know, more than anything, that Gopi cares for me, that I have not been the only one harbouring romantic feelings during those hot, mango-scented afternoons spent teaching him mathematical concepts.

'Ah, you see all the other landlords in neighbouring villages have mostly sons, the few daughters are already betrothed. Also the daughters of city landlords do not want to marry someone from the village. Thus, the landlord has no option but to choose a local girl and you . . . you have brought such fame to the village.'

You are grinning at me, love and pride shining out of your eyes. 'We told the landlord that you want to continue your studies. He wants that for you too. An educated wife, a doctor at that, will be the jewel in his son's crown, you see. All the town landlords look down on our landlord, call him a village hick. So if he has an educated girl for a daughter-in-law, a *rising star* as everyone says the papers have taken to calling you, no-one dare snub him anymore.'

It all sounds so mercenary, so business-like. But the awe-struck elation that has overcome me will not be swayed.

See, Puja, studying has its uses. I might be boring, but I have got everything I want by being so. I have won our parents' approval and the hand of the boy I have secretly liked in marriage.

'How do you know all this?' I ask.

'I have my sources,' you say, tapping your nose and laughing that light-hearted laugh that I haven't heard in a while.

In the fields, Duja's cow moos mournfully, tugging at the rope that tethers her to the post. The banana flavoured breeze ruffles the ears of paddy and they nod hello. It smells of paradise, it is the yellow of maturing pineapples tinged red with dust.

'Look, Sharda,' you say jovially, linking your arm in mine, lifting your sari skirt with the other so it won't be muddied as you skip, like a carefree little girl, down the narrow path towards home, 'there is no hurry. The landlord and his son are coming to see you formally in a couple of years. We've agreed that the wedding will only take place after you've obtained your degree. But the landlord came to talk to us today just to make sure we would not promise you to anyone else.' Your eyes sparkle like a bride's jewels, Ma. 'We wanted to give you girls an education, despite the cost of books and sundries, so you would do better than us. And you have exceeded our dreams!'

If Puja had been with us, she would have said, indignantly, 'Marrying the landlord's son does not really equate to doing better for yourself, Sharda.'

But for me, it does.

All I have ever wanted is to make you and Da happy and proud of me and now I have done so. In a clandestine corner of my heart, I have also wished for the boy who is this village's sweetheart, to be mine. And soon, he will be.

Puja might be Da's favourite. She might flaunt the rules, scoff at tradition, but by following the rules, by being dutiful, I have got what I've always wanted. The jubilation that is pulsing in my veins, coursing through my body is testament to the fact.

'The matrons urged us to take you out of school after seventh standard, and get you to work with us or as a servant somewhere so you could contribute towards your dowry. We are so glad we didn't heed them. Now we must find a suitable groom for Puja, once she's a bit older . . .' Your voice is the starry silver of bliss. 'We will set a date for the landlord and his son to visit nearer the time. No need to tell Puja until then. You know how she is; discretion is not part of her vocabulary. I don't want her telling the whole village when nothing is set in stone as yet.'

And this last is the best part, Ma. It is the syrup that gives crispy jalebis their irresistible sweetness, the saffron that lifts the humble biryani to epic heights, making it food worthy of kings. At last, a secret between us. Just you and me and Da. Like in the days before Puja came along and everything changed.

Chapter 19
Raj

Jewellery of Tears

'That village,' Raj says, 'Wow. Why were they all so hell bent upon reforming you?'

You? He still cannot quite relate that girl he's been hearing about to this woman next to him. His mother.

She smiles softly at him. He clocks the smile in wonder. When was the last time she smiled at him like that? Has she ever?

'That is the way it used to be, Raj,' she says. 'Girls were not allowed minds of their own. Hopefully it has changed now, or is changing. Fingers crossed.'

This tale of his mother's is making Raj see things in a new light. He has been lucky, he thinks, to have grown up in England. He's always had the freedom to do what he's wanted. He has sometimes taken it too far, he knows, and has often made the wrong choices. His addiction to nicotine, for instance, although he must say he hasn't had a craving for a smoke since his mum started narrating her amazing story. And isn't making mistakes how you learn? At least he's been given the choice . . .

Now he understands why his mum was so short with him when he complained that she was always working, never there. He's always had money, he's never had to think about it, or deny himself anything he's badly wanted. He has never known what it is to be poor, to do without . . .

What did his mum have to endure to give him this freedom of choice, this comfortable life? What did she have to go through to gain her independence, to come to the UK? Was losing her sister the price she paid?

He looks at his mother, severe, unyielding, her hair pulled back in a rigid bun, her face subjugated by its armour of makeup, which is now starting to crease a bit at the corners of her eyes. A wispy feather or two of hair dares to escape the stiff restraints of the bun. Hard to reconcile this inflexible woman with the zesty, spirited girl he is hearing about, so full of life, and chafing at the restrictions imposed upon her. And falling in love? This woman, who recoils from the merest touch . . .

'Did that nun really give you a lecture about the "dangers" of touching boys, and having lustful thoughts about them?'

She giggles, an unguarded chuckle, and in that brief moment he gets a tiny glimpse of the girl she once was. Skipping school, daringly spending the day with a boy, something that, obviously, was just not done in that antiquated village of her childhood . . .

'Why? Why were you not allowed to consort with boys? What silly rules!'

'Yes, silly and suffocating,' she sighs, the smile freezing on her face, hardening, like spilling wax from a candle, into a grimace.

He cannot envisage his mother, who balks at the slightest hint of sentiment, (although that has changed a bit since yesterday), daringly touching a boy in a café in a town Raj cannot even begin to picture. A vision of Ellie gesturing to him from the bus, telling him she likes him, looms before his eyes. Love, he thinks, is the one emotion that doesn't change, transcending generations and time and distance. He has been gathering up the courage to talk to Ellie forever and *still* hasn't properly managed it.

Love, he thinks. *It transforms you, and it also binds you in chains . . .*

'You yearned to escape. To be free. Have you? Are you?'

The colour leaves his mother's face like light leaving the sky during a rainstorm, 'Son, I. . .' She gulps, a tremor passing through her.

'I'm sorry, Mum,' Raj blurts, surprising himself. Much as he's resented the remote mother he's known all his life, Raj is waking up to the realisation that he doesn't like seeing his mother like this either, undone, open to hurt. Hearing her story has gone some way in making Raj feel more forgiving towards her. The heated anger that a mere word from her could trigger is not so quick to flare anymore. What he feels instead, as he looks at the woman beside him—a woman who's always been a vexing enigma but who is now gradually revealing herself to be a person he thinks he might be able to relate to—is sadness that circumstances have forced the precocious, fun-loving girl he's been hearing about, to become this remote woman.

His mother gathers herself together. 'Don't be sorry,' she says. 'You've made me think. You're very astute, son.'

He swells from the unexpected compliment, and turns away to look out the window to hide the flush that is taking his face captive.

'This talking to you, telling you about the past is helping me to see myself clearly, scrutinise the girl I was from a distance. I wish I could pluck her out of the past, shake some sense into her and then insert her back in again.' A pause, then, 'You have your whole life ahead of you, son, waiting to be moulded into shape. Mine has settled into the groove of the mistakes I've made, the holes I mindlessly dug and fell into . . . '

Raj turns away from his perusal through the window of the candyfloss clouds stretched as far as the eye can see, disappearing into a cerise gilded horizon and looks at his mother. Her eyes sparkle and glitter with their jewellery of tears.

His distant mother finally doing him the honour of treating him like an adult. This more than makes up for the slap, he thinks.

'You asked if I am free, Raj. Ah . . . I'm beginning to realise that I've bound myself in chains tighter than any the villagers could have conceived, and locked myself in a prison of my own making.' She swallows and anxiety settles over her features—a shadow of pain, as sinister as a masked intruder poised to strike, 'I'm hoping . . . I'm hoping that by seeing my sister again, and meeting Kushi, I will finally be free . . . '

Why am I not enough? Why wasn't I the one who set you free? Raj thinks going back to the window, his earlier good mood dissipating faster than the clouds shifting beneath their plane as his mother continues with her story.

Chapter 20
Puja—Cusp

Gossip Antennae

Second PUC (Pre-University Course) Exam Results for Puja Ramesh, Age 18

Kannada 45/100

English 65/100

Maths 33/100 F

Physics 26/100 F

Chemistry 32/100 F

Biology 30/100 F

We regret to inform you that Puja Ramesh has failed the second year Pre-University Course examination. If she wishes to continue her studies and apply for a place at college, she needs to retake her exams.

❄ ❄ ❄

Puja barely glances at her report card as she rushes down to the shops where he waits for her, the leader of the motor-cycle gang, and the handsomest man in the entire town of Dhoompur.

But that evening, he is not there, revving his bike as he usually does.

She gives up the pretence they have maintained of not being aware of each other until the street empties of gossipy students, busybody doyennes and bored, out-of-work men with nothing better to do than to create trouble by spreading malicious rumours, and approaches his friends.

'Where is he? Is he ill?' Puja grills his friends but they are evasive, their faces going red as carrot halwa when she interrogates them. They mumble something incoherent while furiously concentrating on drawing circles in the mud with their feet and she finally gives up, stomping off in a huff.

The trek home seems to take forever. Puja is annoyed with herself for caring so much, for not being able to get rid of the salty bulge of disappointment lodged in her throat. She hates not knowing where he is and with whom.

Am I that easy to give up?

Then there is the added disappointment of the report card. She was expecting it, of course, but how to show it to her parents, especially in light of Sharda's prodigious achievement? Sharda, who is well on her way to becoming a doctor, and almost three quarters of the way through her medical degree.

Puja has been expecting their parents, especially their ma, to be getting a little anxious by now about marrying Sharda off, but curiously, there has been no mention of marriage.

With their ma being so traditional, Puja is surprised that the subject of Sharda's marriage and Puja's in due course, has not been raised.

At times, Puja wonders if Ma and Sharda are keeping something from her. But she cannot be bothered to push to find out. If it is important, they'll tell her. Sharda has said something obscure about 'fortune favouring the hardworking', she and Ma have lectured Puja about her reputation every so often as usual, but there has been nothing else. At least this means the pressure is off Puja. Ma cannot nag *her* about marriage until Sharda has been married off. And Puja is grateful for this reprieve. It gives her time to plan her future, to run away with him, as he has suggested so many times, although they haven't planned anything concrete yet.

But where is he this evening?

As Puja nears home, she sees a flash of metal, glinting silvery gold in the sunshine. Is that what she thinks it is? Her heart beating a loud tattoo in her chest, she quickens her steps, until she is almost running, and then comes to a panting stop beside the machine parked by the fields leading down to her hut. She glides her hands down the shining chassis, the one that only she has been allowed to ride; the one he keeps so spotless, making sure that one of the many servants in his house wipe it clean of dust every morning, or so he has told her.

'I make them polish it until I can see my face in every part of it,' he has said, proudly.

Gopi, Puja whispers his name, hoarding it in her mouth like a delicious treat. She looks in the wing mirror and tidies her hair, pushing stray wisps behind her ears, catching a lingering whiff of him, motor oil and lemon, as she bends down to check her reflection.

How come he is here?

Puja skips down the fields to her house, her mood suddenly very much improved, breathing in the fragranced early evening air, tasting guavas and hope. Has he decided to tell her parents about his feelings for her, ask for her hand in marriage? But he's never spoken of marriage, only of running away from the village. And why tell her parents before discussing it with her?

Did he gather up the courage to confess his feelings for Puja to his father and perhaps his father made him come here, talk to her parents? She knows how afraid Gopi is of his father, the landlord. He has been so careful about keeping their relationship under wraps, even more so than her. He is worried about being found out—his father is very strict, he says, and will confiscate his bike if he gets wind of any mischief.

So why is Gopi here now, blatantly advertising their friendship to the whole world, if she is right in assuming that Gopi has come to visit her? And if he hasn't come to see her, then *why* has he come?

There is nothing here but fields. The little hut she shares with her parents and sister is slap bang in the middle of nowhere, unlike his huge mansion by the beach . . . oh well, she'll find out soon enough.

She is past the clump of guava trees, and almost upon the hut. She hears loud voices, and laughter. Da is home and so also, it appears, from the booming, sonorous tones, is the landlord, Gopi's father. She's met the landlord at their school feast days; he is always invited to distribute the prizes. She pictures the big, surly man with his bald head and his impressive moustache. Did he sit pillion on Gopi's bike, in *her* place? Why is *he* here?

Puja pulls her salwar down, brushing off the dust accrued from the walk home and bounces into the house, abruptly grinding to a stunned halt as she takes in the scene before her.

Sharda is all decked up and sitting next to Gopi. She is wearing a sari Puja has never seen before, a beautiful garnet and gold affair, and Puja realises, her shuddering heart slowly catching up with her brain, that it is a new one bought for this occasion with money her parents can ill afford. Hasn't she heard her parents and sister worrying time and time again about how to make ends meet? So why spend money they don't have on a new sari for Sharda, when Puja has begged and begged for new clothes but has had to make do with Sharda's drab hand-me-downs which her ma alters, letting down the hems and tightening the waist as Puja is both taller and thinner than Sharda.

Sharda is wearing flowers in her hair and kumkum on her forehead; all of Ma's jewellery is twinkling on her neck and glittering on her arms. She is not wearing her spectacles. She is the picture of a blushing bride.

Gopi is unrecognisable in a lungi and white shirt, a far cry from the checked shirt and trousers that make up his daily uniform. His gaze meets Puja's once briefly before it drops onto his lap, his face going red as his mates', and he squirms uncomfortably on the mat beside her sister.

Da and Ma are laughing the laugh they reserve for visitors and Sharda is coy. Her bangle-laden hands join demurely on her lap.

There is another mat on the floor heaving with laddoos and bondas, bhajis and pedas. Ma has gone all out it seems. The air is heady with excitement and with the smell of fried onions, condensed milk and spices. The landlord is stretched out on the only bench like a snake undulating dreamily after having swallowed a human.

'What is going on here?' Puja asks and her voice is sharp with shock.

'Puja,' Ma says in a voice as false as a wig, 'the landlord has asked for your sister's hand in marriage to his son.'

No! Puja's dumbfounded brain screams in the confines of her head. *No, no, no!*

But, with gargantuan effort, she tries to keep her smile in place and says, charming as ever, looking right at the landlord, her voice steady and not trembling, not even a tiny bit, 'Why can't I marry your son instead?'

And everyone, with the exception of Gopi, who still refuses to meet her gaze, bursts out laughing even though Puja is not joking, even though she is crying inside, her lovesick heart a big bottomless cavern, wet and saturated in tears.

❋ ❋ ❋

The day after his betrothal to her sister, Gopi, as always, waits for Puja outside the shops, and when she walks past, he has the gall to offer her a tentative smile, as if nothing has happened, as if their world has not just shifted on its axis leaning heavily towards her short, squat, bespectacled sister. She ignores him and walks down the road, looking straight ahead.

Instead of keeping pace on the opposite side of the road, as he usually does in order to avoid scandal, he catches up with her.

'Puja,' he calls, in a prayer-like chant that gives her name the meaning it is ordained.

She walks on, pretending he isn't there.

He speeds up and stops right in front of her, blocking her path.

'Fancy a ride?' he asks, his voice slightly breathless.

Puja lifts her hand, and with all her strength, slaps him right across his arrogant, thoughtless cheek.

There is silence. The tinkle of bicycle bells, the honk of the lone, overstuffed, on-its-last-legs rickshaw ferrying schoolchildren home, the chatter of youth, the song of the boatmen, and the laughter of the fisherwomen, pauses in the ringing aftermath. Mouths are agape, welcoming receptacles for swirling particles of grime and inebriated insects drunk on nectar and sunshine. The bitter, woozy smell of shock pervades the dust-bruised air.

Puja's hand smarts and she holds it a bit away from her so it doesn't brush her salwar as she walks away, her head held high. Gopi is the handsomest, coolest boy in all of Dhoompur. The other boys look up to him. And to him, appearances matter.

Puja wills away the tears collecting in her eyes, knowing she has irrevocably jeopardised her chances with him by slapping him in front of his friends. But then she *never* stood a chance. He is betrothed to her sister.

She fights the waves of nausea that threaten to overcome her at the thought of it.

And yet . . . she loves him.

All through the previous evening—as she endured the smiles and the celebrations, as she waved goodbye to the landlord, refusing to meet Gopi's eye, as she hugged her sister and pretended to be pleased for her, as she forced her mother's specially prepared, celebratory sweetmeats down her salt-clogged throat, as she lay on the mat beside her sister and her mother—she had fought her feelings for him, tried to tamp them down, squish them dead.

But they had refused to acquiesce.

She loves him. But she wonders what possessed her to think he cared for her like she has grown to care for him? And now . . .

Her hand stings. She can feel the welts, engorged pink, rising on her palm. Now he will really hate her for daring to humiliate him in front of the entire population.

Well and good.

All those girls waiting in line to win his favours can up their game now, not that he will ever belong to any of them either. That honour has been bagged by her own, nerdy, bug-eyed sister. Acrid bile rises in her mouth.

'Puja.' A hot hand on her sore palm.

She winces, and pulls away.

Despite being slapped, he has persisted in following her, throwing the caution, in which they have always shrouded their relationship (ha!), to the wind.

Everyone is staring at them, noting their every move with keen eyes, gossip antennae bristling. There's an imprint of her palm on his face, red and inflamed. She looks away, unable to meet his gaze. The hurt at his treachery bubbles in her chest, a bitter cocktail that she can taste in her mouth, that congests her nose, and threatens to flood from her eyes.

He has abandoned his precious motorbike, his ubiquitous companion. She sees it lying on its side by the shops, forlorn and discoloured by mud, no longer shiny.

'I am sorry. I didn't know, I swear.' His voice desperate, pleading.

'Leave me alone,' she is pleased that the turmoil she feels is not reflected in her tone, which as she intends, is cold and detached. She gags on the next few words but squeezes them out. 'You are promised to my sister.'

'But I don't want to be. I didn't know . . . '

Is that a wobble in his voice? At last, she looks at him.

His eyes shine as they return her gaze, his luxuriant eyelashes iridescent and glinting in the golden sunshine. As she watches, one perfect little teardrop traverses the wounded landscape of his abused face.

Her aching heart jumps, infused with dawning hope, despite her many doubts.

He cares, sings her foolish heart. *He does. He cares enough to not worry about his status, about how he looks pleading with me in front of the whole street. He cares.*

Gopi senses he is getting through to her and says, urgently, the words tumbling over each other in their hurry to get told, 'I went home yesterday afternoon as usual to change before coming back up here to meet you, but Da was waiting for me. That was surprising in itself as he is never home early. And on top of that, he was in an unusually good mood. He said we were going somewhere and since it was close by could I take him there on my bike? You know, with him, it's always a command, never a request. I gave in, thinking that whatever it was I could finish it quickly and still have time to see you. When he asked me to park by the fields leading down to your house, I started to panic, wondering if he had guessed about us and this was his bizarre way of punishing me. But when we got there and I saw Sharda all decked up . . .' He takes a deep, quaking breath. 'I am so sorry, Puja, I could not tell them, I didn't know how. Especially after I found out that my da had verbally promised me to Sharda long before this . . .'

Really? Puja opens her mouth, suddenly unable to breathe. So this is the secret Ma and Sharda were keeping from her. She understands now why Ma was not stressing about getting Sharda married. The realisation stings like vinegar scooped into the parched mouth of a thirsty man.

'The betrothal yesterday was just the confirmation of that promise my da made to your parents and Sharda without my knowledge. I didn't know! I did not know.' Gopi's voice is choked with emotion, and brimming with fury at his father.

Neither did I know.

'Your parents and your sister looked so happy that my mouth just clamped up . . . how could I tell them that it was not Sharda but you that I wanted?'

Puja does not need to hear any more. Blood rushes to her face and her heart, raw and injured just a minute ago is humming now. The air tastes of happiness, and the drab mud-smudged surroundings are suddenly wreathed in vivid colour.

He cares for me. It will be all right. We will make it all right.

But she has to ask. 'Do you like Sharda? I've heard rumours that you are friendly with her too, but I ignored them before. Is this your latest trick, trying to win over two sisters at once?'

He takes another deep breath. 'I do like Sharda. She's a very good teacher. It was only because of her coaching that I passed Maths in Second PUC.'

His honesty hurts; it is a dart lodged in her heart, skewering it open again, a throbbing wound.

'You pursued her, took it as a challenge to win her over.'

'I . . . I just wanted her to like me, because she is your sister . . .' His voice is urgent, tortured. 'You know me, Puja, better than anyone . . .'

'Do I? Turns out I know nothing at all.'

'Puja . . .' Her name a longing on his lips.

She crushes her sore hand against her thigh, and the jolt of physical pain gives her the courage to ask, above the howling of her heart, 'Do you want to marry Sharda?'

'No!' All the anguish Puja feels is reflected in his voice. 'Puja, *you* are my soulmate. You make me laugh. You incite feelings in me I have never known. My da gave me no warning. I am tired of doing his bidding, bending to his will. He did not even bother to inform me of *my* betrothal until I was actually *being* betrothed. How does he know what's best for me? Why not ask me what *I* want before deciding *my* future, making plans for the rest of *my* life? Why did he not tell me he promised me to Sharda? He has always done this, mapped out my life for me. And I have taken it. But not this time. Puja, *you* are the one I care for. We complement each other. We are made for each other.' He looks right at her with that golden gaze that opens her up and lays her bare, that gaze that takes in who she is and proposes what she can be with him. 'You make my heart come alive. I love you and want to marry you. We'll tell my Da and Sharda. We will.'

Puja's heart swells. She opens her mouth and tastes the jubilant air. Not heeding the watching population, she links her arm through Gopi's and laughs, the sound rivalling the temple bells, which is echoed by Gopi laughing right along with her.

Chapter 21
Kushi

A Hand Dropped at an Airport

When I have finished reading, I rub my eyes and fingers trembling with eagerness, I open the next letter. I am absorbed in Ma's story.

I do not recognise this picture of Ma, this vulnerable, studious girl, battling her envy of her beautiful, carefree sister. I want to know what happens next.

These letters are allowing me to meet Ma as a child, and the girl she was before she became the woman I know—the strong, kind woman with her huge heart, her generosity, and her capacity for caring; the woman who tided me through the death of my father despite the fact that she was grieving her husband. The woman who loves me and has lied to me all my life. The woman who shunned her sister for so many years.

I am reading Ma's story as if my life depends on it. Perhaps it does . . . The way I figure it, if I find out what happened to drive Ma and Puja apart all those years ago, perhaps I'll be able to appeal to Puja's better nature, convince her to donate her kidney to save my life (if it is a match, that is) . . .

The truth is that I prefer to lose myself in Ma's story because it distracts me from my own. When I read Ma's letters, this frantic, fear-splashed present loses its hold on me; it is like a hand dropped at an airport when the person saying goodbye crosses the barrier into another country, another world.

The truth is I am terrified. I don't want to die. I love my life. There is so much I want to do.

I push away the anxiety that threatens to swallow me whole, the dread I am holding at bay and engross myself in my ma's words.

Chapter 22
Sharda—Fissure

Twittering Posse of Busybodies

Dearest Ma,

For a very long time I blamed Puja. I refused to see my part in it all.

Then Kushi came along, innocent, so sweetly perfect in all her human imperfections and my heart flooded with love, crowding out the hate, the hurt, the simmering wrath. My little girl taught me to love again and it was an easing, a great relief. I held her in my arms, this girl with her whole life ahead of her, an empty page awaiting words, and I had an epiphany.

I realised something I should always have known, that we make our own destiny. I understood that I had a choice. I could continue to indulge my hate-shrivelled, rage-tarnished heart. Or I could change. I could wipe clean the half-filled page of my life so far, populated with hurt and hate and regret, and start over. Anew.

Somehow, holding Kushi in my arms made me see beyond the wrongs that had been done to me, to the mistakes *I* had made. She imbued my soul, which had been blackened by wrath, soiled by upset, and dirtied by vengeful thoughts, with the soothing balm of acceptance, and the cleansing gel of forgiveness.

Ma, I have visited this day I am about to narrate a thousand times in my mind. And a thousand times, I have chosen for it a different ending . . .

You know the fights all siblings have: 'She started it.' 'No, *she* did.'

Now I can say for sure that it was me.

Perhaps Puja set things in motion. Or perhaps Gopi did.

But in the end, it was I who lit the wayward match that started the fire, it was I who put events into motion that broke us apart.

It was me.

❄ ❄ ❄

When the matrons come calling I am washing clothes on the granite stone by the well in the dappled shade of the tamarind tree, indulging in fantasies of Gopi now that I am betrothed to him, dreams I denied myself when I was younger due to Sister Seema's dire warnings. And also because I never dared imagine that he would be mine.

Even after you told me of the landlord's intention, Ma, I was nervous, in case it all fell through. I kept pinching myself when you told me of the match, and asked me to keep it a secret from Puja. I was tempted to tell her about it several times, but was worried that by uttering the words out loud, I might jinx my betrothal to Gopi.

When I saw the look on Puja's face when she entered the hut and stumbled upon Gopi and me being promised to each other, I felt guilty for having kept mum. It was the one small cloud in an otherwise perfect day. Puja had recovered though, made us all laugh. What did she say? I can't quite remember. But that's Puja for you, isn't it, ever the charmer.

Ma, you are at our market stall with Da, flush from the success of a match arranged and sealed for me, your eldest daughter, the one you were secretly worried about.

No such worries on Puja's account; in her case, given her looks and charm, provided she manages not to smear her reputation, you know that you will be warding off suitors.

The matrons descend en masse, surrounding me as I rinse the clothes and twist them into ropes, bashing them on the marbled granite stone to bleed out all the water. I feel a finger of dread play up and down the bones of my spine.

You've called me intuitive, Ma. But I suppose I am just cautious.

Everything has gone right for me lately. My medical degree is proceeding smoothly, the expense of tuition and sundries (including the cost of the bus pass to travel to Hosahanapur, where the medical college is, and back), is being paid for by the college because of my brilliant performance in the entrance exam.

'You'll be the first doctor this village has produced,' Da has marvelled countless times, pride burnishing his voice a radiant gold. 'Tell me again, what's the starting salary for doctors these days?' The pride he used to reserve exclusively for Puja.

And when the previous day, the landlord and Gopi graced our hut to formally ask for my hand, the looks on both of your faces were as if you had been bestowed the gift of eternal life.

Gopi had been curiously shy during our betrothal. He would not meet my eye, but looked down and fiddled with his clothes instead. I saw his hands trembling at one point. Did that show the depth of his feelings for me? This softer side to the cocky boy I had known (and begun to care for) at school endeared him to me all the more.

Gopi. My intended. *Mine.*

Wow! To have an arranged marriage where love is already blooming—isn't that serendipitous?

But even in the midst of this joy I cannot tamp down the worry that it is all too good to be true. And so, when I see the matrons Ma, I am petrified. Have the gods realised that I have had more than my share of good fortune and sent this twittering posse of busybodies to prick my bubble of unmitigated happiness?

The matrons flap and chirp and cluck like flustered birds, swamping me with their smell of sweat and spices as they wipe their faces with their pallus and spit their half-chewed paan into the blue sudsy water beside the washing stone, turning it to brown sludge.

'Where's your ma, child?' they ask. 'Any chance of a cup of tea?'

I lead them inside and they crowd our hut, filling it with bustle, making it seem smaller than ever; the news they are bursting to impart gives their substantial bosoms heft as they hold it close for the last few moments before they have to dilute it by sharing it with me.

'We heard, child, about your betrothal.' They say, but their paan-etched, tea-stained grins resemble grimaces.

Please, God. The finger of dread is now an entire hand, taking my spine captive. My stomach cramps.

They sigh. They fidget.

I wait.

'Your sister, Puja,' they say, finally, once they have drunk the tea and complained that it has too much ginger, too little cardamom, and not enough sugar.

Ah, I exhale the huge lungful of air I have been holding in, tasting relief. It's nothing to do with me, or Gopi. *Thank you, God.*

They take fresh paan. They chew noisily. They ask for the coconut shell spittoon.

'She was a delight as a child, but now . . .' they sigh and spit reddish yellow flakes of masticated paan, and their eyes gleam maliciously. 'How will your parents get her married if she keeps mixing with boys, and running riot with them?' They click their teeth to convey disgust.

I nod agreement, and step back imperceptibly to wipe my paan-flecked face with my churidar shawl, which smells of Rin soap and dog. This party of meddlers came here to tell us this? A wasted trip, surely. They know we know all this, they have complained about Puja's antics a hundred times before.

But the matrons never waste energy making a house visit in the oppressive sun; energy they can conserve while nattering on a comfortable veranda being waited upon and plied with sweetmeats, unless there is value to be gleaned by imparting a choice nugget of information, something hot off the press, which has to be shared in person. There is more to come, I am sure.

I wait. Fear clamps my body even as it makes my legs quake.

Please God.

'Child, we would rather be telling this to your parents, but as they are not here . . . '

Please.

They take a collective breath.

God.

'Your sister is running around with your beau.'

Do not react, I tell myself, even as the meaning of what they are saying sinks in, each word a tumbler of acid, burning a path down my insides, reducing to a withering, smoking heap everything it comes in contact with.

Your sister . . .

Puja, whom I have adored from the moment she was born. Puja, whom I have loved more than life itself, and who I always assumed loved me just as much in return. Puja

with whom I have swapped confidences. Puja whom I have
rescued from scrapes, taking the blame myriad times for her
indiscretions. Puja with whom I made a promise that we
would love each other best and look out for each other; a
promise I have kept so far.

Puja who makes me laugh, even when I feel like crying.

Puja, who despite the fact that I have two left feet, took
it upon herself to teach me to dance—'Christian Wedding
Boogie' she called it: her take on ballroom dancing —out
among the fields with our feet sinking in the mud and the
dog nipping at our heels and the cows mooing in surprise.

Puja, who knows how afraid I am of lizards and meticu-
lously chases away each one clinging to the beams above us
every night before we lie down to sleep. Puja whom I have
tended through fever. Puja, who diligently soothed my itchy
skin when I had chicken pox.

Puja, who taught me how to apply makeup, tips she
picked up from God knows where, using wet mud for foun-
dation and the sticky yellow stamen from hibiscus flowers
for lipstick.

Puja who sleeps beside me at night, each of us breathing
in air festooned by the other's dreams.

Puja who still throws her arms around me every so often
and whispers in my ear, 'Sharda, you are the best sister in the
world.'

Puja, who is party to my deepest fears.

Puja, who is my closest friend.

Puja, my only sibling; my precious, beloved sister.

Puja, the traitor, if what the matrons are saying is true.

Your sister is running around with your beau.

Gopi's face, his smiling eyes, his hot breath in my ear: 'You are the best teacher, Sharda.' His hand holding out a Campco chocolate, damp with sweat, thus sealing a friendship. His eyes during our betrothal, evasive as a glimpse of moon on a tempestuous night.

Puja asking, 'Sharda, have you ever been in love?'

I bite the inside of my cheek until the hot, sweet taste of pain floods my mouth with the rusty tang of blood.

I picture again Puja's face when she came upon Gopi and his da in our hut, colour draining from it like waves receding from the shore at low tide leaving forlorn debris behind, the dregs of what could have been. I had felt guilty then and something else . . . unease, sly as an uninvited guest at a wedding sneaking up behind the bride: 'Boo!'

Now I remember what she said that made us laugh. Her words in this very room adorned with my happiness and bedecked with my dreams of a future with Gopi, ringing as clear as an immaculate reputation, 'Why can't I marry him instead?'

'Child, did you hear what we just said?' The matrons squawking like so many hens excited by a cockerel in their midst.

This is why they've come.

I feel their collective gaze upon me like a spotlight shining right into my eyes, keen with the gossip they are itching to spread. They wait for my reaction, which will do very well for their chinwag sessions for the whole of next week. Already, they are rewriting what is taking place in their heads, adding embellishments as they go along, musing on what expressions they will use when they relate this scene to their relatives and loved ones.

'She went pale,' they will say.

'We had to hold her to stop her from falling,' they will murmur.

'She smacked her forehead repeatedly and invoked God while bursting into heart rending sobs,' they will croon.

'What a shame! The poor, deluded sister,' they will sigh.

'Thank God,' they will chant, chomping on their paan and heaving sighs of relief at finally being able to rest their ailing legs, 'thank God our families are normal, our daughters demure. That devastated girl, conned by her own sister, crying her heart out . . . '

'Holding hands without a care in the world! Puja hugging him tight as they conjure up a sandstorm on that motorbike of his! Shameless, that's what . . .' they moan now, nodding like puppets.

'Thank you, I'll tell Ma and Da,' I say, grateful that my voice is steady.

The ladies stand, a collective rustle and whoosh; sighs and cracking of knees. The odour of sweat and stale betel leaves.

I usher them out, even though they are loath to depart without getting more from me. A fit, a tantrum, they'll even settle for a lament, a shocked whisper.

I give them nothing. I wait until they have rounded the corner past Sumatiakka's fields, craning their necks until the last to catch sight of me, to witness my spectacular collapse.

A pity, I think, my mind rejecting what it has learned, and fixing on inconsequential thoughts instead, *that they resemble*

waddling penguins even if their necks can swivel as flexibly as
swans'.

I wash the saucepan in which I brewed the tea and the
dregs of the paan-tinted tea tumblers. My mind is quiet as a
note stripped of music, bland as a tapestry robbed of colour,
empty as art robbed of meaning.

I do not think of that exhilarated girl who had sat beside
Gopi in this very room just one day ago. I do not dwell on
the thrill she had felt at his proximity—this boy she had secretly adored for so long, who was now *hers*.

I do not think of the distance I have traversed in just a
few minutes; it is too big a gap to bridge—the creamy innocence of a few minutes ago besmirched irrevocably by the
chilli-powder red blot of knowledge that I cannot unlearn,
the awareness of having been betrayed by two of the people
who make up my world, two of the people I have loved most.

I look back at the girl I was this morning, spinning dreams
of a happy future with a boy she finally dared own, and I
want to laugh at her. Loudly, hysterically. Laugh and never
stop.

I think of what I have always believed. That being traditional, dutiful, and following the rules, will get me what I want.

Wrong.

Wrong, wrong, wrong.

I hang out the clothes to dry, and wait until one of the
matrons returns under the pretext of looking for a lost hanky,
when all the while, it is fastened securely to her sari skirt with
the biggest safety pin I have ever seen.

And only after I have waved her goodbye, and after I have swept the courtyard and fed the dog, only then do I go inside and pull out Puja's favourite churidar; not one of my hand-me-downs, Ma, but the one you had especially made for her with cloth she had picked out, as a special treat for her last birthday, and I rip it to shreds.

And then, I walk to the market.

You are grateful, Ma, that I have come to relieve you, so you can go home and put your tired feet up for a brief while.

You cup my face in your palms, plant a kiss on my forehead, whisper, 'My sweet girl.'

You cannot contain your happiness at having secured such a good match for me. Even though the landlord's son's proposal has been on the cards for a while, it is only now that it has been formalised, that you can breathe easy that it will actually happen. Your joy gives your face a sheen that makes you look so beautiful, like the mother I remember before Puja was born and sucked all the youth, and the cheerful abandon out of you.

I wait and watch until I am sure you have walked home and are not coming back. Then and only then, do I tell Da.

Da who has always put Puja on a pedestal. Da, in whose eyes my sister can do no wrong.

I know what I am doing. I do not tell you and Da together, Ma, because I do not want to diminish the import of what I am about to do: open Da's eyes to the despicable truth that his favourite child is in actual fact, a traitor. A reckless, unthinking, selfish monster.

She slept next to me last night, Ma, as always, folding into me, her sputtering little snores the soundtrack to my dreams, knowing that this morning she would go to him, hold him, *my* beau. How can she enjoy the sleep of a saint when she is the worst possible transgressor?

I take a deep breath, tasting bile and betrayal.

'Da,' I say. 'I have something to tell you.'

Chapter 23
Raj

Spilled Ink and Tainted Sheets

'It was just a bit of fun at first,' his mum says. Her voice is the bluish purple of clouds at dusk. It is spilled ink and tainted sheets, the smell of sorrow and the taste of remorse. 'But as time went on, Gopi became the drug I needed for survival. I yearned to be free, and he was the embodiment of that freedom.'

'Was he telling the truth when he said it was you he loved?' Raj asks. He is trying to summon the shock his mother must have felt when she stumbled upon the love of her life being promised to her sister.

'He convinced me,' she says softly.

And at that moment, with her face tear-splashed and her makeup collecting in clumps on her cheeks, Raj can see clearly the little girl she once was, and the old woman she will become.

His mother.

He feels a rush of tenderness for her.

And before Raj thinks about what he is doing, he reaches out to touch the tears on his mother's cheek. The tip of his finger glistens for a minute and triggers in him an acute sense of loss.

'I believed him,' his mother says, her eyes glittering in her haunted face. She is thousands of miles away, and years in the past, in a claustrophobic village in a dust ravaged state, in a spice-flavoured country, and he is right there with her, an observer from the future, being introduced to the country as they hurtle towards it, spanning the distance of five thousand miles and nearly twenty years of unspoken words, unforgiven crimes, and unsorted messes—towards a woman and a girl—his unknown aunt and cousin—who are waiting for them to arrive . . .

Chapter 24
Puja—Fissure

The Milky Scent of Ripening Paddy

Puja dances home on a high, breathing in the milky scent of ripening paddy, tasting yellow sunlight on her lips.

He loves me, he does.

But as she reaches home, passing the place where the motorbike was resting the previous day, her steps falter. How to face Sharda? How to tell her? She recalls how yesterday, her sister's face had radiated happiness; how plain, dumpy Sharda had looked almost beautiful.

But she doesn't love Gopi. She doesn't even properly know him!

It will be fine. Puja will convince Sharda and her parents as she has always done.

When she hears the hiss of the stick rushing through the air, and feels the sharp smack of it on her back; when she sees a grimacing stranger inhabiting her da's placid countenance, when she feels her skin split and spurt, she cannot believe it. Even as she buckles and tries to skip away from the stick which makes ripping, stinging contact with her flesh again and again, she wonders if she is dreaming, if she has entered an alternate reality.

'No,' her ma shouts, 'That's enough. What are you doing?'

Ma grabs Da's hand, and tries to stop him, but Da hits Puja with his other hand, repeatedly. She hears a strangled wail, a panicked scream, tastes rust and salt, and realises that it is she who is howling.

The world has gone mad, has tilted on its axis. Puja throws her bag on the ground and cowers under the assault of her beloved Da's hands, the barrage of his words yelled stuttering and gasping, in an unrecognisable voice, so it sounds as if he is crying, and hurting as much as he is hurting her. 'How could you do this? Bring this disgrace upon us? Steal your sister's husband-to-be from right under our noses? Have you no shame?'

The taste of distress and resentment, fury and incredulity—pink tinged brine. Blazing, garnet-hued agony. The dog's howls indistinguishable from the humans'.

Her back is on fire. The stick breaks. Her father collapses.

Her ma tends to her wounds to the accompaniment of salty sobs. She applies Tiger Balm, with its peppermint and eucalyptus aroma of a thousand fevered dreams, of hot milk mixed with barley and bitter pills.

Sharda hunches in the corner, her head in the cushion of her lap.

Her father looks at his hands, the hands that used to lift Puja in the air, twirl her around and around, the hands in whose embrace she always felt safe, the hands that have flogged her, relentlessly, tearing her fragile skin, and breaking her heart.

'You are not my daughter.'

Words she never thought to hear, uttered in a voice that is as familiar as her own name, a voice that used to whisper endearments: 'My princess, my delight, my pride and joy.'

'No,' her mother screams.

Sharda buries her face in her hands, shuddering sobs racking her body.

Puja is numb. Bewildered. Uncomprehending.

Her da, who has just disowned her, examines his hands as if he cannot recognise them—those hands that have wrought such damage. But the words that come out of his mouth are the ones that destroy, that rupture the fabric of her life.

'You will stay with your aunt Nilamma in the village across the river. You will not see that boy again. And you will not see us.'

Chapter 25
Kushi

A Flourishing Growl

I set down Ma's letter feeling chilled and warmed in equal measure.

Chilled because of what happened, and what Puja—whom I was beginning to like, based on the picture of her I have gleaned from these letters—did to my Ma. Stealing her beau, a boy Ma had loved from afar for so long, a boy whom Ma was so thrilled to be marrying.

I am warmed because Ma says I healed her at the beginning of the letter, that it was I who taught her to love again.

'You bring out the best in me,' she says to me often.

I want her here with me. I want to talk to her about what I am learning about her past. I wonder what is happening at the bank. Has she managed to procure the loan needed to see me through this? I really hope she doesn't have to sell the factory. I wouldn't be able to bear it . . .

The bald sister in the bed next to mine is asleep. The grey-haired one sits on the chair, dozing.

The letter I was reading flutters down beside me, onto the bed sheet, and I notice something I missed. A little note tagged onto the end, penned in the margin. Different ink. Her handwriting is slightly different too, more rounded, much as it is now.

I run my hands over Ma's words and picture her carrying these letters everywhere, tucked into her sari blouse, re-reading them and adding follow-ups from the safe distance of a future that is thick with retrospection, but bereft of her sister.

The bald woman moans. The grey-haired one reaches across and cups her cheek. 'Shush,' she whispers imparting solace, and easing her unwell sister back into sleep.

I always thought we would grow old together, Puja and I, Ma writes in the addendum to her letter. *If there is one thing I sincerely wish I could undo, it would be going to Da, and embellishing the matrons' account with titbits fuelled by my rage, and my jealousy. I honestly didn't realise, at the time, what my angry tale would unleash.*

It broke us.

And nothing was ever the same again.

Lost in Ma's words, it is a while before I am aware of a rustle and bustle, a flourishing growl like a swarm of insects converging. I look up, blink, and look again. Up and down the ward, the ailing and their relatives are doing the same.

A throng of villagers, every single one of whom I recognise, hone in on my bed.

I blink back my tears, touched beyond words by my unexpected visitors. They have waited until their chores have finished, and endured a meandering journey on the local bus to make their way here, I know. The trip would have taken them the best part of an hour, and cost them money they can ill afford. When they get back, they will need to cook and feed their families, heat up the water for the family's wash, scour the dishes, feed their dogs and only then get to bed, to be up at the crack of dawn as usual on the morrow for another long day in the fields or working as servants as the case might be.

They place a basket of fruit beside my bed: the ripest bananas, juiciest mangoes, watermelon and guavas. I am overcome by their generosity, and the thought that has gone into this gift. I know that this is fruit they could have sold for profit; it is the best of their meagre crop.

'We weren't sure if you could eat proper food, else we would have got rice and chicken curry with boondi laddoo for afters; we know it is your favourite meal . . . '

'Thank you,' I say through the lump in my throat.

They are out of place in this medicine-suffused room as they crowd the space around my bed. What do they see as they look down at me? Me, whom they used to look up to, whose every word they would act upon. Me, their leader, used to being independent, in charge, always on the go, and now reduced to this . . . this invalid whose body has let her down.

They used to admire me. Do they pity me now?

I understand now what Ma used to say to me about putting myself in others' shoes. This experience has made me vulnerable. I hate having to depend on others for the smallest thing. Now I know why some of the girls who came to me for help wouldn't listen to me. It is hard to have everything taken from you, including your own sense of self. It is frustrating to have someone else dictate what is best for you.

I am awash with shame. I do not want the villagers' pity. Anything but that . . .

And fast on the heels of shame comes the rage, a welcome fiery blast, towards the people who did this to me.

'Kushi,' my visitors mouth my name as if it is a dedication, a celestial gift.

Not pity, no. Thank God. I wouldn't have been able to bear it. And I realise from their benevolent gazes, that despite the fact that my kidneys have failed me, despite the fact I am horizontal and incapacitated, they still admire me. In the villagers' eyes, I can do no wrong.

And just like that, I discover again the confidence I thought I had lost along with kidney function. If I can cajole the Chief Minister of Karnataka into doing my bidding, surely I can persuade Puja to donate a kidney to save her niece's life?

'I am going to get better,' I assure them. 'And then I am going to go after the people who did this to me.' I mean it too.

Their eyes widen in veneration. 'Kushi, you are amazing. Anyone else in your position would be bemoaning their fate. Not you. You are an inspiration.'

I smile, for the first time since I woke up in this strange, anxiety-ridden, malady- soaked bed.

'The police are pretty sure that the people in that car were goondas hired by one of the parents of the boys who were expelled because of your letter. Now they only have to find who . . .' they say.

I can give my inflamed fury no outlet except to grip the sides of the bed as hard as I possibly can.

Once again, the villagers come to my rescue.

'Everyone in the village is asking after you. They send their love. If this hospital wasn't so far away, they would all be here, keeping vigil.'

'I know,' I manage to whisper on the back of a wave of gratitude.

'Everyone is praying for your well-being. The temple is flooded with people offering prayers for your recovery. And the Catholic Church in Dhoompur even dedicated a mass for you. It seems the church has never seen so many worshippers even at Christmas; the parish priest was amazed!'

'Thank you,' I say.

'We'll let you rest. If there is anything you need, you let your ma know, and we'll get it to you, okay?' They squeeze my hand and then they are gone.

I am loved, I think. *I am going to get better,* I think. *I need to, I have to.*

And for the first time I believe I will.

Chapter 26
Sharda—Fissure

The Squelchiest of Seats

Dearest Ma,

Puja was sunshine and moonbeam, star sparkle and fairy dust. She was the glue that held our family together. She danced into our life, dispersing laughter, bestowing love and robbing it, nonchalantly, from me.

And now she is gone.

The weeks that follow are some of the worst of my life.

Da won't look at me. He won't look at anyone. He is a mere shell, going through the motions, existing but not living. He does not talk, will not eat.

When he returns from the market, he sits on the stoop and stares into the distance, as if the horizon contains all the answers to what he is looking for. He doesn't swat at the circling flies, or the whining mosquitoes. He ignores the dog who comes up to lick his face. He doesn't move until the dark drape of night takes the fields hostage.

You cook Ma, frenziedly, all of Puja's favourites, even though we can't afford it, as if by the very act of cooking for her you will bring her back to us again. You cook, using up all the 'good' ingredients—the garam masala that Janakiamma gave you when her son visited from Bangalore, the raisins from Muthamma, a thank you for helping her when her child was gravely ill—that you have been saving for celebrations.

You cook and none of us can bear to eat. For we take one bite and taste loss. Everything, even the kheer you have made with watered down milk and nutmeg and jaggery—just the way Puja likes it—is salty, flavoured with your sorrow, seasoned with your yearning for the daughter you have lost.

Once, when we were younger, in the days when Puja used to follow me everywhere, she and I crouched under the stippled awning of coconut trees at the very edge of Suggappa's field, to take shelter from the sudden shower that had ambushed us.

'You are my favourite person in the world, Sharda. I love you to the sky and back,' she said, as we breathed in the sweet scent of ripe paddy and moist earth, cut off from the world by the curtain of rain that enveloped the bower that shielded us, making the ears of paddy dance and swish. Every once in a while, the wind splattered warm, perfumed drops onto our wet bodies and the soggy mud shifted to accommodate us, making the squelchiest of seats.

'I love you too, and am so lucky to have you for a sister,'
I replied.

She'd run into the rain then, opened her arms wide and
pirouetted, a magenta ballerina glimpsed through the screen
of a glittery, auburn tinged monsoon.

I looped my arm through hers and we ran home to you,
Ma, our feet flying in unison, our laughter echoing above the
patter and rumble of the rain.

I alternate between hating her and missing her, between
wanting to hold her close breathing in her honey and milk
scent and never wanting to see her traitorous face again.

'Who gave you the right,' I want to ask her, 'to steal him
from me?'

'You have always had everything, looks, love, charm,' I
want to say. 'Whereas I . . . I have had to work for every
single thing. Why do you think I studied so hard? To get
Ma and Da's approval, the approval you had with just the
flash of a smile, the gift of a hug. I don't have the face, the
figure or the allure you have. I do not attract love like you
do. Ma and Da knew this, that is why they arranged for me
to marry someone who might learn to love me. Gopi was
mine. He was given to me by Ma and Da, he was their gift
to me, their act of love for me. You had no right to take him
from me.'

❊ ❊ ❊

'The landlord wants to see us,' Da says, not looking at me.

His face is drawn; he is a shadow of the man he once was. He is pining for the daughter he has disowned, and blames the one who caused the rift. I can tell he holds me responsible from the way his gaze does not rest on me for any amount of time, how it wavers and dips.

'Does he know, Da?' I ask, the words tumbling out of my mouth before I can rein them in.

Finally, for the first time since Puja left, he looks at me. I shrink from the cold emptiness in his eyes, all that is left, now that all feeling has been sucked out of him.

I was wrong. He doesn't blame me. He blames himself.

'The whole village does,' he says shortly, his words bitter as lime pips.

'Do we have to go?'

'Yes,' he says shortly, the word ending on a sigh.

Crushed dreams and scattered hopes, I think.

Gopi's face, once beloved, now maligned, looms before my eyes.

We walk up to the landlord's house together, my defeated parents and I. Seagulls screech and the air tastes of rain.

As we near the imposing gates, you falter, Ma, almost tripping. Da pretends not to notice and keeps on walking.

I put my arm around you and squeeze your hand. You squeeze back and straighten your shoulders, ridding them of their defeated slump.

I look at the drive leading up to the mansion and realise that the landlord has made us come here to emphasise the difference between us, to show what a favour he was doing us by agreeing to have me for a daughter-in-law.

The security guard looks us up and down, chewing his paan and spitting noisily, not giving any indication of opening the gates.

He flicks a pebble at a stray dog sitting atop a mound of sand across the road opposite the gates. The dog yelps and limps away.

'You're the ones with the slut for a daughter, eh? You think sending her to the next village will stop her whoring?' he says, insolently.

My cheeks bloom as hot as the sun with embarrassment.

Put him in his place, please, I will Da in my head.

But Da's body droops, as if he agrees with the security guard.

I understand then why he comes home beaten every day, why he sits and stares at nothing at all every evening. Perhaps this is what is happening at the market as well, everyone making fun of his cherished daughter, mocking her.

The taste of disgrace is as bitter as amaranth leaves in my mouth. Your grip on my palm tightens and I realise that you are still holding my hand.

'Open the gates. The landlord is expecting us,' I say to the security guard, keeping my voice level, refusing to acknowledge his derision. 'And while we're in there, I'll be reporting your foul mouth to him.'

He throws back his head and laughs, affording us a glimpse of rotting teeth and paan-ravaged gums. His laughter follows us all the way up the path to the house: the path I had once thought I would be walking up triumphantly as a married woman.

A pack of four dogs are tethered to the wall by the kitchen and they strain at their leads as they build up to a crescendo of howls. A servant comes out, her hands glinting with fish scales, yelling at them to shut up, asking them what all the fuss is about. They smell the fish and turn towards her, but her gaze is riveted by the sight of us.

'Oh,' she says and I can tell by the way her eyes widen that she too has heard about what has happened with Puja.

'What's all the commotion? Rathi, can't you quieten the dogs?' the landlord's unmistakable voice booms from inside and Da flinches.

The landlord emerges, hitching up his lungi, his face flushed and his expression irate as he recognises us.

'I rue the day I agreed to join our two families in marriage,' he yells, pinning us with his arrogant gaze, as if we are dirt under his feet, pebbles that have lodged in his shoe. 'I wanted an educated girl for my son so I overlooked the fact that your family is not of the same ilk as mine. It has brought me nothing but disrepute.'

I have had enough. Da is standing there taking it, but I will not. We may be poor, but I am damned if we are going to be treated as if we're not fit to clean his shoes. How dare he make out *we* are at fault when his Casanova of a son is to blame?

I pull myself up to my full height, which is not much to speak of and looking right at him, I say, 'Yes, we're not of the same ilk and thank God for that. At least *we* have the good manners to invite the people who come to our doorstep inside the house, instead of insulting them in the courtyard, especially when you're the one who asked us to come here.'

'Sh-Sh-Sharda,' Da stammers.

What's happened to you, Da? It is as if everything you are drained out of you when you hit Puja and sent her away.

The servants collect outside the kitchen, one by one, to watch the show. The dogs are still going strong. The security guard walks up the drive hitching his lungi.

The landlord is red as a chilli left too long to dry in the sun. He opens his mouth but before he can find his voice and break off his son's betrothal to me, making a big production of it, which is why he has ordered us here today of course, I say, 'And I do not want to marry your womaniser of a son, thank you very much. He's the one who caused all of this and everyone knows it, however much you stand there abusing us, and trying to shift the blame.'

'It is your whore of a sister who led my son astray with her wiles. After all he's only a man. Everyone knows your sister's reputation precedes her by a mile,' the landlord sputters, sounding much like his son's motorbike.

I smile up at him, 'So does yours, sir, for meanness and cruelty. So does yours.'

And with that, I turn on my heel and walk away, to the servants' admiring titters, to the security guard's open mouthed amazement, and to the landlord's speechless shock.

You and Da follow, Ma.

Da is pale as the milky sap bleeding from a bruised bush; he looks fit to faint.

But what allows me to keep putting one foot in front of the other despite the fact that my whole body is trembling with rage, is the almost-smile playing on your face, Ma, a face that has been marinated in tears and poached in grief since Puja left.

Chapter 27

Raj

The Husky Pink of Rose Blossom

'Your father didn't!' Raj says.

'I'm afraid he did.' His mother's eyes radiate ache and melancholy. Her voice bleeds from old wounds oozing fresh hurt as the scab of time is picked off. 'He was such a gentle man; it came as such a shock . . .'

'I bet.' Raj shakes his head, and his hands bunch into fists. He is surprised at how angry he feels on behalf of his mother.

'And that is why, when I slapped you . . . I am no better than him. I understand now how he could have done it, in the heat of the moment, with fury blinding him to love and what was right.' Her voice breaks.

'But that was different, Mum. One slap is different from lashing the skin off your daughter's back! He hit you and then, did he really kick you out?'

His mum nods, unable to speak.

'Would you like the chicken or the vegetarian meal?' the air hostess asks.

They both decline the meal although Raj asks for another Coca Cola.

The little airplane on the tiny screen in front of him is more than halfway between England and India. Raj is gradually getting a picture of this land he has never visited, despite the fact of his father inviting him over so many times, even going so far as to send Raj the tickets for a round trip which Raj had returned unused.

Raj had refused because he'd always felt that India robbed him of his father.

He did not begrudge his dad for leaving his mother. He understood why he had done so. He even did not begrudge his dad the family he subsequently had. But he begrudged his father for going to India. That had felt final, like his dad was leaving *him*. He couldn't forgive his father that.

Before his father left for India, Raj had always nurtured the secret hope that one day he could leave his unfeeling mum and go stay with his dad. But when his dad emigrated, that option was taken away from him. He used to see his father at least once a month when his dad was still in the country. After that, Raj didn't see him at all, except for the one time his father made the trip to the UK to see his son, after Raj had spurned all his father's summonses and pleas.

'I can't afford to keep coming here to see you, Raj,' his father had sighed. 'I run my own business as you know and I . . . '

'Then don't,' Raj had said. 'And you haven't *kept* coming. You've only come the once.'

'Why don't you visit me over there? You'll love it, I promise. It'll make a nice change from your usual.' His father had
implored.

But Raj had remained implacable, truculent. His father
had given up, and had gone back to India defeated, and did
not invite him there again.

He phoned Raj once every week, stilted conversations
that said nothing at all, that resounded with all the things
unsaid, with old upsets and new reproaches.

*You left, and abandoned me to my robot mother. You had the
choice to leave. I didn't. Why didn't you take me with you?*

Perhaps, Raj muses, his mother is not the cold automaton
he's always assumed her to be. He is beginning to suspect
that she's full of feelings that she has damped down, love
that she has parcelled away, and affection that she shies away
from, as a result of what happened to her, the full extent of
which he is yet to find out.

And India—through his mother's story, he is gradually
getting a picture of a land of contradictions, of people who
love completely and judge harshly, of tempers as hot and
frayed as the weather, of prejudices lingering in a closed soci-
ety, and affection too, oceans of it.

He can see the appeal it might have, this humid, sweltering land. He thinks he understands now its hold on his
father; why he went back. From what Raj has learned in the
course of listening to his mother's tale, everything about this
land is fierce: its weather, its people.

He loathes what it has done to his mother, and hates the
fact that he has been denied the loving woman she could

have been if events had not conspired against her. But, despite that, he is beginning to like the image of the country he is glimpsing through his mother's eyes. He thinks, in time, he might grow to love it. His feelings for this land he is linked to but hasn't yet seen seem to be flowering, while the resentment and anger he's harboured toward his mother is dispelling.

'My da loved me the best,' his mum whispers, bringing him back into the present. 'And I let him down.'

'It wasn't your fault! You loved Gopi. Your father did not even give you the chance to explain.'

'No, he didn't. And that hurt most of all. That is why. . .' Pain tints her voice the husky pink of rose blossom, 'I did what I did afterwards . . .'

Chapter 28
Puja—Fissure

The Lower Lip of the Sky

Puja stands on the rock flanking the beach, listening to the sea hum to the undulating rhythm of the tides. She watches the waves play hide and seek with the sand, mesmerised by the hypnotic way they rise and fall, rise and fall.

She thinks of her father, and his face when he hit her, each fiery stroke branding the virgin skin of her back with the weeping blot of the dishonour she had supposedly wrought upon them; his spittle-flecked, defeat-saturated, loss-smothered words, each one a block of wood stoking the funeral pyre of their relationship: 'You are not my daughter.' Five words that spelled goodbye to the father whose entire being used to soften when she was around. The father who used to say she was his happiness, his reason for living, his world. The father who had indulged her and cosseted her and loved her. Loved. Past tense.

The glimmering expanse of creamy turquoise is beguiling. She pictures herself jumping off the rock. She imagines the canoodling, froth capped waves depositing warm smooches as they welcome her into their salty depths.

She thinks of her last glimpse of her mother before she was forced to leave the house she has called home, the family she is no longer a part of. Her ma broken, her body oozing pain, her eyes raining. Ma had clung to Puja, not letting go, had fallen at Da's feet, begging and pleading. The entire village had gathered to watch, of course, crowding the fields, pushing the grazing cows aside. The crows perched in the coconut trees scattered in alarm at this unprecedented susurration upsetting the placid calm.

Her father had refused to look at Puja, had pretended he was deaf and blind to his wife's agony, her heartrending entreaties.

And Sharda . . .

Sharda had huddled against the mango tree, using it to support her weight, her body having given up on the task. Sharda, who had hefted Puja on her hip when but a child herself, until Puja became too heavy to carry, informing all and sundry, pride dripping from her voice, '*My* sister.' Sharda, eyes leaking, face crushed, trying to disappear into herself.

Puja had walked away from the house where she has always been so adored; the hut that had been home all her life, now smelling of hurt and reeling from grief, rank with shame and trembling under the assault of words that couldn't be unsaid and actions that couldn't be revoked, haunted by the phantom of what used to be, and dogged by the taunting memory of the happiness and contentment that had until recently graced its walls.

She had not cried. Not shed a tear.

All she had felt was anger. Fierce red and burning as the welts on her back, it had pushed away the guilt and the hurt, and ignited a glorious fiery rebellion. What sort of justice was this, where she was not given a chance to explain, to so much as speak? How could her father claim to love her when he went from assuming the best of her to the worst, refusing to indulge the grey areas in between, the faults and indiscretions that rendered her *human*?

When her father took a stick to her back, when her mother and sister went along with it, her family crushed her heart like a cardamom pod being subjected to the ministrations of the pestle.

All her life she has yearned to escape the confines of the village, its narrow-mindedness and prejudice. And she has been justified.

Why does Sharda get to marry Gopi when she, Puja, loves him? What is the sense in that?

When Puja is with Gopi, she feels complete. And if she feels this way about him, how can she stand to see him married to her sister? Her sister, who does not know what it is to be in love, who only knows how to study and cook. Her sister, who doesn't know how to live. For to love like Puja does, with her entire being on fire, her heart aching for Gopi, is to live.

Is it fair, on Sharda, or on Gopi, to be married when their hearts, their whole beings are not consumed by the other? Sharda doesn't *know* Gopi like Puja does. She doesn't know that he has a row of bumpy stitches on his left leg from a dog bite when he was five, that he scraped his knees so much as a child that they are riddled with scars, that he is afraid of heights, that he gets a headache if he drinks ice cold water.

Sharda doesn't know that Gopi got his first bike when he was fourteen, by teaching himself to ride a friend's bike and showing his father what he could do. She doesn't know that his father only bought him the bike and subsequent ones on the premise that Gopi would give him a ride whenever he wanted one.

Sharda doesn't know that Gopi hates raw onions and that he cannot drink tea after four in the evening because if he does then he will be unable to sleep that night. She doesn't know that he always saves half his laddoo for Puja, and that he adores jalebis. She doesn't know that he hates dhal but loves curd rice, that he misses his mother who died when he was three and that he cries when he watches Hindi movies.

Sharda doesn't know that Gopi is a romantic at heart; that *Ek Duje Ke Liye* is his favourite movie and he has watched it 54 times, ten of those times with Puja. She doesn't know that he is extremely ticklish, especially if you tickle him at the waist. She doesn't know that when he laughs his eyes scrunch up into slits and lines radiate from them all the way up to his hairline.

Sharda doesn't know that behind Gopi's cocky exterior hides a scared, insecure little boy who wants everybody to love him. She doesn't know that Gopi's most embarrassing moment ever was when he giggled in fear when his friend Dinu was being whipped by the teacher and Dinu has never forgiven him for it. She doesn't know that he hates getting sand in his shoes, that he loves Rasna mango juice but doesn't like eating mangoes. She doesn't know that he has five moles on his face and that when he is asleep his eyelashes fan his cheeks like unicorn tails.

'You will not see that boy again,' her father had intoned, 'And you will not see us.'

Distress now chases away the wrath, the magnificent surge of ire that had possessed her briefly, making her feel, for a few wild moments, fiercely, vibrantly alive. A shard of agony threatens to rip her soul apart. Her back is on fire from remembered hurt.

Puja looks to the point where the lower lip of the sky meets the upper lip of the sea, sealing all the universe's unfathomable secrets, everything contained in that vast promise, and she wants to walk towards it.

She envisages the hug of watery arms, velvet sand surging under her feet, the saline taste of oblivion.

Hot spicy breath on her neck, the smell of motor oil and lemon.

'Don't even think about it,' he whispers.

She feels him lowering himself beside her on the rock, the brine-infused sea air shifting to accommodate him, and wrapping them both in its tangy embrace.

He leans close and then his arm is around her, and she rests her head on his shoulder, taking comfort from the one thing in her world that hasn't changed, feeling as if she has come home.

Crabs scuttle into shingly holes; men argue; women laugh; infants cry. The air smells of onion and chilli from the bhel puri vendor across from them, mixed with the tang of fish, the taste of moist sand.

How can she give Gopi up, the one constant in her life, the fabric of which has ripped apart, exposing truths she'd rather not have known?

'Shush, it's all right,' he says, and she realises she is crying, the tears she has refused to give in to now find their way out, and huge sobs rack her body.

Gulls squabble. Spices sizzle and curries simmer in the huts by the beach. A man whistles while he urinates right into the sea.

She longs for the days before, when all was right in her world: sitting pillion on his bike, her arms around him, her plaits dancing around her head. A carefree past where she would rest her head on his solid back and taste the air, smacking of fruit and spices and innocence as it whooshed past, loud in her ears, and then dance home to her family, to her studious sister, harassed mother and indulgent father.

'I am so angry with him,' she says when she can speak. She will not call her father Da again. She will call him nothing at all. If he has disowned her, she will damn well disown him too. 'He is paying the aunt to have me stay, probably using the money he was hoarding for my dowry.'

Gopi does not say anything, letting her speak and for this, she is enormously grateful. He understands her. He is the only one who does.

The sky is a kaleidoscope of colour where it converges with the sea. Children screech as they jump in the white and aquamarine breakers, their faces open in expressions of pure delight, their watchful mothers trying to hold them back. Ice-cream vendors and peanut sellers circulate, and in the distance a man hawks tali bonda—palm fruit—for three rupees an eye. A group of churidar-clad girls giggle into their shawls. The frisky sea breeze is infused with the flavour of impending dusk, salty with a garlicky tang.

'It's not too bad with my aunt,' she sniffs. 'Nilamma is old and going blind and glad of the company. He must have asked her to keep strict tabs on me, because I have to account for my every movement.' She cannot help the bitterness veneering her voice the smudged grey of charcoal cinders.

'Where does she think you are now?' His face glows red from the light of the fuchsia sky.

'At the shops. I told her we had run out of oil and lentils.' She manages a watery smile. 'Let's run away,' she says.

'We need money for that, Puja,' he says softly, his hand gently stroking her hair which is in a mess, knotted by the wind rising from the sea. 'My da holds the purse strings and he's ordered me not to see you anymore.' His voice is gritty with frustration.

And yet you are here. You've defied him to be here with me.

'How did he find out about us . . .' she begins, but of course she knows. All those villagers gathered to watch the drama being played out at their hut.

Nothing is sacred in the village, she thinks, *least of all love.*

'I am not betrothed to Sharda anymore. Da broke it off when he found out. I have to accompany him to work every day. It will be harder for us to meet from now on. I managed to get away today because he had an emergency at one of his . . .'

'You are no longer promised to Sharda?' Puja thinks of her sister, the way she had glowed when Puja stumbled upon her betrothal and feels a pang.

But as his words sink in, she is aware of a weight lifting: the burden of guilt and shame she has been lugging around since she found out about Sharda's betrothal.

She smiles up at Gopi, relief flooding her body. Nothing is sorted, everything up in the air. She has lost her family, and yet, there is now a sliver of hope. Gopi is not lost to her.

'I love you, Gopi,' she whispers.

He looks at her, that gaze that tells her everything she needs to know, that looks inside her, into the very depths of who she is. 'I love you too.'

Then he bends down and, while the sun sets and the breeze fondles and the sea gushes and the sky performs, he kisses her. And it is more beautiful than she ever imagined. It is better than her wildest fantasies.

'Arre what are they doing? Chi! Shame on you!'

Somewhere in the corner of her brain, Puja registers the outraged shouts, the scandalized whispers but mostly, she is lost to the world, lost to everything except this man doing to her what she has imagined a hundred thousand times.

'Don't you have a reputation to uphold?' someone shouts and someone else wolf whistles.

Men point; mothers cover their children's faces, but the curious kids peek from between their mothers' fingers: ardent eyes, innocent gazes.

Gopi gives Puja his hand, pulling her up to stand.

'Let's get away from here,' he says and they walk away to a chorus of wolf whistles and jeers.

'Is your da at home?' Puja asks when they are nearing his house, which is right by the beach.

'I don't know if he's back yet. Why?'

'Let's speak to him, Gopi. If I am with you, and we speak to him together, if he sees how much we love each other, perhaps that will sway him. After all, he was willing to have Sharda for a daughter-in-law, why not me?' She is convincing herself as much as Gopi.

She does not allow the sudden vision of her father's face to overthrow her conviction, his hands raining blows on her even as he sobbed: *How could you do this, bring this disgrace upon us?*

Gopi's eyes widen at her suggestion but as they meet her gaze, resolve settles in them, like the sandy grey of wet cement solidifying into concrete. 'Yes. You're right, Puja. I've had enough of him running my life for me. I'll speak to him, tell him it is you I care for and you I want to marry. Come.' He swings open the gates to his mansion.

Her heart soaring like a bird released from the confines of its cage testing the limits of its freedom, Puja falls into step beside him.

A mob of dogs howl as they near the house, but they are tied to their post, so they can't get at Puja.

'He's not home yet,' Gopi says of his father. 'His car is not here. But now that you are, I'll show you my room.'

It is the moment of reckoning. She could go back, having safeguarded the shred of reputation she has left. But since when has she cared for her reputation? And the worst has happened, she has been disowned, what more could possibly go wrong?

'We'll go round the back so the servants don't see.' Gopi says.

Have you no shame? Her father's voice echoes in her ears as she treads softly along the side of the house behind Gopi, holding on to the wall for support.

The dogs are howling fit to rouse the neighbourhood, but the servants do not come outside to check.

'They are probably in the kitchen having a feast,' Gopi whispers. 'Celebrating the fact that my father is away for longer than usual. The dogs bark for the smallest thing anyway, frogs jumping in the garden, a snake slithering past, so no one pays any heed to them. And usually Manu the security guard alerts them to visitors but he must have gone to have his dinner, or perhaps he is in the kitchen with them, making hay while my father's away.'

He turns to her, his face shining in the dim evening light. How she loves him, his beloved profile conjured so many times in the dark of night to soothe her back into sleep.

'And the kitchen is at the opposite side of the house to my room. Nobody will know you are here.'

Puja experiences a thrill when he says this, and sees it mirrored in his eyes, in the way they narrow, in the way his breath comes in gasps of desire.

I am not doing anything wrong, she tells herself, her mind frantically rationalising, keeping the guilt and the haranguing voice of her conscience speaking to her in her father's broken voice at bay. *I love this man and we are going to get married, be together, as soon as we have spoken to the landlord.*

Puja clings to the side of the house, musing what a change this mansion that goes on and on makes from the hut she has called home until recently, with its tiny kitchen and the one room where they all used to eat and sleep.

Do they miss me? She wonders, gagging on a strident spasm of pain.

Gopi turns the corner and Puja bumps her head against an open window shutter.

'Ah, this is it,' Gopi says.

Puja peeps past the shutter into the room, allowing her eyes to adjust to the darkness inside. A space twice the size of the living/dining/bedroom of the hut Puja has been forced out of. A whirring ceiling fan; a table, a chair, a wardrobe; a voluminous mosquito net draped around a monstrous bed that could sleep four people easily.

Gopi is up ahead and Puja quickens her stride until he comes to an abrupt stop in front of a door and she bumps into him, another thrill pulsing through her.

'The back door. It is left unlocked during the day,' he whispers, opening it softly and, once they are safely inside, turning around and gathering her in his arms.

Puja can hear his heart beating wildly in his chest. She has only ever rested her head against his back before, while sitting behind him on the bike, never his chest. She breathes in his scent of sweat and lemon and motor oil, familiar, reassuring. His strong body, muscles rippling, encloses her in the warm cocoon of his embrace. She feels heat rise within her.

I shouldn't be here.

But at this moment, this man's arms are exactly where she wants to be. This man's arms that feel like home, all the more precious now that she is homeless.

After a bit, Gopi gently untangles her and, holding her hand, leads her to his room. He closes the door and standing with his back to it, looks at her, his eyes hungry, alight with want.

You should not be here, alone in a man's room in the dark. Sharda's voice.

Why is *she* here?

Sharda, you haven't loved like I have, loved so much that you forget everything else, throw caution to the wind. What is this big thing that I am doing wrong? Puja queries her sister's spectral voice. *Is being with the man you love so bad? Isn't it the most natural thing in the world?*

Not this man. He belonged to me until you came between us, Sharda says in Puja's head but Puja pushes away her conscience that is daring to masquerade as her sister, thinking, *No. I did not come between anybody. I was there first. He loves me, not you. Me.*

And the very next moment she forgets everything but the man whose mouth is on her hair, her eyes, her nose, her lips. She is all feeling, no thoughts, no pesky conscience raising hell in her family's voices. He gathers her closer to him, and his hand chafes against the healing wounds on her back. She flinches.

'What's the matter?' he whispers. Concern pigments his voice the soft cream of clouds hugging the coral rim of twilight sky.

He turns her around and lifts her churidar top and vest. She lets him, even as she feels the vest tear at the scabs. She hears his dazed intake of breath, a shocked lament, feels his lips tenderly graze each crisscrossing wound, as if by doing so he is trying desperately to right the wrongs done to her, to restore her body, her family, her life back to her. Then he kisses her forehead, a caress so tender that she feels tears collect at the corners of her eyes.

'I love you Puja.' He says and his voice is the ache of night awaiting the tender light of morning. It is the first drop of rain after months of drought. It is a promise and a covenant. It is possession after the devastation of loss. It is the truth.

'I love you too,' she whispers.

Then there is only Gopi and this moment, theirs and only theirs. They lose themselves in each other as shadows creep up the sides of the house, the mosquito net enclosing the entwined bodies of two young lovers not meant to be together.

Afterwards, they are aware of dogs barking, the grumble of a vehicle driving up and coming to a shuddering stop. The thud of doors opening and shutting, the slap of shoes on granite floors, the scurrying of servants. An authoritative male voice calling, 'Gopi?'

The timid knock of a servant on the door and then a hesitant voice, 'Gopi, sir, dinner is ready.'

Gopi turns to Puja and holds her close one more time.

'Let's talk to your father, persuade him that we are meant for each other.' Puja urges, her voice coated with desperation. Now that the reality of what she has done is sinking in, she wants the security of the landlord's approval.

'Now?' Gopi's features, soft in the murky light, are swamped with love.

'Yes.'

He nods, his eyes gleaming glossy gold with determination. 'Da must not know you were here with me or he'll never agree to us marrying. Go back the way you came. I'll make sure no-one sees you and I'll come out when you knock, and we'll speak with him together,' he mouths into her ear, his resolute voice, unwavering in its conviction, instilling her with the confidence necessary to face the ordeal to come.

❄ ❄ ❄

Puja walks back the way she came, hugging the dark walls of the mammoth house, the plan being that she slips out the gate under cover of shadows and then waits to be let in, pretending she has just arrived.

The dogs start their hullaballoo. As before, nobody takes any notice.

Manu the security guard is still missing from his post and Puja boldly walks past the gates and up the drive in plain sight. She knocks on the front door, her heart drumming furiously in the constricted confines of her chest.

'They are eating.' The servant who opens the door is unwilling to let her in.

Where are you, Gopi? You promised you would answer the door.

'I need to speak to the landlord and his son. They're expecting me,' she insists and is allowed unenthusiastic entry and made to wait just inside the front door.

There is no bench to sit on, and Puja shifts uncomfortably from foot to foot for fifteen minutes when the landlord emerges, wearing a colossal frown and scrutinising Puja with knife-point sharp eyes. Gopi follows close behind and walks over to stand beside her. Gopi's presence next to her goes a long way to easing her nerves.

We can do this, Gopi. Together, we'll convince him.

This is like being in court, she thinks. It is as if she and Gopi are about to appeal for their lives. She feels judged by the landlord's truculent presence, radiating animosity and ill will.

Puja wants to hold Gopi's hand, take comfort from his touch, but she knows that would be going a bit too far, that it would sabotage their cause.

'How dare you interrupt our dinner, miss?' the landlord booms, his words clipped, voice tough as granite. 'And why on earth are you standing next to her, Gopi?'

Go on, Gopi, tell him. Tell him how much you care for me. Put into words for him the love you showed me just now, the love I feel pulsing through my body, flowing in my veins.

Gopi rocks on his feet. He seems to have lost his voice, this man who is capable of such tenderness, this man who doesn't deserve this bully of a father.

'I thought I told you not to see her anymore, Gopi. And you . . .' The landlord's eyes are the concentrated slits of a predator stalking its prey. 'Have you no shame? Why are you here?'

A flood of fury swamps Puja, taking her over, reigning strong over the welter of emotions she has been floundering in since her father took a stick to her body. How dare this man lecture her about shame? How dare he use the same words her father did as he was slashing her back open? What right does he have?

'I am here,' her voice ringing high and clear and fearless, reverberating off the walls of this cavern of a room, so Gopi looks up from the perusal of his sandals, 'because your son and I love each other.'

'Oh, you do, do you?' The landlord is smirking now, a widening of his mouth, his eyes hard and cold, like a reptile showing its fangs, like a tiger in the moment before it pounces.

Gopi, help me out, please.

But Gopi seems to be shrinking where he is standing, fear emanating from his every pore, infecting her with its contagious intensity.

Why are you so afraid of your father, Gopi? He is, but a man, just like you.

In the presence of his father, Gopi diminishes, like a car pushed off the road by a domineering lorry.

What happened to your resolve to speak to him, Gopi? Your decision to tell him that you've had enough of him running your life, to inform him of your love for me, your intention of marrying me?

And just as she thinks this, her heart sinking, Gopi surprises her by looking right at her, his eyes shining.

'Da,' he calls to his father.

The landlord turns to his son, his voice dangerously low as he says, 'You want to say something Gopi?'

Gopi falters, looks at her, once, a panicked glance in which she sees a motherless little boy and not the man she loves and then he looks down, his shoulders crumpling, his short spurt of courage vanished.

He's not going to help me out. I'm on my own.

She recalls the scene of his betrothal to Sharda, and how he refused to meet her gaze. She should have known then. She should have stayed away from him, and let things be.

I have loved a weak man.

The air in the room is suddenly too heavy to inhale, and her lungs feel strangled.

'Gopi and I want to marry each other.' She says, her heart hammering like a frenzied woodpecker. Gopi should be saying this, not her. Gopi, whom she can still smell on her, taste on her lips, feel in the slipperiness between her thighs. She cannot look at the landlord, does not want to see the triumph in his eyes.

Where is my courage?

It has slid to the place where Gopi's head rests, as far down his chest as it can possibly go. He seems to be willing himself to disappear, this man she loves.

I knew you were scared of your father, but I never took you for a coward before now, Gopi. I always thought you would stand up for me, for our love, when it mattered. But a coward is what you are.

Why hadn't she seen it before? When he did not break off his betrothal to Sharda even though he did not love her; meekly going along with his father's decision on his behalf?

Why has it taken this long for the scales to fall from her eyes, now, when it is far too late?

The landlord throws back his head and laughs, thundering guffaws that reverberate horribly around the empty, vast room.

Gopi flinches—a puppet, lurching at the end of strings being jerked by the landlord.

Puja does not let the tears pricking her eyes to fall as she stands there, with the evidence of what she has done staining her churidar bottoms.

Did you really love me, Gopi, or was it all just a craven act of one-upmanship on your father and his blasted plans on your behalf?

The landlord laughs for a long time. Then he says, 'I remember you saying something similar the day your parents and I sealed Sharda's betrothal to my boy.'

He leans closer and she can smell his rank breath, feel the hot fumes of it on her face. She wills herself not to recoil.

'Let me tell you something, girl. Do you know why I chose Sharda? Because she is hardworking, she is educated; she is going to be a doctor. What are your prospects? I heard that you failed your pre-university exam. Is that why you've set your sights on Gopi, the only son of a wealthy landlord?'

'I am not interested in money. I love Gopi.'

'Ha,' sneers the landlord, rubbing his palms together.

'Gopi?' she tries again.

He might be a miserable coward, but earlier they were bound by the closest bond possible between two human beings, so surely he can come through for her, just this once.

And surprisingly, he does.

'I want to marry Puja.' His voice wavers, breaking on her name.

The landlord chuckles mirthlessly. 'If you do so, I will disown you. And then we'll see how you manage, with not a penny between the two of you. She has failed her pre-university exams; you have not completed your degree. Will you work in the fields? What will you do?'

Gopi's head sinks once more into the apron of his chest. Puja has an urge to shake him until the words she wants him to say fall out of his throat like cashews from the tree. Does he not remember the avowals of love they made just a few minutes ago? How they sealed the promises they made each other?

'Gopi, we'll manage somehow. Money is not important. We love each other, we'll find a way.'

But he will not look at her. He will not acknowledge her.

She may not be interested in money, Puja realises, suddenly seeing Gopi clearly, now the blinding scales of love have been forced from her naïve eyes, but Gopi is. He cannot survive without the cushion wealth provides. He does not love her unconditionally like she does him, perhaps never has. He has toyed with her to spite his father and now that his father is threatening to disown him, like *she* has been disowned, he is abandoning her to her fate, letting her go, as easily as a fisherman releasing a fish too small and insignificant for his needs back into the water.

'What if someone more beautiful comes along?' she'd asked him once, in the early stages of their relationship.

'What if someone richer comes along?' is what she should have asked.

The closed, stale air in the room, reeking of betrayal, is overwhelming.

'Love!' The landlord scoffs. 'I have heard you've "loved" most of the boys in town. Free and easy with your favours, aren't you? Do you know, I chose Sharda, most of all, because she is a *good* girl. Unlike you.' His contemptuous gaze sweeps over Puja again, marking her as dirty, unworthy.

An all-consuming rage blessedly chases away Puja's misery.

Damned if I will bend to your dominance like your son is doing.

'How dare you speak to me this way! You have no right.'

The landlord comes so close that she can feel his sour spittle dotting her face as he bites out his words. 'I have had enough of members of your family coming here and creating scenes. First your sister and now you.'

Sharda was here? When? Why?

'And don't you dare tell me, in my own house, what rights I have or do not have. *You* do not have the right to be here, whore. You think I will let a girl with loose morals like you come anywhere near my son? Get out, at once and don't come back.' His voice lashes out like a whip.

She stands her ground. 'If I am a whore then your son is a pimp.'

The landlord raises his hand. Puja does not quail or move away.

And finally, too late, Gopi finds his voice. 'Da, No.'

'Hit me, go on. And here I was wondering where Gopi got his spinelessness from. Like father like son. Weaklings, the both of you, turning on defenceless girls.'

The landlord's face is contorted into a purple grimace, his hand still raised.

'Goodbye, Gopi. I'm better off without you.' Puja turns and walks away, holding her head high as she walks out of the gate, and when she turns the corner, she runs, along the narrow path where shadows dance on snoozing fields and the black reflections of waving trees tickled by the evening breeze ripple on the glittering water of the stream, where crickets sing and snakes slither and hiss among the murky foliage, and frogs squat in the damp undergrowth.

The night air carries the perfume of jasmine and the promise of rain; it smacks of intrigue as it whispers to the dozy blades of grass, waking them up and making them jig.

Puja runs, tasting salt and snot. Her churidar flaps around her legs, and the stinging between her thighs reminds her of what she has done, and of what cannot be undone.

Chapter 29
Kushi

Star Speckled Dome

Wow, Ma, I think, putting down her letter, and feeling, for the first time since I woke up in this strange bed bolstered by its armour of machines, something other than bone-weary sluggishness and the dejection and frustration that engulfs me when I realise where I am.

This girl who stands up to the landlord and breaks off her betrothal to his son before he can, she is the woman I know. The woman I love and am proud of. The woman I can see in myself.

Lights have come on in the ward, coating everything in a mellow turmeric glow. I wish Ma was back. I have so many questions I need to ask her. But I suppose trying to organise funds for my ongoing dialysis is not a simple matter of signing cheques . . .

I wonder if the landlord and Gopi have paid for what they did. Where are they are now? Would Ma know? Perhaps I could do something to expose them . . .

Ha! And how will you go about doing that when you are lying broken in a hospital bed?

A burst of air smelling of evening comes through the window. I imagine I am brushing my teeth beneath the jackfruit tree outside our cottage just before bed, and watching the shadows exchange confidences with the star speckled dome of sky, while the neighbourhood dogs howl in the darkened fields, and the paddy undulates in the fragrant dusk in soft, swishing waves, like a hand parting hair.

Then I blink and I am back in the present, in this edifice of discomfort and anguish, of wrecked organs and untold maladies.

When Ma returns from the bank, I want to ask her how she could have let that cowardly man Gopi have such power over their entire family, enough to tear it apart. How could he, a mere boy, have come between Ma and Puja, sisters, bound by blood, and who were once so close?

An orderly pushes what was once a silver trolley, but is now marred by a rash of rust creeping up the sides and eating the steel away; its rattle and swoop along the corridor momentarily punctures the drugged silence of the ward.

If Ma's betrothal to Gopi was off, why didn't she and her parents bring Puja back home?

Did something else happen to prevent their reunion, and to push them even further apart?

I pick up the next letter.

Chapter 30
Sharda—Chasm

A Ribbon of Gossip

Dearest Ma,

Those weeks after our visit to the landlord, I lose myself in my studies. I work extra hard. That way, I do not have to see what is happening to our family. I do not have to breathe in the silences that shout out Puja's absence—an absence that is an aggrieved throbbing presence.

The cracked walls of our hut absorb our heartache, our falling to pieces, as they have absorbed the smoke from our cooking, the smells of spices, our laughter and our tears, our triumphs and our failures, our collective dreams and aspirations, the ordinary passage of our ordinary lives through the years until the extraordinary happened and Puja was wiped out of the family equation.

'Now that Sharda's engagement is called off, bring Puja back,' you plead, Ma. 'We can move to a different village, start over.'

But Da is unshakeable. 'Don't you see what Puja has done? Who will marry Sharda now that the landlord has blighted our name all over the village and beyond? Don't speak about Puja again. She is dead to me.'

The most words he has uttered since Puja left.

In a rare burst of strength, the strength Puja has in spades, you stand up to your husband, Ma.

You, so traditional, so fond of saying, much to Puja's disgust: 'When you get married, your husband is God. Always obey him and do as he asks. Then you will all be happy and your family will be blessed.'

You don't see Da as God now. You tuck your sari pallu into your waist and declare, 'I will go and see her.'

Da looks up at you, and something flares in his defeated face. 'She has brought disgrace upon us . . .'

'No,' you snap, Ma. '*You* have. By hitting her. Sending her away. Bringing the whole village into our business.'

'Stop it. Just stop.' Da covers his ears with his hands and rocks on his haunches. 'You are not seeing her and that is that.' He pauses and then, 'I have been speaking to Nilamma . . .'

Both you and I, Ma, look at him agog.

The mellow summer's evening, the sky a medley of garnets and golds, dark pinks and deep blues, tastes orange, of that afternoon's breathless heat maturing into the placid tones of sundown, spiced with the velvet violet of the night to come.

'Puja is fine. She has settled in well. Bringing her back . . . the landlord will not allow it for one. As it is, he is making life difficult for us, spreading slander, turning our friends against . . . '

'Then let's move to a different village with Puja, find grooms for both of our girls,' you say.

'What about Sharda's degree? And where will I get work? Who will employ me?'

You go to Da, Ma, and fall at his feet. 'Please. I want my daughter back.'

I am still angry with Puja, terribly angry, but I miss her.

And I am tired of missing her. Tired of seeing you and Da suffering, the reflection in your injured eyes of what could have been. Tired of flailing in the dregs of the mire left behind after her departure.

I am tired of tamping down the guilt I feel in the dead of night when I wake, my heart strumming with fear at the nightmare I've had in which I break our family apart with one rash whisper in a well-chosen ear—and find that it is all true.

'I will think about it,' Da says gruffly. 'But until then, I forbid you to see Puja, talk to her. It will only make things worse.'

You nod, Ma, hope and cautious joy budding on your face.

And then, the landlord visits.

❊ ❊ ❊

We spy the motorbike, parked by the road beside the fields, on our way back from the ration shop, Ma, as we lug rice and lentils and oil, inhaling the dust-infused air flavoured with our sweat and exertion.

Drained, we exchange a look threaded through with tentacles of fear.

Now what?

I look at the bike, gleaming as new, and I hear the matrons' words, strung on a ribbon of gossip, laced with intrigue and bedecked with rumour, falling from their paan-glazed predator-like jaws, not caring whom they hurt, or how: 'Puja was hugging him tight as they conjured up a sandstorm on that motorbike of his.'

I set down the bags I am carrying, look around and pick up the biggest cow pat I can find and I smear it all over the bike.

'What are you? . . .' you begin and then you are smirking, Ma.

And we are laughing together and somehow the laughter turns into sobs and we hold each other as we cry for what was and what can never be and what is lost, and we breathe in the smell of cow dung and choke on the taste of our tears.

Then we wipe our eyes and walk down the path through the fields to the hut where the landlord is waiting, pacing up and down, wearing the courtyard thin. His face is dark as a nightmare at being made to wait, which, I suppose he hasn't had to do much of in his privileged life.

I lead the way, walking at a leisurely pace, refusing to rush to pacify the landlord.

There is no sign of Gopi. The landlord has come alone, on Gopi's bike.

Later, I understand that he is making a point, showing us that his son's treasured possession, like everyone and everything else in the village, is his if he decides he wants it.

I glance at the landlord's pristine cream mundu and imagine the patches of cow dung adhering to it as he straddles the bike for the ride home. And that allows me to get through the next few minutes and the torturous exchange with him.

'To what do we owe this honour?' I ask.

I do not invite the landlord inside. Sweat splotches his bald head and beads his face; his clothes cling to him damply.

My voice is calm, even a little amused. 'Have you come to apologise?'

His thunderous face suffuses with red. 'Where is your da?' He snaps.

'Why?' I query, my voice cold as the stream at dawn.

'Tell him to keep his whoring daughter in check. Does he know what she is up to?'

I do not let the shock I am feeling, the latent hurt that gushes like floodwater overflowing the riverbank, show. My voice is as unruffled as the dry bed of a drought-ravaged lake. 'Why should he know what she's up to? He has disowned her.'

'Doesn't your father understand that the duty of a man unfortunate enough to be cursed only with daughters, is to keep them in check? He might have sent her away from home; he might have banished her to another village; but will she stop? She had the gall to come to me and ask for my son's hand in marriage! Gopi confessed that she tricked him into sleeping with her, the shameless whore.'

I see you clutch at your heart and sway on your feet Ma.

The scab forming over the wound of Puja's betrayal re-opens, and blood fizzes out, red and painful.

How could you do this, Puja, bring this added ignominy upon us? Why?

'Thank you, I will let Da know.' I don't know how I manage to speak but I do, my voice steady.

'You tell your da to keep tabs on her, although it is far too late now for the brazen slut. I don't want her whoring body anywhere near my son. I cannot believe I even considered linking myself to your disreputable family.' A pause, then, 'And I will not stand for any of you mosquitoes pestering me any longer, you understand? You are not welcome to stay here anymore.'

'This is not your village to order us around.'

He grins slimily. 'You will find out that it is.'

❄ ❄ ❄

'Sleeping with him! How could she? Giving away her honour, and ours, like a basket of mangoes. Discrediting us even more if possible, stranding us in a quagmire of ignominy,' Da laments, repeatedly hitting his head. 'I will have no more mention of Puja. She is dead to us.'

And this time, Ma, you are too broken to protest.

Chapter 31
Raj

A Stone in a Bag of Rice

Raj looks at his mother, this woman he is finally getting to know—this woman with her gaunt face and her sore eyes with their wine-coloured rims, the makeup of tears. This woman who tells him the story of a girl he never knew, but in a voice he has known from when he lay snug in her womb. The story of a girl who was loved and adored, then shunned and betrayed by the people whom she had cared for the most, discarded by her family as easily as the pith from an orange, wiped away like a dirt stain from a window.

This woman who was let down so completely by the man she loved so completely. No wonder she is afraid to love. No wonder she keeps herself at a remove from everything and everyone. No wonder she has created a buffer around her heart.

It pains him immensely that the wonderful, feisty, brave girl he never got a chance to meet, has become this cold woman who shies away from emotion because of what was done to her.

'Mum, the reason you work so hard, the reason you are so focused . . . is it because Gopi chose money over you?'

She closes her eyes as if she is shutting out the image of Gopi denouncing her. 'I wanted to prove them both wrong, Gopi and the landlord,' she says softly.

Now that he has been afforded a window into the girl his mother was, it hurts Raj to see everything she has lost: her bubbly, infectious personality, her lust for life, stolen from her by the weak people she had the misfortune to love, the pathetic people who did not accept her affection for the gift it was, instead throwing it away as casually as a stone in a bag of rice, the affection *he* has been denied because of what *they* did.

Raj is furious with his mum's parents, her sister, Gopi. Why did her family denounce her so easily? Why didn't they talk to her, give her a chance to explain? Why didn't Gopi stand up for her? Why did she love such a wretched man?

Raj wants to shake Gopi until he sees sense, to wound him like he wounded his mother.

He wants to rewrite history.

The screen in front of him, with its little aeroplane swooping down on the south coast of India blurs. The tannoy booms: 'Ladies and Gentlemen, this is the captain speaking. We will shortly be landing at Bengaluru International Airport . . .'

His mother's hands grip the sides of her seat as the captain announces the temperature in Bengaluru and wishes them a pleasant stay; her knuckles stand out in relief.

Raj reaches across and lays his palm on hers, voluntarily, for the first time since he was a little boy and learned not to touch her. And for the first time that he can recall, she lets him.

Tears fall down the slope of her cheeks, creating more beige tracks in her ruined makeup.

'There are so many ways of giving,' she says softly, awkwardly patting his hand. 'And this is the most important one. Thank you.'

He smiles and she smiles shakily back at him.

'What were you thinking just then, when you looked so serious?' she asks.

'That I would have given anything to have been there that day when you stood up to the landlord,' Raj says. 'I would have put my hands around Gopi's neck and squeezed until he came through for you.'

His mother emits a wet chuckle, and her grip on the seat relaxes.

And Raj is surprised by the urge to put his arms around his mother and shield her from the capricious world she battled alone when not much older than him, an impulse to protect her from her past.

'I was also thinking that it was very brave, what you did, standing up to the landlord. Bet no-one had ever dared go against him before. He sounds horrific. I think you were amazing,' he says.

She smiles, properly this time and her face flowers into beauty, smoothing the etched lines of apprehension at touching down on Indian soil after almost two decades.

Chapter 32
Puja—Chasm

Billowing Seaweed

She dreams that she is flying, Gopi beside her, adrenalin soaring, breathing in the excitement spiced air and revelling in the freedom.

She dreams that she is sitting on the hill above Dhoompur with Gopi making plans to run away. She dreams that they are at the beach, at their favourite hideout among the dunes, throwing pebbles into the sea and spinning fantasies that are out of their grasp, making plans, separately, in the privacy of their heads, for a future together, two figures silhouetted against the setting sun.

She dreams that she is sitting on a rock by the road opposite the gates to his mansion, her back to the sea, the swoop and dive of the waves lulling her tap-dancing heart to a gentler rhythm. After a bit, the gates open and a jeep drives out; she sees the stiff profile of the landlord outlined within and beside him, that of Gopi, who sits by the window on Puja's side of the road.

Look at me, Puja prays and for one minute, one heart stopping minute, Gopi's gaze lands on hers. As recognition dawns, he startles and looks away. And then he is gone.

Puja follows the jeep on foot for a while until it is lost in a haze of dust and sand that smacks at her eyes, rousing tears. She walks back to the gates and peers inside, taking advantage of the security guard's absence—he is in his shack behind the gates, eating boiled rice and pickle from a tiffin box.

She sees the dogs straining at their leads and beside them, lying neglected by the front door, Gopi's motorbike, the very one that was always so polished that you could see your reflection in it from any angle, now sporting a fine red sheen of dust.

Puja jerks awake, her heart pounding with loss and, turning on the mat to hold her ma, realises the space next to her is empty. Her aunt snores in the corner by the hearth. Puja has jumped from one nightmare right into another, one in which she is all alone.

She wakes each morning, her stomach queasy. She thinks it's because of the vivid dreams she's been having, in which she's back at home in the bosom of her family, snuggled between her sister and her mother while her father snores on the bench above. Loved.

She dreams that her father is beaming at her, saying, 'My precious jewel, my darling girl.'

She dreams that it is *her* marriage being arranged with Gopi and it is Sharda who is uncomprehending, devastated.

She yearns for her sister's smile, her mother's arms, her father's absolution. She hears nothing from them. It is as if she doesn't exist, as if, as far as her family is concerned, she is dead.

She is sick, repeatedly, trying to disgorge this knowledge. But the biliousness persists.

She stops eating, hoping that will put an end to the tantrums her stomach insists on having, but it is no use. She keeps telling herself it will get better.

It doesn't.

One day, Puja realises that she cannot tie her churidar bottoms, that they're too tight. She has hardly been eating, how can she be gaining weight? But her stomach has definitely grown, and her waist has become thicker.

And it is then that she has an inkling. It is then, that she counts back to the last time she had her period.

She has always entertained the hope that one day she will return to the hut she still calls home in her head, beg for mercy and be welcomed into the forgiving arms of her family.

Now she knows she can never go back.

✻ ✻ ✻

That evening, she waits until her aunt is fast asleep before slipping out of the hut. She sprints down the hill and across the bridge, the river glowing in the soft starlight, and past her old village, resisting the urge to walk across the fields to the hut that was home, to watch her loved ones sleep.

Are they dreaming about her as she dreams about them? Or is she banned even from their slumbering reveries?

Puja runs up the hillock in the hissing darkness. She is out of breath by the time she reaches the mansion beside the sea where Gopi lives and scales the wall of the landlord's compound, scraping her knees and bruising her shins on the mossy bricks. The dogs howl blue murder and a sleepy voice yells from the servants' quarters beside the kitchen for them to shush. They strain at their leads, wanting to get at Puja.

She ignores them, walking along the side of the house, as she had done once before with Gopi holding her hand. She steps gently, softly, the darkness a comforting cloak, and recalls the way she had felt that day when Gopi had held her, the desire that his kiss had ignited in her, the happiness of knowing he loved her.

Her feet stumble over the pebbles; her heart pounds, and the sickly green taste of guilt floods her mouth.

A new being is growing inside her that has no right to be there.

What has she done?

Night jasmine, roasted cinnamon, dog slobber and settling dust scent the air. Her scraped knees stinging, she holds on to the wall until her head bumps against the window frame of Gopi's room. He always leaves the windows open at night, she knows. She knows so much about him, everything except what is going on in his head, his heart.

Puja stands on tiptoe and peeps inside, squinting to adjust her eyes to the fuzzy dark interior, the only light the red blinking of a mosquito coil. The giant mosquito net that had been their cover that fateful night now shrouds the prone figure of her one-time lover.

How can you lie there so peacefully, she thinks, *while I am in such turmoil?*

She is blindsided by a sudden scarlet spasm of fury. She picks up a pebble, shiny and smooth and hurls it through the bars of the window. It glances off the net and falls to the floor. She lobs another and then a third.

With a twitch and a shudder, Gopi lurches upright on the bed. Puja can just make his shape out through the net. Then he shoves the net aside and strides to the window.

He is wearing just a vest and shorts and despite herself, seeing his naked shoulders rippling, his beloved face close up, Puja feels her broken heart flooding with all the love she still nurtures for him, and, against all odds, hope. Perhaps when she tells him her news he will find his lost courage, his dormant chivalry and declare, 'I'll marry you Puja and to hell with my da.'

After all, isn't that why she is here?

Looking at him now, rubbing the sleep out of his eyes, she is convinced that he must love her too, just as much as she loves him; that he loves her still, however much she has doubted it over the past few weeks. He just needs an injection of daring to stand up to his father and perhaps news of this baby will provide him with it.

His face at the window. His eyes squint and then narrow as he recognises her.

'Gopi,' she says his name; a prayer, a plea.

'Puja! What are you doing here?' His voice a panicked hiss. No love in it.

His head slumps against the windowsill; his voice, when he finds it, is strung with pain. 'Please leave, Puja. This is not a good idea. Leave and don't come back. If he finds out . . .'

'Do you love me?' she queries even though it isn't the question she has come to ask. It slips past the armour safeguarding her heart, the shield of her lips.

'Oh Puja,' his voice is soft, immersed in ache. 'Please. Leave. This is madness. You don't know what he'd do to you if he found you here.' Terror chases the softness from his voice.

Puja used to think, when they sat at their spot on the beach and watched the froth-licked waves flirting with the sand, that he was formulating plans in his head for their future together as she was. She used to think he loved her, completely, wholeheartedly, the way she loved him.

'I am pregnant,' she says and his head snaps up. He stares at her, fear writ large on his face. 'It's yours of course.'

'I cannot do anything. He will never let us marry. Go. I am sorry. Please just go.' His voice frenzied with panic, and his eyes bloodshot. His hands wave at her as if she is an irritating fly buzzing about his face.

Puja wants to close her eyes and shut out his words, pretend he never said them. She wants to rewind this exchange and start over.

She'd come here prepared to forget his cowardice that day in front of the landlord, after he'd made love to her, told her he loved her. But this spineless weakling is the true Gopi, and the boy she's loved so much for so long—the boy she imagined would wholeheartedly accept her and her baby, who would be part of their cosy trio, a new family to assuage the loss of her old one—is just an illusion conjured up by her besotted heart.

How can everything she ever assumed about this man be so wrong? How can he not understand the import of what she is saying? How can he dismiss this new life they have created together, shrugging her words off as callously as a shirt that no longer fits? Doesn't he feel anything, anything at all?

And yet, despite the fresh hurt seeping into every pore of her being and threatening to tear her apart, she tries again. She tries just one more time.

'Has it not occurred to you that you are not your father's puppet? That you have a will of your own? I am telling you about your *child*, for God's sake. Can't you stand up for yourself, for your child for once?' she snaps, and then her bravado deserts her and she is unable to stop the tears, hating herself for them, for this situation, for her pleading. 'Please Gopi, the baby is yours. What will I do? What on earth will I do?'

Despite evidence to the contrary from that fateful day when he had made love to her and then left her to deal with the landlord's wrath by herself, she had still hoped Gopi would stand by her. She had hoped his love for her would triumph over his fear of his father. She had hoped the cowardly side to him she had seen that day had been a one-off, and that now she had explained the situation, he would take charge.

She had hoped . . .

'I can't do anything,' He is crying too. 'I can't Puja. He would kill us both if he found out. Please Puja, just go. I am sorry.'

And with that, Gopi, the boy she has loved so much for so long, the only boy she has ever loved, shuts the window in her face, shutting her out of his life for ever.

And she imagines him settling under the mosquito net and going back to sleep, while she cautiously walks around the house, scrambles over the wall to another howling serenade from the dogs, runs down the hillock, past the snoozing village, over the bridge, and up the hill to the hut that will never be home, where she lies down on the mat opposite her snoring aunt, his baby nestling sheltered and oblivious inside her belly.

The next day she sits at her favourite spot on the beach where a lifetime ago, she had been heckled for kissing Gopi.

Sea gulls squawk, children scream, the salt and pepper whitecaps grumble and bash churlishly against the rocks. The sharp breeze rising from the sea tastes bittersweet, of billowing seaweed and misplaced love.

Everything is the same, and nothing is the same.

The day of the kiss her heart had been full to overflowing. Now it is destitute, undone by what has happened, what she has set in motion.

What to do? What is she to do?

Please God, help me, she prays.

And as if in answer to her prayers, she recalls Chinnamma coming to her ma in tears one summer afternoon . . .

Her ma had asked Sharda and Puja to play with Chinnamma's kids, hollow-bellied, scrawny-legged, bedraggled children who warily catalogued their every move from beneath unruly shocks of matted hair.

Sharda had patiently drawn the kids out, asking questions and sharing jokes, while Puja had eavesdropped on Ma and Chinnamma.

'What shall I do? He spends every penny on drink, comes home and forces himself on me. We are starving as it is, how will I feed one more?' Chinnamma rubbed her belly.

And Ma had said, 'There's a wise woman who lives just outside Dhoompur. Go to her. She will do the needful.'

Afterwards, Puja cornered Sharda where she was sitting with her books under the guava tree. 'Why did Ma send Chinnamma to the wise woman?'

The air smelled green, of new shoots and curiosity.

'Oh Puja . . .' the dog had come up and licked Sharda's face.

'Please, tell me why?' Puja had plucked a guava off the tree, biting into its yielding pink flesh. 'I *am* old enough,' intercepting Sharda's protests.

And Sharda had told her.

❊ ❊ ❊

The wise woman's hut rests picturesque in the flowing emerald fields. It seems obscene that Puja has come to such a beautiful place to commit such an ugly act.

The wise woman is sitting in the courtyard underneath a fragrant lime tree, chewing paan. She is wiry and ancient, with silver hair and silver eyes that shine from a furrowed, leathery face.

She looks at Puja, and then her eyes alight on Puja's stomach. 'Come here,' she beckons and rests her palms gently on Puja's belly.

'No,' the wise woman says softly, after a while, shaking her weathered head. 'You are too far gone. The baby is moving beneath my hands. I cannot do this. It will be murder.'

Puja nods slowly, as the woman's words sink in, realising that, despite the fact that this is the worst transgression a young unmarried girl can commit, and despite the fact that she will be scorned and snubbed even more as an unmarried mother, the feeling that floods through her now, is one of overwhelming relief.

Chapter 33
Kushi

A Sculpture Moulded from Clay

The lights in the ward have dimmed, and I am reading by the yellow glow of my bedside lamp.

All around me grunts and whimpers and mumbling and snores and prayers and pleas. A woman thumbs a rosary. There is the hollow, gushing trickle of anguished tears—tormented relatives giving in to their fears, while their loved ones submit to the drugged sleep of the heavily medicated.

'Stop reading for a bit, Kushi. Try and get some rest,' the kindly nurse who's been checking up on me has urged.

But I can't. I won't.

My body complains as soon as I close my eyes. I feel trapped. I see the car pinning me down, devastating my body like a sculpture moulded from clay; I see my kidneys disintegrating, my leaking blood, roiling red, and my life wasting away.

When I try to rest, the fear I am holding at bay looms. What if this is my future? What if Puja does not agree to donate her kidney? What if she does and it is not a match? What if a suitable donor cannot be found? What then?

The burst of confidence I had felt when the villagers visited has dissipated along with the enticing slice of daylight glimpsed outside the window.

'We'll keep looking for donors for as long as it takes,' my doctor assured me, when I hesitantly ventured my doubts, 'And while waiting for a donor, once you are stabilised, you can go home and come up here for dialysis every other day.' He'd grinned at me as if he was bestowing a special prize.

But I felt as if I were sinking deeper into the morass of an endless nightmare when his words registered. Is this how it will be for the rest of my life? This tie to the hospital? This agony of waiting for a suitable match. This half-life of ailment and injury, this life where I am a patient, a victim like the girls I help. Prone to infection, with death ever closer, chilly fingers dragging up my spine, muttering in my ear, 'Upsy Daisy.'

I have never been good at waiting. I am impatient to the core. If I think of something, I want it done *now*. This is the worst punishment I can conceive of. Waiting for my life to resume.

Why? Why am I being punished? For what sin?

And no matter how many banks Ma visits asking for loans, even after she sells the factory and the cottage, there is no way we can procure enough money for life-long dialysis . . .

I *hate* this situation I find myself in. I have always been a go-getter. I abhor this forced inactivity, this helplessness, this watching my life waste away from the side-lines. I am so *angry* with the people who did this. When I am not reading Ma's letters, I plan my revenge on the perpetrators, thinking up ways to make them pay.

An old woman shuffles her way back to her bed from the communal bathroom, one agonised step at a time, a nurse helping her along.

I have always thought my life was destined for great things. That starting with Bhoomihalli, I was born to change the world. To make waves. To improve lives.

I am not meant to be here, breathing in the sour smell of death and decay that clings to the yellowing walls of this room like the lizards that scuttle between the cracks in the plaster of the ceiling overhead looking for flies to devour.

For as long as I can recall, my dream has been to become a lawyer who fights for justice for the underdog and from there, to becoming one of the few uncorrupted politicians in India.

I never envisioned *this* . . . being stuck in hospital waiting for a kidney, for a piece of meat that will give me new tenancy inside my own body. Waiting for a woman I don't know—the woman who stole my ma's beau, the woman who was my mother's undoing—to visit. Waiting to see if she will consent to being a donor, and my saviour (if her kidney is a match that is).

As I turn Ma's letter over to add it to the stack I have already read, I find that this one too, has an annotated postscript scribbled in different ink.

For a long time, Ma, I blamed Puja for everything that happened. I thought that if only she had stayed within the bounds of propriety, cared for her reputation, taken heed of your warnings and mine, none of this would have happened. A part of me thought that she deserved the beating and the ostracism from our family. That is why I did not do anything, did not plead with Da to bring her back.

And this is my biggest regret: I sometimes wonder if I had begged Da to bring Puja back, would he have? Was he holding back for me, as I was the wronged party? You wanted me to ask Da to bring Puja back, I know, like you had done. You kept dropping hints and I deliberately ignored them.

Jealousy and hurt—they ruined me. They ruined us.

It took Kushi to open my eyes to the truth. Kushi, who is the very best of me and Puja, Ma. She is spirited, like Puja, but she also carries a sensible head on her young shoulders. She thinks before she acts, unlike Puja, who would jump headlong into adventure. That was her undoing, I see now.

Whatever Puja did, she did completely, with all her heart. Kushi is the same but with one small but vital difference. Before Kushi attempts anything, she takes a step back, considers the pros and cons of what she is about to do.

When Kushi does something I am proud of, I want to share it with Puja. The other day, when Kushi told me that women were spectacular in their own right, that they did not need men to underline their success, (I can't for the life of me recall what we were talking about that prompted this observation), I thought of Puja, how she used to sigh and grumble when you served Da first, the best pieces of fish, so we had to make do with only bones.

'Why does Da get to sleep on the only bench and we have to huddle together on the floor? Just because he is a man? What is the fairness in that?' she would ask and you would shake your head at what you considered her contrariness.

I've always regretted not being able to give Kushi siblings. We tried. But it was not meant to be . . .

The bond between siblings is something special. And even though Puja and I have not spoken for years, I realise now that the link is there, between us, a link that stretches across the distance that separates us. It always has been there, even during that horrible time, when I went to Da with my tale-bearing, that time when he hit her and I was too angry to contemplate compassion, too shocked to intervene, too mired in my own misery to realise that I was watching our family fragment like the stick Da was hitting her with.

I miss her so much, Ma, every single day.

As I get older, as Kushi grows and I commit her every quirk to memory, I understand that Puja is the only one who shares my memories of our joint childhood. Who lived through it with me.

I wrote this letter to you when Kushi was just a child, when the memories of what happened were still too raw. Now, she is nearly eighteen, and she is lying here prone and I am rereading this letter as I wait for her to wake and for Puja to arrive.

I pause, realising that my hands are shaking. Ma wrote this addendum very recently, perhaps even this morning, while she was waiting for me to regain consciousness . . .

My eyes drop down again to her words.

And as I read, Ma, I realise that the hate is gone, the rage, the blame.

Now all that is left is remorse for all that we lost, all that wasted time. And hope. Hope that when I see Puja again, I will recognise in the woman she has become, the sister I knew and loved, that we will be able to get past the years apart, the hurt and the upset to the affection we once harboured. And there is faith, that it will all be okay.

I blink. *Will it, Ma?* I want to ask of my mother, who I trust is even now making her way back to me. *Will it be okay?*

I know that in her letter she is talking about her relationship with her sister. But what if Puja is still holding on to the grudge of what happened in the past and does not agree to give me her kidney? What then?

What if Puja is coming here just to gloat? Feast on her sister's misfortune?

No, somehow I don't think so . . .

My ma is so kind, surely her sister will be too? But Ma was not kind where her sister was concerned. Why should Puja be kind in return? What incentive does she have?

In the section of corridor visible from my bed, I glimpse a woman mopping the floor. Why on earth she is cleaning when there are people still milling about, I don't know. The wet floors are an accident waiting to happen. And anyway the once white tiles, now stamped dirty red by hundreds of diseased feet, are beyond the attentions of a phenyl soaked cloth pushed half-heartedly across the floor, I think.

Outside the window of this prison of a room, the day is waning, I imagine, twilight arriving on a cool, cashew-scented breeze, the pink grapefruit of setting sun holding court to graceful black fans—birds flying home to roost—silhouetted against a patchwork sky.

Chapter 34
Sharda—Chasm

A Blackened Big Toe with a Broken Nail

Dearest Ma,

I do not want to think of that horrible time, but I have to. There is no other way.

It happened. And it changed everything. Left everything in its wake burnt and raw, livid and wounded.

Looking back, I wish that we had left the village and moved far away, with Puja in tow, the day the landlord visited. I wish that with all my heart, every single day that's passed since.

But we didn't.

❉ ❉ ❉

It starts with the famine. There's been not much rain for two years running, not nearly enough for livelihoods dependent on agriculture, so tensions simmer along with the earth—parched throats panting for rain and hungry for water.

The farmers do circuits of the temple on their knees; they feed laddoos and milk they cannot afford, and would give anything to have a gulp of to soothe their angry throats, to the Goddess so she will give them rain.

But, every morning without fail, the sky is such a bright blue that it hurts the eyes; the clouds are light and fluffy, frisky as lambs, not wearing a broody black scowl, nor pregnant with rain and fatigued with hefting their moisture-laden burden.

The sun is relentlessly, cheerfully yellow; the green grass now the gold of hay bales, the wells arid as baked cowpats. The ground is cracked, people ravenous, and livelihoods destroyed. Children die from drinking unclean dregs scraped from the bed of the dry lake. The earth starts splintering as do relationships. It is a dangerous time. A time when war can erupt from a mere rumour, a wrong word, a misplaced look.

Da is preparing for our house move, has been for months. He is sounding out farmers in other villages, looking for jobs. But there are none going. The drought has put paid to that.

The longer it takes for Da to organise our move, the more relieved you are, Ma, as am I.

Hurt and angry though I might be, I balk from taking that final step, cutting ourselves off completely from Puja, leaving the hut where her memories thrive. And sometimes I think Da is delaying the move for the same reason.

And then one day, he comes home to say that he has found a job as a bricklayer in a village the other side of Dhoompur. We will be moving in a week.

You look shattered, Ma. Raisin hued shadows ring your pink rimmed eyes as you digest this news.

'Please,' you implore. 'We can't go away without telling her. Please. I want to see her, just once, before we go.'

And to everyone's surprise, including, I imagine, his own, Da agrees.

We decide to go to see Puja the day after next, so you have time to prepare all of her favourite delicacies, Ma. You are hoping that once Da sees Puja, talks with her, he will not be able to leave her behind. You are hoping that meeting with the beloved daughter who was once his world will convince Da to take her with us.

But before we can act on this unexpected sanction from Da, before you can put your plan for reuniting our broken family into action, Ma, our world changes, irreversibly, forever . . .

❊ ❊ ❊

It starts, as these things do, in the marketplace on a Thursday morning, the day after Da gives his permission for all of us to visit with Puja, the day before we are due to meet her. What follows is what I pieced together later, from various disparate accounts as to what happened.

The market sits on a little flat piece of land right next to the highway, and it is permanently cloaked in the peach-coloured dust displaced by the buses hurtling past on their way to the big cities, which stop once in a lucrative (for the villagers) while when the conductor or driver or one of the passengers needs a pee or a bite to eat. Situated where it is, there is always hope that some of these rich people from the cities will buy the produce and meat that the villagers grow but cannot afford to eat.

Now, these potential customers take one look at the wilting produce and the flaccid meat coated in a layer of flies, and climb back into the buses without buying anything. And with each lost sale, starvation and death loom dangerously close for the villagers and their loved ones.

At one corner of the market is the Muslim butcher who sells beef but not pork, of course. In these difficult times, his stall is almost empty, with just a few scrawny cuts of meat from emaciated beasts.

Nobody knows how it happens, but some beef from the sacred cow ends up in the Hindu onion vendor's stall and in one searing heartbeat there is uproar. The villagers, Hindu, Muslim, Christian, upper caste and lower caste alike, who have lived side by side harmoniously for so many years are now up in arms against each other. Shouts rend the air, stippled red, brimming with vitriol. Accusations are hurled; Allah, Jesus, Vishnu and Brahma are all besmirched and reviled.

And then . . . a struck match, and in a moment of unthinking madness, the onion vendor sets fire to the beef and the market is in flames in a matter of minutes.

I am at the convent in Dhoompur, Ma, along with most of the youth and children from Nandihalli. To get our minds off our suffering, dogged thirst a dry gasp at the back of our throats, the nuns have organised a fun day, having managed to procure a barrel of water from somewhere at great cost.

It is the prospect of clean water after days of drinking the trickle of muddy slush jettisoned from the bottom of the well, which, no matter how much you boil, Ma, still tastes of dirt, and leaves me feeling thirstier than before, that finds me at the convent, despite us being Hindus.

Even though most of us are not Christians, we, the youth of Nandihalli, join the nuns in singing a hymn together, thanking Jesus for our blessings, our newly watered throats raised in grateful chorus. Our hands are clapping along as we savour once more in memory the sweet nectar taste of fresh water, when a bedraggled man bursts into the room, smelling of smoke. He falls at the nuns' feet, and asks them to please come at once, to help the injured in Nandihalli market.

'There is a fire,' he says, sobs choking his words out in strangled wheezes. 'Everything destroyed. People have died.'

But even before his words have sunk in, I am on my feet, running as soon as I hear the word 'Nandihalli'. My legs are flying, even though I am short and squat and chubby. Flying like they did when I got my PUC results.

Please God, I pray to a generic god, all gods, *please let my parents be okay.*

But even as I frantically send my entreaties heavenward, I don't hold out much hope. If the gods have not listened to the appeals of an entire village and not sent rain, why would they now listen to me, a mere one of their many supplicants?

Orange heat, sinister and swelling on storm clouds of suffocating navy hits me first. It is a completely different heat from the heavy, over baked, aching-for-rain temperatures we have been experiencing during the drought. My eyes sting and I cannot breathe as I run into the smoke that invades my

lungs. Then, as my sight becomes accustomed to the dark
smog, I come to a shocked standstill.

The market is no more. Just gyrating balloons of dense
blue smoke interspersed with tongues of ruby flames that
a few men are desperately trying to put out, a losing battle
for lack of water. The place where our stall used to be, where
I have spent so many happy, content days, is razed to the
ground, just a charred wasteland.

Where are you and Da?

I grab the lungi of a man rushing past me.

'Please,' I say. 'Where have they taken all the people?'

He nods his head to his left, where the highway used to
be and I see the bodies laid out in a grim, unremitting line.

I walk over on unsteady legs.

Please God. Please.

I don't want to look. I don't want to see anything familiar. At
least then I can hide behind the flimsy skirts of faltering hope.

But I can't not look. What if you and Da have been put
there by mistake, if you need me and I didn't check . . .

I take a quivering breath. Some of the bodies are charred
beyond all recognition. My fellow villagers, every one of
whom I know by name, each with their quirks and their vic-
es, now unrecognisable, their unique traits, their flaws, their
passions wiped out by the impartial brushstroke of death.
And then . . .

No!

I don't want to see this, not here. I want to run away, back
the way I came, but I lean closer anyway, my subconscious
knowing what I don't want to acknowledge.

My da's big toe, with the broken nail, bent out of shape when he fell off the coconut tree. It never got fixed back in place as he couldn't afford to get it seen by the doctor. I follow the leg up to his face, my heart weighted down with the horror of what I don't want to admit.

I will his chest to move. *Up and down, Da, up and down. Please.*

But it doesn't. It doesn't.

He used to carry me on his shoulders, those mornings when we went to meet the boats and I would rest my cheek on his head, the smell of coconut oil and unwashed hair, my arms tight around his neck, until he said, 'Look, Sharda, here we are,' and then he would gently squat down and I would climb down the ladder of his back and jump off, my feet sinking in the soft sand.

'Da,' I whisper, 'come back, come back to me,' and I hold his body, too warm, still burning.

Hands grab at me. 'Come away, girl.'

Where are you, Ma?

I don't want to find you here too. My eyes flicker up and down the line of bodies, Hindus, Muslims and Christians, united in death. My gaze cringes from the gruesome tableau and yet I am unable to look away, coming back agonised, to rest on the one with the broken nail.

Please God, I've got it wrong. Please.

I fight the arms holding me, the smell of ash and cooked flesh, but there is no give. I try to close my ears to the screams emanating from loved ones, the howls that are being wrenched out of me without my being aware of them. I ache to block my heart to the truth of what I have just witnessed.

You are not among the bodies, Ma. At least I cannot recognise any parts of you. I quake as I think this.

Please God, I pray even though God has not heeded a single prayer of mine. Not one. *Are you even there, God? If so, how can you condone this? How?*

'They took some of the injured to the clinic in Dhoompur,' someone says.

And I pray, once again, despite having doubted God just moments before. I pray that you are one of the injured, Ma, and not one of the bodies they are still pulling out of the wreckage.

Puja.

Puja needs to know and I must be the one to tell her. But first, I need to find you. I begin looking for you, Ma, and I get lost in the smouldering crowds. The entire convent, nuns and youth alike, their faces locked in a collective grimace of intense shock, have congregated in this wasteland that was once our bustling market, the repository of so many happy memories.

Just then there is a loud groan, a demonic clap, a flash, and the sky erupts and the rain we have all been longing for explodes onto the blistering earth. It quenches the flames the few straggling survivors have been trying desperately to extinguish, and drenches the dead, these men who have longed for rain but who can no longer feel it—their last rites of fire and water.

And the people who are still alive turn their faces up to the heavens and open their abused mouths, greedily lapping up the ash-flecked drops, and even though it seems sacrilegious to be drinking while their loved ones cannot, their thirst wins out.

❀ ❀ ❀

I find you lying on a mat in the corridor of the clinic in Dhoompur, which teeters under the unexpected weight of this inexorable influx of casualties.

You are unrecognisable. Your body is distended with weeping wounds as you wait your turn for medical attention. Your flesh sizzles to the touch, throbbing and sore. But you are alive.

Your eyes light up when you see me. You manage to wrap your swollen, suppurating fingers around my hand even though it must be agony for you to do so.

'Your da? . . . ' Your leaking eyes plead with me to lie.

I look down, at my blistered and ash sprayed feet, and see a blackened big toe with a broken nail.

'No,' you whisper.

I gather up the courage to look at you. Your eyes are closed, and tormented tears squeeze out of engorged lids.

'I was fifteen when I married him. We were wedded twenty eight years. He was a good man.'

I hold you then, as gently as I can, your hot body pulsing, as we weep for the man we loved. Da's memory colours a space between us, and robs us of words.

'Puja,' you whisper at last, invoking the other person missing from our family tapestry. Your voice is halting, and your breath comes in wheezing gasps. 'Please. Find her. Be the one to tell her. Bring her home.' You try to squeeze my hand, your palm too warm.

I nod, unable to speak, my throat clogged up with hurt and grief and loss.

'Promise me,' your voice is urgent, 'that whatever happens, you will look after your sister.'

'Ma, please, don't speak like that. Nothing will happen to you . . .' Tears prick my eyes.

Your sigh comes from deep within your chest. 'Sharda, listen. You have to be prepared. I cannot . . . I cannot go on much longer. I can feel myself weakening.'

I give in to the sobs building in my chest, willing the tears to wash away my panic and death's ashen presence that I can sense is hovering close, and that I can hear in your laboured breathing.

I cannot envision my world without you. I do not want to. I will take care of you forever; I will wash your wounds, and cradle your body in my arms like a precious treasure, if you would just be with me for always.

'Promise me that you will find Puja, that you will look after each other, look out for each other. Forget what went before, Sharda. Please. You only have one another in this world, you are bound by blood.'

'Ma,' I manage to gasp out between sobs, 'We also have you. Why are you speaking like this?'

'There's a knot in the pallu of my wedding sari, containing my karimani and a necklace. Sell the gold. Then you and Puja go to another village, or even stay with Nilamma, if she lets you, until you finish your degree.' Your breath is straining. 'I know you will succeed somehow to make ends meet, Sharda, I have great faith in you.' Your eyes are soft and filled with such love that it hurts.

It hurts so much. How can you look at me like that and say what you are saying?

My aching heart bleeds to see you are making provisions for us for after you go, Ma. I cannot bear this knowledge.

'We, your da and I . . .' Your eyes shimmer, and silver tears sprout on puffy lids.

Is your breath becoming more uneven? Or is it my imagination?

'We thought we would be around to see you both married and settled, to play with our grandchildren, look after them, help bring them up. Oh never mind.' Your face is creasing with the effort it is taking to speak, your breath coming in winded gasps.

All this talk of death seems to have conjured it up. You are fading right before my eyes. It is as if you have given up.

'Please Ma,' I implore, 'Stay with me.'

I hold you close, trying to inject my need of you into your soul, willing some crucial life into your flagging body.

'Your da and I should have made provisions for your marriage and Puja's,' you are sighing now, spent. 'Please look after Puja, see that she is well settled. And that you are too.

Promise me.' Your boiling fingers are grasping, begging. Your
eyes beseech.

I promise, my voice a jumble of sob-swallowed words.

And just like that, you close your eyes and leave me, Ma, as
if you had been holding on to precious life just long enough
to hear me say I will look after Puja, do my best by her.

You look as if you are sleeping. Your bruised face is peaceful.

But you have gone, leaving me alone in that festering corridor crowded with fear and pain and the smoky scent of
death.

Chapter 35

Raj

A Hug from a Hot Spring

India.

He was expecting high temperatures, of course he was. What he hadn't expected was the physical nature of the heat. It had trounced him with a sweltering, moist slap, had enveloped him like a hug from a hot spring, when they exited Bajpe airport after a hair-raising ride in a tiny aeroplane that he was afraid would not be able to carry his, let alone the other passengers' weight, as well as their luggage. He had sat by the window, and when they commenced their descent into Bajpe, and he had spied those undulating emerald hills and flashes of twinkling, silver rivers snaking between valleys that were coming right at them, he had closed his eyes and prayed. Actually prayed to a god, any god, *some* god to deliver him safely back home.

I want to see Ellie again, please God.

When they finally ground to a juddering halt, in one piece, *thank you, God,* he had turned to grin at his mother, who was gripping the seat rests as if they were her salvation

'We have landed, Mum. We are good to go,' he had said, unable to keep his relief from giving his voice wings.

'I don't know if I can do this,' she had whispered.

'Then you don't have to,' he had said, thinking, *Couldn't you have thought of this before we left?*

'I *want* to see them. But . . . how will I face them? What will I tell them?'

'The truth. That it is all their fault. For shunning you, for discarding you and shrugging you off like the memory of a nightmare in the bright light of morning.'

His mum had rewarded him with a smile, tremulous but filled with purpose. 'I am sorry, Raj, for everything. I know I have been a rubbish parent, and have failed you, let you down very badly. . .'

'Mum . . . '

'I gave you all the material things,' she'd said softly, 'foolishly convincing myself it was enough. I did not give you what really mattered. I did not give you myself.'

'I . . . '

'And yet here you are, so generous, so giving,' she'd said, 'I don't know what I'd do without you. Thank you for forgiving my mistakes. For accepting me, warts and all.'

'Thank you too, Mum, for the same,' he'd said.

She'd smiled again.

And then she'd taken a deep breath, stood up, and walked down the small aisle of that minuscule plane. 'Let's see about finding a taxi and then I'll continue with my story.'

❄ ❄ ❄

Now, he tries to get comfortable in the ramshackle seat of the decrepit taxi that his mother picked at random from the horde of taxi drivers who descended on them like the ducks that flocked to the breadcrumbs he flicked into the pond that his nanny used to take him to when he was little.

He is not prepared for the sheer intensity of the noise in this country, the crowds, the chaos. He is not prepared for the smells, like living things that burrow inside you and take up residence. The piquant zest of spices mingles with the festering reek of open sewers and the aroma of heat and sweat, and earth and dust—billowing apricot clouds of it.

He is not prepared either for colour, the abundance of it, from the saffron hued mud to the kaleidoscopic saris that hang from the garish shop awnings, dazzling in the brutal sunlight. The hawkers' carts proudly bearing mounds of spices: yellow turmeric and red chilli powder, green coriander powder and brown garam masala, or piles of food: crimson fried chicken and heaps of pink-flecked white rice, bright yellow syrup-filled tubes and glossy, treacly ochre balls.

And nor is he prepared for the mind-numbing poverty as gaudily on display as everything else, and as much a part of life. People cooking, eating, defecating, dressing, bathing, urinating, and living their lives by the side of the road: in ditches; in flapping tarpaulin held up with twigs and festooned with holey saris; in huts that appear to be shaped from mud and topped with grass, or even in cement pipes!

Naked urchins weave between traffic, picking up crumbs from the dirt and stuffing them in their mouths. Mothers in bedraggled saris beg for alms with concave bellied, emaciated children on their hips. Vagabonds sprawl by the side of the road, their gaunt bodies infested with weeping sores and swarming flies, their sunken eyes pleading.

What would Ellie make of all this? Ellie . . . he wishes she were here, experiencing this extraordinary country with him.

This country grabs you by the throat, he thinks, breathing in the burnt-orange smell of ruthless heat. *It leaves you gasping. It makes you want to howl and never stop.*

He recalls how he has shouted at his mother for working, earning a living, how he'd brashly claimed just before they left, that he could live without money. Now, after seeing this, he understands why she'd slapped him. He thinks of his huge house, his Xbox and PlayStation, his bedroom that could house three of the huts he's seen, his closet that could house at least one, with its surfeit of designer clothes, most of which he doesn't even wear.

Shame floods his mouth, bitter as an unpalatable truth.

How spoilt I have been. How much I have taken for granted. I've been feeling sorry for myself because I felt unloved, while here, there are people dying of hunger, struggling to live. What wouldn't these people give to be in my situation?

❊ ❊ ❊

His mother's soft voice is saying, 'My stomach had definitely grown. My waist had become thicker. That was when I had the first inkling. I counted back to the last time I had got my period . . . '

The understanding of what his mother is saying jolts Raj out of his introspection, drags him back from the perusal of the world outside the paan-spattered, spit beaded, grimy grey window of this ramshackle vehicle. The windscreen is similarly splashed with marks, and is muddy brown. How the driver can see through it is anybody's guess.

An unmarried mother—not a big deal in the UK—a *very* big deal in the India of his mother's youth and even now, perhaps, he thinks.

The taxi rocks and swings as it judders through yet another pothole, setting off a paroxysm of honks and screeches. The driver of the packed to overflowing bus looming next to them, too close, puts his head out of the window (which is just a gaping hole in the rusting chassis) and yells at them and the bus swerves, almost pushing their taxi off the narrow, potholey road.

'Please. Be careful,' His mother tells their taxi driver.

People ooze out from two openings that pass for doors, one at the front and one at the back of the rickety bus, holding on with just one hand, their feet barely nudging the steps of the bus, their clothes ballooning in the breeze.

Raj looks at his mother and raises his eyebrows, and she smiles briefly before resuming her tale. The bus stops with a clanging and grinding of long-suffering brakes, to add even more passengers to the scrum, and their driver takes advantage of this to race ahead.

Raj listens to his mother's extraordinary story, how she went to the wise woman, and how relieved she was when the wise woman said no.

Much as he hadn't been prepared for the many things he is experiencing in this weird, but strangely familiar country, he is even less prepared for his mother to have been pregnant, a pregnancy that went ahead by all accounts . . .

Mum! Did you keep the baby? Was it me? Is that why you found it so hard to love me, because I was the product of such heartbreak, because I embodied such a difficult time in your life? Is that why you got so angry with me when I said I could live without money, because you had tried your hardest to give me a better life than the one I started out with? he wants to ask, but he cannot find the words.

His mother is sitting hunched as if being here in India is hurting her. Or is it because she is mining the memories? Telling him the truth about his parentage?

'I want to kill Gopi,' he says. 'I want to put my hands around his neck and squeeze. You were very brave, mum, doing it all on your own. Tell me again, why are you going back?'

'Huh?'

'Why are you doing your sister's bidding, uprooting our lives in order to come and visit her and her daughter when she did not once help you, forgive you your perceived mistake in her eyes, come to find you and bring you home?'

'This has gone on long enough, Raj. We cannot keep perpetuating the hurt. Where will it all end?' His mother rubs a weary hand across her eyes. 'And besides . . . '

'Besides?'

'There's more to it than . . .' His mother stops.

He is suffering from the same problem; unable to ask the question that is swelling on his tongue, that has taken over his mind. Has he been living a lie?

He is warming to his mother, in awe of the strong girl she was and the stronger woman she has become, putting the past resolutely behind her, bringing him up almost single-handedly, succeeding in her business against all odds. But if he is the baby she is talking about and she has lied to him about this . . . How can he look her in the eye again?

'I want to know, did you keep the baby?' he manages, obliquely voicing his query, not wanting to jump to conclusions and blame his mother just yet, giving her, finally, the benefit of the doubt.

And she tells him.

Chapter 36
Puja—Chasm

Yellow Striped Marrows

Puja is hanging clothes out to dry on the line that stretches from the coconut tree to the tamarind when the news comes.

The sun reigns strong, lording it over moisture-starved, baking earth, plastering her clothes to her body, and the monsoons show no signs of heeding the prayers being sent up to them by despairing farmers. Every day, the sun rises up in a sky the clear, unruffled blue of a pure conscience, and the hopeful hearts of the villagers sink down to their toes. Wearily they visit the temple yet again, with offerings that wither rapidly in the unyielding golden sunshine.

As Puja pauses to wipe her perspiration soaked face, she spies her aunt's friend, Gangamma, trudging up the hill, her sprightly tread belying her age, her nimble feet deftly finding purchase on the pebble littered path.

Nilamma's hut is housed at the top of the hill on the out-skirts of this new village Puja has been banished to. The hill, red mud dotted here and there with brown rocks and green moss, looks like a giant's fist; the weed-infested, tumble down brick wall, is the giant's knuckle; Nilamma's hut—the squat outcrop wedged within—the giant's finger.

There are no neighbours. Puja surmises that this is why her father sent her here, far away from prying eyes and vilifying mouths, with only an old woman, a cow and a few chickens for company.

The location also deters any visitors. Puja wonders why Gangamma is here now, and what news she brings that cannot wait. For one hopeful, heart-lifting moment, she thinks, *Perhaps she's come with the offer of reconciliation from Da and Ma and Sharda.*

The thought hovers, then Puja pushes it away. Why would they want to see her now, after all this time? She will not allow herself the indulgence of hope, only to be disappointed, and for the hurt she has managed to tamp down to flare up all over again.

'This hut suited my nature-loving, loner of a husband just fine,' Nilamma had said when Puja first arrived. 'Since he has passed, I have toyed with the idea of moving closer to the village but haven't had the energy or gumption to do so. And this place holds all of his memories. It is alive with his presence. If I move, I might not feel him beside me anymore.'

Oh great, Puja had thought, *just my luck to be housed with a mad woman who lives with ghosts.*

The truth is she has come to love Nilamma. The old lady lets her be, gives her space. She is quiet, never intrusive, a blessed relief after the nosy meddling of the matrons in the village Puja grew up in.

'I will not ask you what happened, why you are here,' Nilamma said, that first day. 'It is not my place to judge. But your da asked me to keep an eye on you, so if you are going somewhere, tell me where and why.'

And she has stayed true to her word.

Now that her pregnancy is advancing, Puja is especially appreciative of Nilamma's incurious nature, grateful for the fact that they live up here, secluded from snooping meddlers. Her aunt, as far as Puja is aware, knows nothing of her pregnancy. Puja has been letting down the seams on her churidars, Sharda's hand-me-downs which were wider to begin with, and which her mother had folded in to fit Puja's slimmer frame. It is another thing Puja is grateful for, although at the time she had whinged and sniped that she never got any new clothes.

In the end her mother had given in, taking Puja to Dhoompur and asking her to choose fabric from which to stitch a churidar exclusively for her. Puja had bitten back tears when she found fragments of that churidar when she had packed to come here. It had been shredded to bits, as if someone had taken a scythe to it. Another loss on top of all the others.

She recalls the spangled turquoise fabric threaded through with silver that she had picked out with Ma from the shop in Dhoompur; getting measured at the tailor for her very first *new* churidar after having endured years of Sharda's dowdy hand-me-downs; the joy of choosing a pattern from the huge book the tailor showed her, and then wearing the churidar, that was wholly and only hers, and breathing in the unfamiliar, heady scent of new fabric and feeling transformed. She feels another stab of loss. Oh well, no use for it now anyway.

She unpicks Ma's wayward stitches and wears Sharda's churidars and they hide her bump. As she unpicks the stitches, she imagines her ma sewing them, her hand right here where Puja's is now, and it soothes her to know that she is, in an oblique way, touching her ma as she tracks the path of her stitches.

She shakes her head trying to blink away the yearnings and memories that have been flooding her lately, of a life in the bosom of a loving family that she took for granted, a life she hungers for, a life she wishes she could give this little one who grows secretly within her.

At night, after her aunt is asleep and she cannot get comfortable, or when the dreams of her past life plague her, she talks to the baby, stroking the gentle mound of her stomach, the soft press of it upward and outward the only visible indication of the miracle taking place inside. She narrates stories that Sharda had told her, pushing down the craving for her sister's arms. The baby jumps in her womb, responding to her touch and Puja does not feel so alone anymore.

She's lost her family and she's lost Gopi. But now, she has this baby. A part of her. Something no-one can take away.

On days when her chores are done, Puja sits on a rock at the very top of the hill, and looks down at the huts dotting the fields—once green, now cracked and dry—of her aunt's village. The river, no longer a glinting, silvery blue, is now a mere sliver of muddy red, and beyond that, is *her* village, her hut nestling somewhere within. She feels the nostalgia-scented breeze stroking her face, whispering solace, and fancies she can see Sharda and her ma and da going about their business.

Are they thinking of her? She is overcome by loss and longing and then, her baby kicks and tumbles in her womb and the sadness is replaced by gratitude that her child thrives without needing anything more of her than to exist. To just be. That it doesn't judge her and condemn her. That it has chosen her for its mother.

She loosens her churidar trousers and pats her bump. Her child leaps and cavorts under her touch and she talks to it, sings softly to it. Loves it.

'I will let you do anything you want. I will not clip your wings,' she promises her child. 'We will go far away where your future is not contaminated by the slur of my past. Where people are broad-minded and will not look down on me or you. Where you and I will be free.'

The wind pats and soothes; it whistles and wheezes, and she fancies it carries messages from her ma and Sharda and even her da, and also from her unborn child.

She does not allow herself to think of Gopi.

This far out, the mud road is deserted, and Puja can see Gangamma struggling to walk the last few steps up the hill. The air smells sweet, of honeyed cashews and happy memories, but carries a hint of smoke and Puja imagines she can see speckles of black interspersed amongst the tamarind hued dust swirling in the breeze.

She is tired. She has been feeling out of sorts all day. Sharp points of pain. A periodical gasp-inducing tightening of her stomach, as if someone is clasping it in a pincer squeeze. It can't be the baby surely. It's too soon.

She fancies she can see a flash of red, instantly obscured by a dark curling cloud, in the hazy, auburn blurred distance. She squints, and it is gone. She shakes her head to clear it.

Stop imagining things.

Then Gangamma is upon her, clutching her wrist in her bony clasp, 'Where is your aunt?' her breath coming in puffing pants.

'She's just having a nap. Come sit, I'll make you tea,' Puja says.

Puja could do with a sit down as well. Jobs which were easy before are not anymore. She just doesn't have the energy, as her baby grows inside her.

Sometimes, she is attacked by fear, a shock of panic. She hears the landlord's derogatory words, his sneering snarl. 'How will you survive? You failed your PUC exams.'

How will she look after the baby?

Those times she fingers the secret she carries around with her everywhere, close to her heart, alongside the secret of her burgeoning stomach. The gold bangles her ma slipped into her hand when Puja was forced to leave; bangles that were part of her ma's dowry when she married her da. 'To tide you over until you come back,' her ma had mouthed in her ear.

She will sell the bangles and use the money to go far away. She is just biding her time until the baby is born, so she is close to the wise woman, who has agreed to help with the birth.

But before that she will try one more time. She will visit her family. She will see if they will accept her and her child.

If not (and this hurts, but she has to consider the possibility), she has made up her mind to leave, give her child a fresh start.

But she has to see if this baby will bond their broken family or tear them apart even further. A baby that has no right to exist, a baby pilfered from circumstance, created in one magical moment stolen from time. A baby she already loves more than life itself.

They will go where the breeze of rumour cannot follow, to a town untouched by the air of gossip, unscathed by the wind of calamity. A big town where they can disappear, where no one will have their nose in her business, where they will accept the story she has prepared, that she is a young widow whose husband succumbed to dengue fever.

'Wake your aunt now, child,' Gangamma says, her voice urgent, panic gushing through it.

Without warning, Puja's stomach clenches and she is swamped by a river of agony. It is a concentrated, undulating upsurge of undiluted pain.

When it passes, she looks at Gangamma properly for the first time, and notices the distress in her eyes, widened navyblack with anguish.

'What has happened? Tell me please?'

A clap of thunder.

'Nandihalli market is on fire.'

A sudden breeze brings the smell of smoke and broken dreams.

'No,' Puja yells, 'No, no, no.'

That market stall where she spent so many afternoons, sifting mangoes and bananas from one basket to another,

where Sharda taught her to count using vegetables for counters, the smell of fish and ripe fruit, the excited crackling
of newly minted gossip and the clink of old coins, the taste
of laughter and egg puffs, the soft, comforting feel of her
mother's worn cotton sari and yielding lap—the market stall
that is the hub of some of her happiest childhood memories.

Please God, keep my ma and da and Sharda safe.

She feels a vicelike grip at her waist, as if something is
clamping down. The pain is excruciating. A swell of pure
agony. The baby wants out, she realises, fear a sickly olive
taste in her mouth, even as she tries to assimilate what Gangamma is saying.

It is too early.

*Please God, my baby. Please, I will not be able to survive
more loss. Please.*

Is she bargaining with God? Trading her baby's life for her
family? Is that what it has come to? Is that what He wants?

A shadow looms over the hill, the sky darkening, wears a
scowl of clouds, and emits another warning snarl of thunder.

Her aunt comes running out, bare feet, hair dishevelled,
housecoat awry. 'What happened?'

The first drops fall, fat plops that pigment the dust dark
cranberry. The smell of wet dirt perfumes the shimmering,
rain-freckled air. The clothes that she has just set out to dry
are getting wet but nobody cares.

Another contraction. She waits it out, leaning against the
nearest tree, breathing in the sharp tang of tamarind, trying
not to let her torment colour her face. The baby is coming.

She cannot go to the market, to make peace with her parents and sister. If they are . . . If . . .

Please God.

She opens her mouth dry with dread and regret.

'I'll stay here, you go,' she says to her aunt, a whisper is all she can manage.

She has made her choice. She has chosen her baby.

Keep it safe, God. It is innocent. I made the mistakes. Please. Don't punish my baby.

Does this mean God will take her family?

She cannot think for the pain. She does not know what her role is in this game God is playing with her. She only wants this child, who has tided her through these dark months, who has been her hope, her courage, to be safe and well.

Please.

Her aunt, still in her housecoat, trudges down the hill with Gangamma, each step weighted down with apprehension.

Once they are weaving dots wavering in the distance, Puja clutches her stomach and stumbles in the other direction, and makes her arduous way to the wise woman's hut, praying and pleading and making pacts with a punishing God above the grumble and shiver and splatter and drip of this unforeseen downpour. She opens her mouth in between contractions and tastes the salty pangs of loss, smells the charred remains of her hopes of reuniting with her family. And she knows without a doubt that this is God's way of saying to her—a God as vengeful as her father and the landlord—*How could you, a sinner, a fallen woman, dare imagine a happily ever after?*

❋ ❋ ❋

Grotesquely pregnant, yellow-striped marrows hanging from the ceiling by coconut frond strips looped around their middle grin at her, then fade into oblivion.

'Push,' she hears from far away, 'push, girl, push.'

A flash of silver. Wild hair. Gleaming eyes probing. The wise woman.

Her belly heaves, kicks, has a mind of its own. She cannot think for the pain. It is a separate entity claiming her, owning her. She is tired, so tired. Her eyelids feel as if they are weighted down with rocks.

'Shhh . . . It'll be fine. Don't you worry,' the wise woman soothes.

Sweat dribbles down Puja's face, in between the mounds of her breasts, and navigates the hillock of her belly. She feels a wet cloth on her face, smelling of vinegar—the wise woman kindly trying to help, but she only ends up spreading the sweat unevenly all over Puja's face.

The room is rent with screams—hers, she realises, when she tries to garner saliva from her fuzzy, spent throat.

The torpid air is thick with scents—with rust, pain, sweat, anxiety, and bone-deep weariness—a musty, throbbing aroma that she will forever associate with this . . . afternoon? evening? night?

Dappled shadows hold court on the dank, peeling wall opposite. Pinkish red, lengthening to black. Dusk. The smell of warm hay and fresh cow dung mingling with the other scents. Conjee burbling on the hearth in the far corner. The fraying mat she is lying on soaked through with perspiration and agony. Rotting beams overhead. Marrows dangling.

'Push. Push. Push.' The wise woman's gravelly voice.

I can't, she thinks, but she cannot say it out loud. She doesn't have the strength. She wants to sleep. Out of nowhere, behind heavy eyelids, Gopi's face teasing, tantalising.

No, don't think about him. He is the reason you are here.

Then, her father's face intruding into her thoughts. Beloved. Pale. Fear-embellished. Hovering.

'Push, Puja.'

'Have you forgiven me, Da?'

'Don't call me Da. You are not my daughter.' His face distorted with anger, his love turning to hate in the time it takes for a heart to beat, for a life to be created, his eyes muddy with the shame she has wrought upon them.

'Push, Puja, please.' Her mother's anguished face. Morphing into Sharda's.

'How could you do it, Puja? Steal my betrothed?'

'I am sorry Sharda. So sorry.'

'Shame on you.' All three of them, beloved, turning away. 'You will not see us again.'

No, No, No. I will be good. A dutiful daughter like Sharda. I promise. Please come back. Please.

'Come on, almost there now. One last big push.' The wise woman's voice bringing her back to this blood-splattered, anguish-swathed, fear-cramped room.

Almost there.

She pushes. And pushes.

The scorching pulse of all-consuming pain. The raging agony.

Then . . . a squelch. A scream. A bellow. A wail. A mewling.

'Oh Puja!' The wise woman's voice—overwhelmed, awed, festive as glass bangles clinking on a bride's hand—'A perfect, healthy baby.'

Marrows dance, sunny yellow, joyful.

※ ※ ※

When she comes to, the wise woman is fondling a wispy haired bundle and looking at Puja with eyes that radiate kindness. She holds the bundle out to Puja.

A small, perfect face framed by tufts of coiled black hair. Tiny hands curled into fists. A flawless little body shaped like a question mark. Minuscule legs wiggling, drawing semi circles in the air.

Puja is consumed by the need to hold her baby close and not let go. She doesn't reach for her child.

'My parents . . . '

The wise woman's eyes cloud over. 'I am sorry.'

'Both of them?'

The wise woman nods.

It is my fault, Puj thinks. *Everything, my fault.*

'Sharda?'

'She was spared,' the wise woman whispers.

The tart tang of blood and fluids and decay and drains. The briny, raw taste of loss.

I dared to dream of a happy ending, a new beginning. I hoped this baby could seal us together, mend the fracture in our family unit caused by my waywardness. I sat at the top of that hill and spun fairy tales. I pictured Da's forgiving smile, Ma's welcoming arms. And all the while God was planning his revenge, his punishment for my sins.

'I could not make my peace,' Puja whispers.

'They loved you, child.'

'Did they?'

'Until the last.'

Why can't she believe the wise woman? Why does her sore heart tell her otherwise?

'Your child needs you. Here.' Once more, the wise woman holds Puja's child out to her.

Once more, Puja breathes in her baby, the perfection she has created in her imperfect body, her tainted person bringing forth this unblemished child.

'No.' She will not hold her baby. If she does, she will not be able to let go.

She looks, once more, at this child whose birth called for the sacrifice of her parents, committing every single minute detail of it to memory.

Did you spare me or deny me, child, by deciding to enter the world at the very moment my parents were leaving it, so I was left without one final glimpse of the parents who abandoned me as easily as an out-of-favour toy, a guest who outstayed her welcome?

I thought it would be me who would leave them, running away from the confines of the village that had always bound me too tight, suffocating me. Now, my last vision of them will be my father refusing to look at me, his words, 'You are not my daughter,' his hand lifting the stick and rupturing our relationship like the skin of my back.

My mother pleading with her husband and yet not daring to go against him to stand up for her daughter.

My sister crushed.

Is your soul, child, an intermingling of my mother and father's? Did they have to die for you to live?

Have I chosen you over them?

Everything and everyone she loves, she loses. Her family. Gopi.

She is immoral, wicked. Her family, who knew her best and loved her once upon a time, thought so, which is why they exorcised her from their lives.

She is unlovable, cursed, unworthy.

She aches to hold her child close, protect it from the vicissitudes of a capricious world. But what this baby really needs is protection from *her*, its mother.

This baby is unspoiled, faultless. How can she bear to destroy that purity, taint her child with the filthy brush of her sins, her innumerable imperfections?

This wonderful being deserves so much better, someone who will preserve its innocence, someone who will lead by example. Someone who will be a *good* parent.

She destroys everything good in her life: her parents' adoration; her relationship with Sharda.

She does not want to destroy this baby whom she loves more than she has ever loved anything or anybody else, even her own self.

My darling child, you merit the right to a wonderful life and I can't promise you that. I ventured to think I could, but God asked me how I dared. He showed me the folly of my hopes for a future with you in it by taking away my parents. Instead of the possibility of forgiveness and the expectation of reunion with them, I now have only the burden of their thwarted dreams, their hurt and their anger, the reverberations of the disgrace I wrought upon them.

If I keep you as I yearn to, against God's wishes, I will ruin you as I have ruined myself. And I love you too much to subject you to that, my precious.

Love.

It chokes the life out of one, child.

I love and I lose—

Ma, Da, Sharda, Gopi.

You.

Puja shuts her eyes tight and turns away from her child.

Chapter 37
Kushi

The Vulnerable Frailty of a Fleeting Life

I read my mother's letters to *her* mother, pleas really, for her mother to intercede. To come back from the dead and help her. To guide her. To comfort her. To help her bring up her daughter right.

I cry along with Ma when I find out how her parents died.

I think, how much bad luck can a person endure? To have her parents die in a fire and years later her husband too. How devastated she must have been, how broken, when she found out Da had succumbed to flames as well.

And yet, she hid her pain from me, allowing me leeway to express mine, imparting strength so I could begin to heal.

Ma, I admire you so.

I hear a man curse richly and profusely as he navigates the slippery, wet corridors of this hospital overflowing with people, the sickly wearing expressions of resignation, suffering set into the hollows of their faces as they await their turn to be seen by harassed doctors.

I think of how, all through my life so far, Ma has always been with me, offering comfort and encouragement, supporting me through my every decision, tiding me through every dip and furrow.

All that I am is thanks to my mother. I would be lost without her.

I read on, despite tasting salt and seeing splotches speckling the yellowing pages bejewelled with my mother's beautiful handwriting, the faded blue ink tinted mauve.

Two nurses argue about the dosage of pills allowed a patient right in front of his bed and he looks from one to the other agog, happy to go with the winner. Their voices escalate to screeches, sounding like a company of parrots screaming from amongst the branches of banyan trees, and the few patients who are medicated enough to sleep through the perpetual noise and chaos in this bustling microcosm groan and grumble as they toss in their beds.

I stop reading for a while after my mother promises her mother on her deathbed to look out for Puja and bring her home, to assimilate everything I have learnt.

'Sister,' a weak voice calls from one of the other beds. 'Please, Sister . . . '

It serves to stop the nurses quarrelling over pill dosage and they rush back to what they were doing before this argument put paid to their busyness, leaving the patient over whose medicine intake they were disagreeing with no pills at all. He calls, 'Sister, my pills . . .' but they are gone.

I wonder how any patients in these poky, dirty wards ever get better with the relentless din, the exposure to more infections, the echoes of distress drifting on the dense, germ-laden, somnolent air flavoured with misery and hurt, linctus and the vulnerable frailty of fleeting life.

Why didn't Ma honour the deathbed promise she made to her mother and find Puja?

Or did she? So why are she and Puja still estranged? What happened?

Chapter 38
Sharda—After

Embers and Earth and Damp

Dearest Ma,

I go to find Puja, the morning following the fire, climbing the hill to Nilamma's house.

But the hut is deserted, forlorn looking, the front door left ajar and creaking on worn hinges. There are clothes billowing on a clothes line, soaked in the rain, which hasn't let up since the previous day. I squeeze the water out of them and take them inside, holding Puja's churidars (originally mine) close, trying to breathe in her scent. But all I can smell is the rain, imprinted with the memory of the fire: embers and earth and damp.

The evening after the fire, all the dead are burned together (again, although this time they cannot feel it), you and Da among them.

I wear white, my sari swelling in anguish, curling in the rain.

'The Goddess of Rain wasn't satisfied with milk and produce, she wanted human sacrifice,' the villagers say, flicking their gaze heavenward and wiping their eyes.

'Rubbish. This deluge is because the Gods are mourning the devastation, the senseless loss of precious lives, right along with us,' the matrons aver.

The village is half the size now, diminished, defeated. Muslims and Hindus comfort each other. There is a scarlet, smouldering sensation of loss, of innocence wrenched from even the smallest child. The hiss of a struck match resounds in the survivors' ears.

I imagine maroon as the colour of sorrow. A deep, deathly maroon, the exact shade of viscous, clotted blood, exuding the dusky-rose scent of regret, a smoky odour that will haunt me for the rest of my life.

The moist wood that fuels your and Da's pyre, hisses and spits, the flames radiating bittersweet amber longing—the ache for more time together—and leaving a scorched taste in my mouth. It oozes the grey aroma of wet ash and precious instants lost to the quirks of fallible memory. I stand and I grieve and I promise you, Ma, that the first thing I am going to do after is to find Puja.

After your cremation, I walk down the fields to our hut, thinking to change from my wet clothes before I go looking for Puja again. My steps drag with loneliness and grief, as I near the two-room cottage that feels empty and too large without you and Da and Puja. It is besieged by memories, pickled by grief and strewn with lingering tendrils of happier times.

As I am almost upon the hut, a plaintive, mewling sound, in high contrast to the dog's howl and skitter of rain, startles me. Has Janakiamma's cat had her kittens in the field somewhere?

The dog is circling the mango tree, ears cocked, emitting soft whines. I have never seen him like this before. Does he have an inkling of what's happened, and that his owners are no more?

'What's the matter, eh?' I ask, squatting down to scratch the itchy spot under his neck.

And that is when I see it. Shimmering through a curtain of rain, a basket like the one the fisherwomen use, is set down at the base of the mango tree. It seems to be filled with blankets, and the mewling sound issuing from within.

The dog bounds away from me, towards the basket and stands guard.

And that is how I find her, Ma, a mewling, squirming package under the mango tree—the tree from where I watched Puja being kicked out of our family and life. Its wide branches shield her from the rain. The dog watches over her, somehow knowing that she is precious.

She enters my life at its lowest point, and turns it around, transforming me for the better.

I breathe in the tart smell of raw mango and wet leaves and soggy earth and something else, something fresh and new and green, as I pull away the blankets to find the source of the noise.

A tuft of dark hair, a pointy face, a cherub mouth puckered in a wail.

A baby.

I blink and rock on my haunches. I look again. It is still there. It emits a sorry little excuse for a cry that wedges right into my heart.

I pick it up and hold it close. It snuggles into me. It smells of innocence and milk and miracles and faith.

'There, there, sweetie, shush,' I whisper, rubbing the baby's delicate comma shaped back, soft as lambskin, fragile as fairy wings, and in the process of dispensing comfort, the part of me that has been flailing since I lost you and Da, Ma, fractionally settles.

In the corner of my eye, I catch a flicker of someone running across the fields. I look up in time to see a woman, a lined face, a tangle of silver hair, disappear over the knoll beyond the stream, which had dried up but is now surging again. Before I can cry out, ask if she's the one who left the baby, she's gone.

The baby's cries subside into hiccups.

Cradling the babe, I squat down beside the basket under the fragrant, moisture stippled branches of the mango tree. The dog comes up and crouches beside me.

That is when I see the note in Puja's bold, curvy script, peeking from between the dislodged blankets.

It says: '*Sharda, when I am down, it is your face that flowers before my eyes, that offers relief. Your gentleness, your kind smile.*

You, who used to heft me everywhere on your hip, breathing in my ear, "You are very special, Puja. The most special girl in the world."

I did not mean to hurt you. I am sorry for everything. I am sorry.

Please. Can you find it in yourself to love her like you loved me?'

And at the bottom: *'Could you call her Kushi—happiness, so her name is the harbinger of good things to come for her? And they will—for she has you.'*

The baby has fallen asleep in my arms.

She has you.

I take comfort from its miniature features, peaceful in repose, its little hands clasped in tight fists as if clutching hope in one hand and serenity in another, its lips flickering upwards in sleep as if stroked by an angel that has bestowed it with happy dreams despite what is happening in its immediate world.

I am sorry too, Puja. Sorry that you had to go through all this alone. Sorry that it had to come to this. What did you have to endure to get to this point, Puja? What was going on in your head that you felt you had no recourse but to give up your child?

I open my mouth and the tears I did not even know I was shedding flood my throat and mingle with rain and regret.

❋ ❋ ❋

We move to the my aunt's hut at the top of the hill, Kushi, the dog, (who won't leave Kushi's side) and I, the hut that offered Puja shelter while she was pregnant with Kushi, the hut where she lived until she disappeared on the day of the fire.

And it feels as if we are at the very top of the world, far away from the village and its ash permeated heartbreak, where a hesitant new layer of familiar saffron mud hides the scorch marks, the charred earth, the bloody evidence of the conflagration that has taken place.

Whenever I think of it, (which is almost all the time), I catch a whiff of smoke and heartbreak. I see Da's body, unflinching as the rain battered his poor, charred face. I picture the ghost of our stall where we had such wonderful times and I close my eyes and wish with all my heart to go back in time to how it was before, with Puja safe and happy with us and with the addition of Kushi too now, of course.

And every single time, I open my eyes and hope against hope that my wish has come true, that you and Da are squatting in front of baskets of papayas and guavas as usual and shaking your heads at my fantastic claims of fire and death.

What a romantic fool I am sometimes, eh, Ma!

I suppose this is why I love cooking so much, because while I do so, I feel you are there, somehow, cooking alongside me like you did that very first time, the day you told me the important news that I was going to have a sibling, that I was going to be a big sister.

I imagine telling you and Da about Kushi. I picture the two of you with her. How happy you both would be to have a grandchild! How blessed!

Aunt Nilamma is ill. She is suffering from smoke inhalation from when she went to the market looking for you and

Da, Ma. I tend to her and to Kushi and in between, I scout for jobs.

I have given up the medical degree. I cannot be doing that as well as looking after Kushi. Nilamma is not well enough to care for Kushi and no-one else, with the exception of aunt's friend Gangamma, will come near us. I have become a pariah now, an unwed mother, the lowest of the low.

'Whore,' the inhabitants of Nilamma's village label me. 'Slut.'

They point and jeer, spitting and crossing the street to avoid me. I am not served in the shops. It is Gangamma who gets the groceries for me and I cook for her in return.

Most of the time I don't let it get to me. I am strong and cheerful for Kushi and my poorly aunt. But some days when I collect the shopping from Gangamma and she asks me how I am, I succumb to the tears that I have been suppressing for what seems like forever.

'Look around you, Sharda,' Gangamma says, gently patting my back, 'These people have hardly any food and no proper roof over their heads. They have nothing but the fragile veneer of their respectability to lay claim to. They feel better about themselves when they pass judgement on someone else. Believe me, it is not about you.'

I sniff, wipe my face with my sari pallu, squeeze Gangamma's hand, and begin the long trudge back up the hill. It is a blessing, I think, even as the bags of groceries dig into my palms, that my aunt's hut is so remote, otherwise we would have had to endure much more than just spitting and name calling.

Sometimes I wonder if Puja left me Kushi as a form of punishment for what I, along with you and Da, did to her? I wonder if she knew that this was what she would have to endure as a single mother and decided to pass the baton on to me.

I don't know how I feel about Puja. I am angry with her, still. I am hurt, the hurt having multiplied when I realised that Kushi is Gopi's child. But I also feel sorry for Puja, for everything she went through all alone, without the bolstering support of us, her family. Now I understand why Puja asked the landlord if she could marry Gopi. It was a desperate act on the part of a floundering girl.

Is Kushi Puja's way of giving me something of Gopi because she stole him from me?

I love Kushi like nothing and no one else. It was love at first sight as it was with Puja, Ma, but with none of the jealousy. How could I resent this tiny new life, this helpless minuscule being who had come into my world on the rain ravaged day when I bid adieu to you and Da, a blessing at a time when I had never felt more alone?

Whatever her reasons, I am grateful to Puja for the gift of Kushi, this little girl who floods my heart with love, and chases away the anger and the guilt, the regret and the blame, the taint of smoke and fire, and the bile of betrayal.

'She said she would wait in the hut for us,' Nilamma said bewildered, between wracking coughs, when I asked her where Puja was, the day I found Kushi. She was staying at Gangamma's house, as she was too weak to climb back up the hill to her hut the day of the fire, which is why, when I went to look for Puja on the day of your cremation, the hut was empty.'

'I thought she was at home.' Nilamma's eyes blinked repeatedly in dumbfounded surprise as she took in the fact of the baby. 'I did not even know she was pregnant. I had not an inkling.'

I went to find the wise woman, having placed the wiry hair, and the shambling gait of the woman I'd seen disappearing across the waterlogged fields when I found Kushi.

Marrows dangled from the low beams of her hut, green and yellow dancing bubbles. The piquant fragrance of ripening mulch and ground spices infused the air. Conjee simmered merrily on the hearth, tapping the lid of the pot, and making it dance, the gruel effervescing out of the sides.

The wise woman's eyes lit up when she saw Kushi, who was drifting to sleep in my arms, her hands thrown up on either side of her diminutive head in exquisite surrender, her breath coming in sweet, milk-scented gasps.

'It was you who left her under the mango tree for me to find,' I said.

She nodded. 'I waited until I was sure she had won your heart. And then I left.'

'Why leave her there? Why not just give her to me?'

'Would you have taken her from me if I had held her out to you saying she was your sister's child with Gopi? You would not even have looked at Kushi, this manifestation of your sister's final treachery. I wanted you to fall in love with Kushi, to consider Kushi for herself, and not in connection with anybody else. You needed to look forward not back. To be reminded of the immense love you are capable of and not the hate that has recently begrimed your heart.'

'Where is my sister?'

The wise woman sighed, a deep, weary exhalation and at that moment, she looked her age. 'I don't know. Your ma had given her some gold bangles. I sold them for her. She took the money and left.'

'Why did you let her go?'

She sighed again. 'I tried talking her out of it. But her mind was made up. And it was not my place.' Looking pointedly at me.

'What would you have wanted me to do?' I snapped. 'I didn't even know she was pregnant.'

She raised her eyebrows. *Exactly.*

'You expected me to find her and beg her to come home after she had betrayed me so horribly?'

The wise woman did not say anything but her eyebrows stayed raised.

I was glad I was holding Kushi, as I was beset by a sudden urge to walk up to her and slap them back in place.

'Why did she leave her child to me?' I held Kushi close, breathing in her pure, clean, new baby scent to chase away the anger, the upset.

How dared this woman blame me? When Puja was the one who claimed Gopi from me, destroying our family; Puja who shamelessly went to the landlord, asking if she could marry Gopi; Puja who slept with him, Gopi who was meant for *me*.

Kushi, the miracle blooming out of this chaos, sighed contentedly in her sleep, her little chest heaving up and down. Strips of light sneaked in through the gaps in the mat that masqueraded as the front door of the wise woman's hut and played on her face.

I wouldn't want it any other way, but I have to know why Puja left Kushi with me. I don't want Puja to change her mind again, to come and snatch Kushi away, having decided she wants her child back, after all, when this child is the reason I'm able to survive, go on in a world where I have lost everything and everyone who mattered: you; Da; Puja; Gopi—my unsullied version of him, that is, a sensitive boy beneath the brash façade he presented to the world; and my dream of becoming a doctor.

The wise woman picked up a coconut shell ladle and stirred the conjee. She sighed again and sat down, joints creaking. 'She did not trust herself with her child. She was convinced she was cursed, unworthy of Kushi. She thought her love was not enough, and she could think of only one person to whom she could trust her child, only one person who would give her child everything she herself yearned to, who would bring Kushi up the way she wanted to but didn't believe she could.'

When it mattered, Puja, I let you down. And yet you did not hold that against me.

I already love Kushi more than life itself. I will not let you or Kushi down in this regard, Puja, I promise.

The wise woman came towards me and extended a shrivelled hand to my cheek, her palm cool against my burning skin. It came away wet with my tears.

'She thought you would make a wonderful mother. She told me that with you, Kushi would never want for love.' The wise woman nodded at Kushi slumbering peacefully in my arms. 'She was right.' A breath, then, 'This child is incredibly blessed, to be loved so profoundly. Puja loved her so much she gave her away. Giving Kushi to you was penance for her perceived sins, her attempt at redemption and at securing the best possible future for her child, at the cost of her own happiness. And for you, this cherub is salvation: for allowing a man to come between you and your sister; for wilfully breaking the bond you promised to cherish; for abandoning your sibling whom you vowed to protect. Isn't it?' The wise woman's penetrating stare was like being skewered by light which shone directly into my soul and found it accountable.

I ignored her question, and asked one of my own.

'Will Puja come back?' The words trembled as they fell out my mouth.

Since she loves this child so much, how will she be able to stay away? What if she comes back to claim Kushi—this babe I already think of as mine—as easily as she gave her to me?

The wise woman shook her head, enveloping me, once more, in her piercing, silver gaze. 'I don't think so.'

I believed her.

I let out the breath I had been holding, feeling ashamed and guilty that I was awash with relief.

❋ ❋ ❋

Despite my worries about Puja taking Kushi away from me, I do try and honour the promise I made to you on your deathbed and attempt to look for her, Ma.

I try.

But it is as if she has disappeared into thin air.

No-one knows her whereabouts, least of all Gopi, whom I corner, one dozy cardamom-and-ginger-scented afternoon, at the spice sorting warehouse which I have heard he is managing for his father. I leave Kushi in Gangamma's care when I go to see him.

I am directed to his office, passing mountains of spices, the zesty fragrance assaulting my nose, a heady potpourri.

Gopi stands up when he sees me, his cowardly gaze not meeting mine, resting instead somewhere in the region of my feet.

He looks older, more serious.

'Sharda.' He holds out his hand to shake and I think of this same hand offering a chocolate that began a friendship, that in my mind had developed into so much more.

Silly girl.

I feel nothing for him now, except a faint revulsion. I look at his face and try to link it with Kushi's features. I cannot. Kushi is her own person.

I think of the soft black locks of hair on her delicate head, her wiggling body, her rosebud mouth and I am beset by an ache to be with her, innocence and light, not here with this man I never expected or wanted to see again.

I do not take his hand. He lets it drop to his side.

'What can I do for you?' His tone business-like. A stranger making a polite enquiry.

'Do you know where Puja is?'

And just like that, his impersonal mask crumples and I see the needy boy yearning for affection who I discerned a few times, way back when I used to teach him maths.

'I haven't seen her. Since . . . since . . . '

Since you slept with her.

I hadn't really expected Gopi to know where Puja was. I don't know if what I feel is relief or disappointment.

I do want to find Puja.

And I don't.

Selfishly, I want to carry on being the centre of Kushi's world. I want to be the one she will toddle up to when she is hurt, the one to kiss her bruised knee better. I want mine to be the neck around which she will throw her small arms, the shoulder into which she will snuggle when she is sleepy, and the face she sees when she wakes from a bad dream.

'I. . . I heard that you have a baby now.' He gulps, his Adam's apple bobbing nervously in his throat.

He has lost weight, I realise. He seems to be shrinking into himself.

That is what guilt does to one. I know the feeling.

'Yes.' I look right at him, my voice cool as the wind that warns of a storm.

'It's . . . it's Puja's isn't it?' His voice as faltering as the first shaky steps of a toddler.

'You know?' Heat colours my voice chilli-powder red.

'She came to me one night asking . . . '

'You knew about the baby, *your* baby, and did nothing?' My voice is quivering with rage.

'What could I do?' he shrugs helplessly.

'She carried the baby to term. She gave birth to it. She was all alone. She must have been terrified.' My whole body is trembling. 'You are a cowardly, cowardly man. We are both much better off without you.'

I don't know if I mean me and Puja or me and Kushi. I am all feeling, a hot ball of surging anger.

'Didn't you "love" her?' I throw over my shoulder.

'Didn't you?' he counters and I turn.

He looks at me, eyebrows raised, a challenge in his eyes. He has recovered his composure, is standing tall, shoulders pushed back and in his swagger, I can see the cocky boy he was back then. 'You call *me* cowardly. Ha! She was all alone. Whose fault is that?'

I walk out of his office shaking, unable to control the fury heaving through my body, mingling with throbbing guilt, the knowledge that what he's said is true.

I want to break something. Anything.

I pick up a stone and hurl it at the window of the warehouse, made of glass unlike the wooden shutters of the villagers' huts. It smashes into a thousand kaleidoscopic shards, and the trapped aroma of a multitude of spices escapes in an intoxicating gush of savoury air.

There is uproar.

'Aiyyo, what is she doing? The slut! Has she gone completely mad? Why on earth did Saar agree to see her?'

Two men come up and apprehend me, not daring to touch the tart, of course, just crowding me so I cannot escape.

'Saar, the whore broke the window.'

Gopi comes rushing out, halting to a shuddering stop when he sees me. He runs a hand through his thinning hair.

'It's okay. It's nothing. Let her go and get back to work,' he says not looking at me.

Coward to the last.

❋ ❋ ❋

Week after week, I bundle Kushi in a sari tied snugly around my waist, close to my heart, and trudge into Nilamma's village in order to look for work.

Every morning, I go out into the world boldly and every evening I return defeated, trying to hide the disappointment, etching lines into my face, from Nilamma.

I stand outside the doors to the smaller houses I have been doing the circuits of—none of them are locked, nobody shuts doors in the villages, there's nothing to steal—and call.

The owners come and shoo me away saying there is no job going.

'Anything, I will do anything,' I plead.

'There's nothing here for the likes of you, whore. Do you think we're silly enough to let you steal our husbands? We know how you work, you women with no morals.'

The standard reply I have been getting used to.

In desperation, I decide to try the bigger houses at the other end of the village, the houses I have avoided thus far, knowing that if the lay villagers do not want me, these posh people will want me even less. They are, after all, in cahoots with the landlord—even though he resides in the village across the river, he has made sure to spread slander far and wide. And after my antics at the warehouse, news of which has also circulated, why would they offer me a job?

But, I have to feed this lovely bundle of joy hugging my chest, this diminutive mouth that roots around for milk, somehow.

Gangamma sold your karimani for me, Ma, and we have been surviving on that cash. Once it runs out, there's one more necklace to fall back on. After that . . . I shudder to think.

I need a job, any job. I will beg, if necessary, swallowing my pride and hoping for the best.

I am turned away from the first three houses. Shadows are swallowing the red earth, imbuing it the lacklustre grey of dwindling hope and my precious bundle is getting cranky after having been so patient all day, moving this way and that inside the constraints of the sari sling, trying to bite at my shoulder, at my breast, hoping for sustenance.

'One last house and then we will go home, love,' I whisper.

At the sound of my voice, Kushi looks intently up at me, blinks and then, as if she has understood what I've said, sticks a thumb into her mouth and settles into me, resting her head trustingly on the pillow of my chest. I bend down and press a kiss on her delicate head, breathing in her pink, happy smell: flowers and earth and innocence. She emits a soft coo in response.

The evening air that brushes my cheeks is sweet, fragranced with roses and hibiscus and aboli. I turn the corner and chance upon a little house, set away from the mud path, sitting snug among the fields. The house is encircled by a crumbling moss-embroidered brick wall, and it appears to sprout from a garden busy with flowers, a messy profusion of red, yellow and apricot. Once painted the bright green of new life, the walls are now faded to a weary olive, and it looks for all the world like a fairy-tale cottage set in the midst of a verdant wild wood. And in the soft fuchsia mellifluence of the setting sun, the gloom of early evening lurking up its sides, it gleams a magical, velvety gold.

I walk up to the front door and knock. The door is not as polished as the bigger houses'. In fact, it is going a bit to seed, with evidence of wood lice at the corners.

No answer. I have grown to expect this. I decide to try one last time.

'Hello?' I call.

No answer but my little babe opens sleepy eyes and squints up at me. I plant a kiss on her cheek smelling of sleep, tasting of faith, her whisper-soft skin untouched by the depredations of life.

'Hello?' I call again loathe to go back with nothing to show for a day's worth of job hunting yet again. Kushi starts to cry and I dance from one foot to another to try and soothe her, distract her from the calls of her hungry stomach. When that doesn't work, I move close to the fragrant rose buds and bend down, so her nose is almost touching the smiling magenta blooms.

Kushi breathes the smell in and opens her eyes wide in surprise. I laugh. I am dead on my feet, defeated by the day's losses, worried about how we'll manage when the money runs out. And yet this tiny bundle can make me laugh; make me appreciate the small wonders of daily life.

I think of Puja, of what she is missing, all these small milestones.

Where are you?

So many slip-ups, Puja, culminating in this little miracle who is the manifestation of your immense sacrifice. This angel who is my salvation. She has cleansed my heart of hate, made me whole again.

Thank you, for giving her to me.

In loving her, I love you. In loving her, I repent daily for what I did to you, to us. In loving her, I have learnt to forgive myself.

Have you?

I hope you are happy. I hope you are well.

'Are you enjoying the flowers? They smell wonderful, don't they?' a deep masculine voice says and I almost fall backward into the rose bush in shock.

A strong arm rights me before Kushi wails.

The owner of the strong arm is a small man, with a bushy beard that obscures his face, and crinkly laugh lines that radiate from the corners of his eyes.

I know this man. He has a god-like status in this village. Everyone for miles around has heard of him and looks up to him. He is the teacher who distributes most of his salary among the villagers, the one who educates the slum children in his spare time.

'And who have we here?' he says and smiles down at my babe who peers drowsily up at him. 'Aren't you the cutest sight to behold, more divine even than the flowers?'

I am so surprised that I cannot help it showing on my face. I have never seen a man so natural with babies before, so very at ease. The other village men avoid babies (even their own, especially their own), as they would venomous snakes; infants are, after all, their women's privilege.

And nobody in this village with the exception of Gangamma has talked to me like this up until now, as if I am an equal and not lowly scum from the back of the beyond.

'Is this your house?' I ask when I find my voice.

His eyes shift from the baby to me and I am encompassed by his intelligent, kind brown gaze.

'Yes,' he says.

'I-I . . .' I gulp, and the words come all at once. 'I'm looking for work, do you by any chance need . . .'

'Ha,' he booms, a huge voice for a small man, and claps his hands. 'I have been looking for a housekeeper, as it happens. Providence. Come inside, see if it suits.'

It takes a few minutes for what he has said to sink in. Surely it can't be happening like this, so easily after all that desperate searching. Where's the snag?

Since you and Da passed, Ma, I've become an expert at reading faces; I've had to, in order to survive. Every inch of this man radiates benevolence. And yet, even though I know I cannot afford to turn down this job, I am wary, especially now I have this cherub to care for and protect.

'Your wife, is she in need of a housekeeper?' I ask, more to determine what he is really asking of me.

'I lost my wife last year,' a shadow clouds his face. 'One of the village women comes and cooks for me, but what I would really like is a housekeeper to look after the house, do the cleaning and tame this garden while I'm at school. I am a teacher, you see.'

I know, I want to say. But I keep mum and ruminate on his offer instead.

It sounds ideal. I can picture Kushi sitting in the garden while I hang the washing out to dry, a beautiful bloom among beautiful blooms.

But first . . . I had better tell him. For he must have heard the rumours, surely? Nevertheless, this kind of thing is better out in the open. The words stick in my throat but I force them out. I do not want him finding out and throwing us out, just as we are settling in.

'I . . . I have to tell you . . . '

He smiles at me and his eyes are warm as he waves my words away. 'I've heard all the gossip. News travels fast in this village.'

I've heard about you too. Are you really as good as the stories I've heard make you out to be?

He is party to the rumours. Is he taking them at face value? He's lost his wife. He sees a woman with a baby and no husband. What exactly does he want?

'Then why are you giving me the job?' My voice is belligerent, scarlet as a heart not daring to hope, or to clutch at a lifeline in case it turns out to be poisonous ivy.

He scrunches his face in puzzlement, and then, when my meaning sinks in, his eyes grow wide with understanding.

'Please,' he says, looking right at me. 'Your honour is safe with me. All I want is a housekeeper.'

'Are you really the god the villagers make you out to be?'
I can't help but ask.

What is the matter with you Sharda?

After the experiences I've had since Kushi, I've learnt the hard way not to trust people so easily, lest they bite when my back is turned. They look at me and see the lowest of the low: a woman with a child and no husband, a woman of easy virtue, a woman who will stoop to anything. They treat me the way they wouldn't their mothers and sisters and children and that isn't saying much. You can't be too careful, is what I've learnt.

'Ah, you've heard then.' He pinches the bridge of his nose. 'My wife . . . she died of complications from a fever caused by a mosquito bite. Two days was all it took. She was well on Monday, gone by Thursday. And I . . .' His eyes shine wetly, 'For a while I sank into depression. Not eating. Not talking. Barely managing to survive. And then one of my students came here, a little boy who said he missed me, and that nobody else could teach quite like I did.' He rubs his forehead, takes a breath. 'I dragged myself back to work. And among those children, their innocence and their enthusiasm, I found myself again. A version of myself in any case.' He sighs deeply. 'My wife . . . she adored children, dreamed of having a houseful someday . . . Anyhow, on my way home from school, one evening, I noticed the emaciated children of the slums begging for food . . . And here I was with my cottage and money and food I didn't want to eat. And so, I started giving it away, to help those kids.'

He smiles, a gentle, sad smile that makes me ache.

'People say I am good. Pshaw. Stuff and nonsense. The fact is, I am selfish. I do it for myself. It gets me through the days, and gives me a reason for living.' He nods at me. 'Now, I've never been this honest with anyone in the first few moments of meeting with them. You're a great listener Sharda. I hope you'll be just as good a housekeeper, if you decide to take the job, that is?' He smiles and this time the sadness is confined to the corners of his eyes.

I go with my instincts and nod, hoping I am not making a terrible mistake. 'The villagers won't be happy,' I say.

We'll make a right pair won't we? You the saint and me the sinner, in their eyes.

'Not that my housekeeper is any of their business but I know what you mean.' He rubs his hands together. 'We'll convince them otherwise. I like a good challenge.'

Kushi stirs, whimpers.

'Come and see the house and then you can decide,' he says, ushering me to the door.

He fumbles with the key, and then we are inside, in the foyer smelling of neglect and knowledge, books everywhere, the damp, delightful scent of books.

I breathe in deep. I picture days after my work is done, sitting down and reading, Kushi playing beside me, working my way down all these haphazard piles, my idea of heaven. I lean against the doorjamb, lightheaded suddenly. Is it really this easy? I feel tears sting my eyes. Why now, I think, when everything for once, is working my way.

'Thank you,' I whisper. 'Thank you so much.'

'Well,' he says and I see that beneath his beard he is blushing. I have embarrassed him. 'You can cook, can't you? I didn't think to ask.'

And I smile through my tears and then I am laughing and Kushi looks up at me and then her lips lift upwards and I say, 'Look, she is smiling! Her first smile!' and I am awed.

I am blessed.

❋ ❋ ❋

A procession of villagers comes to my employer's house. They call him 'Sir' and make it their duty to tell him their version of my story: a malign, shameless vamp, who takes advantage of honest men.

Sir nods and tells them that he knows and then he invites them in and asks them to partake of the food I have cooked and they leave singing my praises, saying they have never tasted anything like it.

Bit by bit, I am accepted into the reluctant folds of the village. My name is not uttered in the same breath as 'slut'. Instead I am the woman whose fingers work magic, the fabulous cook who works for Sir, isn't he lucky? And in time, with the inevitable fading of collective memory, I become Kushi's parent, the mother of the amiable child who smiles adorably at everyone.

On my first day at the job, I tell my employer my story, the whole, unabridged truth.

'I'd heard of you,' he says. 'Everybody around here has heard of the local girl who got first rank in PUC. I understood from the papers that you were going to study medicine.' And then, after a pause, his kind eyes earnest, 'Would you like to continue with your medical degree? I could loan you the money.'

Tears flood my eyes at his generosity. 'I . . .' I fiddle with my sari pallu.

'I mean it,' he says and I look up. 'You're so talented. It's a loan you know, you can pay me back in time . . . '

'Thank you so much, Sir,' I rub my eyes with the pallu of my sari. 'But I'll say no for now.'

'Think about it,' he says. 'I think you'd make an excellent doctor.'

But I know it is not going to happen, Ma. That ship has passed. Kushi is now my life. I'll concentrate on bringing her up, making her into the woman I wasn't, the woman Puja tried so hard to be: modern and fearless and unbound by tradition, unafraid to take on the world.

❄ ❄ ❄

Kushi grows a little every day. She's recently started to crawl and she roams the house on all fours, a delightful, delighted little thing, always laughing, extremely sociable, charming all and sundry, so much like her mother.

The stain of my arrival in this village, the stink of scandal has been chased away by the fragrance of my cooking. This is my calling, I realise. Cooking has always made me happy; it is when I feel closest to you. Seeing others savour and enjoy what I have prepared gives me great joy.

Also, I am beginning to have feelings for Sir. Or I should say Naresh, as that's what he's asked me to call him.

'I call you Sharda, so please call me Naresh,' he's said, flashing his earnest smile at me.

I respect Naresh and admire him. He is a man who has tasted sorrow, survived loss, a man who cares, a man who reads, a man with principles, a man I am growing to love.

❋ ❋ ❋

When Kushi is almost a year old, Nilamma passes away, quietly in her sleep, having never quite recovered from the smoke inhalation.

One evening, a month or so after the cremation, as I am cooking potato bondas for Naresh's tea, he asks me to marry him.

'I love you, Sharda,' he says. 'You're the strongest and most intelligent woman I know. I admire you more than anyone I've ever met. You take what life throws at you and make the best of it. You have this elastic and unparalleled capacity to love. You're fiercely loyal and so perfectly wonderful . . . '

'I'm not,' I say, tears streaming down my cheeks and dripping onto my sari blouse. 'I . . . I'm not worthy of your love . . . I've made so many mistakes. My sister . . . I . . . '

'You're only human,' he says softly. 'I'd have done the same.'

'I doubt . . .'

But before I can get another word out, he comes and puts his arms around me and then he lifts my face and kisses me on the mouth.

Kushi toddles up to us while I am still breathless with wonder, and savouring that wonderful kiss that tasted of heaven. It is the flavour I aim for every time I cook and never get quite right; the taste of love, of being loved.

Kushi squats on her bottom and lifts her arms. She looks right at Naresh. 'Da,' she says, 'Dada.'

And Naresh raises an eyebrow at me and says, 'Well, she's made up her mind, at least, and much faster than you too.'

I laugh and I'm crying and he hoists Kushi up and he puts his arms around me, gathering us both in his embrace.

Kushi looks at Naresh and says, 'Da,' and she looks at me and says, 'Ma.'

She touches my eyes and puts her hand to her mouth before either of us can say anything, and her face scrunches up in a look of pure disgust. She opens her mouth, sticks her tongue out and blows raspberries to get rid of the tang of salt.

Both Naresh and I burst out laughing, and her mouth, puckered up to cry, relaxes, and she smiles, brings her palms together and claps, a trick she's recently learned.

And I look at the three of us grouped in Naresh's strong arms in the warm kitchen aromatic with hot oil and roasted spices and think, *We're a family.*

I will not dwell on what will happen if Puja decides to come back and claim Kushi. I will live in the present, with this man who loves me and this girl who has claimed Naresh and me for her own and who lives up to her name and fills our lives with such *kushi*, untold happiness.

Chapter 39
Kushi

The Humble Skin of an Onion

When I read the bit where Ma finds a baby under the mango tree, I am intrigued. Where is this child?

I find out soon enough.

I set down the letters very carefully. They waver and dance before my eyes. The cracked ceiling sways and then rights itself. A lizard hugs the wall. It flicks its tongue at me.

Bile threatens, sluggish, bitter. Nausea heaves; my stomach cringes from the truth it is finding so hard to swallow, from the earthy scent of betrayal and the musty odour of exposed secrets.

I try and fail to reconcile the familiar contours of Ma's beloved face, conjured up by my stunned mind, with this new knowledge that is burning a hole inside me, the words that I've just read, that are percolating through my brain like stones sinking to the bottom of a jar of water.

How can you look like the woman I've known and loved when you've revealed yourself to be someone completely different?

I thought I could rely on Ma. She was my constant. My knowledge of her, the one rigid certainty in this lopsided world.

I remember the time my classmate Sonia told me how she had seen Guru's wife drowning the kittens from her cat's litter in a gunny bag, and described at length their pitiful mews as they sank in the lake.

'But my ma told me that they were all given away,' I'd insisted, 'and my ma doesn't lie.'

'I saw them,' Sonia said. 'Guru's wife put them in a gunny bag, tied it with a string and then threw it in the lake. I heard their mewling.'

'Ma doesn't lie,' I'd yelled then. 'My ma *doesn't* lie. You must have seen some other kittens,' my voice breaking, barely shy of a whisper.

'You don't lie, Ma,' I murmur now, realising, even as I say so that what I had held all my life to be the truth—my mother's honesty—is a lie. My world, already askew, has now upended.

I root around for anger. I find none. Just numbness, shock, and . . . understanding.

Everything suddenly makes sense: why she never told me about Puja; why she kept her past hidden, why she lied. My beloved mother who taught me to value honesty, to be a stickler for truth.

It is like looking through a microscope. I did that once when Da—Da? But what else can I call him?—brought me to the science museum here in Palmipur. At first, I could not make out anything at all through the lens. Then, Da adjusted the focus and I could see, so clearly, all the intricate patterns gracing the humble skin of an onion.

I was amazed, stupefied. For once, I was tongue-tied.

Da teased me about it all the way back.

'You witnessed one miracle and I another,' he said. 'I'll bring you to the museum again just to experience the phenomenon of you not talking for more than a minute.'

You should look at me now, Da. I am rendered speechless, completely mute, by a few squiggly words penned onto ageing paper.

I feel as if I am enclosed in a weird balloon that encompasses this mind-numbing knowledge that has tilted my world, toppled it, and it seems as if the moaning and groaning of patients, the scurrying and tending, soothing and ministering of nurses is happening outside, in the ordinary world which hasn't been warped by this comprehension, this befuddling awareness.

I imagine walking away from here, putting one foot in front of the other, my stride lengthening until I am running, stumbling out of the hospital, with its overpowering smells of medicine and illness and death, and out into the crisp, precipitation-laden coolness of a summer's night.

I want to open my mouth and inhale huge gulps of ordinary air that tastes of dew-seasoned jasmine buds, as if the very act of doing so will take me into before, when I was healthy and whole, when all I was concerned with were my studies and my causes, when I was not scared and defeated and hooked to machines, when I was not awaiting a kidney from . . . from my mother.

Chapter 40
Raj

A God with an Elephant Head

The taxi driver jumps out, leaving the engine running, and lifting his hand, he slaps the boot hard.

Raj's mum flinches as if it is she who has been hit.

Raj looks at her, this woman he has lived with all his life and never knew. This woman who has been hiding a whole other life so carefully under that accomplished, brittle veneer. This woman who had suffered ostracism and endured disgrace, lost her parents and given birth by the time she was only slightly older than he is now. This woman who has been through the wringer and emerged, perhaps not whole, but emerged nonetheless and managed to survive by sheer dint of will.

His mother.

The driver hits the boot of the car again.

'What're you doing?' Raj asks.

The driver grins, yellow, toothless, as, with another hefty thump, the boot yawns open.

'Third time lucky, always,' he says as he hefts their suitcase from the boot.

Ellie, Raj thinks, *I wish you could see this.*

Raj's mum turns and looks at the hospital building, taking in the shrine at the entrance, a god with an elephant head, bedecked with garlands and exuding the scent of sandalwood and incense. The next minute she's standing in front of the shrine, her eyes closed, hands folded in supplication and lips moving earnestly in prayer.

'Mum,' Raj nudges after a bit. 'You've got to pay the driver.'

'Oh,' his mother rummages in her bag and takes out some notes. 'Keep the change,' she tells the driver.

The taxi driver's eyes light up as he counts the notes and pockets them. Thanking Puja profusely and, flashing another yellow grin, he drives away in a blizzard of dust, giving a grateful wave and an ear-splitting honk on the horn—the only part of his unsteady jalopy that properly works.

Although dusk has already painted the sky the colour of ripe grapes, the heat is unrelenting, moist, and clings to Raj's skin, leaching into his very soul.

Hawkers compete with each other in yelling the benefits of their offerings, a last-ditch attempt to sell their wares before they pack up for the day. Specks of grime swirl in the spiced air.

Fisherwomen walk past, nattering busily while simultaneously chewing what looks like spittle-flecked red gloop. Their hips swaying with natural grace, they heft their almost empty baskets on their heads; fish scales glint where they have stuck to skin and cloth.

Men mill around beside a small lean-to, sipping sunset coloured tea from minuscule tumblers, and biting into orange coated snacks that the vendor serves straight from the spluttering oil of a giant frying pan.

'What did you do with the baby?' Raj asks. The question that has been building on his lips, sitting on his tongue, is finally out. 'Mum?'

A bus trundles up to the bus stop opposite and wheezes to a rickety stop, sounding like an arthritic old man.

A pall falls across his mum's face, like clouds hijacking the sun. 'I loved her so much. I ached to hold her. But I didn't so much as touch her. I did not want to blot her with my imperfect love.'

'Her.'

'Yes. I asked Sharda to name her Kushi, in the letter I left with her. I hoped the name would be the herald of good things to come for her. It was so hard to stay away. But I did. I did not so much as call to find out how she was doing. I had left her with Sharda because I'd thought I was doing the best by her. But sometimes I worried that I had limited her life by leaving her behind. I wanted to know if she too yearned to escape the village, if she too was bound by the constraints I had been. I wanted to know if she was happy, if her life had lived up to the name I had given her. I wanted to watch her grow. I wanted to hold her close and not let go.' A quivering breath escapes her. 'I did nothing. I didn't dare keep in touch. I did not want to selfishly uproot her life, the life I had bequeathed her by giving her away, just because I yearned for her. I'd made my decision. I stuck to it. But it's eaten away at me, I realise now. Talking to you, telling you the story of my past, it's opened my eyes. That decision, it affected me, changed me and by extension, it affected you too, Raj. It's reduced me to this person who couldn't love. This shell.'

'Kushi is *your* daughter?'

'She is.'

'That's why you are here. That's why you couldn't say no to your sister.'

He gets it now. Finally he understands why his mother dropped everything to come here. He'd thought it was because of her sister, had surmised Sharda had some sort of hold on his mother.

But it was Kushi all along. His mother's first born child. Her *daughter*. His sister.

'You'll give her your kidney.' It is not a question.

'I'd give her my heart if that's what was needed to save her.' Her eyes glitter like frost ornamenting a winter's night, 'I'd do the same for you.'

And somehow, despite all that's gone before, despite their rocky past, he knows she would too.

He does.

Chapter 41
Puja—After

How to Begin Again

With some of the money from the sale of the bangles, Puja buys a bus ticket to Mumbai.

In the bus, the old woman sitting next to her asks, 'Where in Mumbai are you staying, child?'

The word 'child' conjures up wispy hair, wiggling limbs, a comma shaped bundle held out to her by the wise woman: 'Your child needs you. Here.'

Puja closes her eyes, and tries to will the image away. When she opens them, the old woman is waiting patiently for an answer. Her benevolent eyes seem to peer into Puja's soul.

Through the window, fields and coconut trees smothered in the charcoal tipped shroud of impending night rush past, dizzy silhouettes swaying, taking her towards a future she cannot fathom, and a life she doesn't want.

'I plan to stay in a hostel somewhere, initially, until I find a job.' She manages.

'It's a big city, child. You need to have a plan,' the woman's voice is gentle. She picks up her bag, rummages through it, takes a pen and, tearing a page out of a small green address book, copies something out onto it. 'Here, this is the number for the Ursuline Nuns' convent in Dadar. They take on girls as paying guests.'

'Thank you,' Puja says, her eyes stinging.

The woman lays a gnarled hand on Puja's. 'Take care, child. It's an immense world out there. I will pray for you. Your name is . . .?'

'Puja.'

The woman smiles, her face creasing in a kindly blessing. 'Meaning prayer. There you go.'

Kushi, Puja thinks, as the bus careers through the night towards a city she doesn't know, where she hopes she can lose herself. *Meaning happiness. I hope you are happy. I hope you find the comfort I cannot give you in my sister's arms.*

Gopi, look, I am running away, escaping like we always planned—although I feel imprisoned, not free. Have you escaped? Are you free?

❊ ❊ ❊

Mumbai is chaotic, teeming with people and vehicles, stray animals and hawkers' carts, swarming buildings and overflowing sewers. It is blue with noise and exhaust, clogged with grime and traffic, rent with honks and howls. It reeks of festering rubbish and sizzling spices. It deadens her thoughts. It is balm to her mind, an ointment to her shattered soul.

She dials the number the old woman gave her from a pay phone in the overrun bus station. She takes the overcrowded metro to Dadar, squashed in a seething bubble of people, swimming in their sweat. She breathes in their weary, work-scented thoughts, glad of a respite from her own.

She lodges in the crowded guesthouse for girls run by the Ursuline nuns in the convent in Dadar. Her roommate procures her a job as a receptionist in a multinational company two metro stops away.

Puja keeps her head down and answers the phones. She does not let visions of a wispy haired, rubbery-limbed baby intrude.

Men pay her attention. She ignores them. She has had enough of men. But one of them is persistent. The other girls at the office urge her to go for him. He is one of the top guys in the company, they say, a good catch.

He promises Puja the world. She does not go out with him.

He proposes marriage, says he will make an honest woman of her.

'We will move to England,' he says.

And that gives her pause. If she moves far enough away, then maybe she can outrun the memories, the visions of her child that dig at her at night, the persistent squalling whimpers invading her exhausted reveries.

How to Begin Again:

1) *Run away to a different country, shedding your past like a snake shedding its skin.*

2) *Hide the stomach that gives evidence of what it housed not that long ago.*

3) *Wipe the slate clean of old crimes and concentrate on a new future.*

4) *Do not allow your feelings to take you over again. Keep yourself at a remove from messy emotions, sentimental entanglements, at all times.*

※ ※ ※

England.

A country that is as cold as her heart feels without love to warm it.

She discovers that it is not far enough away.

She watches the single mothers, allowed to live their life and bring up their children without being scarred by disrepute, or brushed by the indelible paint of blame and dishonour. She wonders how Sharda is coping. She tries not to think of her child.

The stink of a sullied reputation and the taint of smoke dog her with a litany of her sins, the procession of her mistakes.

※ ※ ※

Her husband is kind. He is gentle. He gives her space.

But his patience has its limits.

He wants a child. She doesn't; a baby she longed to hold, but dared not touch, haunts her.

'Please, Puja, one child,' he begs.

'I . . . I can't, Dev,' she sighs.

'Leave me,' she says. 'I'm not right for you. You need a woman who'll love you like you deserve to be loved.'

I used you to come here, thinking I could escape my past, the deaths of my parents inextricably linked with the birth of my child.

'I do not want another woman. I love *you*,' he shouts exasperated and insanely upset.

There are fights, anger, recriminations.

She cannot bear to see her husband so upset. But she also cannot bear to bring another child into this uncertain world, fickle as the weather of this country she finds herself in, one more child she couldn't bear to lose, one more perfect being that she won't be worthy of, one more innocent angel she'll love so much that she'll be afraid to blemish it with the ineradicable mark of her countless transgressions.

So she continues to take the pill.

But then she is ill. Spiking temperature. Sickness and diarrhoea. Hallucinations. Visions of rain and fire, of death and birth. The smell of manure and blood. A wispy haired child bawling even though her name spells happiness. A squat, bespectacled girl who promises to love and protect Puja forever. Zooming on a motorbike, pigtails flying, spinning dreams of grand escapes with a boy who says she is his best friend in all the world. Sitting with Ma and Da in the market, counting out coins. Her mother laughing as they spin in the courtyard, raising a curtain of saffron dust. Her father hefting her high in the swing of his arms: *My beloved girl.*

Her husband looks after her. He soothes her. He comforts her. He holds her. And he loves her. Six weeks later, she finds out that she is pregnant.

Dev is ecstatic. She is terrified.

Nine months later, Raj is born.

This time, she is not bespattered with fear, haunted by smoke and fire and the hovering presence of death, with just the wise woman for company, in a hut smelling of drains and cow dung, and populated with marrows.

This time, she is in a sterile hospital room and it is her husband holding her hand, him and the midwife urging her to push.

And yet, she sees pregnant yellow marrows; she breathes in the smell of sewers and compost; she hears the wise woman's voice in her ear, and she is comforted by her piercing gaze.

'I won't be able to give this one away,' she wails.

'You won't have to,' the wise woman whispers gently in her ear.

Raj is born to celebrations and whoops, and there is no accompanying death. No terrifying bargain to make.

But there is penance.

A warm, squiggly being on her chest. Living, breathing, wailing, perfect. Her child. Hers.

She doesn't touch him. She cannot. How can she bear to touch this child when she didn't touch Kushi? How can she comfort this child while Kushi went uncomforted? And what if she brands him with the smear of her mistakes, or punishes him with the stamp of her foul past? She couldn't bear that.

He has his father to love him. He is better off without her cursed love. Her love is a poisonous thing that strikes when you least expect.

Her baby cries, the mournful complaint of a hungry kitten, wanting her breasts, wanting succour, wanting more than she can give. She closes her eyes. The acerbic tang of fluids and fear and fire and death and toxic love intrude into her fatigued trance. Her baby's plaintive laments splotch her battered heart, and stain her snatched dreams the waxy yellow of an oozing wound.

✽ ✽ ✽

Dev tries.

He employs a nanny. He goes to work and when he comes home, he looks after Raj.

He tries to be patient with Puja.

But she can see that it is harder for him to find the forbearance, harder to reconcile this woman who refuses to be a mother.

'Just hold him, look, he wants you to.'

Raj angles his small body towards her, trying to jump from Dev's arms to hers, his little hands stretched out, palms wriggling.

Puja imagines Raj's arms hooked tightly around her neck, her nostrils redolent with his sweet baby boy smell of earth and moisture, of joy and adventure.

She turns away, thinking of a little girl growing up in another country, calling another woman, 'Ma.'

The inevitable happens. Eventually, Dev gets tired of trying. One evening, he comes home and sits her down and from his sombre face, Puja knows what it coming.

'I can't do this anymore,' he says. 'I'm sorry, Puja.'

She nods. She understands. She has been expecting this since she married him.

'I thought my love alone could sustain us. But it's no longer enough.'

'Yes.'

'I will see Raj regularly, of course.'

'Of course.'

And just like that it is over. Another era in her life.

Now it is just her and Raj, bumbling along.

She tries to do her best by her son, but they are like two isolated balloons that will combust if they touch.

❄ ❄ ❄

With Dev's generous divorce settlement, Puja invests in property. She will not countenance going back to the destitute person she was. She hears the landlord mocking, 'You failed PUC. What will you do?' She loses herself in her work.

Raj starts at school, a sturdy, quiet little boy who seems content with the nanny and does not ask much of his mother.

Dev marries again, and his wife is everything he deserves: a plump, happy, loving woman who is always cooking, her kitchen overflowing and heart giving. He moves to Scotland with his wife for his job. But he keeps up his visits with Raj despite having a whole other family, twin daughters and another son.

Then he announces that he is moving back to India. He promises Raj that he will be in touch. Raj walks to his room and shuts the door and refuses to come out to say goodbye.

'You love Raj so much Puja. *I* know it. But I don't think *he* does. Show him. Please. Before it is too late,' Dev urges Puja before he leaves for India.

Puja nods, knowing that Dev knows that he is asking the impossible. After all, isn't this why he is moving back to India with another woman?

As Raj grows older, he and Puja drift further apart. He takes his example from Puja and becomes very distant, a taciturn, sullen child.

Every once in a while, he accuses her, 'You only care about work.'

She bristles and yells at him, although deep down she knows that he's voicing the truth, what he has observed and experienced, his perspective as a child living under her roof, the only other participant in their silent, morose family of two.

And she realises that she is no better than Gopi, who chose money over her. She is also choosing money, the promise and cushion and impersonal security of wealth over the vicissitudes, the capricious travesties of love.

❊ ❊ ❊

She expands her business, amassing more and more properties. She loses her son, accumulating more and more late nights, missed chances and multiplied mistakes.

Somewhere in a hot, dust-glazed country, her other child grows. Sometimes Puja wonders if Kushi yearns to escape like she did, if perhaps it would have been better to bring Kushi here, where personal freedom is not an entity you have to fight for, but is a given. But she baulks at the thought. How can she face her child? What will she tell her? How can she disrupt her life, the life that Puja decided was best for her daughter?

And so she stifles her aching heart, and the longing that threatens to burst out of it.

When on holiday in other countries, she will see a woman cooking on an open hearth, catch a whiff of bubbling rice, breathe in the stench of festering rubbish, the reek of cesspits and stale lives, she will hear a baby's mewling cry, see the mud rise off untarred roads, an asphyxiating cloud of peach smog, and she will feign a headache and retire to the impersonal hotel room for the rest of the day.

Eventually, with the passing of time, she begins to call India home again in that secret part of her heart where she keeps her past locked away.

Every year, on the day her daughter was born in a hut under an awning of swaying marrows, she claims a migraine and retreats to her room. She lies with a pillow covering her face and in the stilted dark, allows herself access to the memories that she has been keeping at bay. She gives her thirsting mind permission to wander, torturing it by conjuring images of the child she knowingly abandoned, a child growing up with no knowledge of her.

She gives in to the cravings she keeps hidden, wave upon wave of painful recollections, the smell of her sister, and the comfort of Sharda's accommodating arms. And in the evening, she cooks marrow soup, the buttery concoction reminding her of a day that she dare not acknowledge, a love she secretly nurses, a past she misses, a sister she hankers for, a child she willingly gave up but would do anything for a glimpse of, for a touch, a word, a smile, a hug, a missive.

Puja realises that she has messed up. She has dug herself into a hole and she cannot dig herself out of it. She has alienated herself from her son. Her daughter has grown up without her. She doesn't know how her sister feels about having been burdened with a child, not having been given a choice in the matter. The child *Sharda* was meant to have with the man *Sharda* was meant to marry.

Late at night, as she catches up on emails and waits for her wayward, uncommunicative son to come home, as she gags on loneliness, she wonders if it was worth it. If perhaps, she should have taken a chance at love again. Perhaps she should have stayed in India, held her child close and opened her heart wide when the wise woman had offered Kushi to her, the day that her parents passed away and her daughter entered the world. What would have happened then? Would everything be different?

Then the police bring Raj home, and Sharda calls, and the past beckons after a silence of almost two decades, and the next thing she knows, she is on a plane to India with her son beside her, recounting to him the story of her past, how she came to be where she is and why.

And now, after the cathartic purging of her past, the whole story that she hasn't dared reveal in its entirety, even to herself, even in the secret confines of her mind, she is able to see clearly, for the first time in years.

Raj. Her boy. She wouldn't have had him if she had stayed in India. He is here. He is hers.

And for now, it is enough.

Chapter 42
Raj

Elusive Dream

'Mum, how you have punished yourself!'

'Yes.'

A rickshaw honks, a dog howls, a little girl skips along right in the middle of the road, pigtails flying.

'Aiyyo,' a man calls.

'I'll take you to visit with your father, after all of this,' his mum says.

Raj nods.

'He tried very hard, son. He tried more than most. He left, Raj, because I vowed to myself not to give of myself anymore. He put up with me as much as he could. I don't blame him.'

Next to where they are standing, a barber has set up shop at a makeshift stand, four poles holding up a roof of coconut frond woven mats. Despite the waning day, he is not short of customers. A wobbly chair, a basin of water, a comb, a blade and a pair of scissors, a towel draped across his shoulders and a mirror he gives his clients to hold, and he is ready to go.

'Yes,' Raj says.

'He loved you; he loves you, very much. He loves you more than I dared.' His mother says.

The barber cuts the hair of his clients at speed, black strands swirling briefly in the grimy air, before gliding down to join the thick carpet of ebony curls around the barber's feet. The clients' shorn necks, sporting minuscule spheres of shiny red from the unruly assaults of the barber's blade, look naked and strangely vulnerable without their armour of hair, the pale flesh blushing maroon from being subjected involuntarily to the brash rays of the evening sun.

'I know, mum,' Raj says, 'I understand now.'

'Love was bad. It made people turn against me. Whoever I loved I lost. I tried so hard not to love you,' she whispers. 'I tried. I couldn't. You and Kushi are two pulses that beat within me. When you used to launch yourself at me, when you were younger, I would ache to hold you, to experience you, to lose the person I had become in the haven of your perfect little smile, to find myself again in your innocent endearments, your sweet perfection. But I pushed you away, kept you safe. It worked a bit too well.' A juddering sigh rocks her whole body, 'I understand now that I did to you exactly what was done to me, pushed you away too much. I thought I was protecting you from me, keeping you safe. But I hurt you. I am sorry.' Tears bleed into her voice. 'In talking to you, telling you what happened, I can see clearly all the mistakes I have made. I wish . . . I wish I could turn back time.'

Raj goes up to his mother and holds her. She is so fragile in his arms, so insubstantial, like the fragmented memory of an elusive dream.

She sobs into his shoulder.

He holds her.

A bus shudders up to the stop, and pushes aside the lone rickshaw trundling along the narrow road. The rickshaw swerves, clipping one of the poles holding up the barber's makeshift stand.

'Lo!' the barber yells, shaking his fist at the rickshaw driver, amid sneezes caused by the mini-tornado of displaced dust. But the awning of the barber's stand crumples and the coconut mats collapse.

'Thank you, Raj,' his mother says, sniffing and wiping her eyes, streaking dirt across her moist face. 'Thank you son.'

The barber abandons his customer mid-shave, and runs away with his towel draped over his shoulder, his scissors in one hand and mirror in the other. The customer stands up and squints, one hand hesitantly feeling his scalp, hairy on one side, shorn and blistering on the other. Then he too, runs, narrowly missing the falling fronds.

'You're welcome, Mum.'

A group of people exit the hospital, four women holding up one in the middle, who is hitting her forehead and sobbing: 'Aiyyo, he's gone. What will I do?'

A gale of fear rousts his mother's eyes, sets her lips aquiver.

'Ready to go inside and meet your daughter?' Raj asks.

She nods, apprehension shining out of her eyes.

'Ready to give her the gift of life again?'

'Yes.' She pushes her shoulders back, her face flushed; anxiety playing peekaboo with the sense of purpose in her face. And then, 'Thank you, Raj. I know I didn't give you much of a choice, but I appreciate you doing this, coming here with me, especially as you can't stand hospitals. It means so much to me.'

He nods.

She swallows and says, her eyes shimmering. 'That evening when you were ill in hospital and you asked me to stay . . . '

He closes his eyes, tries to push away the stab of hurt caused by the memory.

'I did.'

'What?' He opens his eyes, and stares at her.

'I was pacing outside. In the corridor. I just . . . I could not bear to sit next to you and watch you suffer. I was terrified I'd lose you too. I wanted to crush you to me and not let go. I wanted to sob, rail against God and fate, question why it was you, my innocent boy who had to hurt . . . ' A shaky breath, then, 'If I had stayed beside you, I would have gone to pieces, and scared you into being more ill than you already were. And so, I pretended to leave. I went to pieces in the corridor instead. And I kept vigil. I prayed all that night even though I had denounced God the day Kushi was born. I watched that little boy in the bed next to yours being wheeled away and thanked God that it wasn't you, and then felt guilty about it.' A shudder, 'It was me who sent that nurse to you when I saw you sitting up in bed and rocking. And in the morning, when the nurse informed me that your temperature had eased a tiny bit, I was able to give myself a pep talk, comb my hair, spray perfume, paste a smile on my face and come to you . . .'

'Oh Mum. . .'

'I know. I'm sorry.'

He nods. There is an obstruction flooding his throat, tasting of the sea. 'Come on then.' And he gives her his arm and leads her into the hospital that houses his newly discovered sister.

Chapter 43
Kushi

The Makeup of Fabrications

She's here, the woman who taught me right from wrong, who expounded the importance of truth, the necessity of being honest with oneself, the woman whom I had believed in and trusted, whose every word I took at face value, without question, this woman whom I have loved more than anyone else in the world.

She looks at me with the fear spattered, worry infected gaze of a liar who has been found out, a guilty criminal in the dock.

'Why? Why didn't you tell me? All my life I have championed the truth, fought for it and all the while I've been living a lie . . .' Despite myself, my voice wavers. It breaks, as vulnerable as the flimsy foundations upon which our life together has been built.

After all, how can any relationship that has been constructed upon a lie thrive, stay secure and strong? Won't it tremble with every malicious waft of gossip, the whisper of scandal, the insinuation of the truth?

Having the secrets she's been hiding all her life out in the open and shrinking from the spotlight of honesty and directness, seems to have rendered her mute, her face naked without its makeup of fabrications.

Tears glint silver in her eyes like droplets of steam hugging the rim of a dhal saucepan, one travels down her nose and shimmers on her cheek.

She holds out her hand and flexes her fingers, one by one, a plea, a beckoning; her mouth opening and closing like a drowning man gasping for air and finding only water.

I do not want her pleas. I want answers.

I want her to look me in the eye, want to see, finally, the truth laid bare, denuded of its armour of deceits.

'When you held me, and urged me to stay true to myself, weren't you aware of the irony, the hypocrisy? How could you ask me to be true to myself when you weren't?' Each aggrieved word drops like flint from my mouth.

'I tried to tell you, several times. But my tongue refused to push the words out of my mouth; and my throat would dry up.' Her voice falters. 'I didn't want to hurt you. You are so against bias and unfairness of any kind, so vehemently opposed to deceit that I dreaded what knowing the truth would do to you.'

'Ha!' I taste bile, bitter as facts stripped of the sugar coating of palatable falsehoods. 'I trusted you, looked up to you. And you . . . you kept this huge part of my life from me . . . '

'It just . . . it was never the right time,' she whispers. 'I would look at your beautiful face, at your eyes glowing with zeal, at your impassioned appetite for life, at your belief in a righteous, black and white world and I . . . I did not want to be the one who burst your bubble, the one who pointed out the palette of grey interspersed between the black and white of your idealistic world. Your da and I . . .'

'Don't bring Da into it. Not that he is my da anyway. That has been taken from me as well, the certainty that he . . .' I cannot speak any more, my words trapped by a lump, a brine-inflated sponge that is obstructing my throat.

She blanches, her face pale as milky skin skimming the surface of much brewed tea. 'I wish I could absorb all your hurt, your anger, your pain, so you could emerge unscathed from this, Kushi.' Her voice is plaited with grief and regret.

'You should have thought of that before, not now, when it is too late . . .' The lump disintegrates into messy sobs that tear through my body and it feels as if all the bits of me that aren't already broken are breaking now.

The whole ward is silent for once and everyone is staring at us. The ailing, at the other end of the ward nearest the toilets, crane their necks and limp closer, their illness forgotten for a brief while.

I might heal physically if my mother's—*my* mother's— kidney is a match, but will I ever feel whole again? How will I come out of this in one piece? How will I reconcile what I have learnt with what I have believed all my life?

And unreasonable though it is, I want this woman, whose eyes glimmer like raindrops clinging to leaves, to hold me, to tide me through this, to soothe my pain, as she has done a million times before.

No-one else will do.

She tries to reach for me, but I shudder and she slumps back, defeated.

'Kushi,' she whispers, 'Kushi,' as if my name is a magic key that will make everything better. 'My darling . . .'

I cannot bear her endearments, cannot stand to watch her struggle with her emotions. I want her comfort, for her to say, 'It will be okay, it will get better.'

But how? How can any of this get better? How will I rid myself of this throbbing in my chest, this feeling of being let down by her colossal betrayal?

When my da succumbed to fire, (I cannot help thinking of him as Da), there were clear cut villains to direct my anger against, but what do you do when the person you love the most is also the one who has wronged you?

The truth is a splinter in my eye, making everything blurred. I want to remove the splinter. I want everything to go back to the way it was before.

There have been too many sacrifices, too much hurt. Ma's letters, her words, have afforded a glimpse inside her head. I think I understand. I do. And yet, I feel wounded too. Because the people I believed to be my parents did not trust me enough to tell me *my* story, the truth about *my* past.

If I were to find one word to describe what I am feeling, it would be 'confused'.

I want Ma to take me in my arms, chase away the confusion. I ache for the comfort of the platitudes she will utter, every word of which I have always believed, unquestioning, until now. I thought that her arms were the truest things I would ever encounter, where I would always be safe. She was my temple, the solid rigidity of her a constant in the fickle world that stole my da in a blink. In the depths of our grief for Da, she decreed that things would get better and they did. And then . . . . and then she gave me her letters to *her* mother and they changed not only my world, but the way I see her. And that is what I am finding the hardest. She is not the constant I took her to be. I have been ensconced in a fleeting mirage, a house of cards that has toppled with one flick of a careless hand.

Before she returned from the bank, I had reached an understanding, I had thought I had come to terms with this new-found knowledge. But the moment I saw her, the instant her face loomed before me, worry warring with fear, all the hurt and befuddlement I was feeling found an outlet. I lashed out, overcome by rage at her lies.

I am grateful to her for taking me on, loving me unconditionally, in the midst of grieving for her parents and suffering the abuse directed at a single mother. And I am grateful to Da. Da who was brave enough to marry a 'fallen' woman, to take on another man's child, and to tolerate the judgement of the village. But I resent being lied to, being made a fool of.

Ma and Da never gave any indication that I was not theirs, both of them loving me so completely, making me the centre of their world, allowing me the freedom to be the person I wanted to be; which is why this revelation has come as such a shock.

And Puja . . .? I have so many questions for her, the most pressing being why she gave me away. I think I understand .

. . I think I do. I have helped enough young girls burdened by circumstance, undone by fate not to . . .

My head is spinning; my body tied to this bed. Why was I so enamoured with truth? Knowing the truth should not feel like this. I am blindsided by it, and I am reeling from the weight of it, crushed—worse than when that car hit me.

I want to go back to a past where Ma was *mine*, unmarred by this knowledge that she's a liar, that she has been lying to me all these years.

I cannot trust her, not anymore. And that hurts. I feel I cannot trust *anyone* after those closest to me have proved to be capable of such deceit.

I want to run from this angst-charged room, down the claustrophobic corridors of the hospital and out through the door, to breathe lungfuls of the golden air tasting of jackfruit, and fragranced with the incense and entreaties that drift from the shrine by the hospital entrance.

It hurts to open my mouth. It takes effort to form the words I want to say. 'Leave,' I whisper. 'Please, just go. I need to be alone for a bit.'

She stands, and extends a trembling hand towards me. I ignore it.

Her expression: mottled pain as deep and as wide as the Mangalore quarry, and remorse, the sparkling blue of spilled oil on a tarred road, and a plea for understanding, the desolate brown of drought.

I look away from the nakedness of her gaze. 'I need some time to myself.'

My voice is clipped, and harsh. But I am too tired, too worn out by everything that has happened to me to be kind. I want to close my eyes and escape myself, even for a brief while, to seek solace in the soothing nothingness of sleep, if it will come.

'I will be in the corridor just outside this room,' she says. 'I love you, Kushi.'

She turns away, a stooped figure bearing the weight of her falsehoods on her shoulders. I breathe her in, the rounded back and the defeated air of the woman I have known as my mother; the woman I have admired immensely and loved so much; the woman who has loved me and looked after me and brought me up, who has made me the person I am now . . .

Who *am* I?

I no longer know. I am lost, confused, sinking.

I am dying.

Chapter 44
Sharda—Now

A Shadow of a Memory

Dearest Ma,

I am doing what I always do in moments of deep distress: I talk to you. I usually do so via the medium of paper, but I do not have the strength to write just now, so instead I will talk to you in my head.

You who have been dead for the exact time Kushi has been alive, you who are but the shadow of a memory now, you whose face I cannot recall clearly, but a glimpse of which I see in Kushi's smile, in a certain expression she has, in that scowl that pushes her eyebrows together when she is trying to hold a thought.

Does it make me insane, I wonder, this talking to you in my head? I am mad, I suppose. Mad with worry. Mad with grief. Mad with hefting the burden of all the wrong choices I have made, and the wrong paths I have followed in this blind dash that is life.

I so wish I could cook now, Ma. Knead dough for chapathis. Marinate brinjal in a tangy sauce. Deep-fry seasoned, gramflour-coated plantain. Grind masala for fish curry.

I feel so inadequate, my whole being on tenterhooks, as I wait: for Puja's visit, for Kushi to heal, from both the physical injuries inflicted on her by those cruel men and the internal ones I have inflicted on her soul by keeping the truth from her.

My hands feel useless, they should be chopping, stirring, frying—anything except staring at the walls of this disease-ridden hospital corridor, that close in on my desperation, my dread. My head is steeped in regret, marinated in what ifs, and pickled in scenarios—all the ways I could have protected Kushi, all the ways I could have told her the truth of her parentage.

Ma, I cannot stand any longer all these anxiety-swollen, excoriating thoughts populating my brain. I am going to cook instead. If I can talk to a person who only lives on in my head, I can cook in there too, what do you say?

So, I'll prepare the marinade for the spicy squid that you loved so much, Ma. Look, I am adding two teaspoons of chilli powder, a teaspoon of cumin powder and one of coriander powder, a teaspoon of turmeric and one heaped tablespoon of vinegar.

Now I blend in all the spices until the combination becomes a lustrous golden red. I add salt to taste and then add the squid, carefully picked by Da and me from the rejects from the boats which arrived at dawn. I balance the squirming jellylike squid in my hand, helping you pull out the inky black bits from inside. We add it to the marinade and watch the creamy squid turn the pinkish tangerine of a summer sky at sunset.

Somehow I started in the present and have travelled back into the past, Ma, and although I usually love these fantasies where you and Da are home and safe, just now I cannot concentrate.

My mind is enmeshed in the ward next door, where on the fourth bed on the right, my daughter lies, traumatized by what she has learned. It keeps dragging back to Kushi, who also loves squid prepared just that way; Kushi who, when she was little used to hold the fried squid with both hands and stuff it into her mouth. Once she inadvertently rubbed the spicy juices in her eyes. How she scrunched up her face and howled then! I gently washed her eyes with cold water, until she was able to open them again.

'Do you think I'll be able to see again, Ma?' she asked looking right at me, eyes swollen and adorned with tears.

'Tell me what you see, Kushi,' I said holding up two fingers and just as she said 'two', I changed them to three. And we laughed together, her hurt forgotten, the half-eaten squid lying neglected on her plate.

Kushi, my girl, so open with her emotions, Ma, so loving, always declaring her wholehearted affection for me.

'You are my role model, Ma,' she would say often and I'd smile although my heart was aching, burdened by the weight of all I was keeping from her.

And now she knows.

And I wait here in the corridor next to her ward. I wait for my heartbroken daughter to heal—and even though I know it is too much to ask after what I have done, I hope that I will not find Kushi's bright eyes, burning with the zeal to set right the injustices of the world, dulled by the injustice done to her by the woman she trusted, for long.

I hope that her shoulders, always so bouncy with enthusiasm, are not now forever weighted down by my dishonesty and duplicity.

I pray that my sister's—her mother's—kidney will heal my daughter. The girl I brought up as my own, thinking love was enough.

I dream that she will forgive me.

And I wait.

Chapter 45
Puja—Now

The Sepia Taste of Nostalgia

At the shrine at the entrance to the hospital, Puja folds her hands and prays. She pleads with a God she forsook the day her parents died, the day she also gave birth to and gave up her daughter, for her daughter's life.

Please God. I gave her up once. Please don't make me go through it again. Save her. Take me.

All around her is noise: honks and shouts, barks and moos, the trundle of buses and the rattle of auto rickshaws, the laughter of women, and the chatter of children in a language she hadn't realised just how much she missed until she heard it again. The smell of spices and dust, incense and heat, festering garbage and desperation. The taste of grit and ripening fruit, of sunshine and sweat. India. Home.

'Kushi Shankar is in the dialysis ward which is just down through that door there and left along the corridor,' says the harassed receptionist, who is swamped by the maelstrom of people lobbing queries at her from all sides.

Kushi Shankar. The wispy haired baby she's longed for, for nearly eighteen years. Her daughter, and yet, not hers.

Her son, whom she has failed just as much, if not more than her daughter, squeezes her hand and she is grateful for this. She who has shied away from physical contact for as long as her daughter has been alive.

'Remember, Mum,' he says, 'you're doing them a favour.'

'Sharda did me a favour by raising Kushi, Raj. I am only doing my duty. She is my child. I gave her up because I did not want to lose her, and I am losing her anyway.'

'You're not,' Raj says, her wayward son who, in the course of this journey has become a man, a wise one at that. 'She'll be fine.'

'If she asks me why I gave her up, what do I tell her?' She breathes in the universal smell of hospitals and shudders

'You tell her the truth. That you thought you were doing the best by her. At the time you believed it, even though it may not have been the right decision. Be honest, Mum, like you've been with me. It'll be okay.'

'Son, you've turned out so well despite my neglect,' she says softly, giving in at last to the urge of her heart, the yearning she has been clamping down for so long that it has become second nature, and clasping her son's face. The ice that her heart has been encased in for almost twenty years, which started to melt when Raj patted her hand hesitantly in the plane and held her when she cried just now, thaws fully at this contact. 'You are just like your father, thank goodness. Loving and giving.'

'I am just like you,' her son replies. 'Loving and giving.'

She blinks back the warm tears stinging her eyes at his words. 'I've been anything but.'

'You're here now,' her son says. 'You're here when your daughter needs you the most.'

A woman paces up and down the phenyl-reeking corridor. She is hunched, as if warding off blows.

She looks up as Puja and Raj approach. Her face is care-worn, set in deep grooves of worry and fear. But there is something about the eyes, the henna-coloured eyes that are no longer hidden behind unflattering lenses . . . Puja stares. Not Sharda surely? She seems too old.

The woman's face lights up when she recognises Puja. And in that smile, that shy, tentative smile that doesn't quite reach her anxious eyes, Puja sees her sister.

The intervening years fold away like the pleats of an accordion. Puja opens her mouth and tastes the past, earth and love and loss and remorse, fermented and salty with age, and a single word escapes her mouth and populates the space between them like a blessing.

'Sharda.'

That one word, spanning the distance between them, dissolves all the hurt and anger, the guilt and remonstrance, leaving behind only the realisation that what is left after everything has been pared down, is the bond between sisters, a complex weave of love, genes and blood.

This is my sister, who held me while I was being sick, who carried me everywhere on her young hip, who introduced me and my daughter to the world, who's brought my daughter up.

This is my sister, the only person who can see in the adult I have become, the child I once was; the gatekeeper to the hallowed memories of our joint childhood; the only one who can recall, like me, how our mother's eyes changed colour when she laughed, how our father walked with the slightest hint of a limp; the only one whose precious reminiscences of our parents are marked by smoke, contaminated by flames lapping at a village, stealing it of colour, rendering it the grey of ash, the charred husk of a thousand hollow dreams, a myriad wasted lives.

'Puja,' Sharda says, her voice the awed hush of a child waking up to an incandescent world painted the glossy happily ever after of fairy tales by the magic brush of snow. 'Thank God. Thank you for coming.'

Sharda comes up to her and touches her cheek. Her calloused palm feeling just like Ma's, transports Puja right back into childhood. It is sanction and redemption. It is forgiveness and absolution.

'I thank you, Sharda, for all that you did, all you are still doing. Thank you for taking Kushi on,' Puja says.

Hot tears, silvery blue, trickle down the sides of Sharda's face and wet her sari blouse.

'Kushi . . . Sh-She's not . . . Her kidneys . . . '

The terror Puja feels is reflected in Sharda's eyes. And the lingering remnants of the barrier of mistakes and misunderstandings and misjudgements that has built up between the two of them over the years crumbles in the urgency of what is here, what is now, the desperate dread of what might be, binding them together.

At that moment, they are two mothers, united in the fight to save their beloved child.

Sharda pulls Puja to her, holding her close.

'Thank you,' Sharda whispers, 'for giving Kushi to me then. She saved me.' A pause, then, 'And thank you for coming now, to give her to me again.'

It is a warning. Puja understands.

She is mine, Sharda is saying.

'Kushi is not mine to take, not anymore.' Puja's heart aches as she mouths the words, knowing that they are the truth, but feeling as she felt that smoke-scarred, anguish-hued day when her daughter was born and Puja turned away from her, even though every instinct cried otherwise.

Sharda nods, eyes brimming. 'She is all I have.' And softly, 'And now, I have you too.'

Puja's heart overflows.

Raj clears his throat somewhere behind her.

'This is my son, Raj.' She is caught unawares by the pride she feels when she says those words. Her heart blossoms as she introduces *her* son to *her* sister.

'Wow, what a handsome young man. And tall. You look just like your mother.' Sharda, not suffering any of the qualms Puja does, leans forward and folds Raj into a hug.

Raj blushes red as wet mud, as he stands awkwardly in his aunt's arms.

And seeing her son encircled in her sister's arms, Puja, for the first time in twenty years, gets a glimpse into a future that is unburdened by the follies of the past, but lifted up on the tentative wings of optimism, bright as light percolating into an overcast day and feeding it the promise of the brilliance to come. She breathes in deeply and tastes buoyancy, the soft pink of a tender bloom unfurling cautiously in the caress of spring.

'I found your number,' Sharda says softly. 'I've been carrying it around close to my heart, trying to pluck up the courage to call. For the first two years after you left, I was on tenterhooks, worried you would come back and take Kushi away. Then I relaxed, knowing that you had made the ultimate sacrifice. You had relinquished your claim on her.' Sharda swallows. 'I am sorry, Puja. That day . . . '

Puja knows instantly the day Sharda is talking about: the day her world shattered, the day the girl she was died and the woman she is now started to emerge. The memory of it is a throbbing in her back, an ache in her chest, the flavour of blood and sorrow in her mouth.

'It was I who carried the tales from the matrons to Da. It was me.'

Puja lifts up her hand as if to stop now what had happened then. 'Oh what does it matter now, Sharda?' she sighs.

Why does it still hurt?

'I need to say it,' Sharda whispers. 'I have been apologising to you in my head for so many years.'

Puja nods, tasting grief and regret.

'I'm sorry for having allowed it all to happen, for perpetrating it, for not bringing you back home where you belonged. For letting you stay away from all of us, for everything you had to go through alone.' Sharda says, her voice haemorrhaging.

Puja nods again, overcome. The countless mistakes, the guilt, the untold hurt bleeding into so many years of their lives, have stooped their backs and rendered their hearts heavy with the load of feelings undeclared and quarrels unresolved, wrong things said and important ones left unsaid, love unrequited and love taken for granted.

'I am sorry too,' she says. 'For saddling you with Kushi. I know how hard it must have been for you to be a single mother here. But I knew too that if anyone could do it, it would be you, Sharda. At the time, I didn't think myself worthy of my baby. And I could only think of one person I could entrust my precious daughter to—You.'

The cramped corridor smells of aired secrets. It feels light—a heart relieved, confidences renewed, and old wounds throbbing with hurt for so many years, healing

Sharda's eyes flood. 'I loved her. I love her. She is very fragile right now. She's just found out. I . . . I couldn't tell her before.' She takes a breath. 'Kushi's a star, Puja. She's so amazing. So honest, so driven and such a stickler for the truth. She's the very best of me and you. I . . . I should have protected her more.'

Sharda's face is wet with her tears and Puja's mouth is wet with the taste of them.

'Ah, Sharda, don't blame yourself.'

'She will come through. That's what I keep telling myself. But I am beside myself with worry. What with her internal injuries . . .'

'She'll be fine. She has to be.' Puja says, a pledge, a petition, a prayer.

I gave her up all those years ago because I thought I was protecting her. What use the sacrifice I made, all the precious time I lost with her, if I still cannot protect her? God, you owe me.

'If Ma and Da are looking down on us now, they'll be pleased.' Sharda says softly.

'Really?' Puja asks, her voice radiating ache like a wood chip splinter in fragile skin.

'Da pined for you, Puja. He punished himself every moment, every day.'

'Then why didn't he come to get me? Why didn't he bring me back?'

'We were going to, and then the fire happened.' Sharda's eyes are undone with remorse.

'Oh.' Puja breathes in the cobalt scent of erroneous choices and thoughtless slip-ups. Her mouth is bitter with the inky flavour of the thousand moments together with her family denied her. She is ambushed by the sepia taste of nostalgia, the pearly waterfall of myriad happy memories that had made up the life she and Sharda had once shared.

'He loved you most. Right up to the end, he loved you. They both did.'

Puja had not believed the wise woman when she had said the same thing the fateful day when she gave up her daughter, but now, she believes her sister.

'Yes.' She says, her voice light as she feels the burden she has been carrying for what seems forever, slip from her shoulders.

'Gopi died in a motorbike accident a couple of years after you left. No wife or kids.'

'Oh.' Puja doesn't know what, if anything, she feels.

'The landlord went mad with grief, and he died soon after.'

An unpleasant taste at the back of her throat like she has swallowed a mango seed and it is stuck, the asphyxiating feel of grappling for the painfully elusive, silvery essence of life, the whitewashed hum of sadness.

The booming landlord, so full of himself. His cowardly son: the boy who taught her how to love, and also, how not to love.

We are only human in the end, she thinks, trying to picture the landlord, insane with grief. He had loved his son in his own way. Had Gopi known that?

We waste the little time we are given in this world on immaterial things, not the things that really matter, she thinks. *And then, when it is far too late, we long for one more moment together, a moment which, if bestowed, we will draw out and treasure, a moment in which we will say all those things left unsaid, a moment into which we will cram a lifetime's worth of good times.*

I need to tell my children I love them. I need to hold them in my arms, as I have always yearned to do. I need to explain to my daughter why I did what I did. I have squandered enough time.

Puja smiles at her son, still squirming in his aunt's embrace.

Sharda holds out her pinkie finger to Puja. Puja takes it.

'I love you, Puja.' Sharda says, her voice the luminous gold of promise.

'I love you too,' Puja says. The words she thought she would stumble on flow as easily as champagne and she grins as her son stares at her in open-mouthed astonishment.

Chapter 46
Kushi

The Profound Stillness between Roars

Long strands of curly brown hair frame the thin face of the woman standing next to my bed. Her pistachio eyes, under-lined by violet shadows, glisten as they hungrily devour me.

Her lips quiver as she tries on a wavering smile, much like the tremulous lines on one of the beeping machines rigged to my chest.

I look like her. She is a thinner, paler, slightly taller version of me. My mother.

'Why did you give me away?' I ask, my voice watery, clogged with the weight of eighteen years of lost moments.

I think I know why she did what she did but I want to hear what she has to say, understand her side of my story.

She stands there absorbing every inch of me as if she can-not quite believe she is here at last, with me, the daughter she thought she had lost.

Finally she speaks, and her voice is soft as the caress of a dew-spattered leaf, fluid as a lake in the moonlight, grave as the profound stillness between roars. 'I did it because I loved you.'

And then, in that putrid ward, Puja tells me her story which is also the beginning of mine.

By the end of it we are both battling a barrage of tears.

'You loved me,' I sniffle.

'I never stopped loving you, Kushi.' My name on her lips sounds like a dedication. 'I've yearned for you and missed you every single moment of every day of your life.'

I picture a girl not much older than I am now, trying to come to terms with losing her family and her love, a girl who yearned for absolution, a girl who thought that to give up her child was to do penance for sins committed.

I think of all the girls who have come to me for help and advice. And I look at this woman. My mother. Who thought she was protecting me by giving me up.

'But your reasoning was silly,' I say.

She laughs wetly, a chuckle surprised out of her. 'It was, now that I look at it in the cold light of present day. But at the time . . .' Her gaze is sunshine spilling across a rain-swept courtyard. 'I know you are angry. I'll understand if you hate me.'

'You said you longed to hold me.'

'Yes.'

'Well, what are you waiting for?'

She laughs, properly this time, and it is mango juice dripping down your chin on a summer's evening, it is a rainbow glimpsed at the end of a storm battered day, it is warm pebbles skittering on a beach on a drowsy afternoon.

She leans forward and then she is holding me, tubes and all, and I settle into her chest and hear her heart beat and I think that this is how it must have been when I was inside her womb, taking comfort from the rhythmic boom, boom, boom of the blood pumping inside her, the blood that sustained me.

'I did not want to hold you,' she whispers, 'because I was worried I would not be able to let you go. Nothing has changed.'

And I smile in her arms and I can feel her smiling back as she strokes my hair which is matted at the back from the pillow.

'Do you know I haven't touched anyone like this in years?' she says and her voice is awed as a child taking the first bite of cotton candy and discovering heaven on earth, 'I can't for the life of me think why.'

'Being in your arms is like settling into the chair at home that is my favourite, that sags in all the right places and carries my weight so securely, knowing just where to support me and where to let go,' I say and I can feel her hot tears splashing onto me.

She takes a deep breath, then, 'Kushi, Sharda has told me all about you and I am so very proud. I always yearned to escape the village. I felt suffocated in its confines, bound by the stifling chains of tradition. After I left, I wondered if perhaps I had condemned you to a horrible life, a life with only boundaries, a closed life where getting pregnant out of wedlock ruined you. But you, you're something else.' Her voice thick with pride, shiny with love, 'You felt claustrophobic in the village, so you did something about it. You've changed the village, improved it, instead of running away. You're so strong, so very brave, you're the best of Sharda and me.'

'I am as far from brave as you can get. Right now, I am terrified,' I whisper, 'what if . . . what if this is my life?' admitting my deepest fear at last.

She does not let go of me, but pulls back a bit so she can look into my eyes. 'You're going to be fine, I promise.' Her gaze imparts courage to my floundering soul. 'My kidney will be a match and you'll be as right as rain.'

And then she holds me as I cry; as I unburden all the anxieties I've been keeping inside, the worry and the terror.

'You're going to be fine. I know this,' she repeats. 'I love you, Kushi. So very much,' she whispers.

Over her shoulder I see Ma approaching, and behind her a tall boy who looks weirdly familiar, and behind them, the doctor.

Ma's eyes plead with me, they apologise and they love, they tell me a thousand things without one word exiting her lips.

'Mum,' the tall boy says and Puja turns, her whole face transformed, beaming at her son.

'Kushi,' she says, 'this is Raj.'

My brother.

He seems shy, this tall hulking man-boy. He looks uncomfortable and more than a little lost.

'Hey bro,' I say and he laughs, a rumbling growl and snort, his shyness ebbing.

'So,' the doctor says, 'I hear we may have a potential do-nor.'

Ma clutches her chest. Puja squeezes my shoulder, then stands up and turns to look at the doctor.

And hope raises its sunny head and winks at me.

Chapter 47
Puja—Now

Freedom

When she holds her daughter in her arms, Puja feels the chains she has knotted herself in so tightly and for so many years loosen.

She gazes at her daughter with her caramel-gold eyes that radiate courage and valiantly try and mask the anxiety that attempts to steal her smile. Her beautiful daughter with her expressive face, her long hair coiled in a messy plait down her back, with her dimples skipping tantalisingly in her pallid cheeks that should be radiant with the rosy stamp of youth. Her daughter, her grin an exact replica of Sharda's open-mouthed smile.

I never dared hope I would experience this miracle of holding my daughter in my arms. My grown-up daughter. A gorgeous young lady. So very brave. So absolutely amazing.

She holds her daughter and it is the sweetest essence of a magical dream come true.

She holds her daughter and it is hope wafting on a draft of spring air.

She holds her daughter and she finds the freedom she has been searching for all her life.

And then, she sets about the business of healing her daughter, giving her of herself.

Chapter 48
Sharda—Now

Harbinger of Happy Ever Afters

Puja is taken for tests to check if her kidney is compatible.

Raj ventures into the village to bring back a change of clothes for Sharda and for Kushi too if all goes well.

And then Sharda is alone with her daughter.

Alone now that Kushi has met with Puja.

The space beside Kushi's bed which Sharda occupies is pungent with Sharda's fear, rank with her anguish.

Sharda looks at Kushi, breathes her in. This girl Sharda has brought up as her own, this girl she has loved so much, this girl who breathed new life into her just by being, this girl who is her life.

Kushi's eyes are puffy, her face shiny with tears, but her shoulders are not slumped as they were when she had read Sharda's letters and had asked Sharda to give her space, and her head sits straight on the delicate stalk of her graceful neck.

Thank you, Ma. Thank you, God. I thank you. What I did, keeping the truth from her, hasn't broken her. Meeting with her birth mother and brother hasn't either. I would not have been able to bear it if discovering her parentage had defeated her, Ma, if it had turned her into a facsimile of her real self.

Kushi lifts up her hand with its snaking of tubes and says, her voice barely louder than the soft rustle dust makes as it settles, 'I would like a hug.'

Sharda's whole being sings.

I do not deserve this, Sharda thinks even as she enjoys the familiar and much longed for warmth of her daughter in her arms. *I am blessed.*

'I'm sorry, Kushi,' Sharda says tremulously. 'I lied to you because I thought I was doing the best by you, because I did not want you to carry the burden of knowing that your birth mother had given you up. You would have blamed yourself for Puja leaving. And I didn't want that. I wanted you to be the confident girl you are now, not a diffident one crushed by that knowledge.'

Her daughter does not say a word, just burrows her head deeper into Sharda's shoulder and Sharda feels her daughter's hot tears soaking her arm, and her neck.

Sharda swallows down her own tears and, taking courage from her daughter's continued embrace, continues. 'After what happened with Puja, I made up my mind that I would let you be the person you wanted to be. I would not hold you back. And in the process, *you* have made me the person *I* have always wanted to be. You've made me whole. You've filled my life with unparalleled love and joy . . . and Kushi . . . while I was waiting in the corridor, I heard. They have been caught, the people who did this to you.'

Her daughter looks up at Sharda and her eyes are huge with the desire to know.

'It was the parents of the boys involved in your da's death. The parents of the boys who were expelled. All of them were in on it. They hired some goondas to hurt you. They've been caught and are in jail. They'll be tried, and they'll lose their jobs. They'll pay for what they did no matter how high up they are on the influential ladder. The papers are on the case. You're the media darling, sweetie. They'll not let the attack on you go unpunished.'

Kushi sighs, nods, then snuggles into her again.

Sharda takes it as her cue to proceed. 'I promised my ma on her deathbed that I would find Puja and bring her home. You have made me realise that promise, so many years later. You gave me the courage to make that phone call, to talk to my sister, to invite her home. Kushi, it is you who are the adhesive cementing us together, the thread that binds us, the hope, the sunlit promise of a future together. You, Kushi, are our harbinger of happy ever afters. You'll get better, Kushi, I promise you that.'

Kushi nods and still she does not say anything, which is uncharacteristic of her garrulous, vivacious daughter.

Sharda has always known what is going on in Kushi's head because it comes bursting out of her mouth a moment later. But now, there is only silence—an impenetrable heaving sludge. A silence Kushi seems loath to break in case the tide of revelations recedes, trickles once more into a muteness dense with secrets that have been locked up for almost two decades.

RENITA D'SILVA

'I should not have kept the truth from you. It was yours to know and own, I realise that. But I was afraid. You were, you are, so much like Puja, so outgoing, so full of life, and I worried that, if you found out, it would be too much for you. I could not have stomached that . . . I was terrified of the past. I had lost my sister to it. I could not have survived losing you too. I could not have borne my vital, wonderful girl becoming a shadow, overcome by the encumbrances of truth, and never recovering from it.

'I know this is hard for you to comprehend, Kushi, but I thought that, by lying, I was giving you a gift, unshackling you from the past, freeing you, to make of yourself what you wanted, unhindered and untarnished by what had gone before. But to be completely honest, I was not entirely un-selfish. I wanted you for myself and I guess a part of me worried that if I told you, you might want to see Puja, get to know her. I missed my sister. I wanted to see her. But I did not want to share you. I am so sorry.'

'No, *I* am sorry, Ma, for that shameful outburst before,' Kushi says and at the sacred sound of that one word dropping like a blessing from her daughter's throat, that one word exiting the sunburst bud of her lips, the word Sharda thought she'd never hear again from Kushi's mouth, the weight that has been sitting on her heart and constricting her throat melts and the manifestation of the thaw inundates her eyes.

In front of Sharda's blurry eyes, dances the vision of the little girl who used to sit on her bottom and lift up her arms when she wished to be carried, dimples cavorting in her rosy cheeks as she said the one word she had learned before any other, 'Ma.'

She brushes her daughter's velvet curls back from her eyes, and she holds her in her arms as she has done a million times before, imparting and drawing comfort, praying: *Please God let Puja's kidney be a match. Please.*

Chapter 49
Raj

Rainbow of Fireworks

'I need a few things from the cottage at home,' his aunt says, the morning following their arrival, Raj and his mum having spent the night with Sharda and Kushi at Kushi's bedside.

And before he knows what he is doing, Raj says, 'I'll go.'

He doesn't want to stay one minute longer in this hospital stalked by illness, haunted by the ghosts of the dead.

He doesn't want to look at his cousin, no, his sister, who is trying so hard to be brave, but he can smell the fear on her, and in her wan face and tired eyes, he can read the agony she is enduring, and the trauma she is going through.

He can't bear to be party to his aunt's barely concealed terror, the consternation emanating from her in frantic waves.

Most of all, he doesn't want to be in the hospital when the mum he has just discovered, this gentle, loving woman who was hiding behind his remote mother's rigid façade, is wheeled into the operating room for tests. He wants to ambush the doctors, ask them if they are qualified enough to know what they're doing, and subject *them* to tests before trusting them with his mother. He wants to plead with them to please take care of his mother.

He *needs* her.

❈ ❈ ❈

Before he leaves for the village, he speaks to his father.

'Raj!' his father is disbelieving.

Raj has never called his father. It is always the other way round, with his dad calling him.

'I'm in India,' Raj says.

'Wow!' His father's voice is as festive as a rainbow of fireworks. 'To what do we owe this honour?'

'Long story, Dad.'

'I've got time.'

And Raj realises, as he tells his father what has happened, that his father has always had time for him, even when Raj was at his worst.

Like his mother said, his father has tried. He has always tried.

'I'm sorry, Dad, for staying away.' Raj whispers.

'You are here now, son,' his father replies, gentle as a salve on a pulsing wound.

'I'll come and see you.' Raj says.

'No, stay put. You've got a lot going on there. We'll come and see you.'

'Thank you, Dad.'

'And Raj?'

'Yes?'

'Hope it all goes okay with your sister.'

My sister.

He is so lucky, Raj thinks. He has a father who loves him, a mother who he now knows without a doubt loves him with everything she has, and he has a healthy body. He can walk away from this hospital on his own two feet, all parts of him in perfect working condition.

His new-found sister can't.

This is another thing I have taken for granted: my health, he thinks.

❄ ❄ ❄

Raj sprints out of the hospital, into the light and heat, the spicy warm air enveloping him in a humid embrace. Following his aunt's instructions, he crosses the road to the bus stop opposite, narrowly avoiding bumping into a cow and being knocked over by an auto rickshaw.

He waits in the sweltering heat, the sun beating down on his bare head and cooking his brain, sweat trailing tracks down his back and making his clothes cling to him in a soggy embrace.

He climbs into the juddering, rusting jalopy that masquerades as a bus, which pulls up with a jarring screech of brakes at the shack that passes for a bus stop, and gives the name of the village, 'Bhoomihalli', which he has to repeat a couple of times, before the conductor gets his accent. Raj shoves some money from his wallet into the conductor's sticky hand, grateful to his mother for insisting he kept some of the rupees she'd exchanged for pounds at the airport.

The conductor stares at him over the top of his glasses, his khaki uniform tinted ginger with sweat and grime, the collar discoloured, and indistinguishable from the lines of filth embedded into the grooves of his neck. He smells of saliva and spices, and Raj's jet-lagged stomach gives a lurch of nausea. The conductor presses most of the notes, some coins and a sheaf of blue stubs back into Raj's palm, and, not pausing to take a breath, lifts the whistle hanging from a string on his chest to his mouth and emits an ear-splitting shriek.

The bus shudders, once, twice and finally works up the strength to move in a rush of clanging gears and Raj prays that he will reach the village in one piece. He peers between the rusting bars of the window, inhaling the scent of iron and mud, as the hospital fades from view.

Almost an hour later, the old bus grinds to a convulsive halt and the conductor announces 'Bhoomihalli' with another shrill whistle that sounds worse than a horde of shrieking hyenas. Raj stumbles down the uneven steps and he has barely jumped off when the bus takes off again, wheezing and grovelling, in a cloud of auburn dust.

When the grit settles, there are a dozen children clothed in holey rags, apparitions conjured up by the dirt: bare feet, unkempt hair. They are covered in vermilion grime from head to toe, but their eyes glimmer through, eager, excited, starved, hopeful.

What must it be like, Raj wonders, *to go hungry all the time?* He feels a gnawing pain in his stomach at the thought.

They swarm him, these children, holding palms out, their eyes hungry, their bellies sunken, their garments tattered. 'Please saar.'

He doesn't know if begging is legal here, if it is allowed. Oh what does it matter? He has seen more beggars during the taxi ride to the hospital than he had seen in a year in the UK.

He digs in his pockets, checks his wallet. He does not have enough coins, received courtesy of the bus conductor, for all of these kids, so he deposits a ten rupee note in each of the keen little hands.

The children's faces light up. They look at each other, unable to believe the evidence of their eyes. They kiss the notes and they jump in the air, their animated eyes in their dust-coated faces dancing. They lift their hands and whirl, holding the notes high.

And he is inordinately, disproportionately happy.

They say, 'Thank you, saar, thank you,' and touch his feet.

Now, he is just plain embarrassed.

He tries to lift them up, but they cling to his feet as if he is their deliverer.

'Why are you here, saar? Who are you here for?' A shy girl at the back asks.

'I am Kushi's . . . ah . . . Kushi's cousin. You know Kushi?'

'Huh?' they stare at him, their faces scrunched up in befuddlement. 'Why are you speaking that way, saar? All pish pish.'

He smiles at their bemused expressions. Pish, pish. He likes the sound of that!

'Kuuu shiii,' he says, drawing out each syllable slowly and smiles again as he watches their mouths try to follow his. 'Kuuu shiii's couuu sin.'

'Ah,' they grin. 'Kushi's cousin, Kushi's cousin,' they yell in unison, skipping and giggling.

'Yes, that's right,' he nods.

'Kushi's cousin.' A choir of chaotic voices.

He blinks and they are gone, a crew of wide-eyed children running riot in the fields, scattering like beads from a broken necklace, so all that is left is mud settling in a soft orange sigh, in their wake.

What is this village? He wonders. The warm afternoon breeze smells of mangoes ripening in the sun and flicks more grit onto his face. As if he needs it when he is already coated in a dusty turmeric film from sweaty head to perspiring toe!

There seem to be a couple of drowsy huts, a sleepy-looking shop—a tiny oblong with a thatched roof. He has to stoop to enter. There are a couple of glass jars, half filled with small sweets and what looks like peanut brittle, all buzzing with mosquitoes and flies. A few plastic bags of garish apricot crisps hang from the low beams.

Nobody mans the shop. There is nobody about.

A ghost town. Not a town, no. Even village is an overstatement.

Next door, there's another hut, a pungent smell emanating from it. An opening which yawns into darkness.

He cannot see anything else for the swirling dust.

Not a soul.

It is as if the kids have disappeared into thin air.

He should have paid better attention as to which direction they had gone, but he was coughing from the dust which had launched a fresh assault on his eyes and his face.

The sun beats down mercilessly, the heat an insect burrowing inside his very soul. He can see the appeal of going naked here he really can, wearing nothing but a covering of dust which will do for modesty and uniformity. You can't see anything anyway, there's always dust eddying in front of you or yellow sun causing you to scrunch your eyes into squints, and making everything shimmer.

'Hello? Sir?' he hears and turns.

A boy about his age, perhaps a year or two older, is standing before him, holding out his hand.

'Hi, I'm Raj,' he says, taking the proffered hand and rudely transferring the grime he is coated with onto it.

'Nice to meet you. I am Somu,' the boy says in very good English, although he pauses before each word as if he is reading from a page in a book etched onto his memory. 'You are Kushi's cousin?' Somu politely does not mention the dust Raj has transferred onto his hand, gamely wiping it onto the white skirt like thing all the men here wear, and which instantly turns a vivid tangerine.

Raj hesitates, then, 'Yes.' He does not want to get into the whole story, and say, *she's actually my sister, but . . .* This notion of him being known and accepted not for himself, but in relation to Kushi, the wan girl he's left behind in hospital, feels strange, and takes some getting used to.

'We are all so upset about what happened to her.' Somu's face is very expressive and seems to enact every word he utters. 'Kushi is our saviour.'

'Your saviour?' Raj's voice is sprinkled with amused disbelief.

But Somu nods earnestly, his face grave, voice solemn. 'Kushi made sure I got the engineering seat I deserved. She has helped every one of us here in so many ways. She is amazing. The heroine of our village. Is she okay?'

He thinks of his mother even now being tested for a match.

'She's getting there,' he says.

'Good.' The boy nods again. 'Shall I show you around the village?'

Wow, Raj thinks as he walks through the village—so far it is a dusty smattering of huts nestling amongst grime-washed emerald fields—with Somu who tells him all that Kushi has done for him, and for the villagers. Raj is getting a different image of the girl he has to keep reminding himself is his sister, the scared girl trying so hard to be brave at the hospital morphing into this remarkable person who was so incensed by the injustice of her father's death that she wrote a letter that changed everything.

Raj pictures a girl with blazing eyes and fervent views, an incorrigible zest for life and a commitment to change the world around her and her absolute belief that she will do so, a girl aware of exactly where she's headed in life and the knowledge of how to get there.

I wish I knew where my life was headed.

396   Renita D'Silva

What an awesome girl Kushi is. *His* sister. He feels a rush of pride. He is so honoured, he thinks, to be associated with this extraordinary girl.

Please let Mum's kidney be a match, he thinks, even as he shies away from the vision of his mum on the operating table. *Please get better, Kushi,* he thinks. *You have a world to save.*

Somu tells him about the boys who were expelled and how their parents wrought their revenge. Raj is beset by a helpless, frustrated fury on behalf of his sister, much like he was when he heard his mother's story, what had been done to her.

'We are taking action. The media is in an uproar. What happened to her will not go unpunished,' Somu declares fervently, nodding his head.

Gentle-eyed, dirt-crusted cows stalk down the road, flicking away the flies that alight on their backs with a swish of their tails. It is hot enough to fry eggs in and the ubiquitous churning dust makes him feel like he is walking through a carroty haze. It tickles his nose, provoking a perpetual urge to sneeze. The air, thick with soil angst, hangs heavy with a strangely piquant, but overpowering aroma of spices, gutters, and heat.

The huts they encounter look barely big enough to house him, let alone the families he glimpses inside. He would have to crouch to enter one and keep crouching inside, he thinks, they are that small.

Bedraggled children wearing nothing but hungry expressions, thin bruised coverings of brittle brown skin straining over their ribs and dipping into the concave hollows of their stomachs, stare curiously at him, their liquid eyes the colour of ditch water.

I have been so lucky, Raj thinks, *and so very spoiled.*

He samples the pungent flavour of a world completely different from the one he is used to, the soft give of yellowish red soil beneath his feet whispering with every step.

Women in multi-coloured saris cooking on fires out in the open, mud pots simmering and hissing, avert their eyes from his gaze. But all of them wave to Somu and chat with him, in rapid-fire exchanges in the regional language, which Somu tells him is Kannada.

'What are they saying?' Raj asks, curious.

'There's no drinking water in the village. Again! The wells are dry. The borewells that have been installed are far from enough. This year the drought has been terrible and a man was poisoned by the germ-laden excuse for water that the borewells dispense trickle by agonising trickle. Kushi organised a demonstration, before her accident, but we are yet to see any concrete action on the part of the local government . . .'

And once again, Raj is swamped by admiration for his new-found sister, with her passion, her boundless enthusiasm, wishing he had but one ounce of her energy, her fire, her conviction.

What a waste it will be, if Mum's kidney is not a match, he thinks, and instantly pushes the thought, and the accompanying nausea away.

Bony dogs amble up to him, sniffing his feet, hoping for a treat. He breathes in gritty lungfuls of the humid air.

'Ah here we are,' Somu says. 'Would you like a taste of our local wine?'

'Huh?' Raj asks.

They have stopped outside a hay topped shack. When Raj peers into the dark interior, his eyes adjusting, after a bit, to the hazy gloom inside, barely alleviated by flickering lamps, he is surprised by the activity within. Men stooping huddled in the musty, confined surroundings, are taking huge gulps of a creamy liquid spilling from tumblers that shine in the dull murkiness.

Raj inhales the sweet, tart tang of brew as Somu walks in through the opening that stands for the doorway (there is no door) that is so small even Somu, a whole head shorter than Raj, has to crouch to pass through.

The pleasantly drunk men beckon to Somu, and then, when he points Raj out, they stumble outside to speak to him, and Somu translates their rapid-fire Kannada in his careful English. All of them ask after Kushi and send their best wishes; all of them tell Raj how much Kushi has helped them, what she has done for them.

The man at the stool that serves as a counter presses two cloudy bottles into Somu's hands, refusing to take payment, calling after him to convey his greetings to his mother and father and sisters, as he hunkers back out through the opening and blinks in the sunshine.

Everyone knows everyone else here, Raj is beginning to realise.

Somu grins as he holds up the hazy bottles of white foamy liquid frothing at the rim, 'Our version of alcohol. Palm toddy, distilled by cutting into the flower of a palm tree and collecting the sap overnight and letting it ferment. We'll have it with our food. You must eat with us. It'll be a real honour. My parents will be overjoyed.'

Raj takes a bite of something called a veg puff, puff pastry stuffed with spicy vegetables, which he picks at random from a shack crammed full to bursting with pastries, sweets and biscuits, all thrown together haphazardly inside a scratched and dirty glass case, fly-infested and wilting in the sunlight.

'Not bad at all,' he says, as his taste buds process the explosion of spices as the crumbly pastry travels down his oesophagus, adding substance and soothing his stomach which had been on the point of rebellion.

'Wait till you taste my ma's food,' Somu says. 'Not as delicious as Sharda amma's of course. Your aunt is the best cook in the village. I will take you to her factory later, after you've been to the cottage, although she's looking to sell it, now.'

'Why?'

'Medical costs,' Somu says and Raj tastes the scarlet burn of wrath at the people who did this to Kushi in his throat again.

✳ ✳ ✳

Afterwards, after Raj has been to the cottage his aunt and Kushi share, which is like a fairy-tale house in a magic wood, its mouldy scent of trapped air and old phantoms momentarily chased away by his presence, and collected the clothes and sundries Sharda needs, and after he has been to the factory,

a hive of frenzied, bustling, spice-perfumed, laughter-sprin-
kled, gossip-seasoned activity, Somu takes Raj to his house.

It is a one-roomed hut, with a hearth in the corner. A
framed photo takes up most of one crumbling wall. It is of
Somu's family clustered around a puffed-up man who Somu's
father proudly informs Raj in Kannada—with Somu doing
the translating—is the Chief Minister. It seems to have been
taken at the unlucky moment when Somu's father was settling his crotch into place.

'That picture was clicked when Somu got his engineering
seat,' Somu's Da says. 'Kushi's doing.'

Somu's sisters, who have just arrived from school, giggle
when they see Raj. Then, hiding their faces in their churidar
shawls, they run to help their mother who is chopping vegetables at the hearth.

'I am studying very hard to reward Kushi's faith in me,'
Somu says.

'But he still takes the time to help me in the fields in the
evenings when he's back from college,' Somu's father grins
affectionately at Somu, and pride streaks his voice the bright
yellow of happiness. 'Lucky he had the day off today for
exam revision, so he could take you around. He's one of the
few in the village who can speak English fluently.' Again the
barely suppressed joy at his son's accomplishment, a smile
swamped with love as Somu, blushing, translates what he's
said for Raj's benefit.

Love is giving, Raj thinks, *not the other way round.*

*Kushi's father dies and instead of wallowing in grief, she does
something about it. She changes the lives of the entire village for*

the better. Whereas I . . . I have been expecting my mum to not only work and keep me in comfort but also to entertain me. All my life I have blamed everyone for my own unhappiness.

Somu's sisters peel potatoes and chop vegetables, wiping their eyes of streaming, onion-induced tears.

This is real love, Raj thinks. *Children returning from school and helping their parents, in the fields and at home. Children tending to their parents. Children giving.*

Unconditional love. This is unconditional love.

❋ ❋ ❋

When he gets back to the hospital, his mum and Sharda look as if they are the ones who have been run over by the car and not Kushi. They try (not very successfully) to hide the distress that threatens to bubble out of them, the worry that has taken their faces captive so they look, despite their differences, very much alike.

'They couldn't do it. It's not a match.' His mum tells him, after she pulls him out of the ward and into the corridor, and out of Kushi's hearing, her face crumpling like a balled-up sheet of paper.

'My blood group is not compatible with Kushi's.' His mum chokes on her words, her voice furious even as it stumbles, brackish with tears. 'How is that possible? I am her mother. I should be able to protect her. Why is God punishing us like this? Why can't I save my child?'

And once again, Raj holds his mother while she sobs, her thin body plagued by frustrated grief.

'Hey bro,' Kushi says, trying for a smile, when he leads his mum back into the ward.

She looks stricken.

He thinks of everything he has heard about this fabulous girl who he feels privileged to call his sister.

'She wants to be a lawyer and champion the underdog,' Somu told him. 'She then wants to be a cabinet minister and transform the villages and later, if and when she gets the time, she wants to save the world from corruption and greed.'

'Wow,' Raj had laughed. 'Nice and easy ambitions then.'

'You will, Kushi,' he says now.

'Huh?'

'Get to save the world.'

She roots around in her repertoire of smiles again and produces a weak grin. 'From here? This hospital bed?'

'I would like my kidney to be tested for a match,' he says.

Sharda opens her mouth, a relieved moan escaping as she mouths her thanks around salty sobs, finally giving in openly to the tears that have been crowding her eyes.

'Thank you, Raj,' she gulps. 'Thank you.'

Sweat, desperation, entreaty, and gratitude, emanate from his aunt in fusty waves. This woman, who shunned his mum, and then looked after her child like her own.

'You hate hospitals,' his mother says looking up at him.

'I want to do this.'

'You shy away from inoculations.'

'Mum.'

'Your dad was the one who held you in his lap, cuddling you tight and covering your eyes when they were poking you with the needle. I didn't,' her voice wistful.

'Well, you can hold my hand now, while I am being tested, okay?'

She beams at him, eyes shining, and it is just like the look Somu's da gave Somu, and Raj feels joy flooding through him, despite the ordeal that is looming before him.

I can do this. I can.

'I am so proud of you,' his mother says. She cups his face in the palm of her hand. 'I love you, son.' For the first time in his life. Looking into his eyes, hers brimming and overflowing.

'I love you too, Mum,' he turns away so she doesn't notice the tears prickling his eyes but not before he sees her whole being glow, like someone has switched on a lamp inside of her.

Chapter 50
Kushi

Spices and Love

Raj's kidney is a match. I am going to be healed!

When I am better, this is what I will do, in no particular order:

1. Make sure those men who did this to me, the goondas and the people who hired the goondas, are punished.

2) Try and set about raising funds to rescue Ma's factory, save it from being sold to fund my medical bills—make the men who did this to me pay? Need to get legal advice on how to go about this.

3) Organise that rally for better facilities in government schools.

4) Give Raj, my new-found brother and kidney donor, a great big hug.

5) Get to know my birth mother.

6) Cook with Ma, strengthen our bond—which has been somewhat strained by recent events—over spices: a teaspoon of chilli powder, a pinch of cumin, some coriander and turmeric. We'll laugh together as I am attacked by flying mustard seeds, and breathe in the aroma of roasting curry leaves, sautéed ginger, sizzling garlic, bubbling ghee, frying vegetables, warmth and affection and happiness.

7) Realise this dream I have of our new-found family all together in our cottage smelling of spices and love: Ma cooking pickles on the hearth, her sister stirring, one hand on the ladle, the other pushing her hair away from her eyes, their eyes glowing when they alight on Raj and me, dogs howling outside, birds flying home to roost, thick darkness swilling like a drape in the fields and the smell of night drifting in, secretive and fragrant with veiled mysteries, nobody about except Binnu the drunk who will be staggering down the alley singing at the top of his voice until he falls asleep in a ditch and his weary wife hunts him down and drags him home.

8) Become the best lawyer in Karnataka.

9) Become one of the few politicians in India who make a real difference.

10) Save the world from combusting from the corruption and selfish greed of a few grasping people.

Epilogue
Choral Cicada Peace

A shimmering screen of fireflies illuminates the heady darkness smelling of mouldy fruit and mud, of anticipation and exploration. In the distance, a lone beam, (from a torch, Raj thinks), jumps up and down, up and down.

'That's our neighbours going frog and snail hunting so they can have tandoori fried frog legs and snail masala with plenty of coconut and coriander for dinner,' Kushi says, her voice dry, and Raj cannot quite make out if she is joking or serious.

'Really?' he asks.

'I could make some for you?' she offers and now he can definitely detect the smile in her voice. 'Snail masala is very tasty you know. The trick is to not cook the snails for too long, they become rubbery then and you might as well be eating curried bus tyres. I will cook them just right, the sauce creamy, with just a hint of spice.'

She laughs, the sound like wind chimes dancing in the breeze, and he wonders if night vision is among her many talents, if she can see the look of pure disgust on his face, smell his revulsion.

He rests his head against the betel tree, closing his eyes. The soft, scented breeze that strokes his face carries a hint of warmth from the baking hot day that has finally been chased away by night and a sudden shower. It is spiced with the perfume of dusty rain and sun-smothered fruit.

He fancies he hears his mother's voice, faint, carrying over the silvery gush of water from the stream tinkling beyond, and the pitter-patter dripping from the rain-burdened leaves, floating above the call of the night owl and the chatter of crickets.

He opens his eyes and squints into the blackness undulating with blinking lights, mirroring the starry canopy above. How clear the sky here, he thinks, how perfect, how different from the foggy, overcast grey gloom he has been used to seeing above him.

Darkness, like a friend, calls to him benevolently; the smell of adventure, the taste of freedom, the languid bloom of contentment. The gleam and glisten of wet ground, a lustrous sparkle against muddy black. The swish of the sugarcane rippling in the gentle wind.

One day I will bring Ellie here, he thinks. He breathes in the cloying, honeyed aroma of sugarcane and congealing leaves, and smiles in the spirited darkness as he imagines Ellie's reaction.

'My dad is coming here tomorrow with his family,' he says. 'He has twin girls of ten and a boy who's just turned seven.'

'That'll be fun,' Kushi says, softly. 'You'll have to be a model big brother and show them round the village. Hope you've been listening while I've been giving you the tour.'

He laughs. 'You know, that makes four siblings in total. Wow!'

'Huh?'

'You included.'

The wind ripples among the paddy fields beyond—waving arms, black sheaves which will glow honey green later, in the early morning sunshine.

Kushi punches him lightly on his arm. 'I am more than a sibling. We are practically twins, now that we share kidneys.'

He smiles and he can feel her smiling beside him even though he can't see her. His big sister.

Then her tone solemn as a prayer, 'Thank you, Raj. By giving me your kidney, you gave me back my future.'

'By giving you my kidney,' Raj says, 'I found myself.'

It sounds so pompous, said out loud, but he has never spoken a truer word, he thinks.

His sister launches herself at him, and kisses his cheek, the caress of a snowflake.

This is what happiness feels like, he thinks.

❆ ❆ ❆

They walk into the village, Sharda and her sister, looking for their children who disappeared some time ago for a jaunt and haven't come back.

They've just got back from the hospital, Kushi having been given the all clear and while Puja and Sharda have been catching up, Kushi and Raj have gone exploring, Kushi being eager to show Raj around.

'I know you've been here, but I'd like to show you my favourite spots,' Kushi had said, grinning up at Raj and he had smiled back.

And Puja had beamed at her son and said to Sharda, 'I've never seen him smile this much before.'

Night has descended quiet as a whisper in a raucous room. The village is still in the darkness, smelling of the rain that has bathed the earth in much longed for moisture. Master's bakery and Domu's ration shop are boarded up for the night with soggy moth-eaten wooden planks.

They walk past drunks dotted like litter, clutching bottles and mumbling to themselves, having found their version of heaven in the vinegary fug encircling the shack dispensing palm wine.

They hobble down the narrow path toward the fields in companionable silence and after a bit, Puja says, 'Nothing much has changed here, has it? These fields could be the ones near us in Nandihalli! I keep thinking Ma and Da will call us for dinner any second.'

Puja's melodic, chocolatey voice brings back long forgotten memories on the rain-fragranced, nostalgia-seasoned air.

'Except that we are old and our bones creak when we walk,' Sharda quips.

'Speak for yourself,' Puja says, laughing—sparklers tumbling in an explosion of riotous colour.

'Ma made me promise on her deathbed to find you and bring you back home.'

'Really?' Puja's voice breaks.

'You are home now.'

'I am.' Her sister's voice brimming with emotion—bougainvillea bursting down walls, a summer serenade.

They walk alongside Rimmu's hut where she can hear his brood chanting their times tables, their sweet voices laced with the innocence of childhood rising and falling in a tuneful refrain. Thanks to Kushi, Rimmu harbours high hopes for his children.

'Remember when we made that promise to love and protect each other forever?' Puja's voice tentative as hope.

'I do.'

'What happened to us, eh, Sharda?'

'We lost our way for a bit, that's all.'

Past the borewell and hopping over the boulders which pass for a path down the knoll, they cross the stream and push through the constricted, overflowing path between the fields, submerged in water due to the unexpected deluge. The paddy shoots on either side murmur reassurances as they swish in the breeze.

They find them among the sugarcane: two children, shadowy silhouettes leaning against the betel trees at the edge of the orchard. Her daughter is looking up at the brother who has given her a new lease of life; her mouth is open, laughter gushing out of it in silvery waves.

Sharda hears Puja come to a stop behind her, feels her warm, memory-scented breath on her cheeks. Puja slips her hand through Sharda's and squeezes and it is like coming home after a long, tiring day and settling into a comfy chair with a book and a cup of tea and a plate of steaming bhajis.

And in the dark, wet orchard, lit by a host of glittering fireflies, Sharda stands, with her sister beside her. Ambushed by the aromas of the rain-embellished earth and the moist, syrupy sugar cane, they watch their children and listen to their mirth spilling over to join the cricket choir—the blissful choral cicada peace.

Letter from Renita

First of all, I want to say a huge thank you for choosing *A Sister's Promise*, I hope you enjoyed reading Puja and Sharda's story just as much as I loved writing it.

If you did enjoy it, I would be forever grateful if you'd **write a review**. I'd love to hear what you think, and it can also help other readers discover one of my books for the first time.

Also, if you'd like to **keep up-to-date with all my latest releases**, just sign up here:

www.renitadsilva.com/e-mail-sign-up

Finally, if you liked *A Sister's Promise*, you might also like my other novels, **Monsoon Memories** and **The Forgotten Daughter** and **The Stolen Girl**.

Thank you so much for your support – until next time.

Renita.

Author's Note:

This is wholly a work of fiction. I have imagined what might happen in a claustrophobic little village in India. This imaginary village is a combination of various villages from different parts of India and the place where I have set it may not have a village like the one I have described. I wanted to highlight some of the problems villagers face, but also wanted to base it in a setting that is close to my heart. Hence, the villages described in this book are an amalgamation of villages from different states in India where many of the issues that Kushi raises in her letter abound, perhaps not all in one village but at least one in most villages (although not necessarily in the villages in Karnataka where I have set this story).

For ease of reading, I have referred to Bengaluru as Bangalore except in reference to the airport, and to Bombay as Mumbai throughout, even though while Puja was travelling there it would still have been called Bombay.

PUC is the acronym for Pre-University Course.

When Sharda talks of pursuing medicine after her stellar performance in the Second PUC exam, I have not mentioned the Common Entrance test (CET), tacitly assuming that Sharda would have taken it. The CET needs to be taken in conjunction with the PUC exam to gain a medical/engineering place.

The CET seat allocation scam that Kushi mentions in her letter is entirely fictitious, a product of my imagination.

In Kushi's letter, she says, 'The only people assured good futures are those who have enough money to buy their way in.' While this is true to some extent, it is not entirely true all the time.

I apologise for any oversights or mistakes and hope they do not detract from your enjoyment of this book.

FIC DSILVA
D'Silva, Renita
A sister's promise

05/17/18

CPSIA information can be obtained
at www.ICGtesting.com
Printed in the USA
LVHW02s1525060518
576195LV00011B/586/P